INHUMAN
RESOURCES

PIERRE LEMAITRE

INHUMAN
RESOURCES

Translated from the French by Sam Gordon

MACLEHOSE PRESS
NEW YORK • LONDON

MacLehose Press
An imprint of Quercus
New York • London

ISBN 978-1-63506-081-2

Library of Congress Control Number: 2018950985

Distributed in the United States and Canada by
Hachette Book Group
1290 Avenue of the Americas
New York, NY 10104

Manufactured in the United States

10 9 8 7 6 5 4 3 2 1

www.quercus.com

To Pascaline
To Marie-Françoise, with all my affection

I belong to an unlucky generation,
swung between the old world and the new,
and I find myself ill at ease in both.
And what is more, as you must
have realized by now, I am without illusions.

G. Tomasi di Lampedusa, *The Leopard*
translated by Archibald Colquhoun

BEFORE

1

I've never been a violent man. For as long as I can remember, I have never wanted to kill anyone. The odd flare of the temper, sure, but never any desire to inflict proper pain. To destroy. So, when it did happen, I suppose it took me by surprise. Violence is like drinking or sex—it's a process, not an isolated phenomenon. We barely notice it set in, quite simply because we are ready for it, because it arrives at precisely the right moment. I was perfectly aware that I was angry, but I never expected it to turn to cold fury. That's what scares me.

And to take it out on Mehmet, of all people . . .

Mehmet Pehlivan.

The guy's a Turk. He's been in France for ten years, but his vocabulary is worse than a ten-year-old's. He only has two settings: either he's shouting his head off, or he's sulking. When he's angry, he lets rip in a mixture of French and Turkish. You can't understand a word, but you never doubt for a second what he means. Mehmet is a supervisor at Pharmaceutical Logistics, my place of work. Following his own version of Darwin's theory, the moment he gets promoted he starts disparaging his former colleagues, treating them like slithering earthworms. I've come across people like him throughout my career, and not just migrant workers. No, it happens with lots of people who start out at the bottom. As soon as they begin climbing the ladder, they align themselves wholeheartedly with their superiors, and even surpass them in terms of sheer determination. The world of work's answer to Stockholm syndrome. The thing is, Mehmet doesn't just think he's a boss. He becomes the boss incarnate. He *is* the boss as soon as the boss is out the door. Of course, at this company, which must employ two hundred staff, there's not a big boss as such, just managers. But Mehmet is far too important to be a humble manager. No, he subscribes to an altogether loftier, more intangible concept that he calls "Senior Management," a notion devoid of meaning (around here, no one even knows who the senior managers are) yet heavy with innuendo: the Way, the Light, the Senior Management. In his own way, by scaling the ladder of responsibility, Mehmet is moving closer to God.

I start at 5:00 a.m. It's an odd job (when the salary is this low, you have to say it's "odd"). My role involves sorting cardboard boxes of medication that are then sent off to far-flung pharmacies. I wasn't around to see it, but apparently Mehmet did this for eight years before he was made "supervisor." Now he is in the proud position of heading up a team of three office drones, which is not to be sniffed at.

The first drone is Charles. Kind of a fancy name for a guy of no fixed abode. He is one year younger than me, thin as a rake and thirsty as a fish. I say "of no fixed abode" to keep things simple, but he does actually have an abode. An extremely fixed one. He lives in his car, which hasn't moved for five years. He calls it his "immobile home." That's typical of Charles's sense of humor. He wears a diving watch the size of a satellite dish, with dials all over the place, and a fluorescent green bracelet. I haven't got a clue where he's from or how he ended up in these dire straits. He's a funny one, Charles. For instance, he has no idea how long he's been on the social housing waiting list, but he does keep a precise tally of the time that has passed since he gave up renewing his application. Five years, seven months and seventeen days at the last count. Charles counts the time that has elapsed since he lost any hope of being rehoused. "Hope," he says, as he raises his index finger, "is a pack of lies invented by the Devil to reconcile men with their lot." That's not one of his, I've heard it before somewhere else. I've searched for the quote but never managed to track it down. Just goes to show that behind his veneer of drunkenness, he is a man of culture.

The second drone is Romain, a young guy from Narbonne. Following a few prominent turns in his school drama club, he dreamed of becoming an actor and, straight after passing his baccalaureate, moved to Paris. But he failed to make even the smallest of splashes, not least because of his Gascon accent. Like a true young D'Artagnan, or Henri IV arriving at court, his provincial drawl—all r's and ang's—prompted sniggers among the drama school elite with all its urbane courtiers. It amuses us all no end, too. He had elocution lessons for it, but to no avail. He took on a series of part-time jobs, which kept a roof over his head while he attended castings for roles he never had a hope in hell of landing. One day, he understood that his fantasy would never come true. Red-carpet Romain was done. What was more, Narbonne had been the biggest city he had known. It didn't take long for Paris to flatten him, to crush him to dust. He grew homesick, yearning for the familiar surroundings of his childhood. Problem was that he couldn't face going back empty handed. Now he works hard to pay his way, and the only role he aspires to is that of the prodigal son. With this aim in mind, he does any piecemeal job he can find. An ant's vocation. He spends the rest of his time on Second Life, Twitter, Facebook, and a whole load of other networks—places where no one can hear his accent, I suppose. According to Charles, he's a tech wizard.

The third drone is me. I work for three hours every morning, which brings in 585 euros gross (whenever you talk of a part-time salary, you have to add the word "gross," because of the tax). I get home around 9:00 a.m. If Nicole is out the door a bit late, we might run into each other. Whenever that happens, she says,

"I'm late," before giving me a peck on the nose and closing the door behind her.

This morning, Mehmet was seething. Like a pressure cooker. I suppose his wife had been giving him grief, or something. He was pacing angrily up and down the aisle where all the crates and cardboard boxes are stacked, clutching his clipboard so tightly his knuckles had turned white. He gives the impression of being burdened with major responsibilities, exacerbated by personal strife. I was right on time, but the moment he set eyes on me he yelled out a stream of his gibberish. Being on time, apparently, is not sufficient to prove your motivation. He arrives an hour early at least. His tirade was fairly unintelligible, but I got the gist, namely that he thinks I'm a lazy asshole.

Although Mehmet makes such a song and dance about it, the job itself is not very complicated. We sort packages, we put them in cardboard boxes, we lay them on a palette. Normally, the pharmacy codes are written on the packages in large type, but sometimes—don't ask me why—the number is missing. Romain figures the settings on one of the printers must be wrong. If this does happen, the correct code can be found among a long series of tiny characters on a printed label. The numbers you want are the eleventh, twelfth, and thirteenth. It's a real hassle for me because I need my glasses for this. I have to fish them out of my pocket, put them on, lower my head, count the characters . . . A loss of precious time. And if Senior Management were to catch me doing this, it would annoy them greatly. Typical, then, that the first package I picked up this morning didn't have a code. Mehmet started screaming. I leaned over. And at that precise moment, he kicked me right in the ass.

It was just after five in the morning.

My name is Alain Delambre. I am fifty-seven years old. And four years ago, I became unemployed.

2

Initially, I took the morning job at Pharmaceutical Logistics as a way of keeping myself occupied. At least that's what I told Nicole, but neither she nor the girls fell for it. At my age, you don't wake up at 4:00 a.m. for 45 percent of the minimum wage just to get your endorphins going. It's all a bit more complicated. Well, actually it's not that complicated. At first, we didn't need the money—now we do.

I have been unemployed for four years. Four years in May (May 24, to be exact).

This job doesn't really make ends meet, so I do a few other little things, too. For a couple of hours here and there, I lug crates, bubble-wrap stuff, hand out fliers. A spot of nighttime industrial cleaning in offices. A few seasonal jobs, too. For the past two years, I've been Father Christmas at a discount store specializing in household appliances. I don't always give Nicole the full picture of my activities, since it would only upset her. I use a range of excuses to justify my absences. As this is harder for the night jobs, I have invented a group of unemployed friends with whom I supposedly play poker. I tell Nicole that it relaxes me.

Before, I was HR manager at a company with almost two hundred employees. I was in charge of staff and training, overseeing salaries and representing the management at the works council. I worked at Bercaud, which sold costume jewelry. Seventeen years casting pearls before swine. That was everyone's favorite gag. There was a whole load of extremely witty jokes that went around about pearls, family jewels, et cetera. Corporate banter, if you like. The laughter stopped in March, when it was announced that Bercaud had been bought out by the Belgians. I might have had a chance against the Belgian HR manager, but when I found out that he was thirty-eight, I mentally started to clear my desk. I say "mentally" because, deep down, I know I wasn't at all ready to do it for real. But that was what I had to do—they didn't waste time. The takeover was announced on March 4. The first round of layoffs took place six weeks later, and I was part of the second.

In the space of four years, as my income evaporated, I passed from incredulity to doubt, then to guilt, and finally to a sense of injustice. Now, I feel anger. It's not a very positive emotion, anger. When I arrive at Logistics, and I see Mehmet's bushy eyebrows and Charles's long, rickety silhouette, and I think about everything I've had to endure, a terrible rage thunders inside me. Most of all, I have to avoid thinking about the years I have left, about the pension payments I'll never receive, about the allowances that are withering away, or about the despair that sometimes grips Nicole and me. I have to avoid those thoughts because—in spite of my sciatica—they put me in the mood for terrorism.

In the four years we have known each other, I have come to count my job center adviser as one of my closest friends. Not long ago, he told me, with a degree of admiration in his voice, that I was an example. What he means is that I might have given up on the idea of finding a job, but I haven't given up looking for one. He thinks that shows strength of character. I don't want to tell him he's wrong; he is thirty-seven and he needs to hang on to his illusions for as long as possible. The truth is I've actually surrendered to a sort of innate reflex. Looking for work is like working, and since that is all I have done my whole life, it is ingrained in my nervous system; something that drives me out of necessity, but without direction. I look for work like a dog sniffs a lamppost. No illusions, but I can't help it.

And so it was that I responded to an advertisement a few days ago. A headhunting firm looking to recruit an HR assistant for a big company. The role involves hiring staff at executive level, formulating job descriptions, carrying out assessments, writing up appraisals, processing social audits, et cetera, which is all right up my street, exactly what I did for years at Bercaud. "Versatile, methodical, and rigorous, the candidate will be equipped with excellent interpersonal skills." My professional profile in a nutshell.

The moment I read it, I compiled my documents and attached my CV. Needless to say, it all hangs on whether they are willing to take on a man of my age.

The answer to which is perfectly obvious: it'll be a no.

So what? I sent off my application anyway. I wonder whether it was just a way of honoring my job center adviser's admiration.

When Mehmet kicked me in the ass, I let out a yelp. Everyone turned around. First Romain, then Charles, who did so with greater difficulty as he was already a couple of sheets to the wind. I straightened up like a young man. That's when I realized that I was almost a head taller than Mehmet. Up to now, he had been the big boss. I'd never really noticed his size. Mehmet himself was struggling to come to terms with kicking me in the ass. His anger seemed to have abated entirely. I could see his lips trembling and he was blinking as he tried to find the words, I'm not sure in which language. That was when I did something for the first time in my life: I tilted my head back, very slowly, as though I were admiring the ceiling of the Sistine Chapel, and then whipped it forward with a sharp motion. Just like I'd seen on television. A head-butt, they call it. Charles, being homeless, gets beaten up a lot, and knows all about it. "Nice technique," he told me. For a first-timer, it seemed a very decent effort.

My forehead broke Mehmet's nose. Before feeling the impact on my skull, I heard a sinister crack. Mehmet howled (in Turkish this time, no doubt about it), but I couldn't ram home my advantage because he immediately took his head in his hands and sank to his knees. If I had been in a film, I almost certainly would have taken a run-up and laid him out with an almighty kick in the face, but my skull was aching so much that I also took my head in my hands and fell to the ground. Both of us were on our knees, facing each other, heads in hands. Tragedy in the workplace. A dramatic scene worthy of an old master.

Romain started flapping around, no idea what to do with himself. Mehmet was bleeding everywhere. The ambulance arrived within a few minutes. We gave statements. Romain told me that he'd seen Mehmet kick me in the ass, that he would be a witness and that I had nothing to worry about. I kept silent, but my experience led me to believe that it definitely wouldn't be as simple as all that. I wanted to be sick. I went to the bathroom, but in vain.

Actually, no, not in vain: in the mirror, I saw that I had a gash and a large bruise across my forehead. I was deathly pale and out of it. Pitiful. For a moment, I thought I was starting to look like Charles.

3

"Oh my goodness, what have you done to yourself?" Nicole asked as she touched the enormous bruise on my forehead.

I didn't answer. I handed her the letter in a way that I hoped would seem casual, then went to my study, where I pretended to rummage through my drawers. She looked long and hard at the words: "Further to your letter, I am delighted to inform you that your application for the role of HR assistant has been accepted in the first instance. You will shortly be invited to take an aptitude test, which, if successful, will be followed by an interview."

I think she had to read it several times before it registered. She was still wearing her coat when I saw her appear at the door of my study, resting her shoulder against the frame. She was holding the letter in her hand, head tilted to the side. This is one of her classic mannerisms and, along with two or three others, by far my favorite. It's almost like she knows it. When I see her in that position, I feel comforted by the extreme grace she has. There is something doleful about her, a litheness that's hard to explain . . . a languor that is extraordinarily sexual. She was holding the letter in her hand and staring at me. I found her extremely beautiful, or extremely desirable, and was overcome by a furious urge to jump her. Sex has always been a powerful antidepressant for me.

At first, when I didn't regard unemployment as a fatal situation, just a calamitous, worrying one, I was constantly jumping Nicole. In the bedroom, in the bathroom, in the corridor. Nicole never said no. She is very perceptive and understood that it was my way of affirming that I was still alive. Since then, anxiety has given way to anguish, and the first visible effect of this is that I'm practically impotent. Our lovemaking has become rare, challenging. Nicole is very kind and patient, which only makes me more unhappy. Our sexual barometer is all over the place. We pretend not to notice or that it's not important. I know Nicole still loves me, but our life has become much more difficult and I can't help feeling that it cannot carry on like this forever.

But back to her clutching the letter from BLC Consulting.

"Sweetheart, this is unbelievable!" she said.

I reminded myself that I really needed to track down the author of Charles's quotation about the Devil and hope. Because Nicole was right. A letter like this was out of the ordinary, and at my age, having not worked in my field for more than four years, I didn't have the faintest chance of landing the job. A glimmer of optimism stirred in Nicole and me that very second. As though the months and years that had passed had taught us nothing. As though the two of us could never be cured of our hope.

Nicole moved toward me and gave me one of those wet kisses that make me go wild. She's brave. There is nothing harder than living with a depressive. Apart from being depressed yourself, of course.

"Do we know who they're recruiting for?" Nicole asked.

I turned around my screen to show her BLC Consulting's website. The name comes from its founder, Bertrand Lacoste. Serious pedigree. The type of consultant who charges himself out at 3,500 euros a day. When I first joined Bercaud, with my whole future ahead of me (and even several years later, when I signed up for a

lifelong-learning course to get a coaching qualification), becoming a high-level consultant like Bertrand Lacoste was exactly what
I dreamed of: efficient, always one step ahead of my opposite number, producing lightning-quick analyses and a barrage of managerial
solutions whatever the situation. I never finished the course because
our girls arrived around then. That's the official version. Nicole's version. In reality, I never had the talent for it. Deep down, I have the
mindset of an employee: I am the prototypical middle manager.

I said:

"The ad is vague. They talk about an 'industry leader with a global
presence.' Apart from that . . . the job's based in Paris."

Nicole watched me scroll through web pages on employment
regulations and new laws on continuing professional development
that I had spent the afternoon reading. She smiled. My desk was
strewn with Post-its and notes to self, and I had taped various sheets
of paper to my bookshelves. She seemed to realize at that moment
that I had worked relentlessly all day. She is one of those people
who immediately picks up on the slightest domestic detail. If I move
something, she notices as soon as she enters the room. The only time
I've been unfaithful, a long time ago (the girls were still very young),
she found me out that very evening, despite all the precautions I'd
taken. At first, she didn't say anything. It was a tense evening. In bed,
she simply said to me in a tired manner:

"Alain, never again . . ."

Then she curled up next to me in bed. We have never exchanged
another word on the subject.

"I don't have a chance in a thousand."

Nicole places the letter from BLC Consulting on my desk.

"You never know," she says, taking off her coat.

"Someone my age . . ."

She turns toward me.

"How many applications do you figure they received?" she says.

"Maybe three hundred and something."

"And how many do you think have been called up for the test?"

"I'd say . . . around fifteen?"

"So explain to me why they have chosen *your* application out of more than three hundred. Do you think they didn't notice your age? Do you think that passed them by?"

Of course not. Nicole is right. I spent half the afternoon turning the theories around in my head. Each time I come up against the same impossible point: my CV stinks of "man in his fifties" from a mile off, so if they're calling me in, there must be something about my age that interests them.

Nicole is very patient. While she peels the onions and potatoes, she listens to me as I detail all the technical reasons they might have for selecting me. She can hear the excitement bubbling up in my voice despite my attempts to contain it. I haven't received a letter like this for more than two years. At worst, I never hear back; at best, I get told to get lost. I never get called to interview anymore, because a guy like me is of no interest to anyone. So I've come up with all sorts of hypotheses about the response from BLC Consulting, and I figure I have fallen on the right one.

"I think it's because of the scheme."

"What scheme?" Nicole asked.

The rescue plan for seniors. It turns out that seniors are not working for long enough anymore. If only the government had gotten in touch, I could have saved them the expense of some very costly studies. In this case, we're obviously talking about people who are still in work. It seems they stop working even though the country still needs them. And if that's not terrible enough, it gets worse. Apparently, there are seniors who want to work but can't find a job. Whether they're not working enough or are no longer working at all, the older generations represent a serious problem to society. The government has therefore agreed to help by providing cash incentives for companies that agree to employ the elderly.

"It isn't my experience that interests them, it's because they want tax exemptions and other benefits."

Sometimes Nicole does this thing with her mouth to feign skepticism, jutting out her chin slightly. I love it when she does that, too.

"The way I see it," she says, "these sorts of companies have no shortage of cash, so they don't give a damn about government reward schemes."

The second part of my afternoon had been dedicated to clarifying this whole reward scheme business. And, once again, Nicole is right—it's a weak argument. The tax exemptions only last a few months, and the scheme only covers a small part of the salary of an employee at this level. And, what's more, it's on a sliding scale.

No, in the space of a couple of minutes Nicole has come to the same conclusion it has taken me a day to reach: if BLC is calling me in, it's because they are interested in my experience.

For four years I have exhausted myself explaining to employers that a man of my age is just as dynamic as a younger person, and that experience leads to savings. But that's a journalist's argument, fine for the "Jobs" supplements in the newspapers; it just pisses off employers. Now, for the first time, I get the impression that someone has properly read my cover letter and studied my application. This makes me feel like I might have hit a home run.

I want the interview to happen right here, right now. I want to scream.

But I keep it cool.

"Let's not mention anything to the girls, okay?"

Nicole agrees that's for the best. It has been tough for the girls seeing their parents living hand to mouth. They never say a word, but they can't help it—the image they have of me has worn away. Not because of unemployment, but because of the effects unemployment has had on me. I have aged, I have shrunk, I have grown gloomy. I've become a pain in the ass. They don't even know about my job at Pharmaceutical Logistics. Raising their hopes that I might have landed something, only to announce later that I have blown it, is another flop I cannot face.

Nicole cuddles up against me. She delicately places a finger on the bump on my forehead.

"Care to explain?"

I do my best to relate the story in a neutral tone. I'm pretty sure I even put a humorous spin on it. But the idea of me being kicked in the ass by Mehmet does not amuse Nicole in the slightest.

"He's wrong in the head, that Turk!"

"That's not a very European reaction."

But again my attempt at humor falls flat.

Nicole strokes my cheek pensively. I know full well that she feels bad for me. I try to seem philosophical, despite my heavy heart and despite realizing from the mere touch of her hand that we are entering into fragile emotional territory.

"Are you sure this business ends here?" Nicole asks, looking at my forehead.

That's it: next time I'm marrying an idiot.

But Nicole places her lips on mine.

"Screw it," she says. "I'm sure this is the job for you. I'm certain of it."

I close my eyes and pray that, with all his talk of hope and the Devil, my friend Charles is just being a tedious piece of shit.

4

This letter from BLC Consulting has been a real bombshell. I can't sleep anymore. My mood swings between euphoria and pessimism. Whatever I'm doing, my mind constantly comes back to it and creates all sorts of scenarios. It's exhausting.

On Friday, Nicole spent part of the day on her resource center's website and printed off dozens of pages of legal information. After four years out of the game, I'm badly behind. The regulations in my field have changed a lot, especially regarding dismissals (things have become far more relaxed in that department). As for management, there have been plenty of innovations, too. Fashions are changing at breakneck speed. Five years ago, everyone was crazy about transactional analysis, but that's seen as deeply antiquated today. Current trends include "transition management," "sectorial restructuring," "corporate identity," the development of "interpersonal relations," "benchmarking," and "networking." But above all, businesses champion their "values." It's no longer enough to work . . . now you have to "adhere." Before, you just had to agree with the business, nowadays you have to amalgamate with it. To become one with it. Suits me just fine: they employ me, I amalgamate with them.

Nicole sorted and selected the documents, I did some review cards, and since this morning she has been firing questions at me. We're cramming. I am pacing around my study, trying hard to focus. Having composed various mnemonics to help, I'm now muddling them all up.

Nicole makes tea and flops back onto the sofa with papers all around her. She's still in her bathrobe, as is often the case, especially in winter, when she doesn't have anything planned for the day. Wearing her old T-shirt and mismatched woolen socks, Nicole smells of sleep and tea; cozy as a croissant and beautiful as spring. I adore her abandon. If I weren't so stressed by all this job stuff, I would take her straight back to bed. Given my current performance in the sex stakes, I desist.

"No touching," Nicole says, on seeing me finger my bruise.

I don't think about the knock often, but I'm cruelly reminded of its presence the moment I step in front of a mirror. This morning it turned a ghastly color. Mauve in the middle and yellow on the sides. I'd hoped it would make me look manly, but the effect is more grubby. The paramedic told me I would have it for about a week. As for Mehmet, he's off for ten days with his broken nose.

The teams for day-night shifts were swiftly reshuffled to compensate for our absences. I pick up the phone and call my colleague Romain. I get Charles.

"The shifts are a mess," he explains. "Romain did the night and I'm on afternoons for two or three days."

A supervisor is doing overtime to stand in for Mehmet, who has already informed the company that he would like to get back to work sooner. Now there's someone who doesn't need management seminars to learn about adhering to values. The overseer who has temporarily replaced him told Charles that Senior Management cannot tolerate brawling in the workplace. "What is the world coming to when team leaders wind up in the hospital for reprimanding a subordinate?" the guy would have said. I don't know the significance of that, but it's of no value to me. I decide not to say anything to Nicole so as not to worry her: if I get lucky with the job through BLC Consulting, I can deal with all the crap from before with a big grin on my face.

"I'll put some foundation on you tomorrow," Nicole jokes as she inspects my forehead. "No, seriously! Just a bit, you'll see."

We'll see. I tell myself that tomorrow is just an aptitude test, not an interview, by which point the bruise will have more or less disappeared. If I make it that far, of course.

"Well, of course you'll make it that far," Nicole assures me.

True faith is confusing.

I try to hide it, but my excitement is sky high. It's not the same as yesterday or the day before: the closer the test gets, the more my nerves overwhelm me. On Friday, when we started reviewing, I had no idea how badly behind I was. When I did realize, it sent me into a panic. All of a sudden, the girls coming around doesn't seem like such a welcome distraction. The thought of losing prep time sends me into a fluster.

As soon as he enters, Gregory points at my forehead and says, "What happened here, grandpa? Starting to get a bit wobbly on your feet?"

The "grandpa" is his in-joke. In these cases, Mathilde, my elder daughter, usually digs an elbow into his ribs, because she thinks I'm touchy about it. In my opinion, she'd do better to smack him in the fucking face. I say this because she has been married to him for four years, and for four years I've wanted to do it for her. Imagine, a guy with the name "Gregory" ... Plus, he has slicked-back hair, which is another dead giveaway. Mating with a mug like this clearly doesn't bother my daughter, but I'm sorry, it pisses me off. Nicole is right. I do feel touchy. She says it's a result of inactivity. I love this word, even if it's not the first that springs to mind when my alarm goes off at 4:00 a.m. to go and get my backside kicked.

Mathilde is an English teacher. She is a very normal girl. She reserves an inexplicable passion for the quotidian. She adores doing the shopping, wondering about what she's going to cook, thinking six months in advance about finding a good place to go on vacation, remembering the first names of all her friends' children and everyone else's birthdays, planning her pregnancies . . . This ability to fill up her life amazes me. There is something genuinely fascinating about generating such joy from the administration of the banal.

Gregory is a branch manager at a consumer credit firm. He lends to people so they can buy loads of stuff, like vacuums, cars, and televisions. Greenhouses. In the brochures, the interest rates seem completely fine, but in actual fact you end up having to repay three or four times what you borrowed. And if you are having trouble repaying, it's perfectly straightforward: you get another loan, but this time you need to repay thirty times what you borrowed. Standard. My son-in-law and I have spent entire evenings at each other's throats. He represents pretty much everything I hate. It's a real family drama. Nicole is of much the same opinion, but she has better manners than I do, and since she has work, she doesn't spend hours on end thinking about it, whereas an evening with my son-in-law can leave me seething inside for three days straight. I always end up replaying the conversations like a football pundit after a match.

When she's at our place, Mathilde often comes for a chat in the kitchen while I finish the cooking. This is usually a pretext for tackling any dishes left in the sink (she just can't help herself). At her place she's at it constantly; even at her girlfriends' houses she knows where all the glasses go and where the cutlery lives. It must be some sort of sixth sense. I find it quite remarkable.

She passes behind me and plants a kiss next to my ear, like a lover.

"So you bashed yourself?"

Her pity might have made things worse, but it is expressed with such kindness that actually it helps.

I'm about to answer, but the doorbell rings. It's Lucie, my second daughter. She is very flat chested, which causes her great distress. Nice guys find it cute, but try telling that to a girl of twenty-five. She's thin, nervous, skittish. With her, reason doesn't always prevail—she's a passionate girl, quick to anger, more than capable of saying things she immediately regrets. She has a lot more childhood friends than her sister, who never gets cross with anyone. Lucie's the kind of girl who would head-butt Mehmet, after which Mathilde would be waiting with the foundation.

Lucie is flying solo tonight. Her life is complicated. She kisses her mother hello and whirls into the kitchen like a domestic hurricane. She lifts up the lid.

"Did you add a squeeze of lemon?"

"I don't know, your mother's in charge of the *blanquette*."

Lucie sticks her nose into the saucepan. No lemon. She offers to make the béchamel.

"I'd rather do it myself," I say politely.

Everyone is well aware that béchamel is the only thing I can make. Don't take that away from me . . .

"I think we've finally found one," Mathilde says, ready to burst.

Lucie raises an eyebrow in surprise. She has absolutely no idea what her sister means. To buy her a bit of time, I feign bewilderment. "No?!"

Lucie pretends to feel aggrieved, but inside she finds it funny.

Our daughters are a true cross of their parents. Lucie resembles me physically, but she has her mother's temperament; Mathilde's the opposite. Lucie is lively and adventurous. Mathilde is hardworking and resigns herself to things easily. She is courageous and energetic, and does not ask for much from life. Just look at her husband. She was good at English, didn't look much beyond that, and became an English teacher. Chip off the old block. Lucie, however, is more out there. She studied history of art, psychology, Russian literature, and I don't know what else—she couldn't settle on one subject because she found everything so interesting. She did well in studies that she never completed, changing plans as quickly as she did boyfriends. Mathilde did well in her studies because she'd started them, then married a friend from secondary school.

To everyone's surprise, even though we considered her to be unaccomplished in intellectual activities requiring rigor and detail (or perhaps it's because of this), Lucie became a lawyer. For the most part, she defends women who have been abused. As with funerals or taxes, there won't be any shortage of work in this field, but she's hardly about to make a fortune.

"It's a three- or four-room apartment in the nineteenth," Mathilde continues, completely in her element. "Near Jaurès. It's not exactly the neighborhood we were after, but . . . all the same, it's nice and bright. And it's on Gregory's line, which is handy."

"How much?" Lucie asks.

"Six hundred and eighty thousand."

"Wow, there you go . . ."

I find out that they only have 55,000 euros for their deposit and that, despite Gregory's connections in the banking sector, getting a mortgage will be tricky.

This sort of thing hurts. Once upon a time I was in charge of the "Bank of Maman and Papa." They would ask without any hesitation, I would play hard to get, then give in with mock frustration, lending them sums they would never repay, and we all knew I was delighted to do it. It's nice to be useful. Nowadays, Nicole and I have cut back our lifestyle to the bare minimum, which is plain to see everywhere: in what we have, what we wear, what we cook. We used to have two cars, partly because that seemed more practical, but mainly because we never questioned it. Over the years, our level of living rose through a combination of successive promotions and pay raises for both of us. Nicole landed deputy manager at her resource center, and I became head of HR at Bercaud. We used to look to the future with confidence, sure that we'd manage to pay off the mortgage on our apartment. For example, when the girls moved out, Nicole wanted to do some work on the apartment: keep just the one spare room, knock through the dividing wall between the living room and the second bedroom to turn it into a double-sized living room, then shift the water pipes so the sink could go under the window. That sort of thing. So we put some money aside. The plan was simple. We'd put the mortgage repayments on hold, pay for the work in cash, and go on vacation. We were so confident; it was a no-brainer. It would still be a few years before we'd pay off the mortgage, but we had money, and we went ahead with the renovations, starting with the kitchen. In terms of dates, that's very easy to remember: the builders started tearing everything down on May 20, and I was fired on May 24. We stopped the work immediately. After that, the engine tanked, the nose dive began, and we've been in free fall ever since. As the kitchen had already been ripped up, from the plumbing to the tiles, I had to enter DIY mode. I erected a sink on two bits of plasterboard and reconnected some makeshift plumbing. Since it was temporary, we bought three kitchen cabinets that I attached to the wall. We went for the cheapest ones, which unsurprisingly meant the ugliest ones. And the least sturdy. I'm always petrified of putting too many dishes in them. I also laid some linoleum directly onto the cement. We replace it every year. I usually do it to surprise Nicole. I open the door with a grand gesture and say: "We've got a new kitchen!" And she usually says something along the lines of: "Let's crack open a half bottle!" We both know it's not the most hilarious of jokes, but we do our best.

Since my unemployment benefits weren't enough to pay the bills, we dipped into the savings earmarked for the renovations. And when these reserves dried up, we realized that we still had four years of mortgage to pay off before the apartment was ours, and Nicole said we'd have to sell it to buy somewhere smaller that we could pay for in cash. I refused. I've worked for twenty years to get this apartment, and I cannot bring myself to sell it. The longer it's gone on, the less Nicole feels able to say anything about it. For now. She'll be right in the end. Especially if this Mehmet business turns sour. I'm not sure if we'll manage to save face in front of our daughters. Nowadays they are coping just fine by themselves. They can't even do me the good turn of asking for money.

I have successfully completed the béchamel. It's the same as ever. Just like us around the table—we're the same as ever. Before, our predictable conversations and repetitive jokes were fine, but in the last year or two everything has irritated me. I've lost my patience, I freely admit it. This evening especially . . . I am desperate to tell the girls that I've been called in for a job that is absolutely perfect for me, that I haven't had a break like this for four years, that in two days I'm going to pass the aptitude test with flying colors before storming the interview, and in one month, kids, your disappointment of a father will be nothing but a distant memory. But instead of that I say nothing. Nicole smiles at me. She is superstitious. And happy. There is so much confidence in those eyes.

"So this guy," Gregory is saying, "enrolls to read law. And the first thing he does . . . anyone know?"

No one knows. Except Mathilde, who doesn't want to spoil her husband's show. I haven't really been listening, I just know that my son-in-law is a prick.

"He took his college to court!" he announces with adulation. "He compared his enrollment fees to those from the year before and deemed the increase to be illegal because it hadn't been matched by a 'significant rise in the loans available to students.'"

He bursts out laughing in a manner intended to highlight the brilliance of his story.

An intimate blend of right-leaning convictions and leftist fantasies, my son-in-law adores this kind of story. He teems with anecdotes about patients suing their therapists, or twin brothers laying into each other before a tribunal, or mothers with large families attacking their children. In certain variations, customers might get compensation from a contravention by their local supermarket or a car manufacturer. But Gregory verges on the orgasmic when the rulings go against the public sector. Perhaps the railroad has been found guilty because of a broken ticket machine, or the tax office has been forced to hand out a rebate to someone who's filed their return. Another time it might be the Ministry of Education losing against a parent who, after carrying out a comparison of students' marks for an essay on Voltaire, feels that their child has been the victim of some grave act of discrimination. Gregory's jubilation is directly proportionate to how inane the issue is. It's his way of showing that the law allows for the perpetual recurrence of the noble David versus Goliath struggle. In his mind, there is something grandiose about this fight. He is convinced that the law enforces democracy. Once you get to know him a bit, you are mighty relieved that he works in finance. Had the guy been a lawyer, he would have done unimaginable damage.

"That's a bit troubling," Lucie says.

Gregory, not fazed by the idea of giving a law lecture in front of Lucie, a lawyer, pours himself another glass of the Saint-Émilion he brought, visibly delighted to have provoked a heated debate, over the course of which his hypothesis will be demonstrably, indisputably superior.

"On the contrary," he says. "It's reassuring to know that we can still win even if we are the weaker party."

"Does that mean you could sue me just because you think the *blanquette* was underseasoned?"

Everyone turns to me. Maybe it was my voice that alerted them. Mathilde silently implores me. Lucie looks triumphant.

"Does it need more salt?" Nicole asks.

"It's an analogy."

"You might have chosen a different one."

"Well, it's a bit trickier with the *blanquette*," Gregory concedes. "But it's the principle that counts."

In spite of the look on Nicole's face, which is one of extreme unease, I decide to hold my ground.

"But the principle is what bugs me. It's idiotic."

"Alain . . . ," Nicole urges, laying her hand flat on top of mine.

"What do you mean 'Alain'?"

Nobody understands why I'm so annoyed.

"You're wrong," Gregory replies, not a man to back down when he thinks he has the initiative. "This story shows that anyone"—he leans into the "anyone" so that each of us is aware of the weight of his conclusion—"absolutely *anyone* can win if they have enough energy to do it."

"Win what?" Lucie says, to calm things down.

"Well," Gregory stutters, thrown by such a basic jab, "well, win . . ."

"I'm skeptical of anyone who has the energy to chase a tax rebate or thirty euros' worth of enrollment fees . . . surely that energy could be better spent on less selfish causes?"

Here's how this usually pans out. Mathilde jumps to the defense of her prick of a husband, Lucie perseveres, and within a couple of minutes the two sisters are at each other's throats. Then Nicole slams her fist on the table, never quite at the right moment. When the others have gone, she sulks until she can't contain herself any longer, at which point she explodes at me: after the children, it's the parents turn to have a blazing row.

"You're a real pain in the ass!" Nicole says.

In her underwear, she slams the wardrobe door and disappears into the bathroom. I can see her bottom through her panties—a great start.

"I was on fire," I say.

But my joshing hasn't gotten a laugh out of her for twenty years.

When she returns to the bedroom, I'm once again immersed in my notes. Nicole comes back to earth. She knows that we have reached a critical point with this miraculous news. This is pretty much my last chance, and seeing me reviewing my notes in bed calms her down. She smiles.

"Ready for the big moment?"

She lies down next to me, picks up my notes, and moves them slowly to one side, the way a parent might take off their sleeping child's glasses. Then she slips her hand under the sheets and finds me right away.

Ready for the big moment.

From: Bertrand Lacoste [b.lacoste@BLC-Consulting.fr]
To: Alexandre Dorfmann [a.dorfmann@Exxyal-Europe.com]
Sent: Monday, April 27, 9:34 a.m.

Subject: Selection and recruitment

Dear Monsieur Chairman,

Please find below an outline of the main points covered in our recent meeting.

In the course of the coming year, your group is to proceed with the closure of its Sarqueville site and the subsequent wide-ranging layoff plan.

You wish to select one of your current executives to take charge of this difficult mission.

As such, you have asked me to devise a method of assessment to identify the individual who is the most steadfast and reliable: in short, the most competent.

You approved my *Hostage-Taking Simulation Plan*, over the course of which the executives under assessment will—without prior warning—be ambushed by an armed commando.

The ensuing test will make it possible to measure the candidates' ability to remain calm under pressure, their conduct in an extremely stressful scenario, and their loyalty to company values, above all when they are pressed by the hostage takers to betray them.

With your agreement, we will link this operation with our own recruitment process for an HR assistant: the candidates for this HR position will be required to conduct the role play, thereby allowing us to assess their professional aptitude.

Combining these two operations can only be of benefit: at the same time as your executives are being assessed, the candidates for the HR role will be able to showcase their skills as assessors.

I have taken it upon myself to recruit the necessary personnel and to make the material arrangements for the role play. This is, as you can imagine, a rather complex process: we require weapons, actors, a site, a plausible scenario, a concrete plan of action, behavior observation criteria, etc.

In addition we require a watertight premise for calling in candidates to carry out aptitude tests. For this, Monsieur Chairman, your valuable insight will be necessary. And your participation. All in due course.

I suggest we schedule this double operation for Thursday, May 21 (we must choose a day when the offices are closed, and that Thursday—Ascension Day—strikes me as appropriate, if you agree).

I will be submitting a proposal in the near future.

Yours,
Bertrand Lacoste

5

Nicole tells me that I'm very negative and that things always turn out better than expected. She's right again. Two days ago I was extremely depressed. Fine, eleven adults in a room, working away at an exam like schoolchildren, is hardly a massive deal. After all, in life we're constantly being assessed. No, what got to me was the realization on entering the room that I was the oldest. Or rather the only old person. Three women, seven men, aged between twenty-five and thirty-five, all looking me up and down as though I was a casting error or some prehistoric curiosity. It was predictable, but still demoralizing.

We were shown in by a girl with a Polish name, Olenka or something. Pretty girl—sparkling. Icy. Chilling. I don't know what her job is at BLC (she didn't say), but judging by her authoritative attitude and her pushy manner, you got the sense that she gives it everything, that she would sell her soul to be taken seriously. Must have been an unpaid intern. Behind her was a pile of papers, the tests she'd be handing out in a few minutes' time.

She started by briefing us: the eleven of us had been selected from one hundred and thirty-seven candidates. For a millisecond, a silent yet palpable air of triumph filled the room. Then she introduced the position, omitting to name the recruiting company. The job she described suits me so well that during the course of her short announcement, I pictured myself wholeheartedly and delightedly accepting the offer.

But I came back down to earth with a crash when we were handed a thirty-four-page pack of questions that were either open ended, closed, semi-open, half closed or three-quarters open (not sure how they're going to pick through all that) and given three hours to complete it.

I was caught seriously off guard.

I had mainly boned up on legislation, but the questions were very much geared toward "management, training, and assessment." I had to summon all my reserves as I tried to recall information that seemed to date back to the Flood. Since I was sidelined I have lost my reflexes. The new techniques and last-ditch gimmicks I'd discovered two days earlier with Nicole had not stuck. I didn't manage to apply them to the practical examples we were given. At times I found myself just filling in the blank and hoping for the best. That's all I'm good for—autofill.

Over the course of the test I realized that my handwriting is terrible, at times barely legible. I had to try harder with the open-ended questions. I was almost relieved when I had to answer with a checkmark. A real chimp. Or an old chimp, more like.

To my right there was a girl of about thirty who looked vaguely like Lucie. At the start I attempted a complicit smile. She looked at me like I was trying to get her into bed.

By the end I was exhausted. All the candidates filed out and we just gave one another a nod, like distant neighbors who sometimes bump into each other by accident.

Outside it was a beautiful day—it would have been perfect weather to celebrate a victory.

I walked toward the *métro* station, each step leaving me more desperate. It was like a gradual dawning, one layer at a time. I'd left a whole load of questions unanswered. As for the others, the right answers came to me afterward, each one different from the one I'd given. In this sort of game, the youngest ones are like ducks to water. Not me. It was a competition aimed at an age bracket I don't belong to. I tried to tally the precise number of questions I'd got wrong, but I lost count.

When I left I was just tired, but by the time I'd arrived at the *métro* I had sunk into a terrible depression. I could have cried. I realized that I'd never escape this. In the end, head-butting Mehmet seems like the only good solution, the only one that fits what is happening to me. There are terrorists who crash lorries full of explosives into schools, others who plant nail bombs in airports. I felt a strange connection with them. But instead of doing that, I've fallen for something else. Each time, I play the bastards' game. A job ad? I respond. Tests? I pass. Interviews? I attend. Have to wait? I wait. Have to come back? I come back. I'm obliging. For guys like me, the system is there, for all eternity.

It was the end of the afternoon and the *métro* carriages were filling up. Normally I move down the station by walking along by the ticket machines, but this time, I don't know why, I made my way down the edge of the platform, along the white line that you can't cross without putting yourself at risk of being hit by the approaching train. I was like a drunkard, my head spinning. Suddenly there was a great gust to my left. I hadn't been aware of the incoming train, not even heard it enter the station. Each one of its carriages rushed past me, missing me by an inch. Nobody made a start toward me. I suppose everyone here is living dangerously. My cell phone vibrated in my pocket. It was Nicole calling for the third time. She wanted some news, but I didn't have the strength to answer. I spent an hour on a bench at the station, staring at the thousands of passengers piling in to get home. Finally, I decided to board a train.

A youngish man got on just behind me but remained standing at the end of the carriage. As soon as it left, he started yelling to contend with the sound of the train as it whistled round the bends. He relayed his story at such a speed that no more than a few words could be made out: "hostel," "work," "illness." He smelled of booze, rattled on about meal vouchers and *métro* tickets, said he wanted work but work didn't want him. A few other words emerged from his garbled speech: he had children, he wasn't "a beggar." The commuters stared at their shoes or suddenly became immersed in their free newspaper as he passed before them with a polystyrene Starbucks cup in his outstretched hand. Then he left the carriage to get onto the next one.

His display got me thinking. Sometimes we give, other times we don't. Of all the homeless people, we give to the ones who touch us the most, those who find the words capable of stirring us. The conclusion hit me smack in the face: ultimately, even with the destitute, it's the survivors who perform best, since they're the ones who succeed in undermining the competition. If I end up homeless, I'm not at all sure I'll be one of the survivors. Not like Charles.

At home in the evening, I was meant to be tired because—having risen at 4 a.m.—I'd done my morning shift at Logistics before going on to nail the test at BLC Consulting. The truth is I haven't told Nicole that I won't be going back to Logistics anytime soon. The Monday after head-butting Mehmet and my two-day suspension from work, I was greeted by a letter that arrived by recorded delivery. I'd been fired. It was a shocker, because we badly need the money.

I took myself to the job center immediately to see if my adviser had anything up my alley. Normally I fall under the wings of APEC, the recruitment agency for people at executive level, but they don't offer part-time work. I prefer the employees and workers section. It's a couple of notches down the pecking order, where you have a slightly greater chance of survival.

Since I didn't have an appointment, he saw me in the corridor between the waiting room and the cubicles that serve as offices. I told him that Logistics no longer needed me.

"They haven't called me," he said with surprise.

He's young enough to be my son, but frankly I'm relieved he's not. But he is kind to me—he treats me like a father.

"They will call you. In the meantime, you haven't got something quick for me?"

He nodded at the bulletin board.

"They're all there. Right now there's pretty much nothing."

If I had a forklift license or vocational training as a cook, I'd have a better chance at landing something. I had to search the unskilled jobs, but my sciatica counts me out of the rare vacancies on that front. As I left I made a small gesture at him through his office screen. He was interviewing a girl of about twenty. He responded with an irritated look, as though he half-recognized me but was struggling to place me.

The following day I received a letter by registered post from Logistics' lawyer. I'd been reading up on similar cases, and there's nothing complicated: I hit my manager, and he denies kicking me. He's saying he was walking past and "brushed" me. Getting fired is not the worst of it: I could end up in court for assault. Mehmet has cast-iron evidence recording his gravely incapacitating injuries and the potential aftereffects they could cause. The letter detailed his balance and orientation issues, and his severe post-traumatic stress, the long-term repercussions of which will be hard to predict.

He is demanding 5,000 euros in damages.

Just shy of sixty years old, I got kicked in the backside by my superior, yet it seems I have "seriously violated the principle of hierarchy in the company." That's it. I have disrupted the social order. For its part, Logistics is demanding 20,000 euros in damages. That's fifty times the monthly salary that I'm no longer receiving.

Nicole, my love, her patience is wearing thin. She's had her fill. I decided not to bring this up with her. The report I gave her of the test required her to draw on every last drop of energy and encouragement she had left at the end of the day: wait for the results, we're never in a strong position to judge ourselves, you don't know for sure that the young guns did better, just because they seemed so confident doesn't mean they gave the best answers, especially with the open-ended questions it's all about experience, something they lack, and what's more if the recruitment people called you in then it's because they're looking for a more considered approach, someone more tried and tested. I know the spiel by heart. I love Nicole more than anything, but the spiel . . . the spiel I hate.

Later on she finally fell asleep. I got up as quietly as possible so as not to wake her. I do that when I can't sleep: I get dressed and go out for a stroll around the neighborhood. These last few years it's become something of a ritual. After traumatic experiences like the one at the *métro* earlier on, I need to steady my thoughts. This time I walked a bit farther than usual. I was far from home, near the RER station. The gates were open and the cold wind was rushing through the pedestrian tunnels. The garbage cans were overflowing and cans of beer lay strewn across the cement. A heavy neon light flooded the station. I pushed at a little metal placard that read STAFF ONLY and went down a flight of stairs. I was on the well-lit platform. I didn't feel as if I was crying, but all the same the tears started to flow. I was standing up, feet planted on the track ballast, legs apart. I waited for the train.

All that for nothing.

In the morning, I'm shocked to see the envelope with the BLC Consulting logo. I hadn't expected anything for a week, and it's not even been three days. I open it in such a hurry that I tear off part of the letter.

Holy fuck.

I sprint up to the apartment and then back down again, and very soon it's midday and I've been pacing back and forth outside Nicole's resource center for an hour, jittery as a cat, until finally she comes out. She sees me from a distance and can tell from my body language that it's good news. She smiles as she comes toward me, I hold out the letter, she scans it and right away says, "My love," and her voice catches. I am overwhelmed by the certainty that a miracle has just taken place in our life. Both of us have tears in our eyes. I know I must resist the temptation, but I already have a strong urge to call the girls. Mathilde in particular, I don't know why. Probably because she's the more normal of the two, the one who'll process it quicker.

Against all expectations, I have passed the tests. I've made it through.

Individual interview: Thursday, May 7.

This is unbelievable . . . I made it through!

Nicole hugs me tight, but she doesn't want us to make a scene outside her workplace. I kiss a few of her colleagues and shake some hands in greeting as they head out for lunch. Everyone knows I'm looking for work, so when I go there I try hard to look my best, to appear as if I'm bearing up and not letting things get on top of me. For an unemployed person, being there when people are leaving the office is always tough. It's not jealousy. The unemployment itself isn't the hard part: what's difficult is continuing to exist in a society based on labor economics. No matter where you turn, you are defined by what you don't have.

But now everything's different. I feel as though my chest has burst open, that for the first time in four years I can breathe. Nicole says nothing; she is jubilant, holding my arm and squeezing it as we make our way down the street.

In the evening we go to Chez Paul to celebrate, even though we both know this is a real extravagance. We act as though it's no big deal, but that doesn't stop us from selecting our dishes via the price column on the menu.

"I'll have a main course and a dessert," Nicole says.

But when the waitress arrives I order two starters (*œufs en gelée*, which I know Nicole loves), and a half bottle of Saint-Joseph. Nicole swallows hard, then smiles with resignation.

"I'm so proud of you," she says.

I don't know why she says that, but it's always good to hear. I hurry to get around to what I consider the most important point.

"I've thought about how I'm going to handle the interview. I figure they'll have called in three or four of us. I have to stand out. My idea . . ."

And off I go. I'm like an excited teenager recounting his first triumph over a grown-up.

Every now and then Nicole places her hand on mine to let me know I'm speaking too loudly. I lower my voice, but within five minutes I've forgotten again. It makes her laugh. Good God, it's been years since we were as happy as we are tonight. At the end of the meal, I realize that I virtually haven't drawn breath. I try to tone it down, but I can't control myself.

Rue de Lapp is buzzing as though it were summer. We walk arm in arm, in love.

"And you'll be able to stop working at Logistics," says Nicole.

It takes me by surprise, and Nicole raises a quizzical eyebrow. I put on a facial expression that would seem credible enough to me, looking rather ashen in the process. If I don't get this job and end up in court with 25,000 euros to pay in damages . . . Thankfully Nicole doesn't notice anything.

Instead of taking the *métro* at Bastille, I'm not sure why, she carries on walking, stops at a bench, and sits down. She rummages in her bag, takes out a little package, and hands it to me. I open it to find a little roll of fabric with an orange pattern, held together by a small piece of red string, at the end of which is a tiny bell.

"It's a lucky charm. It's Japanese. I bought it the day you were called in to take the test. So far it seems to be doing the trick."

It seems silly, but it makes me very emotional. Not the gift itself. At least . . . I don't really know anymore, but I feel emotional. I must have polished off the Saint-Joseph more or less on my own. It's our life that I find moving. This woman, after everything we've been through, deserves every good fortune. As I stuff the talisman into my trouser pocket, I feel indestructible.

From now on, I'm in the homestretch.

No one's going to stand in my way anymore.

Charles often used to say: "The only certainty is that nothing happens as planned." That's classic Charles. He loves nothing more than a momentous phrase or a lofty stance. I wonder whether he might be an orphan. Long story short, I had horrendous nightmares in the run-up to the interview, but in the end it went pretty well.

I had been invited to BLC Consulting's headquarters in La Défense. I was biding my time in the waiting room, a large space with a luxurious carpet, uplighting, a stunning Asian receptionist, and discreet background music. A place tailor-made for boredom. I was a quarter of an hour early. Nicole had applied a very thin layer of foundation to my forehead to hide any trace of my bruise. I had a constant feeling that it was running, and I had to resist the temptation to check. In my pocket, I played the Japanese charm through my fingers.

Bertrand Lacoste came striding in and shook me by the hand. At fifty years of age, he came across as absurdly sure of himself, but quite affable.

"Would you like some coffee?"

"No, thank you, I'm fine," I said.

"Nervous?"

He asked this with a little smile. Slipping coins into the machine, he added:

"Yup, it's always difficult finding work."

"Difficult, but honorable," I said.

He looked up at me, as if seeing me properly for the first time.

"So no coffee?"

"Thank you, no."

And we stayed there, in front of the machine, with him sipping his synthetic coffee. He turned his back and considered the reception area around him with an air of glum resignation.

"Fucking decorators—can't trust them to do anything!"

Straightaway that set the tone for me. I don't know exactly what happened after that. I was so pumped up it came out automatically.

"I see," I said.

This made him start.

"What do you see?"

"You're going to play it all 'casual.'"

"Sorry?"

"I said you're going to play it all 'relaxed,' sort of 'the circumstances are professional, but at the end of the day we're all human beings.' Am I right?"

He shot me a look. He seemed livid. I told myself I'd gotten off to a decent start, then continued:

"You're playing on the fact that we're more or less the same age to see whether I fall into the trap of being overfamiliar. And now I think you're giving me this look to see if I panic and start backpedaling."

His glare softened and he smiled:

"Right . . . well, we've succeeded in clearing the air, wouldn't you say?"

I didn't answer.

He chucked his plastic cup in the garbage can.

"So, let's get on with the serious stuff."

He walked ahead of me down the corridor, still with that long stride. I felt like a confederate soldier a few minutes before the enemy charge.

He'd done his job well and studied my application carefully, incisively. The moment he came across a weakness in my CV, he pounced on it, exploiting the first sign of frailty in the candidate.

"He carried on testing me, but the tone was different now."

"Did he tell you who he was recruiting for?" Nicole asks.

"No, not at all . . . There were just two or three clues. It's all pretty vague, but maybe I'll manage to find out more. It's in my interest to get ahead of the game. You'll see why. At the end of the interview, I said to him:

"'I must say that I'm very surprised that you should be interested in a candidate of my age.'

"Lacoste pretended to be nonplussed, but eventually he placed his elbows on the table and stared at me.

"'Monsieur Delambre,' he said to me, 'we are just another company in a competitive market. Everyone needs to stand out from the crowd. You with your employers, me with my clients. You are my wild card.'"

"But . . . what does that even mean?" Nicole asks.

"'My client is expecting young graduates, which is what I'm going to give them; they're not expecting an applicant like you—I'm going to surprise them. And then, between you and me, when push comes to shove in the next round, I figure the decision will make itself.'"

"Is there another round?" Nicole asks. "I thought—"

"'There are four of you on the short list. The final decision will be based on one further test. I'm going to be open with you: you are the oldest of the four, but it's not at all beyond the realms of possibility that your experience will make all the difference.'"

Nicole begins to look suspicious. She cocks her head to one side.

"And what is this 'further test'?"

"'Our client intends to assess a selection of their top execs. Your mission is to conduct this assessment. You will be tested, if you will, on your ability to test others.'"

"But . . ." Nicole still doesn't see where this is going. "How does that work?"

"'We are going to simulate a hostage taking . . .'"

"What?!"

Nicole looks as if she's about to choke.

"'. . . and your task involves placing the candidates under sufficient duress for us to test various criteria: their coolness under pressure, their conduct in an extremely stressful scenario, and their loyalty to the values of the company to which they belong.'"

Nicole is struck dumb.

"But that's outrageous!" she cries. "You have to make these people think they've been taken hostage? At work? Is that what you're telling me?"

"'There will be a commando unit played by actors, weapons loaded with blanks, cameras to film their reactions, and you will lead the interrogations and direct the commandos. You will need to use your imagination.'"

Nicole is on her feet, disgusted.

"That's sick," she says.

There's Nicole in a nutshell. You'd think that her capacity for indignation would have lost its edge over time, but not a bit of it. When she feels scandalized, she can't help herself—nothing will stop her. In these situations, you have to try to calm her down right away, to step in before her reaction gets out of control.

"You shouldn't look at it like that, Nicole."

"How should I look at it? An armed commando unit comes bursting into their office, threatens them, interrogates them, for how long? An hour? Two hours? They think they might die, that these people will kill them? All that just so their boss can have a bit of a laugh?"

Her voice is trembling. I haven't seen her like this for years. I try to be patient. Her attitude is understandable. But I'm already fast-forwarding ten days, and it hits me: everything hinges on one single, palpable fact: I have to pass this test.

I try to smooth things over.

"I know it's not very . . . But you have to look at the situation from a different angle, Nicole."

"Why? Because you think this approach is acceptable? Why don't we just shoot them too, while we're at it?"

"Wait—"

"Or better still! Put some mattresses on the pavement without telling them, then hang them out the window! Just to see their reaction! Alain, have you gone completely mad?"

"Nicole, don't—"

"And you're really prepared to go along with this?"

"I understand where you're coming from, but you have to see things from my side, too."

"No way, Alain. I can understand anything, but that doesn't mean I can forgive it!"

She has moved into our train wreck of a kitchen.

I see the two bits of drywall that have been holding up the sink for years. The current linoleum is even less resistant than last year's, already curling up at the corners in pitiful fashion. Nicole, livid as she stands in the center of this mess, is wearing a woolen cardigan that she can't afford to replace. It makes her look diminished. It makes her look poor. And she doesn't even realize it. I take it as a personal insult.

"For Christ's sake, all I know is that I'm still in the running!"

I'm shouting now. The violence of my tone roots her to the spot.

"Alain . . . ," she says, panic in her voice.

"Don't 'Alain' me! Fucking hell, can't you see we're turning into tramps? We've been slowly running aground for four years . . . soon enough we'll be *in* the ground! So yes, it's disgusting, but so is our life—our life is disgusting! Yes, those people are sick, but I'm going to do it, you hear me? I'm going to do what they ask. Everything they ask! Even if I have to fucking shoot them to get the job, I'll do it because I'm fed up . . . I'm sixty years old, and I'm fed up of having my ass kicked!"

I am beside myself.

I grab the wall unit beside me and yank it so violently that it comes away completely. Plates, mugs—everything comes tumbling down with a terrible crash.

Nicole cries out and then starts sobbing into her hands. But I don't have the strength to console her. I can't. Deep down that's the worst thing about it. We've been fighting together for four years just to keep our heads above water, and one fine day we realize it's over. Without knowing it, each of us has folded. Because even with the best couples, each one has a different way of seeing reality. That's what I'm trying to say to her. But I'm so furious that I get it wrong.

"You're able to have scruples and morals because you have a job. For me, it's the opposite."

It's not the best way of putting things, but in the circumstances I can't do any better. I think Nicole has gotten the general gist, but I don't have time to make sure. I pull the door shut as I leave.

At the bottom of our building, I realize I've forgotten to put on a coat.

It's raining and cold, so I turn up my shirt collar.

Like a tramp.

6

It's May 8, a public holiday. We are celebrating Mother's Day at our place because next Sunday Gregory wants to be with his own mother. Nicole has told Mathilde twenty thousand times that she doesn't give a damn about Mother's Day, but to no avail. Mathilde, however, sticks to it. I suppose it's because later on she doesn't want her children to overlook it. She's in training.

The girls are supposed to be arriving at midday, but at 9:00 a.m., Nicole is still in bed, facing the wall. Since her horrified reaction to the selection test that I intend to pass, we've barely exchanged three words. For Nicole, it's simply unacceptable.

I think she was crying this morning. I didn't have the courage to touch her. I got up and went to the kitchen. Last night she didn't pick up the broken dishes, just pushed them into a pile in the corner of the room. It's very large—I must have broken most of our dishes. I can't clean it up now, it would make a dreadful racket.

I turn around, not knowing what to do, so I go and switch on my computer to see if I have any messages.

I gauge my usefulness to society by the number of e-mails I receive. Back in the day, my ex-colleagues from Bercaud would send me a few lines that I'd reply to right away. Just chatting. And then I realized that the only ones who still wrote to me were the ones who had been fired, too. Fellow reduced-to-clear friends. I stopped replying, and they stopped writing. In fact, everything around us got scarcer. We had two old friends: a school pal of Nicole's who lived in Toulouse, and a guy I knew from military service who I had dinner with from time to time. The others were friends from work or holidays, or the parents of the girls' friends from when they lived at home. Maybe people got a bit tired of us. And we of them. When you don't share the same concerns, you don't share the same pleasures. Nowadays Nicole and I are rather lonely. Only Lucie still sends me e-mails, at least one a week. These messages are practically devoid of content, just a way for her to let me know she's thinking of me. Mathilde phones her mother—that's another way.

My inbox consists of newsletters from various job centers and recruitment agencies and a few reminders from management or HR publications that I haven't subscribed to for three years.

When I open my browser, Google gives me some headlines from around the world: *Good news: only 548,000 job losses in the United States this month . . .* Everyone was expecting far worse. It doesn't take much to celebrate these days. *Financial crime reaches all-time high. Business leaders explain it is natural phenomenon . . .* I click onto the next page, not in the least disturbed: I have every confidence in business leaders and their ability to explain away the natural effects of economics.

I hear a noise in the bedroom and move toward it. Nicole appears at last.

Without uttering a word she pours herself some coffee into a Duralex glass. The mugs are in pieces over by the door, with the broom resting on top.

Her attitude infuriates me. Rather than supporting me, she's being all sanctimonious.

"Scruples don't pay the bills."

Nicole doesn't answer. Her face is sullen and she looks exhausted. What have we become . . .

She puts her glass in the sink, takes out some large garbage bags, and fills up four because each one gets so heavy. The jagged porcelain is sharp and cuts through the plastic here and there. You'd normally expect to see plate-smashing antics for the audience's amusement in some vaudeville farce. Here it seems so prosaic.

"I couldn't give a damn about being poor. I don't want to be immoral."

I don't have an answer for that. I take the garbage bags downstairs while Nicole takes a shower. Two trips. When we're back in the room together, we don't manage a conversation and the minutes pass by. The children are going to arrive and nothing is ready. And we need to go and buy some dishes. Short on time, but more important, what with this leaden atmosphere, short on strength.

Nicole is sitting down, bolt upright, looking outside as though there were something to see.

"It's the company that's immoral," I say. "Not the unemployed."

When the girls ring the bell, each of us waits for the other to act. I give in first. I provide a few lame excuses that demand no further explanation, and we take everyone to a restaurant. The girls are surprised and find it odd that, given the occasion, their mother doesn't really seem to be at the party. And what makes it worse is that Nicole is pretending to be happy. I can tell that it's upsetting them. No, not upset . . . They feel that whatever's wrong with us might overwhelm them, too, and it scares them. Mathilde gives her a mother a cardigan. A cardigan, for fuck's sake. I can't remember when it started, but for months now they have been giving us useful presents. If they find out that I've broken all the dishes, I can expect six soup bowls for my birthday.

During dessert, Mathilde announces that they have signed a purchase agreement for their apartment. There are still a few question marks with the bank, but Gregory breaks into a smug smile: he's got it all under control. Their lawyer is putting together the paperwork and it will be theirs by the holidays. Inside, I hope they manage to pay for it.

When I go to settle the bill, I realize that Lucie has beaten me to it without anyone noticing. Both of us pretend not to make a big deal out of it.

"I can help you with anything, Alain," Nicole says before bedtime, "but this . . . this hostage taking doesn't fit with who I am. I don't want to hear any more of it. Don't make me live with that."

She turns toward the wall immediately. I can't expect to persuade her, and it makes me sad.

But I don't leave it there. I start thinking about this final test. Because if I pass, even if it involves methods she finds objectionable, our differences of opinion will be nothing but a distant memory.

That's the way to look at it.

From: David Fontana
To the attention of: Bertrand Lacoste
Subject: "Hostage taking" role play—Client: Exxyal

As discussed, this is where the operation currently stands.

For the commando unit, I have recruited two colleagues with whom I have worked on several occasions in the past and for whom I can vouch entirely.

As regards the role of Exxyal's clients, I have short-listed two men: a young Arab and a fifty-year-old Belgian actor.

In terms of weaponry, I have opted for the following:

—   3 Uzi submachine guns (under 3 kilograms in weight, rate of fire of 950 rounds/min., 9×19 cartridges)
—   2 Glock 17 pistols (635 grams, same caliber, 31-cartridge magazines)

—   2 Smith & Wesson pistols

All weapons will of course be loaded with blank rounds.

The space I am proposing is in a prestigious location, as Exxyal is "inviting important clients" there. It has a meeting room and four offices, with toilets, etc. The site is situated in the outskirts of Paris, with large glass windows overlooking the Seine (see photos and map—Appendix 3).

The premises offer a very favorable layout for what you have planned. We will need to carry out several run-throughs, and so we must finalize a scenario as soon as possible. You will find my proposal in Appendix 4.

Overview: Your client's executives will be summoned to a highly important but confidential meeting, which will explain why it is taking place on a public holiday and why they have been informed at such short notice.

The pretext is that they will be meeting important overseas clients.

The commando unit will intervene at the start of the meeting.

The head of Exxyal Europe, Monsieur Dorfmann, will be evacuated immediately, thereby creating an intensely stressful atmosphere conducive to the aims of your test. It will also give him the opportunity to observe the ensuing sequence of events from elsewhere.

The remaining executives, having been relieved of their personal effects and cell phones, will be held in the office and interrogated in turn. The scenario can if necessary accommodate the option of isolating the hostages for several minutes in order to gauge their capacity for organizing themselves, or indeed for offering resistance, as per your request. The commando head will conduct the individual interrogations as per the assessors' instructions.

The role play will be monitored via cameras and screens.

It is my belief that this fulfills the terms of the brief you assigned me. Thank you for your confidence and for the valuable assistance offered by Madame Olenka Zbikowski.

Respectfully yours,
David Fontana

7

Now that I've stopped working at Logistics, you would think the 4:00 a.m. wake-up would start to wear, but not a bit of it. In fact, I feel so charged up that I barely sleep, and getting out of bed almost comes as a relief. Most nights, Nicole clings to me in her sleep, something to do with holding on to me—it's a game between us. We hold each other, pretend to let go, then grab each other again. We've done this for twenty years and not once spoken about it.

This morning, I know full well that she's awake and that she's just bluffing. But we both remain in our bubbles. A tacit agreement not to touch one another.

As planned, I get to Logistics a little ahead of time. I know the guys from the other teams, and since I have no desire for their questions or their pity, I find a corner where I can survey the entrance without being seen, keeping an eye out for the big, gangling frame of Romain. But it's the unsteady figure of Charles that appears at the end of the street. I have no idea how he does it—the guy must drink in his sleep—but it's not even 5:00 a.m. and already his breath smells like a brewery. But I know my boy Charles . . . tanked up or not, he's always hale and hearty. Although, that said, he does seem to be struggling to place me this morning.

"Well, I never . . . ," he says, looking as if he's seen a ghost.

He slowly lifts his left hand. It's a gesture born of shyness that he makes quite often. It makes his enormous watch slide down to his elbow.

"How are you doing, Charles?"

"The golden days are behind us," Charles replies, as enigmatic as ever.

"I'm waiting for Romain."

Charles's face brightens. He is visibly happy that he can be of service.

"Ah, Romain's switched teams!"

Over the past four years, I have become hypersensitive to screw-ups. Just one word and I can feel them looming—it's become a reflex.

"Meaning?"

"He's on full nights. Thing is he's supervisor now."

It is very hard to know what someone like Charles is thinking. The trancelike state he's permanently in lends him a certain unfathomability. You can't tell if a great deal of comprehension is going on, whether the blank delivery of this harmless news is belying a sort of creeping reflection, or whether booze has addled every last brain cell.

"What do you mean, Charles?"

There's no doubt he registers my concern. He becomes all philosophical, shrugging his scrawny shoulders.

"He's been promoted, Romain. Been made supervisor and we . . ."

"When exactly?"

Charles purses his lips, as if things are about to come to a head.

"Monday after you left."

I ought to be congratulating myself for my intuition, but this is too much of a screw-up. Charles pats me on the shoulder like a Good Samaritan, as if he were offering me his condolences. Maybe his mind does work faster than I've given him credit for, because he says:

"If you need me I was there, too, and I saw everything."

That I did not see coming. For further encouragement, Charles raises a solemn finger:

"When the woodcutter enters the forest with his ax on his shoulder, the trees say the handle is one of ours."

The bit about the ax bamboozles me, but however he chooses to phrase his offer of help, you only need to look at Charles to see how much he means it.

"That's kind, Charles, but I'm not about to make you lose what little work you have."

A sudden look of weariness and regret descends on Charles.

"You don't think I make much of a witness, not presentable enough, is that it? Well, hear you me, that's absolutely right. If you show up in court with a bum like me as your only witness, that risks being quite . . . quite . . ."

He searches for the word.

"Counterproductive?" I suggest.

"That's the one!" Charles bursts out. "Counterproductive!"

He is over the moon. Finding the *mot juste* classes as a major victory. So much so that he forgets the need for any commiseration on my part. He bobs his head, in a state of marvel at this word. It's my turn to pat him on the shoulder. But with me, the condolences are sincere.

I get ready to leave and Charles grabs me by the arm:

"Come and have a drink at my place one evening, if you'd like . . . I mean . . ."

As I attempt to imagine the meaning of "at my place" and the significance of the invitation, Charles is already walking off with his long, lolloping gait.

I mull it over on the way home.

On the *métro*, I check that I still have Romain's cell phone number. Logistics seem to be taking this whole matter very seriously. They are iron-cladding their case. They won't stop at the shirt—I'm going to end up buck naked.

A quick calculation tells me that if he's on nights, Romain might not even be asleep yet.

I call.

He picks up right away.

"Hi, Romain!"

"Oh, hi!"

He recognizes me at once. Makes me wonder if he was expecting me. His voice is chirpy but faint. I detect a little irritation. Nicole says that unemployment has made me paranoid, and she may well be right. Romain confirms his sudden promotion.

"What about you, old man?" he asks.

The more of this "old man" I get, the less I can handle it. Nicole says that unemployment has made me touchy, too.

I tell him about Logistics and the letter from the lawyer. I allude to the threat of a trial.

"No way!" Romain says, flabbergasted.

No point going any further. He's pretending to be surprised by a piece of news that everyone knows already. No doubt it's been a hot topic of discussion for the last three days. If he's trying to pull the wool over my eyes, he's flunked it.

"If I find myself in court, your witness statement will help me out a lot."

"Well, of course, old man!"

No doubt about it this time. If he said it would be tricky to testify in my favor, I might still have had a chance. But no, Romain's mind is made up. He won't be answering my calls two days before he takes the stand.

"Thanks, Romain. Really, thanks a lot, too kind!"

Touché. He got the irony. That millisecond of silence before his response confirms my every fear.

"Don't mention it, old man!"

I hang up, feeling pretty downbeat. For a moment, I entertain the thought of going back to Charles. If I ask him, he'll lose his job, but he'll come all the same. I don't think he will have an ounce of credibility and it would all be for nothing. That said, if it's all I have, I will do it. No choice.

The sword of Damocles is hanging over me, and the higher it gets, the greater the destruction when it's finally released. I feel wild thoughts running through me.

Why do they want to do this to me?

Why do they feel this need to hold my head underwater?

Romain, I understand. I don't hold it against him. In his position, if I had to choose between helping a friend and keeping my job, I'd have no hesitation either. But the company?

I run through the various options available to me. Given the circumstances, I choose the remorseful approach. I'm going to write a letter of apology. If they want, they can pin it up around the workplace or send it to the employees with their next pay stub . . . I couldn't give a shit. Losing this job is hard to take, but it's nothing compared to a trial that might see me stripped of everything.

Back home, I run up to my office. A courier must have arrived first thing since Nicole was still in to accept delivery of a thick envelope with the BLC Consulting logo. My heart is pounding. They didn't hang around.

Normally, when we leave something for each other at home, Nicole and I will pop a little note alongside, make a joke if we're in good spirits, or something frisky if we're in the mood. Or something loving if none of that applies. This morning, Nicole just left the envelope on my desk. No comment.

Before opening it, I grab the letter from Logistics' lawyer that I have hidden in my study and call the number. A girl picks up and puts me through to a guy who explains that the lawyer can't speak to me. It takes ten minutes of negotiating to arrange a telephone meeting with the lawyer's assistant. I have to call back this afternoon at 3:30 p.m. and she'll give me five minutes of her time.

8

The BLC Consulting envelope contains a dossier entitled: "Recruiting an HR Assistant." Inside, a document with the heading: "Role play exercise: hostage taking at the workplace."

Page one announces the objective: "Your mission: to assess senior executives subjected to violent and sustained stress."

Page two details the broad outline of the scenario. Since the hostage taking will be conducted by candidates for the HR position (my competitors and myself), the document sets out the protocols to ensure each of us has an equal chance.

The candidates for one position select the candidates for another: how very in line with the times. The system doesn't even need to exercise authority anymore—the employees take care of that themselves. In this case it's pretty extreme, since we get to fire the worst-performing execs on the spot before they've even secured the job.

The incoming generate the outgoing. Capitalism has just achieved perpetual motion.

I scan the dossier as quickly as possible but, as feared, all the documents are stock, anonymous. We are not therefore supposed to have any way of guessing which company is involved and, more important, of identifying the execs that have been put forward for the test, which would have opened the way for all sorts of secret negotiations among the HR candidates charged with assessing them.

The system does have some moral standing.

We are to assess five executives. Their ages have been rounded to the nearest five.

Three men:
- — Thirty-five, PhD in law, legal department
- — Forty-five, top credentials in economics, finance manager
- — Fifty, top degree in civil engineering, senior project manager

Two women:
- — Thirty-five, business school graduate, sales executive
- — Fifty, top degree in structural engineering, senior project manager

These are senior executives with serious responsibilities. The cream of the company. Champions of the M&M machine: "Marketing & Management," the two heaving breasts of modern business. The principles are simple: marketing involves making people buy what they don't want to buy, while management involves making executives do what they don't want to do. In short, these people are very active in the running of the company and must adhere passionately to its values (otherwise they'd have been weeded out long ago). I wonder why they are assessing these five ahead of any others. Clarifying that will be crucial.

The dossier contains details of everything: their studies, their career paths, their responsibilities. I estimate their annual salaries to fall in the 150,000–210,000 euro bracket.

I go for a walk to think all this through. That's one of my things. My thoughts have a tendency to simmer away. Walking doesn't so much calm them down as channel them. And right now I'm boiling over. I stop in my tracks as I consider how fast everything around me is unraveling. Nicole, Romain, Logistics . . . Getting this job is becoming all the more essential. I am reassured by the fact that I've worked for more than thirty years, and I can confidently say I'm good at what I do. If I carry on being good at it for ten more days, I'll be able to eradicate all these threats. This helps me regain my focus. I fall back into my stride, but I'm still struggling to silence the little voice running through my head. Nicole's voice. Not so much her voice as her words. Acting against her will is unbearable, and I've been in doubt ever since she set out her categorical disapproval. I don't hesitate to do what needs to be done, and that's something she'll never comprehend. Life in her job is a cozy one. Nicole, lucky thing, will never know what it takes to survive in a competitive commercial field. What worries me about her reaction is that ultimately she doesn't believe in my chances; she thinks I'm getting worked up over something that's more virtual than real. My gut's telling me to join the fray, right now. But . . .

I turn all this over and over, unable to think about anything else. My anxiety is like a roly-poly—it always rights itself. I make up my mind.

It's the young Polish girl who picks up. I like her slightly husky tone very much. I find it sexy. I introduce myself. No, Bertrand Lacoste cannot take my call, he's in a meeting. Is it anything she can help me with?

"It's somewhat complicated."

"Try anyway."

Pretty abrupt.

"I'm just about to get underway with my preparation for the final recruitment test."

"Yes, I'm aware of that."

"Monsieur Lacoste assured me that each candidate's chances were the same, but—"

"But you're not so sure."

The girl's not cutting me much slack, here. I'm going to trip up, but I go for it anyway.

"That's exactly it. I find it odd."

Lacoste may well be in a meeting, but she disturbs him nonetheless. My tactic's turning out all right. An evaluation and recruitment firm's image must be rooted in its integrity. That justifies disturbing the boss. He comes on the line.

"How are you?"

You would swear he'd been expecting my call and that he was overjoyed to hear from me. That said, there's still a slight edge to his voice.

"I'm in a meeting right now, but my assistant tells me you have some concerns."

"A few, yes. In fact, no—just the one. I am skeptical about the chances of a man my age in a recruitment process at this level."

"We've been through this already, Alain. And I've given you my answer."

He's good, the wily dog. I'm going to have to keep my wits about me. The whole "Alain" thing is a classic ruse, but still it works: he's playing it all buddy-buddy, even though both of us know full well I can't call him "Bertrand" in return.

My silence speaks volumes.

He knows that I know. At last, we have some sort of understanding.

"Listen," he continues, "I was clear with you before and I'll be clear with you again. There won't be many of you. Each profile is fairly different from the other. Your age is a handicap, but your experience is a bonus. What more is there to discuss?"

"Your client's intention."

"My client is not after looks, he's after skills. If you feel up to the mark, as your test results indicate, your application will stay live. If not . . ."

He picks up on my hesitation.

"I'm going to take this on another line. One minute . . ."

The switchboard fobs me off with forty seconds of music. Hearing this version of Vivaldi's "Spring" makes it hard to hold out much hope for the summer.

"Excuse me," Bertrand Lacoste picks up again.

"Not at all."

"Listen, Monsieur Delambre."

No more Alain. The mask slips.

"The company for which I am recruiting is one of my most important clients. I cannot allow myself to make an error of judgment."

His intimate tone has given way to seriousness. Now he's playing the sincerity card. When you're dealing with managers at his level, it's impossible to know where the lying stops.

"This position requires a high level of professionalism and I haven't found a huge number of candidates who are *really* up to the mark. I can't prejudice the outcome, but between you and me, you would be wrong not to stay in the running. I'm not sure if I'm being clear . . ."

Now this . . . this is new. Very new indeed. I barely heard the rest of his speech. I should have recorded it to play to Nicole.

"That's all I needed to know."

"I'll see you soon," he says as he hangs up.

My heart is pounding. I start walking again to vent my frazzled neurons. And then I get back to work. That has done me a world of good.

First up, focus on the objective facts.

I'm guessing we are three or four candidates: any more than that would be unmanageable. I base my calculations on three since it doesn't alter things dramatically.

So I must beat two rivals to land the job. To manage that, I must perform the best when selecting the five executives. I must eliminate the weakest candidates. Whichever of us registers the most scalps will have been the most selective and therefore the most effective. Five to start with, get rid of four, and finish with a bull's-eye. That's the objective.

I'll have a job if one of them (or preferably several of them) loses theirs.

As I was thinking all this through I had slipped into autopilot and taken a left, ending up down in the *métro*. I have no idea where I'm going. My feet have led me here. I look up and focus on the map. From where I live, every train goes via République. I trace the multicolored lines and can't stop myself smiling: my subconscious is guiding me. I sit down and wait for the connection.

I have to load all the dice in my favor. That involves choosing the best strategy, the one that will result in the greatest number of losers.

I leave République behind and push on to Châtelet.

I'm applying management rule number one: an executive can only be defined as competent when he is capable of anticipation.

As far as I can see, there are two possible strategies.

The first is the one prompted by the dossier: read the anonymous files, study the scenario and imagine, in absolute or approximate terms, how to make the execs surrender to the terrorists' demands, to lose control, to come across as cowards, to betray their company and colleagues—to betray themselves. Classic. Each of them will trust his or her intuition, knowing that in a similar situation, the question is not *whether* they will betray (with a gun to their head!), but *how much* they will betray.

If I were younger, that's the strategy I would use to prep for the task. However, thanks to Lacoste, I know that all my competitors are younger than me—they will definitely approach it that way, too.

I have no choice but to opt for the second strategy. I kick my brain into gear.

Management theory states the following: to attain a goal, set interim objectives. I establish three: it is essential I discover the identity of BLC Consulting's client and of the five executives; then I will need to investigate each one to find out everything about their lives, hopes, expectations, strengths and—most important—weaknesses; and, finally, I have to work out how to give myself the best chance of bringing them down.

I have ten days to go—not long at all.

My subconscious has brought me this far. To the gates of BLC Consulting headquarters.

The heart of La Défense, that vast space bristling with buildings, riddled with motorway and *métro* tunnels, and banked up by wind-battered walkways teeming with myriads of panic-stricken ants just like me. The sort of place where, if I'm victorious, I'll have the opportunity to see out my career. I enter the building's vast lobby and scope out the lay of the land, before making for a set of armchairs with a good view of the elevators.

Even though time is of the essence, I settle down for several hours of (fruitless) surveillance dedicated to the arrival of a person who won't lead me anywhere . . . It's not the right strategy, but it does allow me some time to think, and it's in a place where there's a chance—however slim—of finding something useful. I station myself sideways so that I'm invisible to anyone exiting the elevator, and I take out my notebook. Every twenty seconds I glance over at the elevators. I never thought there'd be so much coming and going at this time of day. People of all shapes and sizes.

I try to focus on my primary objective. BLC Consulting's client is a major company (in terms of scale and resources) operating in a strategic industry (if its executives require regular assessment, that means their responsibilities are more important than they are). But then there are any number of strategic industries. They range from the military to the environment, via international organizations or any area linked to the state, which covers trade secrets, defense, pharmaceuticals, security . . . It's all too wide. I strike them off and retain two key points: a very big company operating in a strategic industry.

Waves of people roll in and out of the interminable elevators. An hour passes. I carry on taking notes.

Administering a hostage-taking role play is no simple task. You need actors, fake weapons . . . what else? A few vague images come to me from the movies: people burst into a bank, police sirens wailing outside; they barricade the doors, yelling to one another as they run behind the counter, employees and customers looking on in terror. Everyone's on the floor. What then?

Another hour later, the intern arrives. She really is very pretty. Her blonde hair is unbelievable. She exits the elevator with an assured step, her eyes focused straight ahead. The sort of girl who wants to show that she never deviates from her path. She's wearing a light-gray suit and very high heels. Half a dozen sets of men's eyes follow her as she crosses the lobby toward the revolving doors. Mine not included. A few seconds later I start tailing her, then watch from the pavement as she strides into the *métro*. I'm left feeling rather frightened by her. I have no way of knowing whether she'll be present on the day of the hostage taking or which bit she'll be overseeing, but I just hope I don't come up against an adversary of her caliber, because this girl is razor-sharp: too young to have done the damage she's capable of, but her time cannot be far off.

At the precise moment I come through the revolving door back into the lobby, I see Bertrand Lacoste leaving the elevator directly opposite me.

Struck by panic, I lower my head and do a complete circuit in the door, then cross the street. My heart is pounding and my legs turn to cotton wool. If he saw me and recognized me I can kiss my hopes good-bye. But I get away with it. In my haste, I had failed to take stock of the details. In fact, Lacoste had gotten out of the elevator alongside a man of about fifty, not very tall but with a muscular, athletic build. His walk is so fluid that he has an almost liquid quality to him.

The two men talk as they make their way across the lobby.

I check that my observation post shelters me from their line of sight. A few seconds later and they are on the pavement shaking hands. Lacoste reenters the building and heads back to the elevators, while the other man stands outside.

He scans left and right, perfectly upright, his legs slightly apart.

I look him up and down. Rectangular face, thin mouth, crew cut. I stop in the middle, armpit-level, where his pecs are. I could swear he's wearing a gun. All I know about this stuff is what I've seen in the movies, but I think I can make out the bulge of a weapon. His hand goes to his right pocket and he takes out a piece of chewing gum that he unwraps as he looks around.

He feels he's being watched. His eyes comb the area and settle on me for a microsecond. Then he stuffs the wrapper in his pocket and makes his way to the *métro*.

That short moment has left me petrified.

This guy might have been anybody, but that one fraction of a second is enough to convince me—beyond any doubt—that he isn't.

I flick through my professional memory in search of a match for a man like that. The spectral face, the economical movements, the very short gray hair . . . the walk.

A type comes to the surface from the depths of my mind: ex-military. What else, though? The answer smacks me in the face: mercenary.

If I'm not mistaken, Lacoste has enlisted a specialist to organize this hostage-taking situation.

Time to leave.

I need to call the lawyer.

On my notepad I have written down the gist of what I'm going to say. My watch indicates that it is 3:30 p.m. when a girl answers with a firm voice:

"Monsieur Delambre? Maître Christelle Gilson. What can I do for you?"

She's young. It feels like I'm talking to the intern at BLC Consulting. For a moment, I picture my daughter Lucie, in her lawyer's outfit, answering the telephone to an unemployed guy like me, with the same peremptory tone, the same air of disdain. Why do all these young people seem so similar? Maybe because wimps like me are so similar, too.

In a few seconds she confirms that I've been dismissed for misconduct.

"What misconduct?"

"Striking your superior, Monsieur Delambre. You would be fired for that at any company."

"And at any company would a superior have the right to kick a subordinate in the backside?"

"Oh, yes, I read that in your statement. But that's not how it happened."

"How can you say that?" I snap. "I was kicked in the backside at 5:00 a.m. What were you doing at 5:00 a.m. that morning?"

The short silence that follows establishes that the interview will be over very soon. I have to iron this out, I absolutely have to find a way in. I glance at my notes.

"Maître Gilson, excuse me for asking, but . . . can I ask how old you are?"

"I don't see what that has to do with anything."

"That's what bothers me. You see, I'm fifty-seven years old. I've been unemployed for more than four years and . . ."

"Monsieur Delambre, this is not the time for pleas."

". . . I lose the only job I have. You summon me to court . . ."

My voice has risen very high again.

"It's not me you should be telling this," she says.

". . . and you demand damages that amount to four years of my salary! Are you trying to kill me?"

I'm not sure if the girl is listening to me, but I think she is. I switch to Plan B.

"I am prepared to make a formal apology."

"In writing?" she says after a pause. I have piqued her interest—we're on track.

"Absolutely. Here's what I propose. Your version isn't right at all, but that's fine. I apologize. I won't even ask for my job back. All I want is for this to stop here. Do you understand? No trial, that's all."

The girl thinks for a second.

"I think we can accept your apology. Can you submit it straightaway?"

"Tomorrow. No problem. Then it's up to you to terminate proceedings."

"Everything in its own time, Monsieur Delambre. You address a detailed apology to Monsieur Pehlivan as well as your former employer, and then we'll take it from there."

I will need to think all this through, but I've bought some time. I am about to hang up, but there's still something I want to know.

"Actually, Maître Gilson. What makes you so sure that the events occurred as Monsieur Pehlivan described them?"

The girl weighs up whether or not to take the bait. Her silence already speaks volumes. In the end, she bites.

"We have a witness statement. One of your colleagues who was present at the scene guarantees that Monsieur Pehlivan only brushed past you and that . . ."

Romain.

"Okay, okay, we'll drop it. I'll submit my apology and we'll leave it there. Deal?"

"I look forward to receiving your letter, Monsieur Delambre."

Less than two minutes later I'm in the *métro*.

A few months ago, I went to Romain's place to pick up a hard drive he was lending me. I don't remember the exact address, but I think I'll be able to find it again. I can picture the street pretty well, with a pharmacy on the corner and his building a bit farther down on the right. I struggle to remember the number, but then it comes back to me—57, same as my age. There's an intercom, I press Romain Alquiler's button, and a sleepy voice answers.

As it happens, Romain is not sleepy at all. I find him pale, anxious, his hands shaking. I had forgotten how small his place is. A shoebox. A sliding door shields the "kitchen space," five square feet lined with stuffed cupboards above a sink the size of a hand. In the main room, his desk—pushed up against the wall and overloaded with computer equipment—occupies half the space. The other half consists of a sofa that must fold out for the night. That's where Romain is sitting. He motions toward an amorphous mass of red plastic on the floor that might be some sort of stool, but I prefer to stay standing. Romain gets to his feet, too.

"Listen," he begins, "let me explain . . ."

I silence him with a curt gesture. We are face-to-face in this tiny space like two rabbits in a hutch. He stops talking and looks at me with blinking eyes. He is scared about what might happen, and with good reason, because I'm not leaving until I get what I came for. Everything depends on him, and that makes me nervous. I spot some beads of sweat on his brow. I shake my head, trying hard to stay calm. I know that this episode between him and me is just a small part of a greater story, the story of our lives. His is easy to understand. Romain comes from a rural, provincial background, and the mentality that stems from those origins governs all his actions and reactions. He has learned to hold on to whatever he has, to guard it jealously. This applies to jobs as well as everything else. Whether he likes it or not, it's a part of him, his property. And I shake my head again, despite agreeing with him wholeheartedly.

To prove the extent of my detachment, I turn to admire his desk, which is dominated by an enormous flat-screen computer monitor. Technology like that sticks out in a hutch like this. I come back to him. He blinks. His shovel-like hands dangle at the end of his long arms. He'd rather be killed on the spot than back down from something that doesn't matter. I don't give a shit. This is an emergency.

"Keeping your job is vital, Romain. I understand. And I don't hold it against you. In your position, I'd be doing the same. But I have a favor to ask you."

He frowns, as if I were trying to sell him a tractor for an unfeasibly low price. I jab my thumb at the monitor:

"It's for a job, to be precise. I'm onto something. I need you to do a little bit of research for me . . ."

His face brightens. He looks mightily relieved to have escaped so lightly and reaches for his keyboard with a broad smile. Everything in this place is within arm's reach. An electronic jingle welcomes us to the virtual world, and I explain to Romain what I need.

"This might be trickier than you think," he says, his provincial prudence getting the better of him.

But his fingers are already dancing over the keyboard. The BLC Consulting website appears, and he spends a second browsing three separate windows that are immediately relegated to the corner of the screen. He's like a conductor. A few clicks later and one, two, three, eight windows burst open in succession. He's only just begun and already I'm lost.

"It's virtually unprotected. What are they, idiots?" Romain says.

"Maybe they don't have anything to protect."

He turns to me, intrigued by such a novel concept.

"Well, looking at it from my point of view," I continue, "I can't see what I would need to protect on my computer."

"Err, how about your privacy?"

Romain is horrified. The idea that you wouldn't protect your data, even if it was of no interest, is completely anathema to him. As for me, I find his indignation astonishing.

"If you had access to my private stuff, what would you do with it? It's the same as yours, same as everybody's."

Romain sits there, stubbornly shaking his head.

"Maybe," he says. "But it's yours."

Like talking to a brick wall. I drop it.

His fingers carry on dancing.

"Here, this is their client file."

A list. One second later, the printer beneath his desk stirs into action. Romain e-mails me some zipped files. He's disappointed that it was all so easy.

"Anything else you want?"

I have more or less everything. The list, with the heading "Current Clients," is short, and leads to eight subfiles. I skim through their names on my way home. I'm at République now. I get off the train and duck into a corridor toward my connection, all the while scanning the list in my hand. *Exxyal.* I stop abruptly. A girl walks into the back of me and lets out a cry, so I move to the side. I quickly go back through the list to check. Exxyal Europe is the only company that fits the brief. Right scale, strategic industry . . . it's all there. I continue slowly down the corridor—all my energy is focused on this name.

Even for someone like me who knows nothing about oil and gas, Exxyal brings to mind one of those monstrous machines, with thirty-five-thousand employees stationed across four continents and a turnover greater than the Swiss federal budget, enough hidden profit in its coffers to pay off Africa's debt twice over. I don't know where Exxyal Europe sits in the multinational rankings, but it's a heavyweight. I'm on the right track. I go back through the list again: the other companies are relatively hefty small- and medium-sized enterprises, along with a few other big companies of no great consequence working in the manufacturing or tertiary sectors. Additional detail: a hostage taking is a much more plausible scenario for a firm working in the oil and gas industry than it is for, say, a company manufacturing cars or garden gnomes.

The day ends on a crucial success, the achievement of my first objective: I am almost certain about the identity of the recruiting company.

I drift off for a moment. Head of HR at one of Exxyal Europe's offices! It doesn't get any better. I step on it with renewed enthusiasm and arrive home a few minutes later.

As I turn the key in the lock and open the door, I immediately grasp the magnitude of the difficulty that awaits me. A glance at my watch: 7:45 p.m.

I go in.

On the kitchen table I see two large paper bags with the words "Discount Dishes" on the side. Nicole is still wearing her coat. She passes me in the corridor without a word. I've screwed up.

"I'm sorry."

Nicole hears me but she doesn't listen to me. She must have gotten home at around 6:00 p.m. Nothing ready for dinner. We've improvised the last three days, but today I had promised to go and buy new dishes. So she must have gone out and done the shopping herself, hence the markedly tense atmosphere at my homecoming. Nicole, without a word, places the new plates, mugs, and glasses in the sink. All of it is horrid.

"I know what you're thinking, but it's the cheapest they had," she says, reading my mind.

"That's why I'm looking for a job."

It's like a broken record. We are starting to resent each other. What is so painful is that we've stuck together, stayed in love, through the hardest times, and just as we're coming out the other side, we start pushing each other away. She has bought something in a container with a brown sauce that looks Chinese. It's all ready—we eat it in silence. The atmosphere is so heavy that Nicole turns on the television. The Muzak to our marriage. *"Tagwell announces 800 job cuts at Reims factory."* Nicole chews, looking at her plate, which seems even uglier now that it's full. I pretend to be engrossed in the news, although it's not telling me anything new (*". . . is soaring. Tagwell was up 4.5 percent at the close of the markets . . ."*).

After dinner, exhausted by the bitterness driving us apart, we go our separate ways without a word: Nicole to the bathroom after doing the dishes, me to my study. She seems to be in a particularly stubborn mood.

My screen doesn't display any of the balletic movement or graceful orchestration of opening and moving windows: just a businesslike webpage with the BLC Consulting logo. A little envelope indicates the arrival of Romain's e-mails. In the BLC Consulting client files, I consult the correspondence between Bertrand Lacoste and his client, Alexandre Dorfmann.

This from the CEO of Exxyal Europe: *"Let's be frank: our initial estimates forecast that the 823 layoffs at Sarqueville will, directly or indirectly, involve more than 2,600 people . . . The entire pool of employees will be gravely and permanently affected."*

A bit later on: *"This complex layoff program will add much value: the executive who gains the opportunity to run this confidential mission will find it to be not just an exceptional experience, but no doubt an emotional adventure, too. He or she will have to be psychologically*

sound, reactive, and will have to demonstrate a great capacity for
shock resistance. Moreover, we must be certain of his or her unfailing
adherence to our values."

On a pad I jot down:

Sarqueville = strategic challenge for Exxyal
→ Essential selection of highly efficient executive to manage the
issue
→ Hostage taking as test to choose the best from potential
candidates

All I need to do now is identify the candidates. But rummaging
through Lacoste's client file reveals no sign of a list of executives for
assessment. I comb through everything again from the start, reviewing files in other folders in case they were simply in the wrong order,
but I already know it's futile. Maybe Lacoste doesn't have it yet. I'll
need to look for it myself.

The only thing on the Exxyal home page aside from a dia-
grammatic overview of the group's structure is a photograph of
the CEO, Alexandre Dorfmann, sitting pretty in the center of the
page. Roughly sixty years old. Thinning hair, a fairly strong nose,
a flinty expression, and a discreet smile at the camera that betrays
the unwavering self-assurance of a powerful man at the pinnacle of
his career, reaping the rewards that his success is due. Sometimes
arrogance can be so blatant it makes you want to throw a punch. I
study the photograph. If I cock my head to the right, I can see my
reflection in the mirror hanging above the corner chimney. I come
back to the photograph. I observe my negative. At fifty-seven, I still
have all my hair, albeit with a few gray strands, a rounded face, and
a boundless capacity for self-doubt. Apart from our determination,
we are complete opposites.

In Lacoste's client files, I find a detailed prospectus for the whole
of Exxyal Europe, which I print off. Armed with the criteria I derived
from my BLC document, I go through all the Exxyal executives that

might correspond with my research, ending up with a list of eleven potential candidates. That's good going, but it's still too many, and that's the problem: the first sift is always the easiest. From now on, I can't afford any mistakes. Every time I eliminate a candidate, my risk of failure is at its maximum. I open a document, copy and paste the eleven names, and rub my hands as though I were placing a bet at the roulette table.

The door opens. It's Nicole.

Is it because of her intense fatigue, or because she's wearing a T-shirt for bed? Is it because she leans her shoulder against the doorframe and tilts her head in that way that always makes me want to cry? I pretend to massage my forehead, but I'm actually checking the time in the corner of the screen—10:40. Too wrapped up in my own business to notice the evening pass by. I look up.

Normally in these situations, if she's happy she'll speak to me. If she isn't, I stand up and walk over to her. This time, both of us hold our ground in our respective corners of the room.

Why won't she understand?

In all the time we've lived together, this is the only question I have never asked myself. Not until today. Never. Today there is an ocean between us.

"I know what you're thinking," Nicole says. "You think I don't understand how important this is to you. You're telling yourself that I have my own little life, my little job, and that I've grown used to having an unemployed husband. And that I think you're incapable of finding a job that's worthy of you."

"It's a little of all those things. Not entirely, but a little."

Nicole walks up to my desk and stops in front of me. I'm sitting down, she's standing. She takes my head and holds it against her belly. I move my hand under her T-shirt and let it rest on her bottom. We've done this for twenty years and still the sensation is nothing short of miraculous. The desire is still there, even today. Except that today the ocean separating us is not between us but within us. We are a couple.

I pull away from her. Nicole contemplates the dancing fish of my screensaver.

"What do you want me to do?" I say.

"Anything but this. It's just . . . it's not good. When you start doing things like this . . ."

This would be the moment to explain to her that Mehmet's kick in the ass will be forcing an additional humiliation on me later tonight: writing a formal apology. But I would be ashamed to admit to it. Same with telling her that the job center is going to have fewer and fewer jobs for me thanks to my dismissal for gross misconduct. And that compared to what we have in store, buying ugly and cheap tableware will feel like the crowning glory of our many years of blissful happiness. I decide against it.

"Okay."

"Okay what?"

She takes a step back and holds me by the shoulders. I'm still cupping her hips in my hands.

"I'll drop it."

"Seriously?"

I'm a bit ashamed of this lie, but like all the others, it's necessary.

Nicole holds me tight. I can feel the relief in every part of her embrace.

"None of this is your fault, Alain," she says, trying to express herself. "There's nothing you can do about it. But this whole job hunt . . . We won't come out of it in one piece if we stop respecting each other. Don't you agree?"

There's too much to say to that. I think I've played my cards right. I nod. Nicole runs her fingers through my hair, her tummy hugging against my shoulder, her buttocks tensed. This is what I'm fighting for, to keep all this. Getting her to understand is impossible. I have to do it without her and then present her with the finished article. I want to be the hero in her life again.

"Are you coming to bed?" she says.

"Five minutes. One e-mail and I'm there."

She turns and smiles at me from the door.

"Will you be quick?"

There can't be more than two men in a thousand capable of turning down an offer like that. But I'm one of them.

"Two minutes."

I think about writing the letter to the lawyer, but tell myself I'll have time to do it tomorrow. My attention is drawn inexorably back to the list. One click and the fish give way to the Exxyal Europe website.

Eleven potential candidates that I need to narrow down to five: three men, two women. I go back through the list cross-referencing ages and degree subjects, then I take them one by one and focus on retracing their careers. I find them on different networks or alumni associations where some people give summaries of their careers. To head up the massive layoff program at Sarqueville, they will need to have solid leadership experience and have already carried out difficult or sensitive assignments that have caught the eye of senior management. This approach helps me reduce it to eight. Still three too many. Two men and one woman. But I can't do any better. It would already be an enormous stroke of luck if the five I'm looking for are in this eight.

I do a bit of flicking between the Exxyal site and the professional networks where I found a few of them and draw up a profile for each one.

My desk isn't that big, so for one of my birthdays Nicole gave me a set of corkboards to pin documents to: six large boards attached to the back of the door that fan open like the pages of a giant book.

I tear down the stuff that's been there for an age: yellowing job ads, lists of potential employers or training schemes that I'm too old to be eligible for, details of colleagues working in HR for other companies and whom I came across frequently in a professional association that I am no longer a member of. I run off large mug shots of each candidate along with their career profiles, leaving plenty of room for notes, and pin the whole thing on the corkboards.

I take a step back to admire my work. Now I can browse my full-size dossier. I have left the outer boards blank, so when I close it you can't see anything.

I don't hear the door behind me open. But the sound of Nicole's tears does attract my attention. I turn around, and there she is in her big white T-shirt. It's been two, maybe three hours since I promised to join her. Since I promised to relinquish everything. She takes in the series of colorful portraits and blown-up CVs, and without a word she moves her head from left to right. It's the most devastating thing she could have done.

I open my mouth, but there's no point.

Nicole has already left. I quickly load the files from Romain onto a USB stick, plug in my laptop to charge the battery, shut down my PC, close the corkboards that make up my wall display, head into the bathroom, and arrive in the bedroom to find it empty.

"Nicole!"

My voice echoes strangely through the night. It sounds like loneliness. I go to the kitchen, the sitting room . . . no one. I call out again, but Nicole doesn't reply.

A few steps farther and I'm outside the door of the guest room, which is closed. I grab the handle.

Locked.

I didn't just make a mistake, I lied, too. I feel terrible. But I have to stay philosophical. When I've nailed down this job, she'll realize I was right.

I take myself to bed. Tomorrow is a big day.

9

My head didn't stop spinning with the same questions all night. If I were in Lacoste's shoes, how would I handle this? There is a hell of a difference between deciding to do a role play and actually staging one. Nicole's questions come back to me: commandos, weapons, interrogations . . .

Soon it'll be 5:00 a.m. I left for "work" like normal and am now settled in a giant brasserie by Gare de l'Est. At the counter, I pick up a copy of *Le Parisien*: *Paris Bourse booming. Ninth consecutive week of growth.* I flick through as I wait for my coffee: . . . *Tansonville factory cleared by police. The 48 employees occupying the premises* . . .

Seated at a table at the very back of the largest room, I open my laptop, and while the system boots up I drink the revolting coffee. Besides a handful of Togolese street sweepers joking around on their break, the other early birds include insomniac drunkards, night workers finishing their shifts, taxi drivers, exhausted couples, and wasted kids. This dawn underworld makes for a depressing sight. I'm the only person in the room slogging away, but I'm not the only one in distress. I open the files saved on the USB stick from last night.

Among Lacoste's correspondence, I find two notes written by a certain David Fontana, possibly the man I saw at BLC headquarters. The first is about hiring Arab actors and acquiring weapons loaded with blanks. The second contains a map of the premises where the hostage taking is to be held. Judging by his style and given his field, this Fontana must be ex-military. I log on to the brasserie's WiFi and look him up. My failure to find him confirms my suspicions. So discreet he doesn't feature anywhere, at least not under that name. I jot down a mental reminder: establish his identity, find out where he comes from.

Right from the start, I know I'll need help. Another essential quality for any HR manager is the ability to assemble skill sets. That's management rule number two.

I love the internet. You can find anything on it, however vile. The web really is made in the image of Western society's subconscious.

It takes me a little over an hour to find the site I need. It has police officers, former police officers, future police officers, police fans—and there's a whole lot more of them than you might think. I spend a while chatting with the other users online, but without much success. At this time of day there's just the dropouts and the unemployed. No interest. The safest bet would be to place an ad. I'm a novelist searching for very precise information on hostage taking. I need a user with experience in this type of situation. I give an e-mail address created especially for the occasion, but I change my mind. Time is of the essence: I give my cell phone number and cross the first item off my pad.

The following part of my research brings very bad news. Private detective rates vary from 50 to 120 euros per hour. I do the numbers—it's disastrous. Yet I'm struggling to come up with an alternative solution. I have to investigate these eight execs, not just their professional bios but their private lives, too. I gather three or four addresses of detective firms offering their services to businesses, and which don't seem either overly prestigious or patently suspicious. Even if it is a bit of a lottery, I choose the ones located closest to where I am now. It's just before 8:00 a.m. when I hit the road.

It doesn't matter what the office or company, the manager I meet with always resembles the person I was before, back when I was confident in my skills and still had somewhere to apply them.

"I see," he says.

Philippe Mestach. Mid-forties, calm, organized, methodical, normal build. Basically the sort of person who goes unnoticed. I decide to tell it to him straight. I talk about a job opportunity, but I don't mention the nature of the role play, simply explaining the aims of the assessment the five employees are to undergo. He clocks exactly what I'm up to.

"So you're definitely loading the odds in your favor," he says. "But the timescale's not on our side. We often investigate people on behalf of their employers—it's a growth market for us. Unfortunately, in our line of work, the quality of the result is often contingent on the time invested in it."

"How much?"

He smiles. Let's cut to the chase.

"You're right," he says, "that is what it comes down to. Shall we run through everything?"

He tallies up all my requirements, does some calculations on a little pocket calculator, and pauses for a long moment's reflection. He stares at the figures, returns the gadget to his pocket, then looks up at me.

"All in: 15,000 euros. No hidden costs. Thirteen thousand if you pay in cash."

"What can you guarantee?"

"Four full-time investigators and—"

I cut him off.

"No, I mean results! What can you guarantee?"

"You give us the names of your 'clients,' we find their addresses, and then for each one we give you their marital status, detailed family

history, information on assets, the salient aspects of their private and
professional lives, as well as a broad outline of their current financial
situation (obligations, availabilities, and so forth.)."

"That's it?"

He raises a perplexed eyebrow. I carry on:

"What do you expect me to do with general stuff like that? I'll end
up with a whole bunch of Mr. Averages."

"The country is populated entirely by average people, Monsieur
Delambre. Me, you, them—everyone."

"I'm looking for something more targeted."

"Like?"

"Debts, professional misconduct at a previous job, family problems, younger sister in hospice, alcoholic wife, shameful hab-
its, speeding fines, orgies, lovers, mistresses, secret lives, Achilles
heels . . . That sort of thing."

"Anything's possible, Monsieur Delambre. But there again, the
clock's against us. What's more, to dig this deep, we must use very
specific channels, nurture relationships, follow up leads, not to mention get lucky."

"How much?"

He smiles again. It's not so much the wording he enjoys as the
directness of the request.

"We must be methodical, Monsieur Delambre. Here's what I suggest. Two days after your first payment, we will provide you with the
main information pertaining to each of your clients. You study these,
you focus your research criteria so that we can target our approach,
and I give you a quote."

"I'd rather pay a flat rate."

He takes out his little calculator and taps in some numbers.

"For an additional two days' investigation: 2,500 euros per client.
Including bribes."

"And in cash?"

"That's the price in cash. By invoice, that would be . . ."

More number crunching.

"Don't bother. I get it."

It's colossal. If I only pay the additional fee for half my execs, I'm still looking at 23,000 euros. Even with the entire remainder of our savings, I'm 95 percent shy of the sum.

"Think it through, but don't take too long. Once you confirm, I will need to assemble a team very quickly . . ."

I stand up, shake his hand, and get back on the *métro*.

This is the moment of truth. I've known it since the start. The arguments with Nicole, the nerves of the last few days, the tension surrounding the aptitude tests and the interview with Lacoste . . . everything has just been a precursor to this final stage, which rests on one single, critical issue: the question of how far I'm willing to go.

To succeed, I must take every risk.

I can't make up my mind.

I feel terribly depressed.

My eyes skim over the ads on the *métro*, over the relentless boarding and disembarking of passengers. My feet carry me up the escalator automatically, and here I am at the street where we live, in this neighborhood we fell in love with immediately from the second we first saw it.

It was 1991.

Everything was going well for us. We had been married for more than ten years. Mathilde was nine and Lucie seven. I called them all sorts of silly names, "my princesses," and all that. Even then Nicole was radiant, you just need to look at the photos. We were a very French couple, with fixed jobs and reasonable, climbing salaries. Our bank informed us that we could make it onto the property ladder. Acutely aware of the responsibility, I took a map of Paris and marked out the areas where it was realistic to look, and almost at once we found somewhere right on the other side of town.

That's where I am now. I leave the *métro*. I remember. I can replay the scene perfectly in my mind.

The charm of the place struck us right away. The neighborhood sits on a little hill, the streets weaving up and down; the buildings, like the trees, have been there a century. Ours is a tidy red-brick job. Without saying anything, we hoped that our apartment would be one of those with bow windows. As the elevator juddered. I swiftly estimated that we'd be able to fit all the household appliances in it except the sofa. The real estate agent looked at his feet, very professional, opened the door, and the apartment was incredibly light because it was so high up, and it only cost 15 percent more than what we could borrow. We were eager and panicky in equal measure. It was exhilarating. The bank manager rubbed his hands and offered us additional funding. We bought it, we closed, we picked up the keys, dropped off the girls with some friends, and returned: with just the two of us, the apartment seemed even bigger. Nicole flung open the windows that look out behind over a schoolyard with three plane trees. The rooms echoed with the emptiness to be filled and the fun to be had, with the life that was smiling on us, and Nicole grabbed me by the waist and pinned me against the kitchen wall, taking my breath away with a ferocious kiss, buzzing with excitement, but I realized I'd have to hold fire until later because she was off again, walking from room to room, outlining her grand plans with big birdlike waves of her arms.

We were in debt up to our necks, but despite the impending disaster, by some miracle, by some fate we weren't even aware of, we got through those years unscathed. The secret to our happiness in those days was not love (we've always had that), nor was it the girls (we still have them, too): no, the secret to our happiness was that we had work, that we could, no questions asked, enjoy the innumerable positive consequences of our unimaginable good luck: paid bills, vacations, outings, university enrollment fees, cars, and the certainty that our diligent, determined work would reward us the way we deserved.

I am at this same place again almost twenty years later, but I feel a century older.

I hear Nicole's tears, I'm in my study, I see her tattered cardigan, the discount dishes, and I dial a telephone number and ask for Gregory Lippert. The linoleum in the kitchen is curling up again (it'll need changing), and I say "hi, it's Grandpa," trying to apply a jocular tone, but my voice betrays my true intentions. The makeshift sink is more desperate than ever, and I need to find a unit to stick on the wall. He says "huh?," surprised because I don't call him often, and I say "I need to see you," and he says "huh" again. It disgusts me already but I need him, I'm insistent—"immediately"—and he realizes it's really, truly urgent, so he says: "I can manage a few minutes, shall we say eleven?"

10

The café is called Le Balto. There must be about two or three thousand just like it in France. Typical of my son-in-law to choose a place like this. I bet he has his lunch here every day, first-name terms with the waiters, enjoying a quick scratch-card with the secretaries while cracking hilarious jokes about "lucky jerks." There's a *tabac* in the corner of a large room with tired seats, Formica furniture, shiny tiles on the floor, and on the terrace window a roll-down menu with pictures of hot dogs and sandwiches for customers too stupid to read the words "hot dogs" and "sandwiches."

I'm early.

A big flat-screen, positioned very high on the wall, is tuned to a rolling-news channel. The volume is way down. Even so, the customers propping up the bar are glued to the screen, watching the headlines streaming across the bottom: *Business profits: 7% to employees and 36% to shareholders—Forecast: 3 million unemployed by end of year.*

I reflect on how lucky I am to be job-hunting in this climate.

Gregory is keeping me waiting. I'm not convinced there is any particular reason—I can picture him deliberately making himself a little late, his way of showing me what a big deal he is.

At the next-door table, two young guys in suits, insurance types, not unlike my son-in-law, are finishing their coffee.

"No, no, I promise you," says one, "it's ridiculously funny! It's called 'On the Streets.' You play a homeless guy. The aim of the game is to survive."

"What, like integrate back into society?" asks the other.

"Don't be so fucking stupid! No, the aim is to survive. You have these three key factors—three compulsory things . . . You can't avoid them, you just do what you can to keep them in check. There's cold, hunger, and alcoholism."

"Brilliant!"

"It's hilarious, I swear! Shit, we had fun! You play with dice, but it's a game of tactics. You can earn free meals, nights in hostels, a spot in a heated *métro* entrance (those are the hardest to get!), cardboard boxes for when it's cold, access to railway station bathrooms to wash . . . No, I promise, it's fricking hard!"

"But who do you play against?"

The guy hesitates for a second.

"You play for yourself, buddy! That's the beauty of the game!"

Gregory arrives and shakes hands with the two guys (I called it). They leave as Gregory sits down opposite me.

He's wearing a steel-gray suit with one of those pastel shirts that always bring to mind a kitchen color scheme, all sky blue or pale mauve. Today it's waxy yellow with a beige tie.

When I left Bercaud, I had four suits and a shitload of shirts and ties. I loved it, the whole dressing-up thing. Nicole used to call me an "old tart" because I had more clothes than she did. I was the only dad you could give a tie to for Father's Day two years running without being reprimanded. The only ties I never wore were the ones from Mathilde. She has appalling taste: her husband is living, breathing proof.

So, I used to have four suits. Shortly after I was laid off, Nicole started insisting that I throw away the oldest ones, but I refused. From my first day of unemployment, I wore a suit every time I left the house. And not just for appointments at the job center or the occasional interviews I managed to line up. No, I went to Pharmaceutical Logistics at 5:00 a.m. wearing a suit and tie. A bit like a prisoner who shaves every morning to hold on to a shred of the self-respect he fears he has lost. But one day, on my way home, the stitching on my favorite suit came undone on the *métro*. It ripped open from the armpit to the pocket. Two girls standing next to me burst out laughing. One of them held up her hand in apology, but she couldn't help herself. I maintained an air of dignity. All of a sudden, a few of the other passengers started giggling, too. I got off at the next station, removed my jacket and slung it over my shoulder, like a trendy businessman on a hot day, even though we were in January. When I arrived home, I threw away everything that was more than four or five years old. All I kept was one clean suit and a few shirts, which I'm saving. They still have the see-through plastic cover from the last trip to the dry cleaner's. My clothes are like antiques on display in a glass cabinet. The first thing I'll do if I land this job is get measured for a tailored suit. That wasn't even a luxury I allowed myself when I was working.

I'm tense.

"You seem tense," Gregory says, with his usual subtlety.

As he scrutinizes me more closely, however, he notices my desolate expression and remembers how I'd told him that I needed to see him, something that has never happened in all the time we've known each other. He gathers himself, clears his throat, and offers a little supportive smile.

"I need a loan, Gregory. Twenty-five thousand euros. Today."

I realize this is a lot of information for him to take in. But after thinking through all the possible approaches, I'd come to the conclusion that it was better to get straight to the heart of the matter. It works. My son-in-law's mouth hangs open in silence. I feel an urge to shut his lower jaw with my fingertips, but I resist.

"It's vital, Gregory. It's for a job. I have a onetime opportunity to land my perfect job. All I need is 25,000 euros."

"You're buying a job for 25,000 euros?"

"Something like that. It's too complicated to explain everything in detail, but—"

"No chance, Alain."

"What, buying a job?"

"No, lending you that amount. No way. In your situation . . ."

"Exactly, son! That's why I'm a reliable customer. I'll be able to repay you easily once I've got the job. It's a very short-term loan I need. A few months, that's it."

He's struggling to keep up, so I clarify.

"Okay, you've got me . . . I'm not literally buying a job. It's . . ."

"A bribe?"

I make a pained expression and reluctantly agree.

"That's shameful! They can't make you pay to get a job. It's illegal, apart from anything else!"

This makes my blood boil.

"Listen, my boy. What's allowed and what's illegal is another matter entirely! Do you know how long I've been unemployed?"

I'm shouting. He tries to simmer things down:

"It's been . . ."

"Four years!"

My voice has become very shrill. This is driving me close to the edge.

"Have you ever been unemployed?"

I'm bellowing now. Gregory looks around the room, afraid of making a scene. I have to ram home this advantage, so I raise my voice a notch higher. I want this loan, I want him to back down, I want a memorandum of understanding. I'm determined he will give me his word.

"You can shove your stupid morals up your ass! You've got a job, and all I'm asking you is to help me find one! Is it that complicated? Hey—is it that complicated?"

He motions at me to calm down. I try a different tactic. I move closer and talk in a hushed tone.

"You could lend me 25,000 euros for whatever, a car, a fitted kitchen . . . There we go, that'll work, a fitted kitchen—you've seen ours. And then I repay in twelve months. One thousand seven-hundred euros per month plus interest is not a problem, I'm telling you, there's no risk for you."

He doesn't answer but looks me in the eye with renewed self-assurance. The look of a professional. In just a few seconds my status has changed. Now I'm negotiating a loan. Before I was his father-in-law. Now I'm a client.

"It's out of the question, Alain," he says firmly. "To lend an amount like that, we need guarantees."

"I'll have a job."

"Yes, maybe, but right now you don't."

"The job title is HR manager. It's for a very big company."

Gregory frowns. Another change of status: now he's taking me for a fool. The situation is slipping away from me. I attempt a reboot.

"Fine, what do people need to get 25,000 euros from you?"

"Sufficient income."

"How much?"

"Listen, Alain, this is no way to go about it."

"Okay, what if I have a guarantor?"

His eyes light up.

"Who?"

"I dunno. You."

His eyes close.

"It's impossible! We're buying an apartment! Our debt ratio will never stretch—"

I grab his hands across the table and grip them in mine.

"Listen to me, Gregory."

I realize I've only got one round left, and I'm not sure I have the courage to fire it.

"I've never asked you for anything."

This is going to require a lot of energy. A whole lot.

"The thing is, I don't have any other options."

I look down at our intertwined hands and rally my thoughts. Because this is tough, really tough.

"You're my only hope."

I gather my strength between each word, trying hard to focus elsewhere, like a first-time prostitute limbering up for her debut blow job.

"I must have this money. It's vital."

Good God, I'm not going to have to stoop this low, am I?

"Gregory . . ."

I swallow back my saliva. Fuck it.

"I'm begging you."

There, I said it.

He's as stunned as I am.

His profession as a usurer has led to countless family disputes, and now here I am, sitting in front of him begging for the charity of a loan. The situation is so improbable that it leaves us both feeling dizzy for a while. I took the gamble that this surprise strategy would make him do a U-turn, but Gregory shakes his head.

"If only it were up to me . . . You know I would. But there's no way I can fast-track a case. I have bosses. I don't exactly know what your income is, Alain, or Nicole's, but I doubt . . . If you needed three thousand, or even five thousand, we could see, but . . ."

What happens next is, I think, attributable to just one word. Begging. I shouldn't have begged him. I did something that can never be undone. I realized it was a mistake before I'd even said it, but I did it anyway. As I lean back in my chair and twist around to my right, like I'm about to scratch my ass, I am not completely conscious of my actions, but I am sure that they are the inevitable consequence of a single word. Ghastly wars must have been waged like this, because of a single word.

I wind up, gather all my strength, and slam my fist into his face. He wasn't expecting that at all. It's instant chaos. My clenched fist strikes him between the cheekbone and the jaw, his body is flung backward, and his hands reach out in a desperate reflex to grab hold of the table. He's flung back six feet, crashing into another table and taking two chairs with him, his arms flailing around for support as he falls, his head smacking into the post behind him and his throat letting out a rasping, bestial yelp. All the regulars turn around as the din of shattered glass, broken chairs and upturned tables is replaced by stunned silence. The space in front of me is clear. I clutch my fist so hard against my stomach that it hurts. Then, to everyone's bewilderment, I stand up and leave.

I have gone from never hitting anyone in my entire life to doing it twice in the space of a few days: first my Turkish supervisor, now my son-in-law. There's no escaping it. I have become a violent man.

I'm back in the street.

I have yet to grasp how damaging the results of my actions will be.

But before worrying about that, I intend to solve my one problem, my one and only problem: finding this 25,000 euros.

11

Having laid my son-in-law out for the count, I continue on my way. From the outside, anyone might think I've lost all feeling.

Once upon a time, I knew myself well. I mean that my behavior rarely surprised me. When you've experienced most situations, you also learn the correct responses to them. You even notice the circumstances where self-control isn't necessary. Family scuffles with pricks like my son-in-law, for example. Past a certain age, life starts repeating itself. The thing is, anything you do or don't acquire through experience alone you can learn in two or three days' worth of management seminars, with the aid of grids that class people according to their character. The process is practical, it's playful, it boosts your spirits at little cost, and it makes you feel clever. It even lets you imagine you might become more efficient in the workplace. In short, it soothes you. Over the years, trends have changed, and so have the criteria. One year you get tested to see if you are methodical, energetic, cooperative, or determined. The next it might be to check if you're hardworking, precocious, pioneering, persistent, empathetic, or imaginative. If you have a new coach, it turns out you are protective, directive, putative, emotive, or responsive, while the next session you attend helps discern whether you're action, method, idea, or procedure oriented. The whole thing's a hoax, but no one can get enough of it. It's like with horoscopes, where you always end up identifying traits that match your own. The reality is that you never know what you're truly capable of until you find yourself in extreme circumstances. Right now, for example, I'm surprising myself a lot.

My phone rings as I'm leaving the *métro*. I'm always wary when things are moving too fast, and things are moving too fast now.

"My name is Albert Kaminski."

A pleasant, open voice, but it's too soon. Come on, I only posted the ad this morning and already . . .

"I believe I can offer you what you're looking for," he tells me.

"And what is it I'm looking for?"

"You're a novelist. You're writing a book that revolves around a hostage taking and you need practical, concrete advice. Precise information. Unless I misread your advertisement?"

He is well spoken and not at all fazed by my direct question. Seems solid. I get the impression he is calling from a public place where he has to keep his voice down.

"And you have personal experience in this field?"

"Of course."

"That's what everyone says."

"I've experienced several real hostage situations, all with different circumstances and in the recent past. Last few years. If your questions are about how this sort of operation unfolds, then I think I'll be able to answer most of them. If you want to meet me, here's my number: 06 34 . . ."

"Wait!"

There's no doubt he's skilled. He speaks calmly, he doesn't get annoyed by my deliberately aggressive questions, and he's even managed to wrest back the initiative, since I'm the one requesting a meeting. This could well be my guy.

"Are you free this afternoon?"

"Depends what time."

"You tell me . . ."

"From 2:00 p.m."

It's a date. He suggests a café near Châtelet.

What will have happened since my departure? It must have taken my son-in-law some time to get back on his feet. I picture him spread-eagled on the floor right in the middle of the room. The owner comes running up, slips his hand under his head, and says: "Wow, you seem pretty shaken up! Who was that guy?" Ultimately, though, I don't know Gregory that well. I have no idea whether he's brave, for example. Maybe he stands up and dusts himself off to salvage some dignity. Or maybe he starts yelling: "I'll kill him, the bastard!" That line always seems pathetic. The big question, of course, is whether he'll call Mathilde now or wait until this evening. My entire strategy hinges on that decision.

The entrance to the *lycée* where Mathilde teaches English is located down a side street. At lunchtime, there are always loads of kids loitering on the pavement outside. Plenty of heckling, noise, rowdiness—boys and girls spilling over with white-hot hormones. I keep my distance, huddled in the doorway to an apartment building. Mathilde picks up quickly. There's a racket going on at her end as well as mine. She's surprised. I can tell that her husband hasn't called her yet. The window of opportunity is very narrow, and it is essential I don't let it close.

"Here? Now? Is it Maman, is something wrong? Where are you? Outside, but where?"

"No, it's not Maman, don't worry, nothing serious, I need to see you, that's all, yes it's urgent, in the street, just here . . . If you've got five minutes . . . Yes, straightaway."

Mathilde is prettier than her sister. Less beautiful, less alluring, but definitely prettier. She's wearing a delightful printed dress, the sort of dress you notice on a woman right away. She has an attractive, swaying walk that reminds me a bit of Nicole, but her expression is anxious, fearful.

It's so hard to explain, but I get there in the end. My request is hardly crystal clear, but Mathilde latches onto the bottom line: 25,000 euros.

"But, Papa! We need it for the apartment. We've signed the preliminary contract!"

"I know, my angel, but the sale's not for another three months. I'll have paid you back well before then."

Mathilde is very flustered. She starts pacing around the street, three angry steps this way, three mortified steps back.

"Why do you need this money?"

I tried the same tactic on her hubby an hour ago, and I know it won't go down well this time either, but right now it's all I have.

"A bribe? Twenty-five thousand euros for a bribe? That's crazy!"

I nod bitterly.

Four more nervous paces along the pavement, then she turns to me:

"Papa, I'm sorry, but I can't."

She has a lump in her throat, and she's looking me straight in the eye. She has summoned up all her courage. I'll have to tread carefully.

"Angel . . ."

"No Papa, don't 'angel' me! No emotional blackmail, I'm warning you!"

Looks like I'll have to tread very, very carefully. I put forward my argument as calmly as I can.

"How do you intend to pay me back in two months?"

Mathilde is a practical woman who never strays from concrete fact, and she always asks the right questions. Even when she was little, the moment we needed to plan anything—a trip, a picnic, a party—her hand would be the first to go up. Her wedding required almost eight months' preparation. Everything was arranged with military precision . . . I've never been so bored in my whole life. Maybe that's why she seems so distant from me sometimes. She's standing in front of me. I suddenly ask myself what I'm *really* doing here. I shoo away the image of Gregory sprawled across the café floor, his cheek pressed up against the pillar.

"Are you sure they'll pay an advance to someone they've only just hired?"

Mathilde has agreed to discuss the matter. She doesn't realize it yet, but her refusal is now long gone. She's still prowling up and down the pavement, just more slowly now, keeping nearer and returning quicker.

She's hurting, and it's starting to make me hurt, too. I've been so caught up in my own helter-skelter situation that I've lost all qualms. If I had to lay out her cretin of a husband again, I'd do it in a flash, but now, suddenly, I feel bereft. My daughter is before me, torn apart by her conflicting obligations, a genuine moral dilemma: her home or her father. She has saved up this money; it is the sum of her life's hopes and dreams.

It's her printed dress that rescues me: I realize that the shoes and bag are matching. The sort of outfit that Nicole should be able to afford.

Mathilde is canny when it comes to hitting the sales, one of those women who goes on scouting missions two months in advance and who, by sheer force of preparation and strategy, one day manages to purchase her dream outfit despite its being wildly beyond her means. Mathilde must be the result of some freak genetic quirk, since neither of her parents is capable of such an achievement. I'm sure it's what attracted her husband to her.

Speaking of whom . . . I picture him back in his office. A secretary will have brought him a freezer bag full of ice cubes as he considers whether or not to sue his father-in-law. He'll be fantasizing about a judge—the long arm of the law—issuing the sentence loud and clear. Gregory gleefully immerses himself in the scenario: he leaves the courtroom in triumph, his wife weeping by his side. Mathilde looks down, forced to recognize that her husband's values are superior to her father's. She is torn. But not Gregory. Awash with sanctimony and righteous anger, fearless and upstanding, Gregory sweeps down the steps of the Palais de Justice, which has never before been so deserving of its name. Behind him is me, his father-in-law, broken and battered, gasping for breath, begging . . . There's that word again. Begging. I had to beg him.

Me.

I press on:

"Mathilde, I need this money. Your mother and I both need it. To survive. I'll pay back whatever you're able to lend me. But I'm not going to beg you."

Then I do something terrible: I bow my head and walk away. One step, two steps, three . . . I walk quickly because the momentum is in my favor. I'm ashamed, but I have to be resilient. To get this job, to save my family, to save my daughters, I have to be resilient.

"Papa!"

Score!

I close my eyes as the scale of my deceit dawns on me. I turn back. I will never forgive the system for what it is doing to me. Fine, it's me who is rolling around in the mud, me who is being vile, but in exchange, may the gods of the system give me what I'm due. May they let me back in the game, back in the world. Let me be human again. Be alive. May they give me this job.

Mathilde has tears in her ears.

"How much exactly do you need?"

"Twenty-five thousand."

The die is cast. It's over. The rest is just formalities, and Mathilde knows how to take care of those. I have won.

My ticket to hell is guaranteed.

I can breathe.

"You have to promise me," she begins.

She detects so much confidence in me that she can't help but smile.

"I can swear to whatever you want, my angel. When do you exchange?"

"We don't have an exact date. Two months . . ."

"I'll have paid you back, angel, cross my heart."

I pretend to spit on my hand.

She hesitates.

"Because . . . I'm not going to say anything to Gregory, all right? So I'm counting on you . . ."

Before I can even answer, she has grabbed her cell to call the bank.

All around us the schoolchildren are yelling, jostling, joking with each other, drunk with the joys of being alive, and of being attracted to one another. For them, life is nothing but one huge prospect. We are here, my daughter and I, standing in the midst of them, both of us bolt upright as the tide of youthful enthusiasm pitches up from side to side. All of a sudden Mathilde seems less pretty, somewhat faded in her dress that now seems less elegant, more ordinary. I have a think and it comes to me: my daughter looks like her mother. Because she's afraid of what she is doing, because her father's situation is wearing down her resistance, Mathilde seems jaded. Her chic outfit even takes on the appearance of a tired cardigan.

She's on the phone and gives me an inquisitive look.

"In cash, yes," she confirms.

It's a wrap. She raises an eyebrow at me and I close my eyes.

"I can be there around 5:15 p.m.," she says. "Yes, I realize twenty-five thousand is a lot in cash."

The bank manager is not taking this lying down. He likes his money.

"The sale won't be happening for another two months at least . . . By then . . . Yes, no problem. Five o'clock, yes, perfect."

She hangs up, terrified at having crossed the point of no return. My daughter resembles me, now. She's broken.

We stay there without saying anything, just looking. A wave of love rolls right through my body. Without thinking I say, "Thank you." It hits Mathilde like an electric shock. She helps me, she loves me, she hates me, she's scared, she's ashamed. No father should provoke so many powerful emotions in a daughter or take up so much space in her life.

She returns to the school in silence, her shoulders limp.

I have to be back at 5:00 p.m. to accompany her to the bank. In the meantime, I call Philippe Mestach, the detective.

"You'll get your advance tomorrow morning. Nine a.m. at your office? Go ahead and assemble your team."

Châtelet.

It's sort of a brasserie, but with leather armchairs. The chic end of shabby-chic. The kind of place I would have loved when I had a salary.

When I see him, the first thing that comes back to me is his voice. It seemed borrowed, as if speaking irritated him. He barely stirs, or if he does it's very subtle, like slow-motion. He's thin. I find him very strange looking. Like an iguana.

"Albert Kaminski."

He hasn't stood up, just leaned forward a little, holding out his hand indifferently. First impression: minus ten. It's a poor start, a major handicap, and I don't have much time to lose. I have objectives.

I sit straight-backed at the edge of the armchair, no intention of staying for long.

He's the same age as me. We sit in silence as the waiter takes our order. I try to figure out what is bothering me about him, then it hits me. He's a junkie. Drugs are a tricky area for me, because, as astonishing as it might sound, I've never touched them. For a man of my generation, that's nothing short of miraculous. So when it comes to drugs, I'm not exactly a natural, but I think I've put my finger on it. Kaminski is all over the place. He's in free fall. We could be cousins. Our fall might not be the same, but our desperation is. I back away. I need strong people: skillful, operational.

"I used to be a commandant in the police," he begins.

His face is creased, but his eyes are dry. Nothing like Charles. Alcohol ravages you in a different way. What's he on? I don't have a clue, but it's clear that this inspector has lost none of his self-esteem.

Latest score: minus eight.

"I spent most of my career doing special operations at RAID. That's why I answered your ad."

"Why aren't you there anymore?"

He smiles and looks down.

"I don't mean to pry, but how old are you?" he says.

"More than fifty, less than sixty."

"Roughly the same as me, then."

"What's that got to do with anything?"

"By the time you get to our age, you can spot certain types right away: gays, racists, fascists, hypocrites, alcoholics. Drug addicts. And you, Monsieur . . . ?"

"Delambre. Alain Delambre."

". . . I can tell you see me for what I am, Monsieur Delambre. So that's my answer to your question."

We smile at each other. Minus four.

"I used to be a negotiator. I was let go from the police eight years ago. Professional misconduct."

"Anything serious?"

"There was a fatality. A woman, a desperate case. I was a little high. Ecstasy. She threw herself out the window."

Anyone who can cancel out a ten-point deficit in just a few minutes is someone capable of faking compassion, proximity, similarity. In short, a good cheat. In the Bertrand Lacoste mold. Either that or they're extremely sincere.

"And you think I can trust someone like you?"

He thinks for a moment.

"That depends on what you're looking for."

He must be taller than me. Standing up, I figure five foot nine. He's broad shouldered, but everything tapers in the farther down you get, like someone from the nineteenth century with consumption.

"If you really are a novelist and you're looking for information about hostage taking scenarios, then I meet your needs."

The subtext is clear: he's no fool.

"What does RAID stand for?"

He frowns in total despair.

"No, seriously . . ."

"Research, assistance, intervention, dissuasion. I was in charge of the dissuasion part. At least I was until I was given the heave-ho."

He's not bad. Even if the two of us do make for a right old pair of sad cases. How does he make his living? He's poorly dressed. Seems an opportunist type, in poor health: can't imagine he turns much down work-wise. Sooner or later, this guy will end up in the slammer or in a dealer's garbage can. In terms of rates, that gives me some bargaining power. The thought of money overwhelms me with sadness. Mathilde's face enters my mind, followed by Nicole, my wife who doesn't want to sleep by my side. I am tired.

Albert Kaminski looks at me with concern and offers me the carafe of water. I'm struggling to catch my breath. I'm taking this too far, it's all going too far.

"Are you all right?"

I down a glass of water and shake myself.

"How much do you charge?"

From: David Fontana
To the attention of: Bertrand Lacoste
Date: May 12
Subject: "Hostage-taking" role play—Client: Exxyal

The preparation of the location is underway. We will be employing two main zones.

First, the larger room (Sector A on the diagram) will be where the hostages are held. It is separated from the corridor by a partition with a glass window that the commando can cover should you wish to carry out any isolated interrogations.

Second, there are the offices.

D marks a rest area and debriefing room. B denotes the interrogation chamber. As outlined in the scenario, the executives will be interrogated in turn, with the interview based on their individual areas of expertise.

The interrogation will be viewed by the assessors, who will be monitoring events on screens located in Sector C.

In the current configuration, the candidates for the HR position (marked in gray on the diagram) will be sitting in front of their screens.

We have carried out some tests: the soundproofing between the rooms is satisfactory.

Two sets of cameras will relay the footage live to the assessors. The first camera will be in the hostage "waiting room"; the second will be in the interrogation chamber. As soon as these rooms are fitted out, we will begin full trial runs.

Finally, I feel I must reiterate that it is not always possible to predict how participants will react in a role-play scenario.

Regardless of the outcome, the parties commissioning the operation will be held responsible.

Please find attached in Appendix 2 the disclaimers to be signed by you or your client.

Yours sincerely,
David Fontana

Jeu de rôle « Prise d'otages » – Schéma d'implantation

[[
Top heading: **"Hostage-taking" role play—Master plan**
Ascenseurs: **Elevators**
Évaluateurs: **Assessors**
caméra: **camera**
Interrogatoire: **Interrogation chamber**
WC: **WC**
Salle de retenue des otages: **Hostage waiting room**
M. Dorfmann: **Monsieur Dorfmann**
Issue de secours: **Emergency exit**
]]

12

At 5:00 p.m., the first thing Mathilde sees as she leaves the *lycée* is her father. Me. There I am, standing stock-still as the youths flood out from every angle, shouting, running, barging. She doesn't say a word to me—doesn't even break her stride—tight lipped as though heading to the slaughter.

Iphigenia.

I think she's overdoing it a bit.

We enter the bank and up pops her "customer adviser." A dead ringer for my son-in-law: same suit, same hairstyle, same bearing, same voice. Heaven knows how many clones have come off the same production line. But it's best I avoid thinking about Gregory, because he might yet be the precursor to some colossal problems.

Mathilde sees the bank manager by herself for a moment and then comes back. It's crazy how simple it is. My daughter hands me a fat envelope.

I go to hug her but she mechanically offers me her cheek. She regrets her coldness, but it's too late now. She thinks I'm cross: I look for something to say, but it doesn't come. Mathilde squeezes my forearm. Now that she has relinquished half of what she owns to me, she seems calmer. She simply says:

"You promised, remember . . ."

Then she smiles, as if ashamed of repeating herself, of showing me so little trust. Or so much fear.

We go our separate ways outside the *métro*.

"I'm going to walk for a bit."

I wait for her to leave, then go down into the station myself. I didn't have the courage to prolong the contact. I put my phone on vibrate mode and slide it into my trouser pocket. By my count, Mathilde will be home in less than half an hour. One station follows another, I change and walk through the corridors, my phone slapping against my thigh. At the interchange, instead of boarding the train, I take a seat and scoop up a crumpled copy of *Le Monde*. I browse the article: *Employees currently represent 'main threat' to businesses' financial security.*

I look at my watch nervously as I continue to leaf through. Page 8: *Auction record: Emir Shahid Al-Abbasi's yacht to sell for 174 million dollars.*

My feet are on hot coals and I can barely concentrate.

I don't have to wait long. I fumble for my phone and look at the screen. It's Mathilde. I swallow hard and let it ring through. No message.

I try hard to focus on something else. Page 15: *After four months of strike action at factory, Desforges employees lift blockade after accepting 300 euro payout.*

But two minutes later she calls again. A glance at my watch and I do a quick calculation. Nicole won't be home yet, but she will get back before me and I do not want Mathilde leaving a message on our machine. The third time I pick up.

"Papa!"

Her words catch. So do mine.

"How could you . . ."

But that's all she can manage. She's back home. She has just discovered her husband's face all smashed up and heard that I had gone to her because I'd failed with him.

Mathilde must have confessed to her husband that she'd given their apartment money to her father.

They are livid, I understand that.

"Listen, angel, let me explain . . ."

"STOP!"

She yells this with all her strength.

"Give me back my money, Papa! Give it back RIGHT NOW!"

I reply before I lose my courage.

"I don't have it anymore, angel. I just put it toward the job."

Silence.

I'm not sure if she believes me, because all that I used to represent in her eyes has now melted away to form a new image of me, one that is unimaginable and unbearable.

It's not only that she has to revise everything she thought she knew about her father. It's worse: she has to live with it.

Right, I must reassure her. Tell her she has nothing to worry about.

"Listen, my angel, you have my word!"

Her voice is serious, measured. This time, the words come easily. She is able to distill all her thoughts into a few simple syllables.

"You are a bastard."

This is not an opinion, it's a fact. As I leave the station, I hold the envelope tight against me. My ticket for the top spot in the pantheon of bastard fathers.

13

Mathilde did not call back. She was so furious that she came in person. The finger she pressed on the buzzer seethed with such rage it felt as though it were still ringing when she was upstairs and hurling abuse at me in front of her mother. She demanded I give back the money she lent me, yelling at me like I was a crook. I didn't want to dwell on the fact that the envelope containing her money was in the top drawer of my desk, and that it would have taken me a second to put her mind to rest, to restore order. I focused, drawing on all my reserves of courage, like when you're at the dentist and he's wrestling with a tricky tooth.

Everything went terribly. It was to be expected, of course, but it was painful all the same.

Why won't they understand? It's a mystery. Actually, it isn't really. In the beginning, for Mathilde and for Nicole, unemployment was an abstraction, a concept: something written about in the papers or spoken about on television. Later, reality caught up with them: as unemployment spread, it became impossible to avoid contact with someone personally affected or someone with a close relation out of work. Yet the reality was still foggy, an undeniable presence, but one you could live with; you know it exists, but it only concerns others, like world hunger, homelessness, or AIDS. Or hemorrhoids. For those not directly involved, unemployment is background chatter. Then one day, when no one is expecting, it comes knocking on your front door. Just like Mathilde, it presses its fat finger on the buzzer, except the sound doesn't carry on ringing in everyone's ears for the same length of time. Those who go to work in the morning, for example, stop hearing it there and then, only to be reminded of it when they get home in the evening. If at all. That's if they live with someone unemployed, or if it makes a brief appearance on the news. As for Mathilde, she only ever heard it mentioned on the odd evening or weekend when she came to visit. That's the big difference: unemployment bored into my eardrums, and it's never stopped. Try explaining that to them.

As soon as Mathilde gave me the chance, I tried to reason that this was an unprecedented opportunity (a job I had a genuine hope of securing), but one word in she started yelling again. I wondered for a second whether she might re-smash all our new crockery. Nicole said nothing. Slumped in a corner of the room, she looked at me and wept in silence, as if I were the sorriest specimen she had ever witnessed.

Eventually, I gave up explaining myself. I went back to my study, but that wasn't good enough. Mathilde flung open the door with a fresh volley of insults—nothing would appease her. Even Nicole started trying to reason with her, to tell her that shouting and screaming wouldn't change anything, that she had to take a more constructive approach, see what can be done in practical terms. Mathilde's anger then turned on her mother.

"What do you mean 'what can be done'? Can you pay back what he took from me?"

Then she turned to me:

"Do you REALLY want to pay me back, Papa? Do you REALLY want to give back the money before we buy the apartment, because . . ."

At that point she stopped dead.

She had been so overwhelmed by fury that it hadn't dawned on her until now: there was nothing she could do about it. If I don't pay her back, the sale will fall through and she will lose most of her deposit. Nothing can be done. She choked. I said:

"I gave you my word, angel. I will repay you, in full, before your deadline. Have I ever lied to you?"

It was a low blow on my part, but what other option did I have?

Once Mathilde had gone, a long, droning silence filled the apartment. I heard Nicole moving from one room to another, then finally she came to me. Her anger had given way to utter despondency. She had dried away her tears.

"What was it for, this money?" she asked.

"To load the dice in our favor."

She waved this aside with furious disbelief. For several nights now, ever since she's been sleeping in the spare room, I've been wondering whether I'd be brave enough to say when she asked me that question. I'd devised plenty of theories. Of all the possible solutions, however, it was Nicole who unwittingly chose one.

"You said to Mathilde that it was for . . . a bribe?"

"Yes," I said.

"Who for?"

"The recruitment firm."

Nicole's face changed. I thought I detected a glimmer of hope in it. I went for it. I know I shouldn't have gone this far, but I was in need of some comforting, too.

"BLC Consulting is in charge of the recruiting. They're the ones who will choose. That's what I paid for. I bought the job."

Nicole sat down on my desk chair. The computer screen woke up and displayed the Exxyal website, with its oil wells, helicopters, refineries, and all the rest.

"So . . . it's certain?"

I would have given all my remaining years not to have to answer that, but none of the gods came to my rescue. I was left alone to consider Nicole's burgeoning hope, her wide-open eyes. The words wouldn't come. I smiled and spread my arms as a token of proof. Nicole smiled, too. She found it utterly marvelous. She started crying again and laughing at the same time. All the same, she carried on looking for the catch.

"Maybe they asked the other candidates to do the same?"

"That would be stupid. There's only one job up for grabs! Why get the others to do it if it only means repaying them after?"

"It's so weird! I can't believe they suggested this."

"It was my idea. There were three candidates whose profiles matched. We were neck and neck. I had to stand out from the others."

Nicole was stunned. I felt some small relief, but it had an extremely bitter taste to it: the more I presented this version of events as infallible, the more menacing the uncertainties of my plan seemed. I was jettisoning my last chances of ever being understood, even though victory wasn't even guaranteed.

"And how are you going to pay Mathilde back?"

As anyone knows, the first lie spawns the second. In management, we learn to lie as seldom as possible, to stay as close as we can to the truth. That's not always feasible. In this case, I had no choice but to escalate it a notch.

"I negotiated 20,000 euros. But for 25, they'll do what they can to convince their client to pay me an advance."

I wondered where I was going with this.

"They'll give you an advance while you're still on probation?"

In any negotiation, there is a tipping point. Make or break. I was there. I said:

"Twenty-five thousand euros . . . it's just three months' salary."

A veil of skepticism continued to linger between us, but I felt that I was on the brink of persuading her. And I knew why. Because of hope—inescapable, rotten hope.

"Why didn't you tell Mathilde all this?"

"Because Mathilde can't see beyond her anger."

I went up to Nicole and took her in my arms.

"So," she said, "this hostage taking . . . what's that all about?"

All that remained was to play this bit down. I felt good, as though I had started believing my own lie.

"It's nothing more than a charade, my love! In fact, it's utterly pointless now because the game's already been decided . . . We're talking about a couple of guys with plastic guns who'll scare everyone for a bit and then it's finished. The role play will last about fifteen minutes, just a way of seeing whether or not the folks completely lose their cool, and then the client will be happy. Everyone will be happy."

Nicole carried on thinking for a second, then said:

"So, there's nothing more you have to do? You've paid and you've got the job?"

I answered:

"Correct. I've paid. All we have to do is wait."

If Nicole had asked one more question, just one, it would have been my turn to break down in tears. But she had nothing left to ask—she was satisfied. I was tempted to point out that she didn't have such a big problem with the hostage taking now that she knew I would get a job out of it, but I'd already tried my luck and, in all honesty, I was exhausted with myself, with all my lies and trickery.

"I know that you're a very brave man, Alain," she said. "I know how desperate you are to get out of this. I know full well that you do menial jobs that you never talk about because you're afraid I'm ashamed of you."

I'm astonished she knows all that, too.

"I've always admired your energy and willpower so much, but you have to leave our daughters out of this. It's up to us to overcome this, not them."

In principle I agree, but if they hold the only solution, then what? We pretend not to see? Does solidarity only work one way? Of course, I don't say any of this aloud.

"This money thing, about buying your job, you have to explain all this to Mathilde," Nicole continued. "Reassure her. I'm telling you, you have to call her."

"Listen, Nicole, all of us are caught up in anger, emotion, and panic. In a few days, I'll have a job, I'll give back her money, she'll buy her apartment, and everything will be back to normal."

Deep down, each of us was as exhausted as the other.

Nicole gave in to my scummy reasoning.

14

I've more or less finished my research into Exxyal Europe's activities.

I know the European group's organization chart by heart (as well as the major shareholders in the American group), and I'm proficient in the key growth figures from the last five years, the backgrounds of all the top dogs, the detailed breakdown of their capital, the main dates relating to the group's market history, and their future plans, especially the initiative to trim back production sites and close down several refineries across Europe, including the one at Sarqueville. The hardest was getting acquainted with the sectors in which Exxyal operates. I spent two whole nights familiarizing myself with the principal aspects of the industry: deposits, exploration, production, drilling, transport, refining, and logistics. At first it all frightened me because I'm not that hot on the technical side, but I'm so pumped up that I'm ready for the challenge. It's weird, but every now and again, I feel like I'm already there, already in the company. I even think that some of the execs might be less well informed about the group than I am.

I've made myself flashcards. Almost eighty of them. Yellow for the group's finances and stock market history; blue for technical aspects; white for partnerships. I wait for Nicole to leave, then recite them to myself as I pace around the living room. I'm completely in the zone—the immersion technique.

Four days now I've been cramming. This is always the most thankless part, where the ideas have registered but are still muddled. A bit longer and everything will start settling in my brain. I'll be as ready as anything when the test day arrives. Nothing to worry about from that perspective.

According to their role in the group, I start envisaging the questions I'm going to put to the exec hostages, ones that are likely to derail them. The lawyers must have access to confidential information on previous arrangements with subcontractors, partners, or clients; the finance guys must know about various bits of foul play in the negotiation of major contracts. That side of things is still a bit vague . . . I need to dig deeper, prepare more, be totally ready for the big day. I'm also making notes about hostage taking, which I then revise with Kaminski.

Yesterday I received the first investigation reports from Mestach's agency. Reading them terrified me: in terms of their private lives, these people are perfectly ordinary. I mean representative-sample ordinary. Degrees, marriages, a few divorces; children who get degrees, get married, get divorced. Humanity can be so fucking depressing sometimes. Looking at their details and track records, these people are commonplace. Even so, I have to find their faults, to lay them bare.

I'm waiting for Kaminski. Despite being on the ropes himself, he managed to take advantage of my urgent situation to negotiate favorable terms. He's expensive, and I'm scraping the financial barrel, but I like the guy, he's decent. I couldn't keep the novelist act up for long. I told him the real story, which has simplified our working relationship no end.

Yesterday he read the "hostage" profiles, which I find so lackluster, and he saw my concern.

"If you were to read your own profile," he said, "it would look like that. But you're not just some average unemployed guy: you're planning a hostage taking."

I knew this, but in Nicole's absence, I don't have anyone to tell me the simple things I need to hear.

So I read and reread the profiles. As Kaminski said, "However exhaustively you prepare, when it comes down to it you're always forced to follow your intuition."

If I bear in mind the possible mistakes in my list of hostages, my chances of success are moderate at best. But even if I slip up in my preparations, I'm still banking on the fact that none of my competitors will have the same level of insight into the hostages' private lives.

I only need to crack two or three to come out on top. And to achieve that, I need to source some "hard-hitting" information.

I can afford supplementary investigations into five people, no more. After a huge amount of deliberation, I kept two men (the economics specialist Jean-Marc Guéneau, forty-five years old, and the civil engineer in his fifties, Paul Cousin) and two women (Évelyne Camberlin, fifty, structural engineer, and the business school grad, Virginie Tràn, thirty-five). And I threw in David Fontana, the organizer from Bertrand Lacoste's e-mails.

With Paul Cousin, there wasn't a shadow of a doubt: his bank accounts show that his wages are not paid into either his personal account or his family account. Very mysterious indeed. His wife has an account that he tops up himself each month. He doesn't transfer huge amounts—smells like separation. Or if their relationship is stable, she must be in the dark about the real situation. The fact is that Cousin's salary (he's a civil engineer in his fifties with more than twenty years under his belt, so it's hardly inconsiderable) doesn't show up anywhere: it's stashed elsewhere in an account under a different name.

Very promising indeed.

Bonus information.

I examined Jean-Marc Guéneau's file in microscopic detail. He is forty-five years old. At the age of twenty-one, he married one of the Boissieu girls—tidy little fortune. They have seven children. I found virtually nothing on Guéneau's family, but on the flip side, his wife's father is none other than Dr. Boissieu, a fervent Catholic and a very vocal anti-abortion lobbyist. As such, they're at it like rabbits at Guéneau HQ, firing out an offspring every five minutes. You don't need to be too cynical to suspect he's got a few beauties waiting in the wings. The moment people start wearing their morals on their sleeves, you can be positive there's something unmentionable going on behind closed doors.

Bonus information.

Out of the ladies, I kept Évelyne Camberlin. Fifty, single, high ranking . . . scratch away at a woman like that and something is bound to come up. My decision to keep her was very much based on her photographs: I'm not sure why, but I find her interesting. When I told Kaminski as much, he smiled and said: "Well spotted."

I rounded off my lineup with Virginie Tràn. She's in charge of several major accounts, Exxyal's biggest clients. She's ambitious, calculating, moves up the ladder quickly: I don't think this girl is held back by scruples. Surely some leverage somewhere in there.

There's every possibility that these additional investigations won't come to anything, but I'm making progress.

How am I ever going to get out of this shitstorm? Sometimes the thought makes me dizzy. Not least because the rest of the landscape is looking so bleak.

I've not heard a peep on the Pharmaceutical Logistics front since sending off my letter to the lawyer. Every morning as I pretend to come home from work, I empty the mailbox to find that nothing has come. I've called Maître Gilson two or three times a day but never managed to get hold of her. A gnawing sense of anxiety has set in. So when the postman makes me sign for a letter sent by registered mail, and I see the Gilson & Fréret firm heading, I feel an unpleasant tingle run down my spine. Maître Gilson informs me that her client has decided to uphold their complaint against me and that I will receive a court summons to make a statement on the assault committed against my supervisor, Monsieur Mehmet Pehlivan. To my astonishment, Maître Gilson picks up this time.

"There's nothing I can do, Monsieur Delambre, I've done everything I can. What more do you want? My client is taking this complaint seriously."

"But didn't we have an agreement?"

"No, Monsieur Delambre. It was your idea to write a formal apology. We didn't ask you for anything. You did that on your own initiative."

"But . . . why go to court if your client has accepted my apology?"

"My client has accepted your apology, true. He then forwarded it to Monsieur Pehlivan who, by my understanding, was quite satisfied with it. But you must be aware that this letter represents a comprehensive confession."

"So . . . ?"

"So . . . insofar as you acknowledge the facts fully and freely, my client feels he is within his right to claim for the damages he is due in court."

When I offered to write this letter of apology, it did occur to me that things might turn out this way, but I didn't think it was possible for an employer and his lawyer to be capable of such a craven move toward someone in my situation.

"You're a fucking bitch."

"I understand your point of view, but I'm afraid that won't stand up in court, Monsieur Delambre. I advise you to find a stronger line of defense."

She hangs up. This hasn't made me as angry as I expected it to. I only had one card to play and I played it. No point beating myself up about it, and I can't even blame them: it's hard to leave the table when you know you have a winning hand.

That doesn't stop me from hurling my cell against the wall, where it explodes. When I realize I need a new one (in other words, about five minutes later), I start looking for the pieces underneath the furniture. Patched up with tape, it now looks like a rag doll, or an old fogey's glasses down at the hospice.

I've spent everything Mathilde gave me, and even though Kaminski has agreed to lower his rate from 4,000 to 3,000 euros for the two days' work, I've still had to withdraw 1,000 euros of the 1,410 left in our savings account. Let's hope Nicole doesn't feel inclined to check the balance before all this is over.

Right at the start, Kaminski suggested a plan of action: day one would be dedicated to the nuts and bolts of the hostage taking; day two, we would tackle the psychological side of the interrogations. Kaminski doesn't know David Fontana, but having read the organizer's messages, he tells me that the guy knows exactly what he's doing. Bertrand Lacoste and I each have our adviser, our expert, our coach—we're like a pair of chess players the day before the world championships.

As far as Nicole is concerned, everything's still fine. She has calmed down, and despite my reservations, I suspect she's phoned Mathilde to reassure her and explain the ins and outs of the situation.

So when Kaminski arrives just before 10:00 a.m., I don't imagine for a second that I'm on the brink of disaster.

As agreed, he's brought along a camera and tripod that we can connect to the television so we can look back over what he calls the "respective positions," and for rehearsing the interrogations.

To help me get to grips with the technical side of things, he's also brought two firearms: an eighteen-round 4.5mm Umarex pistol, which is a copy of the Beretta, and a Cometa-Baikal-QB57 to stand in for the Uzi submachine guns that, according to Fontana's e-mail, will be used in the real thing. Kaminski proposes replicating the layout of the two main rooms, as per the site map from the e-mail, to show me where the pivotal action spots will be, and we've rearranged the sofa, table, and chairs to create the zone where the hostages will be held.

It's just after 12:15 p.m.

Kaminski tells me how the commando will maneuver itself in the premises to ensure it retains overall control of the situation. He's sitting on the floor—back against the partition wall, legs folded—impersonating a hostage.

I'm standing in the doorway with the little submachine gun slung across my shoulder like a bandolier, the barrel trained in his general direction, when Nicole arrives home.

It's quite a spectacle.

If she'd walked in on me fucking the next-door neighbor, that would have been absurd and therefore easier to process. But this . . . The sight that greets Nicole belongs in the realm of hyperrealism: the weapons Kaminski brought are terrifyingly present. This is training. The man hugging his knees and staring up at her from the ground is a professional.

Nicole is speechless. She holds her breath in bewilderment. I'd pretended to her that the interview was just a formality. Now she's fathoming the extent of my duplicity. Her eyes dart over the gun in my hands, the furniture pushed into the corners. It is such a calamity that neither of us can find anything to say.

In any case, my lies spew out so loudly that they're unintelligible. Nicole just shakes her head and leaves without a word.

Kaminski's being decent about it. He manages to find something to say. Later on I defrost some food in the microwave and we eat standing up. I reflect on the horror of the situation. Nicole hardly ever comes back for lunch. It would be quite extraordinary if she did it twice a year. And she always calls ahead to make sure I'm there. Of all the days! Everything is conspiring against me. Kaminski smiles and tells me that it's in situations like this that true strength of character shines through.

It's now early afternoon and the atmosphere is heavy. I need to dig deep to summon the energy to get back to work. The image of Nicole in the doorframe, her eyes—it's giving me hell.

He's a good guy, Kaminski. He's going the extra mile, telling me real-life anecdotes so I can envisage all the possible scenarios. He's very cagey about his own life, but one thing leads to another and I end up pretty well piecing together the details of his career. He did clinical psychology before joining the police, then he became a negotiator with RAID. My guess is that he wasn't a user by then, or at least that the effects weren't so visible.

As the day draws on, he gets more nervous. Withdrawal. From time to time he claims he needs a cigarette to recharge his batteries. He goes downstairs for a few minutes and comes back calmer, eyes gleaming. His drug of choice remains a mystery to me. His addiction doesn't bother me in the slightest; what pisses me off me are his diversion tactics. In the end I snap:

"Do you think I'm stupid?"

"Screw you!"

He's furious, a mutinous look in his eyes. I hesitate for a second before carrying on:

"I know you're high as a kite all day long, but at this price I'd hope for more than a wreck!"

"What difference does it make?"

"Every difference. Do you think you're worth what I'm paying for you?"

"That's your call."

"Well, I'd say no. The girl you killed, she jumped out the window while you were shooting up behind some truck . . ."

"So what?"

"So that wasn't your only fuckup! Am I wrong?"

"That's none of your business!"

"It's not the same in the police as it is in the private sector. You don't get fired the first time you mess up. How many were there before? How many deaths had you been drugged up for before they decided to throw you out?"

"You've got no right!"

"And while we're at it, this girl . . . did you see her fall or did you just see her body on the pavement? I've heard it makes a nasty sound. Young girls especially. Am I right?"

Kaminski slumps back in his chair and pulls out a pack of cigarettes. He offers me one. I await his verdict.

"Not bad at all," he says with a smile.

I feel mightily relieved.

"Not bad: you held your line, remained focused on impactful subject matter, and proceeded with short, incisive, well-chosen questions. No, I'm telling you, for an amateur, that wasn't bad at all."

He stands up and stops the camera. I hadn't realized it was filming.

"We'll keep that for tomorrow and go back over the sequence when we discuss the interrogations."

Good day's work.

He leaves at around 7:00 p.m.

Evening falls and I'm alone in the apartment.

Before he went, Kaminski suggested we put all the furniture back in place. I told him it wasn't necessary; I knew Nicole wasn't coming home. I scraped some change together and went to buy a bottle of single malt and a pack of cigarettes. I'm on my second whiskey when Lucie arrives to collect her mother's things. I open the windows wide because it's warm and the smoke from my first cigarette is going to my head. When she comes in, I must look like I'm completely off the rails, which I'm not. But appearances matter. She doesn't comment. All she says is:

"I can't stay, I have to look after Maman. How about lunch tomorrow?"

"I can't do lunch. Tomorrow evening?"

Lucie nods and hugs me with great tenderness. It hurts.

But I still have plenty of work to do.

I light a second cigarette, grab my notes, and start studying, pacing around the big, deserted living room: "Capital—47 million euros. Composition—Exxyal Group: 8 percent, Total: 11.5 percent . . ."

Over the course of the evening, Mathilde leaves two short, violent messages.

At one point she says: "You're the exact opposite of what I expect my father to be."

It breaks my heart.

From: Olenka Zbikowski
BLC Consulting
To the attention of: Bertrand Lacoste
Subject: End of internship

As you will no doubt be aware, my second internship finishes on May 30. This six-month period followed an initial four-month internship.

You will find enclosed with the present note a full report on my activities at BLC Consulting since you were kind enough to place your confidence in me. I would like to take this opportunity to offer my sincere thanks for the roles you have allocated me in these ten months, roles which, in several cases, have far exceeded the responsibilities ordinarily attributed to an intern.

Almost ten months of unpaid activity, during which I have demonstrated constant willingness and unfailing loyalty, represents a sufficient trial period for me to expect a decision on your part regarding permanent employment.

Allow me to take this opportunity to declare once again my dedication to the company's business activities, and my strong desire to continue to collaborate alongside you.

Best,
Olenka Zbikowski

15

Charles said: "I live at number 47." Which really means that his car is parked opposite number 47.

Number 47 is the only number on the street, along with 45, which is three hundred yards away. Between the two lies the enormous brick wall of a factory, the neighborhood's only attraction. Opposite, construction fencing and scaffolding. The street is straight as a die, dark, with lampposts at thirty- or forty-yard intervals.

Charles greets me with the little Indian sign he makes with his left hand.

"Before," he tells me, "I was over there right under the street-light. Forget about sleeping! Had to wait for a space to free up in the shade."

Charles had burst out laughing when I called him.

"Is that drink still on?" I said.

His joy was genuine, despite having already drunk enough for both of us that day:

"Seriously? You want to come to my place?"

And so here we are, almost 11:00 p.m., standing outside his place: a bright-red Renault 25.

"Nineteen eighty-five," Charles says, proudly patting the roof. "Six-cylinder 2.5-liter turbo V6!"

The fact that it hasn't been driven for more than ten years doesn't faze him in the slightest. The car is up on blocks to avoid flat-spotting the tires, which lends it the impression of floating a few inches above the ground.

"I've got a pal who comes around every few months to pump them up for me."

"That's great."

What's really astonishing are the bumpers. Front and rear. Huge great chrome bars, way too big, that rise to about four feet off the ground. The sort more commonly seen on American trucks. Charles notes my amazement.

"It's my neighbors in front and behind. The last ones. Every time they came home from a ride they'd bash into my car. One day I got fed up. So here we go."

Here we go indeed. Quite something.

"Down there farther along," he says, pointing to the other end of the street, "there used to be another Renault 25. An 'eighty-four GTX! But the guy moved."

His voice is tinged with the regret of lost friendship.

A good part of the street is occupied by tired old vans and other cars up on blocks, all housing families of immigrant workers. The mail carrier leaves the mail under the wipers, like fines.

"There's a good atmosphere in this neighborhood, you can't complain," says Charles.

We go inside for drinks. It's very organized, Charles's apartment, ingeniously arranged.

"Well it has to be!" he answers when I remark on it. "It's not very big so it has to be . . ."

"Functional . . ."

"Yes! Functional!"

As ever, Charles is bowled over by my vocabulary.

He places a tray between the seats to serve as a sort of liquor cart for the bottle and the peanuts. It's mild outside so I lower my window, and I feel the night air caressing the back of my neck. I brought a drinkable whiskey: nothing too swank, but not bad either. And a few bags of potato chips and other snacks.

We barely speak, Charles and I. We look at each other, smiling. Not that there's any ill will between us. It's a moment of calm. We're like two old friends in our rocking chairs on the terrace after a family meal. I let my mind drift and it fixes on Albert Kaminski. I look at Charles. Which of them do I feel closer to? Not Charles. He sips his whiskey, his lost eyes gazing through the windshield, past the huge bumper and beyond to his peaceful neighborhood. Charles is a victim; that's the only profile he fits. Kaminski and I are severe cases, car crashes: either of us could end up a murderer. It's a serious point. We are dabbling with radicalism. Having abandoned all hope, Charles might just be the wisest of the three of us.

On the second whiskey, Romain's shadow looms before me, a reminder of the long procession of grievances I have in store. I've made my decision. I won't ask Charles to testify.

"I figure I'm going to take care of this myself," I say.

This comes right out of the blue, and it's obvious Charles doesn't fully grasp what I am talking about. He inspects the bottom of his glass in a dreamlike state, before grumbling a few words that might amount to an agreement, but who knows. Then he thinks and shakes his head, as if to say that it's better this way, that he understands. I turn to the line of cars, the pavement glistening under the yellow smudges of the streetlights, and the factory wall that looks like a prison. I'm on the verge of the Big Test, the one that I've dedicated all my energy to, more than all of it. I savor this moment of peace as though I might die tomorrow.

"Funny when you think about it . . ."

Charles agrees that, yes, it's funny. This is the moment where, helped along by the whiskey, I ask myself the question: why am I here? It terrifies me to think that I came to gather my strength. If I miss my shot, this may well be what I can look forward to—a car up on blocks in a derelict suburb. That's a bit harsh on Charles.

"That wasn't very nice of me . . ."

Without hesitating, Charles places his hand on my knee and says: "Don't worry."

I'm still ashamed. I try to change the subject.

"So, have you got a radio?"

"Well, now you're talking!" says Charles.

He reaches out and hits the button: . . . *with the CEO receiving a golden handshake of 3.2 million euros.*

Charles turns it off.

"Good system, hey?" he says proudly.

I don't know if he's talking about the news or if he's just happy to be showing me his home comforts. We stay there for a good while.

Then I tell myself it's time to go back. I've got studying to do, I must stay focused.

I didn't say anything, yet Charles motions to the bottle:

"A little one for the road?"

I pretend to think about it. I actually do think about it. It's not a good idea. I decline, saying I need to be sensible.

Several more sedate, gentle minutes pass by. The calm makes me want to cry. Charles pats me on the knee again. I focus on the bottom of my glass. It's empty.

"Right, time to call it a night . . ."

I turn to grab the door handle.

"Let me show you out," says Charles, opening his side.

We shake hands in silence at the back of the car.

As I walk to the *métro*, it occurs to me that Charles might be the only friend I have left.

16

Five days until I'm up against the wall on Thursday. The countdown is both reassuring and frightening. For now, all I want is reassurance.

Despite the half-bottle of whiskey I knocked back last night, I'm up and ready for battle at dawn. As I drain my coffee I realize that my review notes are starting to stick. On Monday or Tuesday I should be receiving the results from the additional investigations, leaving me a day or two to come up with a strategy, provided there's even an ounce of dirt to go on.

Since Nicole left, the apartment has been desperately sad.

Mathilde has stopped giving me grief via the answering machine. She'll be having a tough time stopping her husband from suing me straightaway. Maybe he already has.

Kaminski arrives on time, to the second. On the agenda: reading and analyzing several RAID training documents focusing on the psychological aspects of hostage taking and interrogation.

First he refers to an itemized list of maneuvers that make hostages confess—so long as they've been held long enough—and the precautions the commando would have to take. That gives me a better understanding of the various psychological phases the victims go through, not to mention the points at which they'll be their most vulnerable.

We summarize what we've covered at the end of the morning session, then dedicate the afternoon to the interrogations. My management experience has already given me a solid grounding in manipulation techniques. Interrogating hostages is simple: take a job interview, multiply it by an annual performance review, then add weaponry. The principal difference is that in business, your fear is latent, whereas in a hostage taking, the lives of the victims are in danger. On second thought, it's the same in business. Ultimately, the only real difference lies in the nature of the weapons and the length of time they're left to stew.

In the evening, as planned, I have dinner with Lucie.

Her treat, so her choice of restaurant. Sooner or later, as we grow older, we become our children's children. They're the ones who take charge. But I'm in denial that the moment has already come, so I insist on a change of restaurant. We go to the Roman Noir, which is just down the road. It's warm. Lucie looks as pretty as a flower, even though she's making out that this dinner isn't a special occasion. The fact is that by talking about other things, the occasion becomes an event. Lucie tries the wine (it's common consensus that she has the best nose in the family, not that there's ever been any proof of it). Perhaps she doesn't know where to start. In any case, she opts to talk about everything and nothing, about the apartment she wants to move out of because it's so dingy, her work at her firm, the low pay that's forcing her to live hand to mouth. Lucie only talks about her love life when she's not having any joy. She's avoiding the subject, so I ask the question:

"What's his name?"

She smiles, takes a glug of wine, and looks at me as though she's announcing bad news:

"Federico."

"Of course, you always go for the exotic ones! What was the last guy called, again?"

"Papa!" she says, smiling.

"Fusaaki?"

"Fusaaki."

"Wasn't there an Omar, too?"

"You make it sound like there have been hundreds!"

It's my turn to smile. Bit by bit we keep pretending to forget why the two of us are here. To put her at ease, as soon as we've ordered dessert I ask her how her mother is doing.

Lucie doesn't answer straightaway.

"She's sad," she says eventually. "Very stressed."

"It's a stressful time."

"Are you going to tell me why?"

Sometimes you have to prepare for a meeting with your children the same way you do a job interview. Of course I don't have the energy or the inclination this time around, so I improvise, keeping it very general.

"Come on, spell it out," Lucie says after my bungled account.

"Well, your mother refused to listen, and your sister refused to understand."

She smiles.

"What about me—where do I fit in?"

"There's room in my camp, if you're interested."

"Wow, it's a pitched battle, is it?"

"No, but it is a battle, and right now I'm fighting it alone."

So I have to explain. More lies.

As I repeat what I said to Nicole, I realize how many lies I've heaped one on top of the other. I'm keeping the whole, wobbling pile together, but the slightest knock and it'll come crashing down, bringing me with it. The ad, the tests, the bribe . . . That's where it snags. Lucie's more perceptive than her mother and doesn't fall for it for a second.

"A well-established recruitment firm is entertaining a bullshit idea like this for a few thousand euros? That's really quite astonishing . . ."

You'd have to be blind not to detect her skepticism.

"It's not the *whole* firm. The guy's doing it solo."

"That doesn't mean it's not risky. Doesn't he care about his job?"

"I have no idea, but once I have my contract, he can go to the slammer for all I care—I couldn't give a damn."

There's a lull as the waiter arrives with the coffees, and afterward the conversation struggles to pick up again. I know why. So does Lucie. She doesn't believe a word of what I'm telling her. As if to prove it, she drinks her coffee and places her hands on the table.

"I need to go . . ."

She's surrendering, no doubt about it. She could have scratched away at the sore point, but she chooses not to. She'll still come up with a few platitudes to say to her sister and her mother; she'll think of something. As far as she's concerned, I'm caught up in some tawdry affair, and she's not in any hurry to find out the details. Lucie is running away.

We walk together a little. Eventually she turns to me:

"Right, well, I hope everything turns out how you want. If you need me . . ."

And there's so much sadness in the way she squeezes my arm and kisses my cheek.

After this, my weekend takes on an eve-of-battle feel.

Tomorrow in the battle think on me.

Except that I'm alone. I don't just miss Nicole because I'm alone, but because my life without her has no direction, no sense. I'm not sure why I've been unable to explain this all to her, how things have become so complicated. This has never happened to us. Why would Nicole not hear me out? Why did she not believe in my chances of success? If Nicole no longer believes in me, I'm already dead.

I need to hold on for a few more days.

Until Thursday.

The following day, I review my notes and run through my accounts to see how much I've spent, nausea overwhelming me at the thought of what might happen if I screw this up. I study the photographs and the biographies of the hostages. I go for a walk to keep my concentration fresh. I bring all my notes, my beginner's guide to the oil and gas industry, and a photocopy of the RAID document from Kaminski.

When I get back, there are three messages from Lucie. Two on my cell phone, which I'd left at home, and another on the landline. After our futile dinner last night, she would like an update. She's a bit worried, she doesn't say why. I don't want to call her back—I can't afford to lose my focus. In four days, I'll be back in the race, and I'll be able to explain how hard it was holding up without them.

17

Mestach called last night to say that the additional investigations were now available. As I still owe him half his fee, he doesn't miss the opportunity to remind me that his investigators have met a very tight deadline and that it's miraculous they've obtained so many results—a classic technique to make me think I'm getting value for money. I don't fall for it.

Mestach counts the money twice before handing me a large envelope. He starts to show me out, but I take a seat in the armchair in the corridor leading up to his office.

It dawns on him that if I don't feel I have enough bang for my buck, then he'll know about it right away. This is my daughter's money, and I have no intention of frittering it away on nothing.

To be honest, given the time constraints, it's good. In places, it's even very good. I don't want to let this on, so as soon as I've taken stock of the first few results, I slip out of the building. Seems he won't have to know about it after all.

Back at home, I clear my desk and line up the findings.

Jean-Marc Guéneau. Forty-five years old.

This guy is straight out of the nineteenth century. People from Catholic families like his have been intermarrying for generations. The men are all generals, priests, professors; the women are all housewives, little more than laying hens. His family tree is more of an elaborate tropical shrub. Like the rest of the spineless upper middle classes, his little clique has been diligently leaching income from land and property ever since the start of the industrial revolution, a term they hold in particular disdain because it reeks of the proletariat. Predictably enough, the last few generations have been particularly hard-line. They live in the sixteenth, the seventh, the eighth *arrondissements*, Neuilly—only the classiest neighborhoods. Our Guéneau marries at twenty-one and proceeds to produce a brat every eighteenth months for the next ten years. They called it a day at seven. Madame must be taking her temperature every five minutes between Hail Marys, insisting on the withdrawal method, too, because you can never be too careful. So it's unsurprising that Guéneau needs to come up for air; rather seedy air, as it happens. I have two photographs of him: the first is taken at 7:30 p.m. as he enters a side door on rue Saint-Maur; the second, taken at 8:45 p.m., shows him leaving. That means getting home around 9:15 p.m. For his trip to the "gym," he's carrying a sports bag.

This is a real stroke of luck. His credit card shows that he spends two hours a week on rue Saint-Maur, usually on Thursdays. He's bound to have some friends among the regulars. That cracks me up. This one's a done deal—dead man walking.

Paul Cousin, fifty-two, is less classic, and all the more exciting because of it.

A man with a CV like this is untouchable. He's got nothing that will let him stand out from the rest of the pack. I'll need to ensure that his interrogation falls to one of my rivals. That's the plan, at least.

In the photographs, he has a worrying physique: an unbelievably voluminous head with eyes that bulge out of their sockets. He goes to work every day at Exxyal, he has his own underground space in the company parking garage, he's a senior project manager, he

travels, he submits reports, he attends meetings, he visits facili-
ties . . . and yet for more than four years he's been signed up with an
executive recruitment agency and receiving unemployment benefits.
I check his employment record and—with the help of an accompa-
nying note with precise details, dates, and facts—I manage to piece
together his strange career.

Paul Cousin worked for Exxyal for twenty-two years until he was
fired four years ago (the victim of a staff cut in the department he'd
been assigned to a few months previously). At that point, he was
forty-eight years old. What happened in his head? Was it a mental
block or a desperate tactic? He decided to continue coming in to
work, as if nothing had happened. His superiors cited him and the
case went right to the top, where the powers-that-be ruled in his
favor. If he wanted to carry on coming into work, that was fine with
them. He doesn't get a salary, he works, performs well, but there's no
other way of putting it: for four years, he's been volunteering!

He must be holding out some hope that he can prove himself. He
is working to get his job back.

In doing so, Paul Cousin is embodying capitalism's oldest dream.
Even the most imaginative of bosses couldn't hope for better. He's
sold his apartment because he can't afford the mortgage, traded in
his car for a cheaper model, and receives a minute sum in unemployment benefits, and all the while he's got loads of responsibility. It's
not hard to see why he's so interested in the Sarqueville layoff plan:
if he does a good job heading up this round of staff cuts, then he'll
be back in the fold once and for all. This is his return ticket to the
giddy heights of the Exxyal Group. A man with this level of ambi-
tion will give up his life without flinching—he is unstoppable. He
will never surrender, not even when he's staring down the barrel of
a submachine gun.

Then there's Virginie Tràn, the Vietnamese girl. Now she's a fine
customer.

Mestach and his team couldn't be sure when her affair with
Hubert Bonneval began. Judging by her phone records and various
hits on her credit card statements, you could hazard a guess that

they've been together for eighteen months. I have several photographs taken two days ago showing the couple at the food market on rue du Poteau: eying each other up lustfully in front of the cheese; kissing next to the peppers. The final shot shows them entering Mademoiselle Tràn's apartment arm in arm. Must be less than eighteen months if you ask me—either that or they're genuinely in love. The notes suggest they met in professional circumstances: a seminar, trade fair, or something. Possible. But even more interesting than Mademoiselle Tràn is her lover. He's thirty-eight and a senior project manager at Solarem, a subsidiary of Exxyal's main business rival. She is quite literally in bed with the competition. Excellent.

I get straight online and in no time at all I've found the big sites run by Solarem. I have a very clear idea of the situation I'll put little Virginie in to crack her, to show her what sort of an assessor I am: I will push her to betray her lover for her company, forcing her to reveal technical information pertaining to the offshore rigs installed by Solarem. She will have to call her man and explain that, for work purposes, she *must* have certain pieces of confidential information about her competitor's sites. To demonstrate her loyalty to her employer, she'll have to make him be unfaithful to his. Perfect. Textbook.

As for Évelyne Camberlin, nothing. Odds and ends. Money farted into the breeze.

They saved the best until last.

David Fontana. The pro brought in by BLC Consulting to organize the hostage taking. I recognize him in the photograph: definitely the man I saw with Lacoste.

Six years ago he set up an agency specializing in security. Checks, installations, surveillance. His company is kosher. Nothing wrong with cashing in on the latest wave of collective paranoia. Every year, he and his team install more cameras than you can shake a stick at. His balance sheet is not entirely positive: the investigator's theory is that a decent amount of his profit is stashed away with the help of some creative accounting before being paid to the boss on the sly.

The hidden part of his business activities is more opaque, almost as much as his past. Business intelligence for companies, debt collection, protection in all its forms. His clients only see the agreeable side of his CV. He began his career in the army, the paratroopers, before making a long transition into the intelligence services. As far as his clients are concerned, his official pedigree ends there. He keeps quiet about his "freelance" (read "mercenary") activities. Scratch below the surface and in the past twenty years we see David Fontana popping up in Burma, Kurdistan, Congo, former Yugoslavia . . . The man likes to travel. After that, he jumps on the modern bandwagon by joining various private military contractors, whose client lists include governments, multinational corporations and organizations, and diamond merchants. His main job is combat training, his skills getting plucked by the most famous agencies: Military Professional Resources Inc., DynCorp, Erinys, and the rest. Seems he's been more than happy to lend a hand in several different theaters. You get the feeling that this guy is full of goodwill.

In the end, Fontana is forced into early retirement following a slight hiccup: he's suspected of involvement in the massacre of seventy-four people in South Sudan at a time when the company employing him was propping up the Janjaweed, the government-supported militia.

After that he sensibly decides to settle down and establish his own surveillance and security company.

No doubt Bertrand Lacoste knows nothing of all this. Neither do Exxyal. His company brochure is squeaky clean, his CV meticulously sugarcoated. Not that they'd give two hoots anyway: no matter what domain they're dealing with, they want skilled people, and there can be no doubt that David Fontana is an expert.

I think back to my fear at being found out by him outside the BLC Consulting building. My intuition wasn't wrong.

I create a sheet for each of the three execs with my personal notes. As I imagine the questions I'm going to put to them and how I'm going to conduct the interviews, I can't help feeling apprehensive.

My selection process was rigorous, but if the execs who turn up on the day are different from the ones I've investigated and invested in, it will be catastrophic—I would be going in empty handed.

This prospect makes me so anxious that I instantly chase it from my mind. In life, you need luck, too. Having had my fair share of bad fortune over the years, it's reasonable to suppose that I'm due some favorable odds. All the same, I go back over my selection criteria, and I'm relieved to reconfirm my choices. Now that the apartment is empty and I'm all alone, I have to resort to self-congratulation.

Bertrand,

So. After ignoring my message about my internship finishing and the permanent position you promised me, I hear you've awarded an unpaid internship to Thomas Jaulin, a friend of mine from college.

I notice that the role he's been offered is absolutely identical to the one I've been carrying out for the past ten months at BLC (you just copy and pasted my contract when you drew up his!).

I'm keeping things "professional" for now, but I seriously hope that I've misread the situation.

Call me at home tonight, pls.
    I don't care what time.
Olenka

P.S. I left my little necklace in your bathroom, please keep an eye out for it . . .

From: Bertrand Lacoste
BLC Consulting
To the attention of: Olenka Zbikowski
Date: May 18
Subject: Your internship

Madame,

I have given our various discussions due consideration and can confirm that we cannot foresee a situation whereby you are granted permanent employment.

A number of recent contracts have allowed us to secure the company's short-term future, but they are not sufficiently longstanding to enable us take on new colleagues on a lasting basis.

With the exception of one or two isolated incidents, your time at BLC Consulting can on the whole be described as satisfactory, and we are glad to have been able to offer you the opportunity of such a worthwhile experience that will strengthen your *curriculum vitae* as you approach potential employers.

I appreciate your surprise with regard to the approval of Monsieur Thomas Jaulin's application for a five-month unpaid internship at BLC Consulting. Our acceptance followed your categorical refusal to extend your internship beyond May 30. It goes without saying, however, that, given your intimate understanding of our activities and the seamless manner in which you have engaged with your fellow team members, Monsieur Jaulin's offer would immediately be withdrawn should you wish to extend your current internship.

I very much look forward to hearing your response.

Kindest regards,
Bertrand Lacoste

18

The situation couldn't be clearer: the odds are in my favor.

I can't imagine any of the other candidates being better prepared. I'll be the best because I've worked the hardest.

This thought is running through my head when, at around 7:00 p.m., the telephone rings.

It goes to the answering machine, but it's not Lucie's voice on the speaker this time. I know this voice. It's a woman. A young woman.

"My name is Olenka Zbikowski."

I approach the speakerphone with a combination of intrigue and suspicion.

"We met at BLC Consulting when you came in for your tests. I was the one who . . ."

When I realize who she is, I rush to the telephone so quickly that I knock it over. I have to run my hand under the sofa to recover the handset.

"Hello!"

I've only taken three steps and done one squat but I'm as breathless as if I'd run a marathon. I am terrified by this call—it is not at all in the ordinary running of things.

"Monsieur Delambre?"

I confirm that yes, that's me: my voice betrays panic, the girl apologizes, and I realize that it's definitely her, the girl who handed out our test papers.

She wants to meet me. Immediately.

This isn't normal.

"Why? Tell me why!"

She can hear how shaken I am by this call.

"I'm not very far from where you live. I can be there in twenty minutes."

These twenty minutes feel like twenty hours, twenty years.

The meeting takes place in the little garden by the square. We're sitting on a bench. The streetlights illuminate one by one. There aren't many people around. She's not as pretty as I remember, perhaps because she's not wearing any makeup. She composes herself and, in very simple words, informs me that the world has ended.

"Officially, you're one of four candidates, but three of you are just there to make up the numbers. The position is going to be allocated to a candidate named Juliette Rivet. You don't stand a chance. You're just a foil."

This information whirls around in my brain, but it doesn't break through the cortex. It carries on its journey before worming its way between my two synapses. The scale of the calamity starts to dawn on me.

"Juliette Rivet is a very close friend of Bertrand Lacoste," the young woman continues. "She's the one he will pick. So he has chosen three candidates for show. The first because he has an international profile that will satisfy the client, and another with a vaguely similar CV. But Lacoste is going to make sure they get marked down. As for you—you were chosen on account of your age. According to Lacoste, 'It looks good to have an old guy in the picture these days.'"

"But Exxyal will choose the candidates, not him!"

She's taken aback:

"How do you know that it's Exxyal recruiting?"

"Answer me . . ."

"I have no idea how you know that, but Exxyal won't contest Lacoste's verdict. They're looking for someone with a similar skill set and will be happy to take the candidate favored by the firm they've hired for the recruitment. End of story."

I look around but it's like a mist has descended. I'm about to faint. My stomach is in knots, my kidneys aching.

"This job is not for you, Monsieur Delambre. You have absolutely no chance."

I am so disoriented, so bewildered that she wonders if she was right to warn me. I must be a frightening sight.

"But . . . Why are you telling me this?"

"I've informed the other two candidates as well."

"What's in it for you?"

"Lacoste used me, squeezed me, drained me, then discarded me. I'm doing everything in my power to make sure his glorious operation fails because no one is there to take part in it. His candidate will be the only one who turns up. It will be a personal kick in the teeth and, as far as his client is concerned, an absolute disaster. I appreciate it's a bit childish, but it makes me feel better."

She stands up.

"The best thing you can do is not go, I guarantee. I'm sorry to have to tell you, but your test results were very poor. You are no longer in the running, Monsieur Delambre, you shouldn't have even been called in for an interview. Lacoste kept you for show, so even if by some small miracle you manage to pull something out of the bag, you don't stand a chance. I'm sorry . . ."

She makes a vague hand gesture.

"I admit that I'm doing this mainly for selfish reasons, but I'm also telling you so that you don't have to go through a fruitless and potentially humiliating experience. My father must be roughly the same age as you, and I wouldn't want . . ."

She's sufficiently thin skinned to realize that her attempt at demagoguery might be taking it one step too far. She purses her lips. My stricken expression is enough to tell her that she's found her target.

I feel like I've had a lobotomy.

My brain has ceased to react.

"Why should I believe you?"

"Because you've known from the start that it was too good to be true. That's why you called Bertrand . . . I mean Monsieur Lacoste a few days ago. You wanted to believe it, but it defied all logic. I think you know it . . ."

I wait for my brain to kick back into action.

When I look up, the girl is gone; she's already at the edge of the square, heading slowly toward the *métro*.

It's dark now. The lights are still off in the apartment. The window in the sitting room is wide open and the dim glow of the streetlights is trickling in.

I'm alone in my chaotic apartment. Nicole is gone. I've beaten up my son-in-law. He and my daughter are waiting to get their money back. The Logistics trial will be underway in a few weeks.

Suddenly the intercom rings.

Lucie. She's downstairs.

She has called and called and now she's worried.

I stand up but I barely make it to the door. I collapse to my knees and start crying.

Lucie's voice is imploring.

"Open up, Papa."

She knows I'm there because of the open window. I can't even move now.

It's finished. Time to bow out.

Tears come and keep on coming. Crying like this is my first real respite for a long time. The only thing that's been absolutely true. Tears of disarray. I am devastated, inconsolable.

Lucie eventually leaves.

I have been crying, crying so much.

It must be very late. How long have I stayed here, slumped against the front door, sobbing? Until the tears run dry.

Finally, I summon the strength to get up, despite my exhaustion.

A few thoughts pick their way through my head.

I take a deep breath.

Anger overwhelms me.

I look up a telephone number and dial. I apologize for calling so late.

"Do you know where I can get myself a weapon? A real one . . ."

Kaminski leaves me hanging for a few seconds, unsure how to respond.

"In theory, yes. But . . . What exactly is it you need?"

"Anything . . . No! Not anything. A pistol. An automatic pistol. Can you? With real ammunition."

Kaminski concentrates for a second.

"When do you need it for?"

DURING

19

An hour before the start of the operation, Monsieur Lacoste came to me and said:

"Monsieur Fontana, there's been a slight change of plan. There will just be two candidates for the HR post, rather than four."

His tone suggested that this was a minor detail that had no bearing on proceedings; but the tense expression I'd noted a few minutes earlier when he received his second text message of the morning led me to believe otherwise. His client, Exxyal, had requested four candidates, and it was hard to imagine that reducing this by half would be without consequence. Monsieur Lacoste didn't give me any indication as to why these two candidates had pulled out at the last minute, and it wasn't my place to ask.

I kept quiet. Not my problem. My job exclusively involved organizing the technical aspects of the operation: finding the premises, sourcing personnel, and so forth.

The fact is, I've run a fair number of operations in my time—many of them a lot more complex than this—and if my experience has taught me one thing, it's that they are as vulnerable as living organisms. They're like a chain: all the links must hold. So when little hitches start stacking up in the minutes before liftoff, alarm bells ring. You always have to trust your intuition. Except by the time your intuition tells you something's wrong, it's usually too late.

From a distance, I saw Monsieur Lacoste deep in discussion with Monsieur Dorfmann, the CEO of Exxyal Europe. He had that air of detachment that people affect when they're delivering bad news as though it was of little importance. If Monsieur Dorfmann was annoyed by this, he didn't show it. Now there's a man who knows how to stay cool under pressure; there's a man I can respect.

A little after 9:00 a.m., someone called to say that two people had arrived, so I headed downstairs. The deserted main lobby made for a truly depressing sight, with twenty or so enormous armchairs and two lone people. They were sitting more than thirty feet apart and hadn't even dared to greet each other.

I immediately recognized Monsieur Delambre. As I approached him, I rolled back the tape in my head, pausing on a frame from a few days earlier. I had just come out of a meeting with Monsieur Lacoste. I was on the pavement, about to move out, when I sensed I was being watched. It's a very particular feeling, and years of hazardous exercises have taught me to pay great attention to it. It has saved my life on more than one occasion. So I stopped right where I was, took out a piece of chewing gum to buy myself some time, and while I was unwrapping it I mentally scoured the area to identify the enemy's position. As soon as my intuition turned to certainty, I looked up with a snap. On the corner of the building opposite, a man was watching me. He pretended to look at his watch, before—just by chance—his cell phone decided to ring. He took out the device and clamped it to his ear, turning around as though he were engrossed in the call. It was Monsieur Delambre. He must have been on a reconnaissance mission. But the person in front of me was unrecognizable from the man I'd seen on the pavement that day.

From the start, his anxiety struck me as disproportionate. A real bundle of nerves.

His face was haggard, almost deathly pale. He had clearly cut himself shaving as there was an unpleasant red scab on his right cheek. A nervous tic made his left eye twitch intermittently, and his palms were sweaty. Any one of these symptoms would have been enough to suggest that he was feeling extremely out of his depth in this situation, and that he had little chance of seeing it through to the end.

Picture it: two withdrawals in quick succession, Mademoiselle Zbikowski AWOL (Monsieur Lacoste was leaving her endless messages, and with greater and greater urgency), and one candidate on the brink of cardiac arrest . . . The whole adventure was threatening to be a lot more perilous than expected. But that was none of my business. The premises met the brief and were suitably equipped, the devices all worked, and my team had been well trained. I had done my part, and whatever the reasons for their monkeying around, they didn't concern me. All I cared about was receiving the balance of my fee.

Having said that, part of my brief did involve "consultancy" services, so I decided to cover my back: after shaking hands with Monsieur Delambre and Madame Rivet (sorry, *Mademoiselle* Rivet), I asked them if they'd be so kind as to wait a moment. I went over to the reception desk and put an internal call through to Monsieur Lacoste to explain the situation.

"Monsieur Delambre strikes me as being in very poor shape. I think he's a nonstarter."

Monsieur Lacoste didn't react right away. After the series of mishaps he had sustained since our arrival, this news seemed to knock him further. It even occurred to me that if Monsieur Lacoste himself were to show signs of weakness, then that would be game over; but he pulled himself together just in time.

"What do you mean, poor shape?"

"He strikes me as very nervous."

"Nervous? Of course he's nervous! Everyone's nervous! Me included—I'm nervous!"

In my head, I added the raw tension in Monsieur Lacoste's voice to the growing list of calamities blighting this affair. He quite literally wouldn't hear another word said about it. The wheels were in motion, and even though the operation was starting to resemble the mad runaway train from *La Bête humaine*, he could see no way of halting it without losing face in front of his client. He was making these problems out to be nothing but minor inconveniences. I've seen a lot of this since I started working with businesses. Like heavy machinery, these projects gather so much momentum (in terms of energy, capital, and time) that no one has the balls to stop them. You see it with advertising or marketing campaigns or big events. When their backs are against the wall, the people in charge always acknowledge in hindsight that the warning signs were there—they just chose not to acknowledge them. But they only admit this to themselves, never out loud.

"We'll manage just fine," Lacoste said to me with a reassuring tone. "And anyway, there's nothing to say that Delambre won't turn around and prove himself a much stronger candidate than we're giving him credit for."

Faced with such willful blindness, I decided to hold my tongue.

At the far end of the lobby, Monsieur Delambre's shrunken figure seemed apprehensive; a bomb ready to blow. Barring a technical screw-up (which would have brought my role into question), I didn't foresee any danger. This was just a little role-play exercise.

If I'm honest, it didn't bother me much to see the operation foundering. To begin with, at least, it even amused me. Understand that I've spent twenty years in various theaters of operation. I've risked my life as many as twenty times, and I've seen a lot of people die. So when a company shows up wanting to stage a virtual hostage taking . . . Fine, I'm sure they had their reasons (linked to their balance sheet, undoubtedly), but over the course of the planning, I noticed the schadenfreude they were taking from it. Monsieur Dorfmann and Monsieur Lacoste have mind-blowing levels of responsibility, but this hostage-taking escapade had gone further: it frightened them, and they relished the fear. The consequence of this was now plain to see.

Monsieur Lacoste joined us downstairs soon after. It was hard to tell whether his nervousness was merely caused by the situation or whether, like me, he had an inkling that the exercise was entering a tailspin. This is typical of successful people: they don't have a shred of self-doubt and consider themselves capable of overcoming any difficulty. They think they're untouchable.

Monsieur Delambre's whole demeanor jarred with that of the svelte, ethereally pretty Mademoiselle Rivet, in her figure-hugging gray-flecked suit. She knew what she was doing when she picked that outfit. Slumped in his sizeable lobby armchair, Monsieur Delambre suddenly appeared old and jaded. It seemed like an unfair contest. Not that it was a fashion competition . . . No, this was a test in which the participants would need to demonstrate considerable interpersonal skills and genuine proficiency, and on this front, Monsieur Lacoste was right: Monsieur Delambre still had every chance. In fact, now that there were two of them instead of four, on paper his chances had doubled.

The two candidates stood up in a single movement. Monsieur Lacoste made the introductions:

"Monsieur Delambre, Mademoiselle Rivet . . . and Monsieur David Fontana, who is our noble stage manager."

A warning light immediately started flashing in my head: there was something about the woman's collectedness and Monsieur Lacoste's insistence; a certain manner about them . . . I remember being convinced that these two were already—what's the word?— acquainted. And I couldn't help feeling sorry for Monsieur Delambre, because if I was right, he was in danger of being nothing more than a walk-on part.

I also noticed that Monsieur Delambre was carrying a briefcase, while Mademoiselle Rivet just had her handbag, which only served to further highlight their difference. It looked like he was on his way to work, while she was on her way home.

"It's just the two of us?" Monsieur Delambre asked.

The tone of his voice stopped Monsieur Lacoste in his tracks. It was low and shaky. The voice of a man under intense pressure.

"Yes," Monsieur Lacoste replied. "The others have withdrawn. Your chances are all the higher . . ."

The news didn't seem to please Monsieur Delambre in the slightest. He had a point: even if it did improve his chances, it still seemed . . . all this rigmarole and only two candidates? Monsieur Lacoste sensed his misgivings.

"Forgive me for speaking frankly," he added, "but the fundamentals of this operation have nothing to do with you!"

He glared at Monsieur Delambre, realizing the importance of wresting back control of the situation.

"Our client needs to select the most suitable candidate from five executives to carry out a vital restructuring process. This is the primary objective of the exercise. However, an HR assistant will be recruited simultaneously over the course of the assessment; after all, the main role of an HR executive is, of course, to evaluate personnel. We are simply killing two birds with one stone."

"Thank you, understood," Monsieur Delambre said.

It was difficult to tell whether his tone carried bitterness or a thinly veiled anger. Whatever the case, I felt it better to change the subject, so I showed the candidates to the elevator and took them upstairs.

We entered the meeting room at precisely 9:17 a.m. Yes, I'm certain of that. In my line of work, precision is paramount. Over the years, I've managed to internalize my timekeeping: at any hour of the day, I can tell you the exact time, correct to within a few minutes. But that morning I also had my eye on the clock. The meeting had been called for 10:00 a.m. and the Exxyal Europe execs were scheduled to arrive at least ten or fifteen minutes in advance: all the final arrangements needed to be made before then.

I introduced Monsieur Delambre and Mademoiselle Rivet to the team, starting with the two actors who would be playing the role of the clients. Malik was wearing a large, brightly colored djellaba and a violet keffiyeh with geometric patterns, while Monsieur Renard was wearing a traditional suit.

"At the start of the role play," I explained, "Malik and Monsieur Renard will play the clients that the Exxyal Europe execs are invited to meet. Malik will exit right away; Monsieur Renard will stay until the end."

Throughout this presentation, I paid particular attention to the candidates' reactions because, while Monsieur André Renard may not be an actor of any great renown, a few years ago he did appear in a fairly successful ad for a household product, and I was worried that the participants might recognize his face. But Monsieur Delambre and Mademoiselle Rivet's concentration was already fixed on the three members of the commando. It's important not to understate their impact, complete with their fatigues, balaclavas, and combat boots, and their three Uzi submachine guns lined up on the table alongside rows of ammunition. Even though everyone knew full well that this was a role play, the whole thing made for quite a spectacle, not least because (without wanting to brag) I had picked my teammates well. Kader, the commando chief, has a calm, determined face; and Yasmine is capable of looking terrifyingly stern. Both of them started their careers in the Moroccan police, and their records speak for themselves. As for Mourad, in spite of his shortcomings, I'd decided to keep him on because of his rugged features: with his full, unshaven cheeks, he has a brutal face that suits his role perfectly.

Everyone greeted each other with a simple nod of the head. The atmosphere was fairly tense. That's always the way in the minutes before the start of an operation—it can be misleading.

Next I showed them the three rooms: the meeting room where the role play would begin and where the group of hostages would be held; then the interrogation chamber where the executives would be called individually or in pairs, should Monsieur Delambre or Mademoiselle Rivet want to play them against one another. There was a laptop computer connected to the Exxyal Group system sitting open on a small table. Lastly, I took them to the observation room, from where the two candidates would administer the interrogations. One monitor would display images from the waiting room recorded on two different cameras; another showed images from the table in the interrogation chamber. The final room, from where Monsieur Dorfmann and Monsieur Lacoste would oversee the operation, was none of their concern.

Monsieur Lacoste left us at that point. We could see that he had some concerns. My guess is that he went to call Mademoiselle Zbikowski yet again, even if, given the time, we both knew she wouldn't be coming. I have no idea what happened between the two of them, but it wasn't hard to guess that his assistant had stood him up, leaving him to take care of things on his own.

Mademoiselle Rivet attempted a smile at Monsieur Delambre, probably as a way of easing the tension, but he seemed far too anxious to respond. They sat down next to each other and turned to the screens that were relaying live footage from the meeting room.

That was when Monsieur Dorfmann arrived. I had only met him once before, a few days earlier at our only rehearsal. He had been very gracious and very receptive to my suggestions; both of which were effective ways of emphasizing his authority. For a man of his age, he is remarkably flexible—it took him no time at all to learn how to collapse the right way.

We went into the rest area so that I could bring him up to speed. I reminded him of his instructions, but Monsieur Dorfmann was less accommodating than at the rehearsal. It irritated him hearing information for a second time, so I kept it short, and he promptly returned to the meeting room. Everyone was on edge.

As per the plan, Monsieur Renard was seated to his right. He seemed to be getting in the zone for his role as an important client, while Malik was sipping a very strong coffee on Monsieur Renard's other side.

And we began the wait.

20

The images relayed by the cameras were clear. I was happy with everything from a technical perspective.

Monsieur Lacoste was stationed just behind Monsieur Delambre and Mademoiselle Rivet with a pad of paper. I pulled up a chair and watched them. I was a bit nervous myself. Not because of what was at stake, no—there was nothing in it for me—but because I like a job well done. And because I was still owed a third of my fee, to be paid on completion of the operation. The mission was very well paid, I have to admit. The truth is that business role plays come with a serious price tag, but they're not all that interesting. They're there for the amusement of companies and managers. I like my missions a bit more real.

In any case, I always get nervous before the start of a mission, regardless of how major it is. But nothing compared to Monsieur Delambre. He was staring straight into the monitors, as though he were expecting them to reveal some hidden truth, and when he switched from one screen to the other, it wasn't just his eyes that moved, but his entire head, a bit like a chicken. Mademoiselle Rivet seemed more concerned with her neighbor than with the test itself. She was looking at him surreptitiously, the way you might eye a messy eater at the table next to you in a restaurant. Monsieur Delambre didn't even seem to notice her, and carried on with his mechanical actions. I found his behavior so worrying (it's normal to be nervous in this kind of situation, but *this* nervous?) that I touched him on the shoulder and asked him if everything was all right. I hadn't even finished my sentence when he leapt up as if I'd just electrocuted him.

"Huh? What?" he said, spinning around abruptly.

"Is everything all right, Monsieur Delambre?"

"Huh? Yes, fine . . . ," he replied, but he was somewhere else entirely.

That's what is so hard to take: right then, I had all the confirmation I needed that everything was about to go down the tubes. My concern had given way to certainty. Yet still I did nothing. Monsieur Delambre had a screw loose. We could easily have canceled the test for the HR candidates without interfering with the assessment of the execs. It was just that the two operations had always been linked in my mind, and so the idea never occurred to me. And from then on, everything went too fast.

As the start of the operation approached, Mademoiselle Rivet seemed less and less composed. In fact, she hadn't regained her color since seeing the members of the commando with their black shiny guns—little did she know that her tribulations were far from over. I stood up to show the two of them how to use the microphone to speak into the earpieces of the different members of the commando. Monsieur Delambre answered with a series of groans, but he had clearly understood the instructions because he operated the controls correctly when it was his turn for a trial run.

The Exxyal execs were beginning to trickle in: Monsieur Lussay first, followed by Mademoiselle Tràn.

Monsieur Maxime Lussay is a legal executive. Just as well, if you ask me, because he looks like a natural-born lawyer: immaculately turned out, every movement underpinned by a certain stiffness. His eyes seemed to twitch in staccato fashion, as if they had to revert to their original position before moving to the next spot. I had read their files closely: I remembered that Monsieur Lussay had a doctorate in law and had drawn up and overseen numerous Exxyal Group contracts.

As for Mademoiselle Tràn, you could tell right away that she worked in sales. A very dynamic woman—a little too dynamic, if you ask me, almost like she was on something. She walked with assurance, standing square in front of people. She gave off the impression that nothing could faze her, and that if you dithered at all, she would finish your sentences for you. With her physique and her six-figure salary, she must be highly attractive to men her age.

These young executives . . . you could tell how modern and confident they were just by the way they swaggered into the waiting room. Every shake of the hand screamed: "We are powerful, productive, happy people."

The Exxyal executives went up in turn to greet their boss, Monsieur Dorfmann, and he treated each of them with that sort of familiar attitude you see all too often in business. I find it so puzzling. From the top of the ladder to the bottom, everyone is friends with everyone, calling each other by first name even though traditionally it should be *Monsieur* this or *Madame* that. I think this confuses the picture. In that sort of environment, people end up mistaking their office for the local café. I spent part of my career in the army, and things there are a lot more clear cut. You know why you're there. Your colleagues are either superiors or subordinates, and when you meet someone, you know straight off whether he's one or the other: whether he's above you or below you. In business, it's all become blurred. You play squash with your boss, you go for a jog with your line manager . . . it's a mess, quite frankly. If people aren't careful, there won't be any leaders left; companies will be controlled by spreadsheets alone. Although sooner or later, there'll be a return to hierarchy—make no mistake. And quite right, too . . . when the spreadsheets show that your performance isn't up to scratch and the higher-ups demand answers, then you can't complain just because you've confused them with school friends for too long.

That's how I see it, at least.

Anyway, there was Monsieur Dorfmann holding court at the end of the table. One by one, his colleagues came in and, amid all the backslapping, advanced straight past "Go" and landed on the square marked "Power," shaking their CEO's hand before schmoozing with Monsieur Renard and Malik, who Monsieur Dorfmann took a moment to introduce. Then they took their seats.

Back where we were in the observation room, Monsieur Lacoste named each executive as he or she arrived, pointing out each one in turn to Mademoiselle Rivet and Monsieur Delambre against the list they had been given. For example, he'd say: "Maxime Lussay, PhD in law, thirty-five, legal department"; or "Virginie Tràn, thirty-five, graduate in business, sales executive."

Monsieur Delambre had clearly done his homework. He had sheets for each candidate and was taking lots of notes, on their behavior I suppose, but his hand was shaking so much I wondered if he'd manage to read them later on. Mademoiselle Rivet's approach was less intensive: she was working directly on the document she'd been sent, and was marking the names of the people with a cross as they entered. The overall impression was that she hadn't taken her preparation very seriously.

Monsieur Jean-Marc Guéneau and Monsieur Paul Cousin arrived within a few minutes of each other.

The former is an economist, and the first thing that struck you was how pleased he was with himself. He strutted around with an air of entitlement, puffing out his chest, reeking of self-confidence. His lazy eye was irritating—you couldn't tell which one was true.

His neighbor, Monsieur Paul Cousin, was the exact opposite. I remember noticing that Monsieur Cousin had a very large head, at the same time as being frighteningly thin. He had a fanatical look in his eyes, like an overzealous churchgoer. A raft of engineering degrees, a decent part of his career spent in the Persian Gulf, followed by a return to HQ four years ago with considerable levels of responsibility. This guy is Captain Technical, the Emperor of the Oil Well.

Madame Camberlin is around fifty, a senior project manager. She was sufficiently sure of herself not to mind arriving last.

Monsieur Dorfmann seemed eager to make a start, so he tapped his fingers on the table before turning to Monsieur Renard and Malik.

"All right, then. First of all, allow me to wish you a warm welcome on behalf of Exxyal Europe. The introductions were a little swift, so if I may . . ."

The atmosphere in the observation room had hardly been light in the first place, but at that point it became oppressive.

The voices we heard through the speakers seemed to come from a faraway and sinister world. I looked over at Monsieur Lacoste, who responded with a small nod of the head.

I left the room to join my team in the area next door. Out in the corridor, I could hear Monsieur Dorfmann's voice filtering through from the meeting room.

(. . . *with this highly promising synergy, which we are absolutely thrilled about . . .*)

All three of them were prepared. True professionals. All I had to do was adjust the angle of Yasmine's submachine gun, a reflex on my part. Then I held my arms out to the side.

The signal was clear: it is time.

Kader gave a nod.

They were on the move immediately. I watched them file down the corridor (. . . *and represents a major turning point in global strategy for stakeholders across our sector. This is why . . .*). I followed them before making a sharp turn and falling back in behind Monsieur Delambre and Mademoiselle Rivet.

In under seven seconds, the commandos reached the meeting room and burst through the door.

"Hands on the table!" Kader screamed, while Mourad headed to his right and stalked around the perimeter of the room.

Yasmine nimbly circled the table, banging her Uzi barrel loudly on the desk to make sure everyone obeyed the order.

They were all so shocked that no one moved a muscle. Not a sound was uttered as everyone held their breath. The Exxyal execs looked aghast at the submachine gun barrels a few inches from their faces. They were too hypnotized to register who was holding them.

In front of his screen, Monsieur Delambre tried to write something on his pad, but his hand was trembling too much. He glanced to his right, where Mademoiselle Rivet was trying to keep a certain distance. Everything happened so suddenly that her face had gone almost as white as her neighbor's.

Using the remote control, I activated the camera recording the scene and panned around the table: the five execs were wide eyed with terror, no one attempting even the smallest movement. They were petrified.

On our screens, we saw Kader approach Monsieur Dorfmann.

"Monsieur Dorfmann," he began, with his thick Arabic accent.

The Exxyal boss slowly looked up. He suddenly seemed smaller, older. His mouth hung open and his eyes looked as if they might burst out of their sockets.

"You're going to help me clarify the situation, if you don't mind," Kader continued.

Even if someone had been crazy enough to intervene, he wouldn't have had time to lift a finger. In less than two seconds, Kader took out his Sig Sauer pistol, extended his arm toward Monsieur Dorfmann, and fired.

The sound was deafening.

Monsieur Dorfmann's body was flung backward, his chair tipping back for a moment into thin air before snapping forward and throwing his upper body onto the table.

Then the action sped up. Malik stood, his huge djellaba billowing around him, and started yelling at the leader of the commandos in Arabic. There was an urgency to his words as he unleashed a stream of furious, panic-stricken insults, the sentences flooding from his mouth. The torrent dried up when Kader fired a bullet into his chest, striking him near his heart. Malik did a quarter turn that he didn't have time to complete as the second bullet hit him full in the stomach. He folded under the impact and collapsed to the ground with a thud.

Hostage behavior falls into three categories: physical resistance, verbal resistance, and nonresistance. As a matter of course, we favor nonresistance, since it helps the remainder of the operation run more smoothly. During the preparations, I had selected a hostage to "symbolize" a losing strategy (Malik had just achieved this task perfectly) in order to demonstrate that nonresistance represented the group's best chance of survival. Our client had asked us to test their employees' shock resistance, which requires—as Monsieur Lacoste had reminded me on several occasions—assessing their level of cooperation with the enemy on a scale that runs from total resistance on one end, to barefaced collaboration on the other. For this to happen, it was essential that they agreed to negotiate, and the best way to do this was effectively to show that it was the only option available to them.

But let me return to the action.

With the first bullet, everyone let out a muffled cry. Try to imagine . . . by that point the room was shuddering with the sound of the three explosions, which completely dominated the room, and two men were lying on the ground, each of them with a bloodstain spreading around their bodies.

Madame Camberlin clasped her hands to her ears, while Monsieur Lussay—eyes screwed shut, palms flat on the table, completely disoriented—thrashed his head from left to right as though he was trying to bounce his brain from one side of his skull to the other.

"I think the rules have been made clear. My name is Kader. But we have plenty of time to get to know one another."

His voice seemed muffled to them.

Kader looked down at Monsieur Guéneau and frowned with mild disdain.

There was a clear sound of dripping liquid; a large, dark puddle was forming beneath Monsieur Guéneau's chair.

Despite the fact that all people have distinct characters and temperaments, hostages always respond in more or less the same way.

The brain reacts to suddenness, terror, and threat in a fairly narrow way. It is common for hostages—as seemed to be the case with Monsieur Cousin, who was clasping his head and gazing directly ahead of him—to remain in a state of incredulity because of the suddenness of the attack, as though refusing to believe it, preferring to think they've fallen victim to some sick practical joke. But it doesn't take long for them to come around to a more rational state, especially when you kill one or two people in front of them. That was why I'd chosen to "take out" Monsieur Dorfmann immediately, since he represented a figure of authority in their eyes. This maneuver served to flip the pyramid on its head, and consequently the commando's message was clear: we're in charge. The fact that Monsieur Dorfmann had played his role to perfection, bursting the pouch of blood I had provided him with and falling just the way I had shown him, only added to the effect. I'd reassured him beforehand: at the end of the day, no one would notice if he didn't pull it off perfectly, since people's brains are so frazzled by the unexpected nature of the situation.

Monsieur Delambre and Mademoiselle Rivet froze. A hostage taking on television and a hostage taking in real life are not at all the same thing. I know, I know, this wasn't exactly "real life" but, without wanting to blow my own trumpet, it was quite realistic. The two candidates experienced the action as though they were in the meeting room themselves. The reason I say that? Their reactions. Going back to what I was saying about the different behaviors exhibited by victims in this sort of situation, they encompass nine key emotions: shock, astonishment, anxiety, terror, frustration, vulnerability, powerlessness, humiliation, and isolation. Monsieur Delambre's reaction corresponded with anxiety and isolation, while Mademoiselle Rivet was displaying shock and terror.

In the event that the murder of the Arab client didn't have the desired deterrent effect, my plan was to cut short any attempt at physical resistance by the hostages.

"Everyone over here!" Mourad shouted, gesturing toward the wall opposite the windows.

Struck dumb with fear, they all stood up and started shuffling around uncertainly, as though they were afraid they might knock over a valuable object, keeping their heads down to avoid any missile that might come their way.

"Hands against the wall, legs apart!" Mourad shouted.

Monsieur Lussay, who had no doubt seen this done before on television, spread his arms and legs wide, his buttocks tensed as he waited to be frisked. Next to him, Mademoiselle Tràn's tight skirt was inhibiting her legs. Yasmine approached her from behind and yanked up the material with the tip of her gun, before kicking her feet apart harshly. Mademoiselle Tràn placed her hands against the wall, too, fingers splayed. Having her skirt hitched up like that was degrading, especially with men around: another effective technique to emphasize a hostage's vulnerability. As for Monsieur Guéneau, his trousers were sodden down to his knees and his whole body was shaking, while Monsieur Cousin's eyes were screwed shut as though he were expecting a bullet to shatter his skull at any second. Wedged between the Exxyal execs, Monsieur Renard, our actor, was mur-muring away softly and incomprehensibly. Madame Camberlin, at the end of the line, seemed all the more unnerved when she realized he was reciting a prayer (just as I'd instructed him). The sound of someone praying for their life is another good way of guaranteeing cooperation in hostage situations.

A few seconds later, their backs still turned, everyone heard foot-steps, then a door opening and closing again. Each of them must have sensed a figure moving back and forth behind them. They could make out the sound of tables being dragged, and then some panting. The commandos were busy removing the two bodies.

After two or three minutes, Kader ordered them to turn around. The tables had been lined up along the partition wall, and the blood-stains on the carpet were glistening black. The center of the room was entirely empty; in situations like this, nothing is more unsettling than emptiness.

When Mourad came back into the room, his submachine gun hanging limply in his hands, it was clear he had wiped his bloodied chest with the back of his sleeve. Like a carefully choreographed routine, each member of the commandos assumed a position in front of the line of hostages: Kader in the middle, Yasmine to the right, Mourad to the left.

A few seconds went by, during which the only sound was Monsieur Guéneau's sobbing as he stared at the floor.

"Okay," Kader said. "Everyone empty their pockets!"

Wallets, bunches of keys, music players, and cell phones were collected into the two women's handbags on the big conference table.

Yasmine walked down the ranks and began searching them with her expert hands. She left nothing to chance: pockets, belts . . . everything. Mademoiselle Tràn felt the young woman's hands skim dexterously over her breasts and between her thighs. Madame Camberlin wasn't paying attention to anything; she was simply trying to keep herself upright, even though it was obvious that all she wanted was to collapse in a heap. Yasmine then frisked the men, running her skillful hands over their buttocks and the inside of their legs. Even Monsieur Guéneau's drenched trouser legs were patted down without any compromise before she took a few steps back and signaled to the leader that all was in order.

The hostages were lined up again, still on their feet, with the commandos fanned out in front of them.

"We are here for a sacred cause," Kader said calmly, "a cause worthy of every sacrifice. We require your cooperation, and we are prepared to lay down our lives to get it. Yours, too, should that be necessary. We will leave you to reflect on this for a moment. *Allahu akbar!*"

The other two commandos repeated "*Allahu akbar*" after him in unison. Then the leader walked out, followed by Yasmine, leaving big Mourad to guard them on his own.

No one knew what to do.

No one moved.

Monsieur Guéneau fell to his knees and huddled on the floor, sobbing.

21

Malik had changed out of his costume into jeans and a pullover, and his sports bag was sitting next to him on the floor. I gave him his envelope, we shook hands, and he disappeared off to the elevator while I went back to Monsieur Delambre and Mademoiselle Rivet.

After putting on a fresh shirt and suit in the rest area, Monsieur Dorfmann poked his head in. I gave him a thumbs-up to confirm that he had played his part wonderfully. He smiled at me, and I realized at that moment that I'd never seen him smile before.

He slipped away and, along with Monsieur Lacoste, went back to the rest area, where the monitors were showing footage from both the meeting room where the hostages were being held and the interrogation chamber where his executives would soon be taking it in turns to sit down across the table from Kader.

From then on, Monsieur Dorfmann and Monsieur Lacoste worked away in their room. They were the sleeping partners: it was their job to discuss the test and comment on the executives' performance. I was alone with the other two candidates to oversee the technical developments of the hostage taking. It's funny, but despite the extensive (and, as it would emerge, memorable) operation I'd put together for Monsieur Dorfmann, I don't think I'd exchanged more than twenty sentences with him. I had no idea what state of mind the man was in. He must have been certain that it was necessary and in the best interests of his company. He was the god of his world. But who was *his* god? What did he worship? His board of directors? His shareholders? Money? I was still pondering this when Monsieur Delambre started fidgeting in his chair. I assumed he needed to use the bathroom. Mademoiselle Rivet was deathly pale, jotting down the odd word on her pad, clicking her ballpoint pen, and pulling her suit jacket around her as though she were suddenly cold.

"We'll get them into position. Then it's up to you how you play it," I said. My voice made them jump. They both turned toward me, which meant I could see them face-on. They were no longer the same. I've seen it so many times: strong emotions contort people's appearances, as though their true faces, their true selves, come to the surface in extreme circumstances. Monsieur Delambre was the worst—his grimace looked like a death mask.

"Mourad, arrange them in a circle as planned, please," I said into the microphone.

As I was speaking to him, Mourad cupped his hand around his ear like a singer. He nodded, standing in the middle of the room, but as he moved away the earpiece fell out.

"Alright," he said.

Six pairs of frantic eyes turned on him, then on the earpiece dangling comically on the end of its wire.

"We're going to, uh . . ." Mourad said. "We're going to change. Position. We're going to change it."

The message didn't register. Right from the start, I'd never been a hundred percent sure about him: even in the practice runs, he hadn't covered himself in glory. I'd brought him on board because of his physical presence, but frankly the guy's as thick as a board, which ensured I kept his involvement to a minimum. He's Kader's cousin, and I agreed to have him on the basis that this was a role play—I wouldn't have given his CV more than three seconds if this had been a real operation. In fact, if you want the truth, he kind of cracked me up. But I have to admit he'd surpassed himself with the earpiece gaffe. If the situation hadn't been so fraught, I would have burst out laughing, but in the circumstances, all I could do was join the others in watching the scene anxiously.

The hostages were aware that they had to act, but the "position" instruction had baffled everyone. Madame Camberlin looked at Mademoiselle Tràn, who was examining Monsieur Cousin. Monsieur Renard had stopped praying, while the sniveling Monsieur Lussay stared at Monsieur Guéneau. Nobody knew what was going on.

"Okay, you," Mourad said.

He pointed at Monsieur Cousin, who straightened up immediately. In the face of adversity, that's what he does: he straightens. I made a mental note that he'd be a tough one to crack.

"You come here," Mourad said (he motioned to where Madame Camberlin was standing) "... you, there ..." (gesticulating to Monsieur Renard) "... and you, around here ..." (somewhere between Madame Camberlin and Mademoiselle Tràn) "... next to you ..." (pointing at Monsieur Guéneau) "... and you ..." (Mademoiselle Tràn) "... you come and stand here ..." (this time the intended destination was very unclear, a spot somewhere near Madame Camberlin, but it was hard to tell) "... and you, uh ..." (Monsieur Lussay was on tenterhooks) "... okay, you, here ..." (he was pointing at his feet) "... but in a circle!" Mourad blurted out for good measure.

The hostages didn't feel remotely threatened. Mourad's orders lacked any edge—he came across as finicky, almost relishing the moment, like a greedy teenager picking out his favorite treats at the *patisserie* counter. And to top it off, he now stood there looking pleased to bits with his job. Except no one had moved. In the hostages' defense, even I—the person responsible for designing the desired configuration—had no idea what he was trying to get them to do.

"Come on, move!" Mourad said, in the most convincing voice he could manage.

Understand that when a character like Mourad tries to act all
assertive with a submachine gun slung over his shoulder and the
barrel swinging around in front of him, it makes the weapon considerably less maneuverable. So despite his attempt at vigor, the order
fell flat—everyone hesitated yet again.

That was Monsieur Cousin's cue. As I've said, it's in situations like
this that a person's true character comes through. No one knew what
to do, but Monsieur Cousin kicked into action. In retrospect . . . no,
let's not get ahead of ourselves.

Monsieur Cousin stepped forward and stood in his assigned
space, as did Mademoiselle Tràn, followed by Monsieur Guéneau.
Then Madame Camberlin moved to her right and Monsieur Renard
headed left before everyone stopped, uncertain. Monsieur Lussay
bumped into Monsieur Cousin, who sent him back toward Madame
Camberlin.

Mourad was disappointed: he thought his orders had been nice
and clear. But what he did next was inexplicable. I'm telling you,
this guy was full of surprises . . . He put down his Uzi and walked up
to the hostages. He grabbed Madame Camberlin by the shoulders
and peered at the floor as if he were looking for specific markers on
the carpet. It was as if he'd invited Madame Camberlin to partner
him in a tango lesson and was desperately trying to remember his
steps. He shoved her three feet along and said: "There." He was so
absorbed in his task that it didn't even occur to him that the hostages might take the opportunity to seize the submachine gun and
attack him. Mademoiselle Tràn, her body extremely tense, took a
step toward the weapon . . . I felt an icy chill run down my spine. But
Mourad turned around just in time, busily taking Monsieur Renard
by the shoulders and positioning him a little farther away. Then it
was Mademoiselle Tràn's turn, followed by Monsieur Lussay, Monsieur Guéneau, and Monsieur Cousin. The hostages were arranged
back-to-back in a broad semicircle, each one about three feet apart.
No one was facing the door.

"Sit down."

Mourad had picked up his weapon again.

"That's good like that," he announced with a satisfied tone, before turning to the camera, as though hoping the lens might congratulate him on his outstanding performance.

Then the hostages heard the door open and close again.

Silence fell. Two or three minutes passed by.

Mademoiselle Tràn risked a sideways glance.

"He's gone," she said, blankly.

22

"I . . . I have a telephone . . . ," Monsieur Renard said, turning to the others. His face was very white, and he had to swallow back his saliva a number of times. "It's my wife's, I'd forgotten about it . . . ," he went on, speaking in a bewildered tone.

He sank his hand into his inside pocket and pulled out the tiny cell phone.

"I've . . . They didn't find it . . ."

He examined the phone lying flat on his palm.

The revelation fell like a bombshell.

"You'll get us killed, you bastard!" Monsieur Guéneau cried, beside himself.

"Calm down," Madame Camberlin said.

Monsieur Renard looked thunderstruck, his eyes flicking between the phone and the faces of the execs.

"They're watching us," Monsieur Lussay added through pursed lips, his voice hushed.

With a discreet movement of his chin, he indicated the top corner of the room, where a small black camera had been installed. Everyone turned either left or right to look at the ceiling.

"When the red light's blinking, it means it's not working," Mademoiselle Tràn said.

"You can't be sure of that," Monsieur Lussay replied.

"It's true! When it's on, there's a green light, if it's red it's off," Mademoiselle Tràn said with a tone of pure disgust, even hatred.

"These cameras . . . ," Madame Camberlin cut in, "they don't have sound. They can't hear us."

Only Monsieur Cousin remained silent. He was still ramrod straight, inflexible, as stiff as a corpse.

"So what do I do?" Monsieur Renard asked.

He made his voice quiver to perfection. It was a remarkable performance, which I found reassuring after Mourad's woeful display.

"We've got to call the police," Madame Camberlin said, who was trying to sound calm.

"We have to give them the phone!" Monsieur Guéneau shouted.

"Shut your face for a second!"

All eyes turned to Mademoiselle Tràn, who was glaring at Monsieur Guéneau.

"Try thinking for a second, you idiot," she snapped, turning to Monsieur Renard and holding out her hand. "Give it to me."

It was my turn to intervene.

"Mourad! Quick, get back to the hostage room!" I hissed into the microphone, and a second later I heard him crashing down the corridor.

Monsieur Renard had put the handset on the floor and was about to slide it over to her like a puck across an ice rink. He drew it back and forth on the ground, summoning all his concentration, before releasing it with a flourish. The telephone careened across the carpet toward Mademoiselle Tràn, whirling around like a spinning top, but his aim wasn't good.

On the screens, we saw Mourad open the door right at the moment the phone came to rest at Monsieur Guéneau's feet.

Caught by surprise, he slipped it up his right sleeve and tried to look calm, as if he hadn't moved a muscle since his captor had left.

In front of me, Monsieur Delambre was furiously taking notes, which at the time I found encouraging, I suppose. Perhaps at the start he was only suffering from pre-match nerves. Now he was in the zone, fully focused. Mademoiselle Rivet was scribbling away, too.

A long silence ensued. Mourad was fiddling with his earpiece, struggling to keep it in place. In fact he was so consumed with his earpiece-insertion maneuver that he seemed to have forgotten about the hostages. All eyes (with the exception of Mourad's) were bearing down on Monsieur Guéneau, who looked as if he might expire at any moment. I zoomed in on his arm momentarily: he was clearly holding the little cell phone in his sleeve and trying to cup it there, before clearing his throat.

"Excuse me . . . ," he said.

As Mourad turned toward him, the earpiece fell out.

"The bathroom . . . ," Monsieur Guéneau said, his voice barely audible. "I need the bathroom."

Not only was he failing to demonstrate any sangfroid, he wasn't being very creative either. His trousers were as wet as a mop, and there he was asking for the bathroom . . . But Mourad is not the sort of person who thinks like this. In fact, he seemed delighted at the opportunity that had presented itself.

"We've got a plan for this," he said. "You need to be accompanied," he added, reeling off the lines he had learned by heart.

Monsieur Guéneau immediately realized that he'd made a strategic error, and so he made eye contact with Madame Camberlin, who cottoned on right away:

"Me, too! I need the bathroom, too."

Mourad closed his eyes then opened them again.

"Okay, there's a plan for that, too," he said triumphantly. "You have to go one at a time. You asked first, so you get to go first," he said to Monsieur Guéneau.

I breathed a "very good" into Mourad's earpiece and he smiled like a giant baby. Monsieur Guéneau hesitated, unsure what to make of this sudden show of happiness.

"On you go," Mourad said, holding out his hand as reassuringly as possible, before opening the door. Standing there was Yasmine, stony faced, her legs set, as though they were planted in the ground. She looked Monsieur Guéneau in the eyes without blinking.

"Go!" Mourad repeated.

So Monsieur Guéneau stood up, both fists clenched at the end of his straightened arms, the only way he could prevent the phone from slipping out of his sleeve.

Monsieur Delambre looked up. He seemed to be mulling over an intriguing idea, made a few notes on his pad, then laid down his pen.

And we waited. A few minutes passed. Provided my instructions were being carried out to the letter, I knew that Monsieur Guéneau had made it down the corridor, all the while under close guard. He'd entered a cubicle, turned, and tried to shut the door, but the barrel of Yasmine's Uzi had blocked him.

"Do you mind . . . ," Monsieur Guéneau said, scandalized that she was standing there facing him.

"Up to you. I could always take you back?" Yasmine said coldly.

Monsieur Guéneau turned and lifted the toilet seat with a frustrated motion before opening his fly, rummaging around a little, and then urinating noisily. He kept his eyes down as he slid the telephone along his wrist. On his own cell phone, he could have written a text with his eyes closed. They're all the same, he told himself: same functions, same keys. Head still lowered, he clutched his tummy to gain a few more precious seconds, then ran his index finger down the keypad to find the button at the bottom, and started typing discreetly.

That was when the phone started ringing. The volume was so loud we could hear it all the way down the corridor.

On hearing the blaring ringtone echo around the toilet cubicle, the blood drained from Monsieur Guéneau. He fumbled for the phone as it vibrated in his sleeve and only just managed to catch it in his fingertips. Then he froze for a second, his eyes closed, probably waiting for his captor to unleash a burst of gunfire into his kidneys. But nothing happened. He blinked and turned toward Yasmine. What was he expecting? A blow to the face? A bullet in the head? A kick in the balls? He had no idea, but his whole body trembled. Yasmine didn't move, even when the phone rang a second time. She pointed to it with her submachine gun as it continued to vibrate in his hand. He shivered from head to toe as though he was being electrocuted.

Yasmine jerked her weapon toward his waist.

Monsieur Guéneau looked down and closed his fly, blushing, then held out the device to Yasmine, who simply repeated the same, categorical gesture.

He looked at the flashing screen—unknown number—pressed the green button, and heard a man's voice. Kader's voice.

"Do you think this is acceptable behavior, Monsieur Guéneau?"

23

The first thing Monsieur Guéneau saw as he entered the room was the Uzi on the table by Kader. Submachine guns always make so much more of an impression than a simple pistol. And should a hostage try his luck and grab it, they're just that little bit harder to maneuver, allowing the captor plenty of time to intervene. Kader is very experienced: these amateurs didn't pose any threat, not least because the weapons were loaded with blanks. Plus, I had the utmost confidence in Kader and Yasmine, having enlisted their services for several challenging operations. I was aware of their quality. Kader just sat there holding the Sig Sauer he had used to "kill" two men a few minutes earlier. Monsieur Guéneau turned in a panic, only to meet the steely expression of Yasmine, who shoved him in the back with her Uzi toward an empty chair.

This was the moment of truth.

The first interrogation would set the tone for the remainder of the role play. If it went well, it would mean that the strategy was right for the task. Up to that point, my scenario had proved effective, and everything had gone according to plan. That's experience for you.

But now we were entering the "active" phase, in which Monsieur Delambre and Mademoiselle Rivet had to interrogate the executives to assess their behavior, and which would involve a certain amount of improvisation. I therefore remained attentive to every little detail.

Mademoiselle Rivet approached the microphone between herself and Monsieur Delambre and let out a faint, dry cough.

Monsieur Guéneau sat down. He was shaking violently—his sodden trousers must have made him cold. On the screen, we could see him mouthing words, but we couldn't hear anything through the speakers.

Without waiting for any instructions, Kader leaned toward him and asked:

"Excuse me?"

"Are you going to kill me?" Monsieur Guéneau mumbled.

His voice was barely audible, which made his fear seem even more pathetic. Mademoiselle Rivet must have picked up on this, because she kicked into action:

"That is not our primary intention, Monsieur Guéneau. Unless, of course, you leave us with no other option."

Kader interpreted the words very well and relayed them carefully. Coming from his mouth, the word "intention" sounded like a threat—maybe because of his accent, or maybe because of his controlled, convincing tone. Mademoiselle Rivet could hear her own words being echoed. It gave all three of us the peculiar impression of being in both places at once.

Monsieur Guéneau shook his head, eyes closed.

"Please . . . ," he murmured through his tears.

He thrust his hand into his pocket and slowly withdrew the phone, placing it on the table as though it were a stick of dynamite.

"I'm begging you . . ."

Mademoiselle Rivet turned to Monsieur Delambre and indicated the microphone so that he could have his turn to intervene, but he didn't move and carried on staring at the screen. I realized that he was sweating, which was surprising bearing in mind how cool the air-conditioning was. Mademoiselle Rivet ignored him and continued:

"Were you going to call the police?" she said into the microphone for Kader to repeat. "You're seeking to undermine our cause, is that it, Monsieur Guéneau?"

Monsieur Guéneau looked up at Kader, ready to swear by Almighty God, but he thought better of it.

"What . . . what do you want?" he said.

"No, Monsieur Guéneau, that's not how this is going to work. You're a member of the finance department at Exxyal Group. As such, a lot of confidential information passes through your hands: contracts, agreements, transactions . . . So, my question to you is this: what are you willing to do for our cause in exchange for your life?"

Monsieur Guéneau was stunned.

"I don't understand . . . I don't know anything . . . I don't have anything . . ."

"Come on, Monsieur Guéneau, we both know perfectly well that in the oil and gas industry, a contract is like an iceberg: most of it is under the surface. You've negotiated several contracts yourself, if I'm not mistaken?"

"What contracts?"

Monsieur Guéneau thrashed his head from side to side, as if he were pleading for help from some invisible bystander.

Wrong move. From the start of the interrogation, there was a feeling that Mademoiselle Rivet hadn't taken into account Monsieur Guéneau's current circumstances; that she didn't have the measure of the situation. She'd gone fishing for information, but Monsieur Guéneau hadn't bitten, and now he seemed to have guessed her strategy, even if he was yet to pin it down completely. A few uneasy seconds passed.

"What exactly do you . . . want from me?"

"You tell me," Mademoiselle Rivet said.

The interview was foundering.

"But you do—you do want something from me, don't you?" Monsieur Guéneau asked.

He was extremely distressed. The questions he was being asked seemed at odds with the brutality of the situation. It was as if the commandos didn't know what they wanted.

I never like it when things start drifting. I swallowed hard.

That was when Monsieur Delambre snapped out of his lethargic state, stretching out a hand and taking the mike for himself:

"You're married, are you not, Monsieur Guéneau?" he said.

Kader was taken aback, not only by the change of voice in his earpiece, but no doubt by Monsieur Delambre's deathly tone.

"Uh, yes . . . ," he replied to Kader's forceful question.

"And that's going well?"

"Pardon?"

"I'm asking you whether everything's going well with your wife."

"I don't understand . . ."

"Sexually . . . with your wife?" Monsieur Delambre persisted.

"Listen . . ."

"Answer me."

"I don't see . . ."

"Answer me!"

"Yes, uh . . . everything's fine."

"You're not . . . hiding anything from her?"

"Pardon?"

"You heard me."

"Well, uh . . . I don't see . . . no . . ."

"And your employer, too—you're not hiding anything from him?"

"What . . . that's not the same . . ."

"It often amounts to the same thing."

"I don't understand . . ."

"Take off your clothes."

"What?"

"I said take off your clothes! Now! Hurry up!"

Kader realized the objective and put down the Sig Sauer and picked up the Uzi instead. Monsieur Guéneau looked on in horror, babbling incoherently.

"Please, no," he implored.

"You have ten seconds," Kader added, standing up.

"No, I beg you . . ."

Two or three long seconds passed.

Monsieur Guéneau wept, looking in turn at Kader's face and the submachine gun. At a guess, he was trying the utter the words, "Please, please, I'm begging you . . ." But at the same time, he was taking off his jacket, which fell to the floor behind him as he started to unbutton his shirt.

"Trousers first," Monsieur Delambre barked. "And take a step back . . ."

Monsieur Guéneau stopped and did as he was told.

"Farther back!"

He was in the middle of the room, in full view. He set to work on his belt, letting out a groan as he went. He wiped his eyes clumsily.

"Faster . . . ," Kader urged him, under Monsieur Delambre's instructions.

Monsieur Guéneau had taken off his trousers and was hanging his head. He was wearing a pair of women's panties. Bright red ones. With cream lace. The kind you might see in the window of a sex shop.

If you want the absolute truth, I was disgusted by him. I'm no fan of homos at the best of times, but there's something about deviant homos that I find even harder to stomach.

"The shirt," Monsieur Delambre said.

When Monsieur Guéneau had taken everything off, we could see that he'd been wearing the full outfit beneath his suit: matching bra and panties. He made for a truly pathetic sight. His arms dangled at his side, his head bowed, sobbing more violently than ever. He was fuller in the chest than his bra size could cope with, and the bright-red material was slicing into his tubby, hairy body. His stomach was white and saggy, and the piss-soaked panties were wedged right up his fat buttocks.

It was impossible to say where Monsieur Delambre's intuition had come from, but it had come from somewhere. How had he suspected Monsieur Guéneau of his dirty secret? Mademoiselle Rivet did not know what had hit her: this first interrogation had gone way beyond anything she could have imagined.

Monsieur Delambre took to the floor again:

"Monsieur Guéneau!"

The man looked at Kader in a state of bewilderment.

"Do you think anyone can trust a man like you, Monsieur Guéneau?"

He was doubled up with the humiliation, his shoulders drooping forward and downward, his chest heaving and his knees almost knocking against each other. Monsieur Delambre took his time before moving in for the kill.

"For political reasons that we don't have time to go into, we would like Exxyal Group to hit the headlines. Our cause requires us to damage the reputation of various large European corporations. Exxyal Group must be made to look its absolute worst, if you follow me. To achieve this, we need to provide the press with tangible proof. We know that you have access to information that can aid us in our cause: confidential clauses, bribes, kickbacks, secret deals, undisclosed backing, aid, sweeteners . . . You know what I'm talking about. So you have a choice. I can either kill you now. Or if you'd rather take some time to think through my proposal, I can send you back to your colleagues for a couple of hours. No doubt they'll be amused to see you in this—what's the word?—*decadent* outfit."

"No . . ." Monsieur Guéneau murmured, whimpering now.

He was in an awful way—totally and utterly humiliated.

He must have been aware of Yasmine looking at him from behind. Even though she was in uniform, she was still a young woman. He clawed at his sides as though he were trying to rip his skin off.

"Unless, of course, you are prepared to support us in our cause?"

It all happened very quickly.

Monsieur Guéneau fell on the pistol, and before Kader could move a muscle, he'd grabbed it and jammed the barrel into his mouth. Yasmine's reflexes were excellent. She caught his arm and jerked it toward her. The pistol bounced onto the floor.

Everyone froze.

Monsieur Guéneau, in his red lingerie, was lying spread-eagled on his back across the table, one arm flung over his chest, the other hanging in midair. He had the air of a wretched victim on a sacrificial altar, like something out of a Fellini film. You couldn't help thinking that the man had just lost a part of his self-esteem that he would never recover. He wasn't moving and was struggling to breathe. Eventually, he rolled onto his side, huddled into the fetal position, and started crying again, silently this time.

It was clear that Monsieur Guéneau wanted to die.

Monsieur Delambre leaned into the microphone again.

"Time to do it," he whispered to Kader. "Get his Blackberry."

Kader said something in Arabic to Yasmine, who went to fetch the little box where the hostages' telephones, watches, and other personal effects had been put, then laid it by Monsieur Guéneau's face.

"Over to you, Monsieur Guéneau," Kader said. "What do you choose?"

The wait was interminable. Monsieur Guéneau was numb, his actions very slow. He seemed dazed, but managed to roll over, prop himself up, and, with great difficulty, stay upright. He tried to unhook his bra, but Monsieur Delambre rushed to the microphone:

"No!"

Not a chance.

Monsieur Guéneau shot a look of pure hatred at Kader. But once again, it was futile: he was dressed in women's underwear, soaked to the bone, terrified of losing a life he no longer had. He was crushed. He rummaged through the box and picked out his Blackberry, which he switched on with a familiar hand. The scene was all the more pitiful because it was so drawn out. Monsieur Guéneau connected his device to the laptop computer linked to the Exxyal Europe system. Kader was behind him to keep a close eye on things. Monsieur

Guéneau punched in his code and started digging around the files of various contracts, I suppose—on our screens we couldn't see what was happening in any detail.

After that, I believe opinions differ.

As far I'm concerned, I heard Monsieur Delambre say: "Bastard." Whether it was one "bastard" or several "bastards," I'm not a hundred percent sure. He didn't say it loudly—it was more like he was saying it to himself. Mademoiselle Rivet said she didn't hear anything herself. But I'm certain that's what he said. The interrogation was over, Monsieur Guéneau was finished—how it had come to this, we weren't even sure ourselves—and Monsieur Delambre turned his head and said "Bastard" (I'm sure of it). The operation he was conducting was far from complete, but the impression we got was that he'd lost all interest in it. Kader turned toward the camera, waiting for his instructions. Monsieur Guéneau, slumped over the laptop keyboard, continued to sob like a baby in his skimpy red lingerie. After a bit, Yasmine looked up at the camera, too.

It was amid this general confusion that Monsieur Delambre decided to stand up. I was looking at him from behind, so I couldn't tell you what his expression was like. My guess is that there was an element of—what do I mean?—*relief* about it . . . Like a calmness. Of course, it's always easy to say that in retrospect, but you can check, I said this in my first statement.

Anyway, Monsieur Delambre was on his feet throughout this weird silence, during which Mademoiselle Rivet's disquiet was plain to see. Then he picked up his briefcase, turned, and left the room.

The effect was odd. You'd have sworn he was heading home at the end of a day's work.

As soon as he left, I knew I had to act. In the interrogation chamber, Kader was still wondering what to do as the wretched Monsieur Guéneau sobbed over his keyboard. I grabbed the microphone and said hastily: "Stop that and get dressed!" before switching the mike to Mourad's earpiece, causing him to crane his neck with great concentration. "Keep an eye on them," I said. I turned to run after Monsieur Delambre before he did anything stupid, but I'd barely taken a step before Monsieur Dorfmann and Monsieur Lacoste came into the room.

They were standing stiffly upright and staring straight ahead. Next to them, Monsieur Delambre was clutching his briefcase in his left hand. In his right hand, he was holding a pistol, a Beretta Cougar, which was pressed against Monsieur Dorfmann's temple. I could tell at once that he wasn't playing around—there was a wild look in his eye and he was determined. And when you see one man holding a gun to another man's head, it's always best to assume he's prepared to pull the trigger.

"Everyone into the meeting room!" Monsieur Delambre yelled.

He yelled because he was afraid, and his eyes were wide open, which made him look as if he were hallucinating.

Mademoiselle Rivet let out a cry.

"What's going on?" I started saying, but Monsieur Delambre cut me off. He swung the gun over to Monsieur Lacoste's head, aimed just in front of him, closed his eyes, and fired. Not a moment's hesitation. The bang was horrific: two screens exploded (Monsieur Delambre had fired at random), glass was everywhere, smoke, a stench of burning plastic. Mademoiselle Rivet fell to her knees screaming; the two men he was holding at gunpoint buckled under the blast, hands to their ears.

I held up my hands as high as I could to show that I wasn't going to put up any resistance, because with the exploding screen and the foul smell of cordite, there was no doubt he could have killed any one of us, all of us.

Monsieur Delambre was using live ammunition.

24

"Hands up! Move! Step on it!"

Monsieur Delambre was shouting constantly, filling the space with sound to prevent us from thinking, and making the most of the element of surprise.

In a few seconds, he made us cross the corridor, picking up Kader, Monsieur Guéneau, and Yasmine on the way, and—still screaming—shoved us violently in the back as far as the meeting room, where the fake hostages had just become real ones.

For good measure, he then turned to the right-hand camera, took aim, and fired. The device disintegrated in a cloud of smoke. Next he swung to the other side and let off another bullet, but he had less luck: it struck well wide of the camera, making a hole the size of a football in the partition wall. But Monsieur Delambre was not about to lose face. "Fucking hell!" he yelled, before firing at the camera again, this time striking his target.

It's impossible for you to imagine the effect of three gunshots from a 9mm Beretta pistol in a 500-square-foot room. Everyone felt as though their head had just exploded like the cameras themselves.

This Beretta had a thirteen-round clip. That meant he still had nine left to shoot, and whether or not he had a backup magazine, this was no time for fooling around.

What struck me most was Monsieur Delambre's *professionalism*. Sure, he was screaming like a man possessed and had lost all his composure (you could tell from his nervous, jerky motions—precisely what made him so dangerous). But he was continuously scanning around him, and each gesture was measured and deliberate. Kader shot me a glance to see if I was on the same page as him: there was method to Monsieur Delambre's madness. It suggested some sort of coherent security protocol, and it was a sign that he'd received some training from a professional. For starters, he was holding his weapon with two hands. Amateurs often keep their arms locked, like they've seen on television, instead of simply tensing them (and more often than not, they place their weaker hand farther back on the weapon). Monsieur Delambre, however, was holding his weapon perfectly: poised and ready for the recoil should he need to shoot. It was surprising, but at the end of the day, I was there as Monsieur Lacoste and Monsieur Dorfmann's adviser—why shouldn't Monsieur Delambre have his advisers, too? And if he had sought guidance, then it was a necessary precaution, because there was nothing simple about what Monsieur Delambre was preparing to do.

You see, waving a Beretta around in front of a couple of people is one thing, but taking twelve or so people hostage is another matter. And I must confess, Monsieur Delambre had made a pretty decent start, and our response needed to take this into account. I don't mean to brag, but if he hadn't shown such discipline or method, if he hadn't made some of the right moves, Kader or I would have eaten him for breakfast.

Deep down, I have to admit, I knew the tables had turned.

It was as though the man on stage was entirely different from the one who'd been waiting in the wings. I had the unpleasant feeling that I'd been outplayed by a fellow professional, and, for a man of my experience, that was extremely hard to take. For the purposes of the operation, and as per our orders, until now we'd been "play-ing" at hostage taking, and just like that, someone had changed the rules of the game. I didn't take it well. I don't like being challenged, over and above the fact that Monsieur Lacoste was paying me to ensure everything ran smoothly. He'd agreed to my very high rates so that everything *would* run smoothly. And for some pathetic, unemployed little middle manager, prompted by God knows who, to come along and start brandishing a gun at us and thinking he'd get away with it . . . No, I didn't like it one bit.

Monsieur Delambre was holding a Beretta, a gun I know very well.

Kader, Yasmine, and I looked at each other in silence and came to the same conclusion. The smallest window, the slightest error, and Monsieur Delambre was a dead man.

By that point, everyone in there must have thought they'd gone mad. Those who'd known that this was a simulation realized that we'd switched from a role play to the real thing. The others must have been totally bemused to see the commandos who'd taken them hostage moments before were now prisoners themselves. That must have been quite hard for them to process. The Exxyal execs, who had seen Monsieur Dorfmann shot dead a few minutes before, must have been surprised to find him alive and well, at the same time as discovering they'd been the victims of a hoax. Various new people had now entered the fold, including a man holding a gun to their boss's head and blowing cameras to smithereens. This state of astonishment played into Monsieur Delambre's hands.

Before anyone could take stock of the situation, he made all of us lie flat on our stomachs, arms and legs spread apart.

"Fingers too, spread them! Anyone tries anything and I shoot!"

That's not something you make up on the spot. You've really got to know your stuff to say the "spread the fingers" thing. That said, despite the shrewd pointers he'd been given, you could tell from his technique that he was a first-timer. He must have recognized his error when he went to search the newcomers: everyone was lying down all over the place, and there was no way he could properly frisk everyone at the same time as keeping them all in his field of vision. This is the lone gunman's primary problem. Working alone requires a lot of technical organization and anticipation, and if one aspect doesn't go according to plan, you can be sure you'll run into problems. What's more, Monsieur Delambre's mental state was not up to the task. He was still yelling things like: "Don't move! First person to move gets it!" Deep down, he didn't mean it. At least that was my impression when I felt him stand over me and pat me down. His movements weren't so clumsy that I had reasonable cause to intervene, but they weren't as systematic and precise as they should have been. He might slip up, I remember thinking—in fact I was sure he would. Stretched out in the middle of the room like a customer caught in a run-of-the-mill supermarket holdup, I resolved to show no mercy should I gain the upper hand.

Little did he know, but Monsieur Delambre had never been so close to death.

When he searched me, even if his technique was a little graceless, he had an advantage: he knew what he was looking for. Cell phones, mainly. One for each person. And then watches, to deprive us of any time markers. He had no difficulty relieving us of these objects, which he stashed in a drawer he'd pulled out of the table.

After that, he went to the windows and shut the blinds before proceeding to the next phase of the operation—namely, reconfiguring the room:

"You!" he shouted in Monsieur Cousin's direction. "Yes, you! Get up, KEEP your hands in the air, and move over there! HURRY UP!"

He was still shouting, but some words he was screaming. It was hard to tell whether this was a sign of increased panic or whether he was still filling the space with sound to prevent us from thinking. The problem was, it was preventing him from thinking, too. I was one of the first he ordered to stand up, and this gave me the chance to observe him for a second. I remember noting how agitated he was. The idea that he was so impatient, so irritable, made us all scramble. We felt he wasn't far from committing a blunder of some sort, or being seized by a murderous impulse at any point.

When you look back on events as I am now, everything seems to play back in slow motion. You take in every gesture, every intention, but the fact is it all happened very fast. So fast that I didn't even have time to consider the fundamental question: why was Monsieur Delambre doing this? What did he want? Why was an exec who'd been called in for a recruitment test taking his future employers hostage? And why with real bullets? Behind all this there were stakes that were beyond my understanding, and I realized that the best thing was to wait for the dust to settle.

He made each of us get back up in turn and assigned us all a space. Then he ordered us to place our hands flat on the ground and sit on top of them, with our backs to the wall. The opportune moment was not going to be presenting itself anytime soon, because this position is one of the hardest to get out of. I've used it myself in countless operations.

It was clear he hadn't planned this in minute detail, because he'd often point to someone, hesitate, and snap: "There!" before changing his mind with a "No, there!" The effect was unsettling.

Eventually everyone was in position. I'm not sure if it was deliberate, but there was a certain logic to the order we were in. To his right, he had the Exxyal Europe group: Madame Camberlin, Mademoiselle Tràn, Monsieur Cousin, Monsieur Lussay, and Monsieur Guéneau (who'd had time to slip his trousers and jacket back on). To his left, he had my team: Mourad, Yasmine, Kader, Monsieur Renard, and myself. And finally, alone in the middle, wedged between the two groups, were Monsieur Dorfmann, Monsieur Lacoste, and Mademoiselle Rivet. The result, though improvised, was impressive, because these two men immediately took on the appearance of a pair of defendants before a tribunal. They must have felt it: they were deathly pale. It was maybe more striking in Monsieur Lacoste's case, who's naturally suntanned (all that time on the ski slopes, at a guess).

Contrary to what people might think, in such circumstances it's not the women who cry the most or the loudest. Monsieur Guéneau, who was maxed out on the tear front, stared at the ground between his legs, his jacket wrapped firmly around him. Monsieur Lussay, on the other hand, had picked up the baton and was now whimpering like a puppy afraid of being smacked. Madame Camberlin was crying in silence, her makeup a total mess, with black streaks down her cheekbones and only a small bit of rouge left on her lower lip. I always find it a little off-putting when middle-aged women look in such a state. Mademoiselle Tràn was very pale. She looked as if she'd aged ten years in the space of a few minutes, all the volume gone from her hair. I notice this a lot. When people are under duress, the first thing they let go is their appearance—their life is the only thing that matters anymore. And generally speaking, they become quite ugly.

Most impressive of all was Monsieur Cousin. Normally, his extreme skinniness was extraordinary enough, but sitting there he was as upright as an altar candle, and his hawk-like eyes seemed to be scanning for obstacles. Unlike the others, who were prepared to abandon all dignity if it meant saving their lives, he was glaring at Monsieur Delambre as though he were a mortal enemy: unblinking, unflinching. It was as if they were on an equal footing, and his obedience to Monsieur Delambre's every order betrayed a silent yet radical opposition, while his shrinking co-hostages moved as little as possible.

The ones we could hear most clearly were Monsieur Lussay, who was moaning relentlessly, and Monsieur Renard, our actor, who looked as though he wanted to melt into the carpet to escape what was, undoubtedly, the most challenging role of his career.

There was a thirty-second silence.

Monsieur Dorfmann had managed to stay poker faced. As I've said before, his composure was quite remarkable.

Monsieur Lacoste was just about regaining his senses. He looked over at me and raised his eyebrows, proof that he was prepared to stage an intervention. But this was my responsibility, not just because I was the organizer of the operation, but also because I had the longest track record in this field. I caught Yasmine's eye, as I was aware of her experience in the psychological aspects of crisis situations. She responded with an ambiguous look—it was hard to read her opinion. I felt I was able to take the initiative, and so I made the most of this short lull to establish first contact:

"What do you want, Monsieur Delambre?"

I did my best to keep my voice serene, composed, but in retrospect I realize this wasn't the best opening gambit. Monsieur Delambre came hurtling toward me, and we all recoiled, starting with me.

"What about you—what do *you* want, you bastard?"

He struck me with his gun, square in the forehead, near my hairline, and since I'd not seen him apply the safety catch, I'll admit I was alarmed. I shut my eyes as tight as possible.

"Nothing, I don't want anything . . ."

"That's why you're giving me shit, you bastard? *For nothing?*"

A bead of cold sweat pricked at me, and I was overcome with nausea. You know, in my line of work, I know what the fear of death feels like, and I can assure you it's unmistakable . . .

The best thing was not to answer, to avoid agitating him any further.

The barrel of his gun was pointed at my brain. The man was verging on pure insanity, and I told myself that at the first opportunity, I'd have no hesitation lodging a bullet in that same spot, right in his brain.

25

There was no doubt my intervention had been premature, but it was too late for regrets. I had presented Monsieur Delambre with a breach, and he'd charged right into it.

"Alright then, big guy!" he said to me. "Where's all your wonderful organization, now? Where is it now, eh, you prick?"

I can't tell you how the others reacted to this, because I kept my eyes closed.

"It was all going so well . . . such a shame. Your little team, your little cameras, your shitty little machine guns!"

He drilled the gun into my forehead, as if he wanted the barrel to pierce my skull.

"But this one . . . this is a real one, my friend. With real bullets, that make real holes. We're not playing Cowboys and Indians now. In fact, speaking of Indians, where's the big chief?"

Monsieur Delambre was standing up again, hand on hip, pretending to search around.

"That's a very good point . . . where's the head honcho?"

He knelt down in front of Monsieur Dorfmann, just as he had with me. He placed the tip of his Beretta in exactly the same position, right in the middle of his forehead. He was fizzing with hatred. He wanted to belittle us, humiliate us. This answered my question about his motives and went a long way to explaining what would happen in the future: deep down, Monsieur Delambre didn't want anything. He wasn't after money; he wasn't demanding a ransom. No, he wanted revenge. Bitterness and resentment had driven him to these lengths. He was craving retribution of the symbolic kind.

This aging, jobless executive was starting to take a perverse pleasure in brandishing a gun in the face of a major European CEO, so much so that a bloodbath had become a plausible outcome.

"Well, then . . . ," he continued. "He's so discreet, our generalissimo. He seems worried sick. Of course he does—he's got such mighty responsibilities! Must be tough, eh? Eh? Yes, it is, it's tough . . ."

Monsieur Delambre had adopted a theatrical, mocking, sympathetic tone.

"Mass layoffs . . . Now that really is tough. But wait! That's not even the toughest part, is it now? No, no, no . . . the toughest part is planning them all. Now that really is complicated. They're just coming so thick and fast, aren't they? You've hit your stride. It takes some expertise to manage all this firing—some real willpower. Got to bargain with the bastards, don't you? And for that you need men, good ones at that. Soldiers, boots on the ground for the great capitalist cause. You can't just pick any old so-and-so, can you, O mighty Caesar? And when it comes to choosing the best, nothing does it quite like a good old-fashioned hostage taking. Well: you're in luck, dear leader. You've got one."

He leaned forward, turning his head to the side, as if he were about to kiss him on the lips, and I managed to catch a glimpse of Monsieur Dorfmann's face. He was keeping his cool, holding his breath and thinking about what to say. But he never got the chance—Monsieur Delambre was on a roll.

"In fact, your higher-than-highness, tell me about Sarqueville: how many exactly are you firing there?"

"What . . . what do you want?" Monsieur Dorfmann managed to say.

"I want to know how many people you're firing from that plant. I could easily kill everyone here for you, right here, right now. That would make twelve. A decent start. But I'm just a lowly sole trader. You—you work on an industrial scale. How many are you planning to mow down at Sarqueville?"

Monsieur Dorfmann felt it wise not to venture down that road, and he decided to keep quiet. Good job, too, if you ask me.

"I remember reading the number 823 somewhere," Monsieur Delambre continued. "But I don't know if that last count's up to date. How many is it, exactly?"

"I . . . I don't know . . ."

"Oh, but you do, you do know!" Monsieur Delambre insisted, brimming with confidence. "So come on, enough false modesty . . . How many?"

"I don't know, I'm telling you!" Monsieur Dorfmann shouted. "Just tell me what you want!"

Monsieur Delambre ignored him.

"It'll come back to you. You'll see," he said.

He turned, raised his, arm and fired at the water cooler, smashing it to smithereens and sending five gallons of water cascading onto the floor.

Eight bullets left. And nobody was in any doubt that he was capable of inflicting far more damage with that much ammo.

Once again he leaned toward Monsieur Dorfmann.

"Where were we? Oh, yes. Sarqueville. So, how many exactly?"

"Eight hundred and twenty-five," Monsieur Dorfmann whispered.

"There you go—it did come back. So let me see . . . that's two more. But, two doesn't mean anything to you, does it? My guess is that those two people see it rather differently."

Up to that point, Monsieur Delambre had been organized and meticulous, but since he'd started addressing Monsieur Dorfmann, his strategy seemed less coherent, as though he had lost track of what he wanted to achieve. This backed up my theory that his sole aim in taking us hostage was to frighten or humiliate us. As hard as it was to believe, this was the most likely explanation, judging by his behavior.

Stress. It's sort of like a thread that each of us carries inside, a thread whose resistance we can never really predict. Everyone has their own threshold. Madame Camberlin must have reached her breaking point, because she'd started moaning, quietly at first, then louder and louder. As though this were a signal or a form of consent, all the others started wailing, too. The collective effect reminded me of a pressure valve being released. With this cry, everyone gave free rein to their fear and anguish, and as it drew out, the voices of the men and women melded into a single bestial lowing that filled the room, and I thought it would never stop.

In the midst of this astonishing cacophony, Monsieur Delambre couldn't meet anyone's eye, since they all had their chins pressed into their chests, their eyes screwed tight shut. He staggered back into the center of the room and started yelling himself, and his shriek was so powerful, so harrowing, that his pain seemed to stem from somewhere far deeper . . . The others fell silent, cut off in their stride, and looked up at him. It was a curious scene, you know: this man standing in the middle of a meeting room, pistol in hand, his eyes raised to the heavens as he howled like a wolf, as though he were on the brink of death. In a split second, Kader and I reached an agreement. We flung ourselves at him, Kader at his legs, me at his waist. But Monsieur Delambre dropped to the floor, like a house of cards, the best possible way to check our attack. His bullet struck me in my right leg, and Kader held up his hands in surrender after Monsieur Delambre had cracked him over the head with the butt of his pistol.

"Nobody move! Stay where you are!" I shouted though the pain. I was afraid someone else might try to attack and make him start spraying bullets all over the place.

Kader and I crept back toward the wall, me clutching my leg, him his head. The sight of blood marked a new stage in events, and everyone was aware of the escalation. Until this point, there had been noise and fear, but the blood made things more physical, more visceral. It took us one step closer to death and drew another collective whine from the hostages.

I've thought long and hard about whether I did the right thing. Kader assures me I did. He figures we couldn't have let the situation unravel without trying something, and that had been the most opportune moment. The way I see it, a course of action is only correct if it's successful. This episode heightened my frustration and made me all the more determined to show Monsieur Delambre that he wouldn't escape so lightly forever.

Back against the wall, Kader and I established that neither of us was seriously injured. He only had a slight gash on his scalp, but it was still bleeding freely, quite spectacularly, in fact. As for me, I was clasping my leg and grimacing, but as soon as I ripped open my trouser leg, I realized that the bullet had grazed me without causing much damage. But Monsieur Delambre was oblivious of this, and so without exchanging a word, Kader and I exaggerated our pain.

Monsieur Delambre had come around and was back in the middle of the room. He retreated within himself, not knowing what to do.

"You need to call an ambulance," I murmured.

He was disoriented, lost, unhinged. It fell to us to provide him with solutions.

He didn't answer, so I pressed on, trying hard to keep my voice level.

"Things aren't too bad for now, Monsieur Delambre. You can still come out of this okay. It's fine, we're only wounded. But you see, I'm losing a lot of blood. Kader, too . . . You need to call an ambulance."

I didn't have my watch anymore, but I knew that the real hostage taking had only been going on for about twenty minutes so far. Monsieur Delambre had fired five shots, but the building was in a business park, and on a public holiday like this, there was little chance that anyone had raised the alarm. There was only one remaining solution: for Monsieur Delambre to give himself up. Our wounds provided good leverage for this outcome, but Monsieur Delambre was showing no sign of going down without a fight. He shook his head over and over, as if hoping the problem would take care of itself.

"Wounds . . . Anyone here know first aid?" he said after a brief silence.

No one answered. Everyone knew instinctively that a new power struggle was about to unfold.

"So? Anyone? Okay, let's try this another way!" Monsieur Delambre said. "Fuck, if we're going to cause irreparable damage, we might as well do it properly!"

Two strides and he was in front of Monsieur Dorfmann, crouching down and resting the barrel of his gun on the CEO's knee.

"Come on then, The Great Helmsman. Time for some heroics!"

Judging by the speed with which he'd made his decision, there was no doubt whatsoever that he was going to shoot, but a loud voice stopped him short.

"I'll do it."

Monsieur Cousin was on his feet. He looked like a ghost, there's no other way to describe it. He had a milky-white complexion, almost translucent, and a wild look in his eyes. Even Monsieur Delambre was thrown.

"I know a bit of first aid. I'll have a look."

And Monsieur Cousin was on the move. It was so surprising that he seemed to be walking in slow motion. First he approached Kader.

"Look down," he said, leaning down next to him and fiddling with his hair for a second.

"It's nothing," he said, "just an abrasion to the scalp. It's superficial. The bleeding will stop on its own."

He spoke with immense authority, as if he himself had become the hostage taker. His assurance and gravitas meant that he had switched roles with Monsieur Delambre, who stayed kneeling in front of the Exxyal chairman, unsure what to do.

Then Monsieur Cousin stooped down to inspect my leg. He lifted it from underneath the tibia like paramedics do, and moved the fabric to one side.

"Same—this one's not serious either. It'll be just fine," he said.

He stood up and turned toward Monsieur Delambre.

"Okay, so . . . What do you want exactly? Let's get this over with! Who are you, anyway?"

Monsieur Cousin was holding his captor to account.

In the space of a few seconds, this hostage taking had become a battle of two wills. The hostages were still sitting around the room, forming a sort of ring around the two men glaring at each other in the middle. Monsieur Delambre was at a major advantage: he had a gun. He had used it six times, making several holes in the wall, injuring two people and annihilating a water cooler. And he had seven bullets left. Monsieur Cousin, however, was not about to feel intimidated by his opponent. His hackles were up, and he looked ready for a fight.

"Aaaaaah!" sighed Monsieur Delambre. "The model exec swoops in to rescue his boss—how touching!"

He had taken a backward step, so that he was pressed against the door, his pistol still held in both hands. He swung toward Monsieur Dorfmann again.

"Congratulations, your Excellency, for what you've achieved with this man. He's almost the prototype! You fire him, but he carries on working for free, hoping you'll take him back on. Isn't that just wonderful?!"

As he spoke he pointed his gun skyward as if he might fire at the ceiling, or as though calling everyone to witness. Then he thrust it toward Monsieur Cousin, nodding his head in admiration.

"And you, you want to defend your company, is that it? Risk your life for it, if need be? It's your family, your gang! They've been running you into the ground for months . . . no qualms whatsoever about giving you the boot. But that doesn't mean a thing to you: you're willing to die for them! That's not just submission—that's martyrdom."

Monsieur Cousin looked him square in the eyes, not in the least bit shaken:

"I repeat," he said. "Who are you and what do you want?"

He didn't seem at all fazed by Monsieur Delambre's performance, nor by the weapon training at him.

Monsieur Delambre brought his arms to his sides with a false air of remorse:

"But, the same thing as you, old boy. All I want is a job."

He then stalked up to Monsieur Lacoste, whose face contorted with fear. This time, instead of resting the barrel on his forehead, he aimed it directly at his heart.

"I did everything to get this job."

"Listen . . ." Monsieur Lacoste stammered. "I think you have . . ."

But Monsieur Delambre silenced him by pressing the weapon farther into his chest. His voice was calm now, and that's what was so frightening—how measured his tone was:

"I worked harder than anyone to get this job. You led me to believe I had every chance. You lied to me, because in your mind, I'm not even human."

He started tapping Monsieur Lacoste's chest again with the barrel of the gun.

"The truth is, I'm better than her! Miles better!" he yelled, jerking his head toward Mademoiselle Rivet, whose presence only seemed to add to his fury, because suddenly he shouted:

"I deserved this job! And you stole it from me! You hear me: you stole it from me and it was *all I had left!*"

He fell silent. He leaned in close to Monsieur Lacoste's ear and, loud enough for all of us to hear, said:

"So, because you won't give me what I am due, I have come to take my pound of flesh."

Suddenly we heard the sound of hurried footsteps.

As soon as he realized that Monsieur Cousin had fled down the corridor, Monsieur Delambre swung around and shot at the main entrance, but his aim was too high and he only managed to make a hole in the partition wall. He started running, careered into a chair that Monsieur Cousin had knocked over on his way past, nearly crashing to the floor with his gun, but making it to the corridor. We saw him raise his weapon with both hands, hesitate, then lower his arms. It was too late.

He now only had two bad solutions to choose between: running after Monsieur Cousin and leaving us unguarded with our telephones, or staying with us and letting Monsieur Cousin go and call for help.

He was trapped.

There was still no shortage of possible outcomes, but at that point it ceased to matter what happened, or whether some people came out dead or alive: one way or another, it was over.

The experience taught me that it only takes a couple of seconds for a man to become a maniac. The basic ingredients (a sense of humiliation or injustice, extreme loneliness, a weapon and nothing to lose) all resulted in Monsieur Delambre's decision to barricade himself in with us as the police arrived outside.

When he reentered the room, his gun dangling by his side and his head bowed in defeat, I thought it was Monsieur Delambre's turn to start crying.

26

Monsieur Delambre could have chosen to back down, but I don't think he had the strength. He had reached a point of no return, and he clearly had no idea how things were going to finish. That's always the hardest part—finishing.

He pulled up a chair and just sat there, back to the door, facing the hostages.

He was no longer the same man. He was beaten, spent. Worse than that, he was crushed. With his elbows resting on his knees, he held his pistol limply in his right hand, gazing at the floor. In his left hand, he was fingering a small piece of orange cloth, which had a sort of miniscule bell that made a sharp ringing sound. It looked like a lucky charm.

Monsieur Delambre had positioned himself at the opposite end of the room, too far away for anyone to reach him before he could raise his gun.

What was I thinking at that moment? Well, I was wondering what he had been hoping would happen. He had brought a loaded gun, which suggested he had always been prepared to use it, but what was his objective? No matter how much I turn it over in my head, the vision he presented at that instant confirmed everything: Monsieur Delambre had acted out of desperation. So desperate, so devoid of hope, that he was willing to kill.

As Monsieur Cousin had predicted prior to his escape, Kader's bleeding had effectively stopped. As for me, I'd made a tourniquet to stem the flow of blood, and now it was just a matter of patience.

A calm composure had settled over the group. It felt like a vigil. The tears had stopped, along with the groans, moans, and grievances. The whole thing had lasted well under an hour, but enough had happened to leave everyone traumatized.

The stage was set for the final act.

Everyone was apprehensive, retreating within themselves to summon as much strength as they could. If Monsieur Delambre's will to keep us there appeared to be faltering, then there was some hope, but you only needed to look at him to see that he was in it for the long haul, and there was no telling how long.

And so when the first police sirens were heard a short while later, everyone was wondering what the next twist in the saga would be. Would Monsieur Delambre surrender or make a stand? Heads or tails? Everyone placed their bets; everyone waited for the outcome.

When the sirens drew nearer, Monsieur Delambre didn't look up; he didn't make even the slightest movement. His spirits had been sapped. I listened closely and discerned at least five police cars and two ambulances. Monsieur Cousin must have been efficient and persuasive, since the authorities had taken him seriously. We could hear the heavy tramping of boots in the parking lot. The police were assessing the scale of the problem. First the building had to be secured. In a few minutes' time, vanloads of RAID counterterrorist teams would arrive. We would then enter into a negotiation process lasting five minutes or thirty hours, depending on how comprehensive, skillful, and resistant Monsieur Delambre proved to be. As he was still looking at his feet, lost in thought, the hostages stared at one another, communicating silently as their personal uncertainty accumulated to form a collective anxiety. Monsieur Dorfmann, collected as ever, tried to calm everyone down by looking reassuringly at each person in turn. Monsieur Lacoste, however, had been found wanting from the start of the ordeal and still hadn't managed to get back on track. He looked defeated.

A megaphone crackled to life, and a voice was heard:

"The building is surrounded . . ."

Still slumped in his chair and his head still lowered, Monsieur Delambre held his arm aloft and—without a second's hesitation—fired a bullet into the window. The glass behind the blind shattered with an almighty crash, and all the hostages instantly rolled into a ball to protect their heads from the falling shards.

Then Monsieur Delambre stood up, went over to his briefcase, and opened it, taking no precautions whatsoever with regard to us, as if we were no longer an issue. He removed two Beretta magazines—enough for a siege—and returned to his seat, laying the fresh ammunition at his feet. This didn't bode well at all for the final phase.

After their first announcement on the megaphone, the police didn't push it. A few minutes later, more sirens. RAID had just arrived. They would need about twenty minutes to consult the building's architectural plans, establish eyes and ears where possible to observe what was happening in our room, and assemble teams at the key access points with a view to sealing the premises. At the same time, elite RAID snipers would be positioned opposite the windows, each one of them capable of slamming two bullets into Monsieur Delambre's head should he make the smallest slip.

I estimated first contact from the negotiator to come after about ten minutes, and I figure I wasn't far off. He called on an inside line that was located on the floor near the wall to Monsieur Delambre's right.

All eyes converged on the device, but it took a good twelve rings before Monsieur Delambre decided to react. He seemed exhausted. The handset was a standard-issue thing with buttons and a digital screen.

"Hello," Monsieur Delambre said, picking it up, but without initial success. Then he pushed a button, then a second, before getting very angry very quickly and pushing almost all of them, following which all of us could hear the person speaking at the other end—he'd pressed the loudspeaker button by mistake, not that this seemed to bother him.

"Monsieur Delambre, this is Captain Prungnaud."

"What do you want?"

"I want to know how the hostages are doing."

Monsieur Delambre looked around the room.

"Everyone's fine."

"You've wounded two of them."

The conversation adhered to normal protocol and advanced as predicted. It didn't take long at all for Monsieur Delambre to declare that he wouldn't let anyone go, and that they would have to "come and fetch him." To punctuate this announcement, he took aim and shattered two more windows. The laminated blinds he'd pierced now had large holes burned out of them, which gave a solid impression of what might happen if Monsieur Delambre decided to start firing at us instead of the windows. At that moment, the RAID snipers would no doubt be squirming in the hope of catching a glimpse of Monsieur Delambre through the gaping holes in the blinds, but he was too far from the windows for them to risk anything.

Neither Kader nor I could wait any longer to intervene. While we were waiting for the police, I had stolen a glance at Yasmine, who until now had been keeping a low profile, which was quite out of character for her. Throughout the long wait, she had—moving by fractions of an inch—managed to change position, stealthily bringing a foot beneath her backside, shifting her opposite arm: on her mark, set, and ready to pounce. A true pro. She was sitting about twenty feet from Monsieur Delambre, and I knew that she was ready to take him out at the first sign of weakness. A little earlier, when Monsieur Delambre had gone to get his extra ammunition, I signaled to her that it wasn't the right moment. The perfect window would be just after he fired his final bullet. In the few seconds it would take him to realize his magazine was empty, get a new one, and replace it, Yasmine would have all the time in the world. I wouldn't have given

Monsieur Delambre a one-in-a-hundred chance against that perfectly trained live wire. For the moment, he had three bullets left and seemed primed to fire at anything that moved; paradoxically, this was good news for us, since it meant our opportune moment would arrive sooner. We therefore had an unexpected chance to take action before RAID.

And to be perfectly honest, that was my sole objective.

I felt thwarted, and I'd vowed to resolve the situation myself before the security forces arrived. It was a matter of honor. I was all the more determined since Monsieur Delambre was armed: I could kill him in cold blood without any fear of the consequences and claim self-defense. In front of the other hostages, I would let off a quick burst, pretending I didn't have time to take aim, even though in truth I'd need just a few tenths of a second to lodge a bullet right in the middle of his forehead. Which was precisely my intention.

But things didn't quite pan out like that, you might say.

Monsieur Delambre seemed more confused than ever, and was trying to remember all the advice he'd been given. He was back on his chair, facing the group, but as we waited for him to fire his last round, he ejected his current magazine and replaced it with a fresh one. The whole thing took him less than four seconds, and before we knew it Monsieur Delambre was holding a newly loaded pistol with thirteen good bullets, ready for action.

Yasmine kept her cool, but inside I could tell she was devastated. We were heading for a RAID assault, with all the consequences that entailed.

Our room was on the fourth floor of the building. Three of the four windows had been shattered by gunshots, and the wind was blowing in through the gaps. At first the air had been rather pleasant, but now it was making things extremely uncomfortable. Would the RAID team opt for this entry point? Not impossible . . . My money was on a simultaneous double offensive targeting the corridor and the exterior: a two-pronged attack that Monsieur Delambre would be incapable of resisting by himself. And after seeing him blast out three windows without warning and with real bullets, the security forces would never give a man holding twelve people hostage (including two injured) any chance of escaping with his life.

From an investigation point of view, the police and RAID had moved very quickly: Monsieur Delambre had been identified, allowing the negotiator to call him by his name from first contact. In fact, from the information supplied by Monsieur Cousin, it must have been easy for them to pull up Monsieur Dorfmann and Monsieur Lacoste, and maybe even collar Mademoiselle Zbikowski, who surely held the keys to this mystery.

The first round of negotiations had been over and done with very quickly—the three gunshots made sure of that. It wouldn't be long until RAID turned up the heat again. Only ten minutes, as it happened.

Monsieur Delambre stood up at the second ring. Yasmine watched his every movement. So did I. Would he look away while he was talking? Where would he leave his weapon during the conversation? Would he move as far as the telephone cord let him? He jabbed at the buttons again, one undoubtedly canceling out the other, and the loudspeaker stayed activated.

"Monsieur Delambre, what do you want?"

Captain Prungnaud again, whose clear, calm voice oozed professionalism.

"I don't know . . . Can you find me a job?"

"Yes, I had a feeling the problem might have been along those lines."

"That's correct, just a small problem. 'Along those lines.' I have a proposal for you."

"Go ahead."

"The people here with me all have jobs. If I kill one of them—any of them—and free the rest, can I have their job?"

"We can talk about anything, Monsieur Delambre, and I mean anything, including your job hunt, but before that we'll need you to release some hostages."

"Talk about money, for example?"

The negotiator let that one lie for a second, just to size up the problem.

"You want money? How m—?"

But before he could finish his sentence, Monsieur Delambre had fired at the last window, sending more glass crashing onto the crouched hostages.

We'd barely opened our eyes before Monsieur Delambre had hung up and resumed his position. A huge commotion could be heard downstairs in the parking lot. The fact they were dealing with someone hell-bent on exterminating windows at random intervals was not making the security forces' job any easier.

The telephone rang again about five minutes later.

"Alain . . ."

"That's *Monsieur Delambre* to you! It's not like we're old pals from the job center!"

"Okay, Monsieur Delambre, as you wish. I'm calling because I have someone next to me who wants to speak to you. I'll pass her over."

"NO!"

Monsieur Delambre shouted and smashed the receiver down. But he stayed put, paralyzed in front of the phone, mute and motionless.

Yasmine stared intently at me, asking whether now was the moment, but I was sure the negotiator wouldn't pass up a response like that. Indeed, a few seconds later the telephone rang again, but this time it wasn't the RAID negotiator at the other end. It was a woman. Young, no more than thirty, I don't think.

"Papa . . . ?"

Her voice was trembling with emotion and Monsieur Delambre was squirming uneasily.

"Papa, answer me, please . . ."

But Monsieur Delambre couldn't speak. He held the phone in his left hand, the gun in his right, and it seemed nothing could pull him out of the turmoil the woman's voice had just plunged him into. Hearing that voice was harder for him than firing a bullet into

Monsieur Dorfmann's head, but maybe it boiled down to the same thing: unambiguous proof of the desperate stalemate he was in. For a second—just a second—I felt sorry for him.

There was confusion on the line. No one knew where to go from there.

Another woman's voice on the line, older this time.

"Alain?" she said. "It's Nicole."

Monsieur Delambre was absolutely rooted to the spot.

The woman was crying uncontrollably, choking and unable to speak. We could barely hear anything over her sobbing. And it was upsetting to us, because she wasn't just crying for our sake, but for the sake of her husband, the man who'd taken us prisoner and been threatening to kill us for over an hour.

"Alain," she said. "I'm begging you . . . answer me."

That voice, those words had a devastating effect on Monsieur Delambre.

"Nicole . . . Please forgive me," he said in a very low voice. That was it. Nothing else.

After this, he replaced the telephone and grabbed the drawer with all our cell phones and watches. Then he went up to the window, lifted the blind, and flung the contents out of it. One motion, everything at once. I have no idea why he did that—I'm telling you, it was very odd. In any event, I didn't have long to speculate.

The first bullet whisked past his left shoulder, and the second went right through the space where his head had been half a second earlier. He fell to the ground and turned toward us, holding his gun in his outstretched hand. Which was just as well, because Yasmine was already on her feet, ready to spring on him.

"Get down!" he cried at her.

Yasmine did as she was told. Monsieur Delambre crawled on his belly and stood up a few yards away. He went to the door, opened it, and turned to us.

"You can go," he said. "It's over."

Astonishment all around.

Did he just say it was over? No one could believe it.

Monsieur Delambre stayed like that for a few seconds, his mouth hanging open. He was right—it was over. I think he wanted to say something to us, but it didn't come, the words catching in his head. The telephone carried on ringing, but he didn't even flinch at it.

He turned and left.

The last sound we heard was the key turning in the lock from outside in the corridor.

We were locked in, but we were free.

It's hard to describe what happened next. All the hostages leapt to their feet and rushed to the windows. Once the blinds had been torn open, it took a good amount of persuasion and effort from me and my team to stop them from clambering onto the ledges and throwing themselves out. It was pure panic.

On seeing the hostages congregated at the windows, the police officers in the parking lot were not immediately sure what had happened. The negotiator called on the inside line. Yasmine answered and informed the police of the apparent situation, because we still weren't sure whether Monsieur Delambre would change his mind or not. It was deeply uncertain, and I shared the officers' concern. We didn't know, for example, where he was with his loaded gun and all that spare ammunition. Had he genuinely stood down? Or was he waiting in ambush somewhere else in the building?

Kader was struggling to calm Monsieur Lussay, Madame Camberlin, and Monsieur Guéneau. Monsieur Renard was the most agitated. He kept yelling: "Come and get us! Come and get us!" Yasmine had no other choice but to let off two deafening whistles that quieted him down in an instant.

Limping as best I could, I took hold of the phone and introduced myself before having a brief conversation with the RAID captain.

Ten or so minutes later, ladders were placed against the outside wall of the building. Two RAID teams wearing bulletproof vests and helmets and armed with assault rifles scaled them in seconds flat. The first made sure we were protected, while the second went down to open the inside doors to make way for the other teams, which immediately scoured the building for Monsieur Delambre.

Moments later we were down in the parking lot wrapped in those foil blankets . . .

There—that's more or less what I told the police and repeated to the investigating magistrate.

It emerged that Monsieur Delambre had laid down his weapon and the remaining full magazine on the floor by the entrance of the office he'd retreated into. The RAID team discovered him crouching at the foot of a desk, head between his knees and his hands clutching the back of his neck.

He didn't put up any resistance.

I must have taken part in a good fifteen or so operations that were considerably more dangerous and complicated than this one. Yasmine, Kader, and I carried out a thorough debriefing the following day. Every operation has its learning outcomes, so it's always worth playing back the film in slow motion, frame by frame, pulling out every detail, however insignificant, to feed into our experience. After all, experience is what earns us our bread and butter. Then we move on to new destinations, new missions.

Except this time it didn't work out that way.

The images from that half day whirled through my head on repeat, as if they contained some subliminal message that had eluded me.

I told myself this was pointless, that I should focus on other things, but to no avail—for days later the images were still coming back to me.

Always the same.

We were in the parking lot. An air of relief had descended on everyone. The RAID team that discovered Monsieur Delambre in an office radioed down to the agents positioned outside to inform them that the operation was over. My leg was receiving attention. Paramedics were all around us. The RAID captain came to shake my hand and we exchanged a few passing comments.

I could see the freed hostages from where I was standing. Each person's reaction matched his or her temperament. Monsieur Guéneau was wearing his full suit again, in complete disarray; Mademoiselle Tràn had already touched up her makeup; Madame Camberlin had also regained some color and wiped away the smudges that had covered her cheeks just moments before. They were all in a circle around Monsieur Dorfmann, who was answering their questions with a smile. Authority hadn't taken long to restore itself. It even seemed like the hostages needed it, as though it were a vital touchstone. What was extraordinary was that none of them resented the Exxyal Europe boss for organizing the hostage taking, an ordeal that had been cruel and violent in equal measure. To the contrary, everyone seemed to find the whole thing perfectly worthwhile. For some of them, this was to garner credit for their performance; for others, to atone for their weaknesses. It was remarkable how quickly normal life resumed. Monsieur Cousin's hulking frame stood out from the others. The verdict was clear: he was the man of the moment, the embodiment of altruism and courage, the day's big winner. He wasn't smiling. He looked like an election candidate whose victory had just been announced but who was pretending to take the result in his stride to demonstrate mental superiority. Yet all you had to do was consider the position he occupied alongside Monsieur Dorfmann, or gauge the invisible, admiring circle his colleagues had formed around him—colleagues who just a few hours before must have scorned him—to understand that he was the undisputed champion of this adventure. No one was in any doubt that he'd just sealed his ticket to the Sarqueville refinery.

Monsieur Lacoste was already on the telephone. Animal reflex, without a doubt. He was speaking animatedly. I think he had a lot on his plate. He'd have to answer to his client, Monsieur Dorfmann, and with that I wished him luck . . .

A little farther away, Monsieur Renard was already relaying the details of our incarceration and release to the press, his measured movements becoming increasingly flamboyant. His finest role to date. I remember feeling that he'd have been quite happy to die in his sleep that night.

The flashing lights were turning slowly, engines purring, lending the entire scene a reassuring sense that the crisis was over.

That's how I remember it.

And then there were the two women I didn't know. Mother and daughter. Monsieur Delambre's wife is a very pretty woman. I mean, really lovely. Her daughter, thirty or so, had her arm wrapped around her mother's shoulder. Neither of them was crying. They gazed at the entrance to the building. They'd been told that Monsieur Delambre had been apprehended without resistance, and that he hadn't been injured. A third woman arrived, also around thirty. Her face, although very pretty, was drawn and aged. The three of them held one another's hands tight as the RAID team left with Monsieur Delambre.

There you have it—these are the recurring images that have come back to me since that day.

I'm at home, by myself. All this happened about six weeks ago.

It's Tuesday. I have some work to do, but nothing urgent.

Yasmine called me from Georgia the day before yesterday for an update. She asked if I was still "mulling over" the affair. I laughed it off, but the fact is that I was. This morning again, as I was stirring my coffee and looking out on the tall trees in the square, I replayed Monsieur Delambre's exit.

It's funny sometimes how it plays on repeat. It was 10:00 a.m. Again I watched the RAID agents bringing out Monsieur Delambre.

As soon as they had secured him in the interrogation room, they fastened him into a straitjacket made of black material. This was not a method I was familiar with, but Captain Prungnaud assured me it was highly practical. In short, Monsieur Delambre was handcuffed underneath, and the straitjacket formed a sort of hammock to carry him on his back. The RAID officers were holding him up by four straps, his body swinging to the rhythm of their running as they headed for the vehicle. We could only see his face. He passed by a few yards from the three women, who started crying when they saw him in this position. His wife made a futile gesture in his direction. The police were running so fast that he was past us in less than a second.

This is what's been lingering in my mind since the end of the ordeal. The look in his eyes. His face . . . It was almost impassive, which was hardly out of the ordinary for anyone who saw it. It was even to be expected that Monsieur Delambre's expression should be so relaxed, so relieved after this saga.

But it was the way he looked at me as he went by. It lasted a fraction of a second. It wasn't the defeated loser's look I might have anticipated.

He held my stare very deliberately.

It was the look of a winner.

And beneath it, I could have sworn there was the hint of a smile. The image is vague, but it's there nonetheless.

Monsieur Delambre departed the scene with an air of triumph, satisfaction, and the faintest of smiles. He may as well have winked at me. It was bizarre . . .

I played back the film one more time.

Now I'd put my finger on the right memory, I could see his face clearly. That smile—it wasn't the final revenge of a loser; it was the smile of a winner.

The image had become crystal clear.

I rewound the film even farther. RAID swooped in throwing smoke grenades. Before that, the hostages flocked to the window. And before that, Monsieur Delambre said: "It's over."

Shit.

Monsieur Delambre was alone in that room waiting to be arrested. *The RAID team discovered him crouched at the foot of a desk, head between his knees and his hands clutching the back of his neck.*

That's the reason I highlight the coincidence, because it was at that precise moment my telephone rang.

It was Monsieur Dorfmann.

I had never spoken to him on the phone. He was the end client. My only point of contact had been my employer, Monsieur Lacoste, a point I tried to make to him.

"There's no more Lacoste," he replied.

His tone was direct. As you have no doubt noticed by now, Monsieur Dorfmann is not a man who takes kindly to being contradicted.

"Monsieur Fontana, would you be willing to accept a new mission? It follows on from the one you were previously assigned."

"In principle, yes. It's a matter of—"

"Money won't be an issue," he said, cutting me off with disdain.

After a moment, Monsieur Dorfmann said:

"You see, Monsieur Fontana, we have . . . a serious problem."

Yes, they did, as I'd just realized myself.

"This is not coming as a great surprise," I responded. "With all due respect, sir, I do believe we've been fucked. Hard."

Silence.

"You could say that, yes," Monsieur Dorfmann concluded.

AFTER

27

I used to think I'd stop at nothing to get a job, but that was because prison had never crossed my mind.

I realized I had none of the necessary genetic traits for survival in this habitat. In Darwinian terms, my capacity to adapt to the prison environment placed me at the bottom of the hierarchy. Like me, there are some who have landed here by chance, accident, or lunacy (all three, in my case) and who are struggling with the deep anxiety of their situation. They may as well stroll around wearing a placard with the words "Easy pickings: help yourselves!" This condition is known as "cell shock," and it's the primary cause of early suicide.

To establish which subspecies you belong to, you just need to take one step outside your cell. It turns out I belong to the group that gets punched in the face right away, and then relieved of any possessions the officials haven't already taken. I didn't even see the guy coming, but there I was sprawled across the floor with my nose split open. He crouched over me, took my watch and my wedding ring, then entered my cell and swiped everything that took his fancy. As I got to my feet, I realized that my altercation with Mehmet had anticipated my new circumstances very accurately, but with two crucial differences: first, I was on the losing side this time; and second, for a single agent like myself, there were plenty more potential Mehmets out there. The opening exchange had not gone well for me. All the others were watching me with their arms folded. Taking one in the face like that (the first time I step out of my cell) wasn't the most humiliating thing; in one way or another, it's what I've had to endure since day one of unemployment. No: the humiliating thing was being the victim of an action that had been predictable to everyone except me. The guy who stole everything I owned just happened to be at the front of the line. In the space of a few seconds, he taught me that this place is a zoo, that at some point everything ends up with a fight.

Since I've been here, I have seen about thirty new prisoners arrive, and the only ones who avoid this initiation are the reoffenders. Being a first-timer at my age didn't let me off the hook. Now I'm part of the club: I fold my arms and watch the show.

Nicole visited me at the start of my detention. My nose looked like a pig's snout. We made an odd couple, because unlike me Nicole had made herself pretty as a picture, with lovely makeup and the beautiful patterned dress that crosses over at the front, and which I love because I always used to pull at the little cord . . . In short, she wanted to project confidence, desire; she wanted to do me a good turn, to put on a brave face despite the circumstances, because she felt it was necessary for enduring the long road ahead of us. When she saw me, she acted as though everything was normal, which was impressive. The nurse, a brutish fellow, had just changed the bandages, leaving me with large bloodied cotton wads up each nostril so I had to breathe through my mouth, and the scar running beneath the two sets of stitches was still covered in dried blood. I was also struggling to open my right eye because the lid had tripled in size. The antiseptic cream was a pissy yellow and gleamed beneath the neon lights.

And so it was that Nicole sat down in front of me and smiled. She swallowed back the "How are you?" question and started talking about the girls, all the while staring at an imaginary point in the middle of my forehead. She talked about the house, day-to-day stuff, and in a few minutes silent tears began streaming down her cheeks. She carried on talking as though she hadn't noticed them. Finally, the words stuck in her throat and, afraid of seeming weak when I needed her to be strong, she said: "Sorry." Simply "sorry," just like that. And then she lowered her head, devastated by the scale of the catastrophe. She decided to get a tissue out of her bag, fumbling around for an eternity. We were both dejected, defeated.

It occurred to me that this was the first time we'd been so apart since we met.

That "sorry" from Nicole unsettled me deeply. Things have been hard enough for her already, and it's only just getting started. There are stacks of paperwork—the whole thing is a fucking mess. I told her that she mustn't feel she has to come and see me, but she replied:

"It's already enough that I have to sleep without you . . ."

Those words suffocated me.

After that, in spite of her distress, Nicole managed to compose herself. She had some questions for me. There was so much she didn't understand. What had happened to me? I no longer resembled her husband, not even physically. The man she'd lost would never have done those things.

This was the essence of her question: what have I become?

A bit like in accidents, her brain was fixated on peripheral details. She was in shock.

"How did you find a gun with real bullets?"

"I bought it."

She wanted to ask me where, how much, how, but her real question was too pressing.

"Did you want to kill people, Alain?"

Now that was a tricky one. Yes, I think I did.

"No! Not at all . . . ," I answer.

Nicole clearly didn't believe a word coming out of my mouth.

"So why did you buy it?"

I got the impression that this gun was going to stay between us for some time.

Nicole started crying again, but this time she didn't try to hide it. She took my hands in hers, and there was no hiding the proof anymore: my wedding ring had disappeared. Our wedding ring had probably already changed hands for a blow job from a young rent boy, who'd worn it in his ear for a few days before trading it for some weed, a couple of pills, or some methanol . . . Nicole said nothing. She simply filed the information away in the spreadsheet that one day will calculate the sum total of our shared losses. Or perhaps in our statement of affairs when we file for bankruptcy.

I'm now aware that the one question burning on her lips was also the one she'd never ask me:

Why have you abandoned me?

Chronologically speaking, however, the first visit was from Lucie. Not unexpectedly, in fact. The police remanded me in custody and asked if I had a lawyer. And I said Lucie. She was willing enough to come. The second RAID arrested me, she knew I'd call her first. She squeezed me in her arms and asked me how I was, without a single word of judgment or criticism. It was incredibly comforting. That's why I would have called her ahead of her sister even if she hadn't been a lawyer.

The police installed us in a little room and hit the timer. We cut short the gushing to avoid being overwhelmed by the emotion of it all, and I asked Lucie how everything would pan out, and in what order. After giving me a broad outline of all the procedures, the penny dropped.

"Oh, no! No, Papa, not a chance!" she protested.

"Why not? Come on: I'm in prison and my daughter's a lawyer . . . it makes perfect sense!"

"I might be a lawyer, but I can't be *your* lawyer!"

"Why, is it illegal?"

"No, it's not illegal, but . . ."

"But what?"

Lucie aimed a gentle smile at me that reminded me of her mother. Given the circumstances, this made me enormously depressed.

"Listen," she said with as much composure as possible, "I don't know if you realize, Papa, but what you did was really . . . disturbing."

She spoke to me as if I were a toddler. I pretended not to notice because at that stage in the conversation, it seemed a fair assessment on her part.

"It all depends on the charges the investigating magistrate decides to bring forward. At the very least, he'll get you for 'false imprisonment,' maybe 'aggravated,' and because you fired at the police—"

"I didn't fire at the police, I fired at the windows!"

"Yes, fine, but the police were on the other side of the windows, and that's known as 'armed assault against a police officer in the execution of his duty.'"

For someone who doesn't know the first thing about law, this was a terrifying expression. It raised just one question:

"So how long are we talking? Worst-case scenario . . ."

My throat was dry, as was my tongue, and I felt like my vocal cords were lined with sandpaper. Lucie stared at me for a moment. She had the hardest task, namely giving me a reality check. And she did it very well. My daughter is a mighty fine lawyer. She spoke slowly and clearly.

"What you did is about as serious as it gets, Papa. Worst-case scenario: thirty years in prison."

Until then, the number had been hypothetical. On Lucie's lips, it became real and terrifying.

"Any chance of a reduced sentence . . . ?"

"We're a long way from that, believe me." Lucie sighed.

Thirty years! She could tell that the prospect shattered me. Things had been desperate enough before, but this news finished me off. I must have seemed shrunken in my seat, and I couldn't hold back the tears. I knew I mustn't, because nothing is worse than seeing old men cry, but it was beyond my control.

Two days before the hostage taking, before throwing myself into the fray, I spent a mere hour weighing up the legal risks. I consulted two or three law books, reading them in the mad grip of my fury.

I knew I was embarking on something desperate, but the consequences were far less tangible than my anger.

As I gazed at Lucie, I felt convinced I would die in prison. And the look in her eyes indicated that she thought the same. Even half this sentence, a measly fifteen years, was unthinkable. How old would I be when I got out? Seventy-five? Eighty?

Even if I managed to avoid getting my face smashed in on a bimonthly basis, it would still be impossible.

I sobbed like a baby, and Lucie swallowed hard.

"We'll fight this, Papa. First, that's the maximum sentence, and there's nothing to say that the jury will . . ."

"What do you mean 'jury'? Won't I be tried by a magistrate?"

"Nooo, Papa."

She found my ignorance bewildering.

"Your actions mean you'll be tried by a judge in the high court."

"High court? But I'm not a murderer! I didn't kill anyone!"

My tears had reached the next level, fueled by my indignation. For Lucie, the situation was becoming more and more complicated.

"That's why you need a specialist. I've done some research and I've f—"

"I don't have the money to pay for a specialist."

I wiped my eyes with the back of my hand.

"We'll find the money."

"Oh yeah? How's that, then? Hold on, how about this for an idea: let's ask Mathilde and Gregory if we can dip into their savings!"

That pissed her off. I carried on:

"Forget it. It's fine, I'll defend myself."

"Don't even think about it! In this sort of case, naivety will only go one way: the maximum sentence."

"Lucie . . ."

I took her hand and stared her in the eye.

"If it's not you, it's me. No one else."

My daughter saw there was no point persisting. Her arguments would fall on deaf ears, and the realization left her despondent.

"Why are you asking me to do this, Papa?"

I'd calmed myself down. I had a huge advantage over her: I knew what I wanted. I wanted my daughter to be my lawyer. I'd thought of nothing else over the last few hours. As far as I could see, there was no other solution. My decision was made.

"I'm going to be sixty, Lucie. That is what's at stake for me—the rest of my time on this earth. I don't want that to be in the hands of someone I've never even met."

"But Papa, this isn't psychotherapy, it's a high court trial! You need a professional, a specialist!" she said, grappling for the words. "I don't know how it all works. The high court is . . . it's very particular. It's . . . it's . . ."

"Here's what I'm asking you, Lucie. If you don't want to, I understand, but if it's not you . . ."

"Yes, so you've said! This is blackmail!"

"Absolutely. I'm banking on you loving me enough to agree to help me. If I'm wrong, then please let me know!"

The tone settled as quickly as it escalated. We'd come to an impasse, neither of us saying anything. She blinked nervously. I thought she might back down. There was light in the tunnel. There was still a chance.

"I have to think about it, Papa, I can't give you an answer just like that . . ."

"Take your time, Lucie, there's no hurry."

But the truth is, there was a hurry. We needed to go through a whole lot of processes, and soon: the investigating magistrate will need to elect a suitable interlocutor, I'll need counsel to establish my line of defense, and several other grim complications besides.

"I'll think about it. I don't know . . ."

Lucie hit the buzzer. There was nothing left to discuss. We said our good-byes quickly. I don't think she had any hard feelings against me. Not yet, at least.

28

My case hit the headlines in no time. Even the eight o'clock news ran it, which wouldn't sit well with the investigating magistrate—they never take kindly to media exposure. Two days after my arrest, I'd hoped against hope that the spotlight on me would fade when the CEO of some big company wound up in prison for embezzling an eye-watering sum of money (he's in the same jail as me, but in the VIP wing). Maybe it's because guys like him are ten a euro cent nowadays, or just because their cases aren't considered that news-worthy anymore, but the diversion was short lived and the cameras were back on me soon enough. My story was more media-friendly than his. After all, more folk out there can identify with an unem-ployed guy blowing his fuse than with some bigwig who siphons off six times the value of his share options.

The press have treated my hostage taking like one of those nasty news items in which a teenager shoots up his school. They're mak-ing out as though I were in some sort of unemployment-induced stupor. A fanatic. Reporters rushed to question a few idiots on my street ("Oh, well, you know, he was an easygoing sort of neighbor.

If I'd had any idea . . ."); a few guys from work ("Oh, well, you know, he was an easygoing sort of colleague. If I'd had any idea . . ."); even my adviser from the job center ("Oh, well, you know, he was an easy-going sort of unemployed person. If I'd had any idea . . ."). It's funny to see such unanimity on the matter. It feels like you're attending your own funeral, or reading your own obituary.

On the Exxyal front, there's been plenty of noise, too, not least regarding the hero of the day, Crown Prince Paul Cousin. His display of courage did more than enough to restore the company's faith in him. He's back in the fold. Everything I'd dreamed of for myself. I can just picture him, already back at Sarqueville heading up a round of layoffs that will affect several hundred families. Perfect man for the job.

In front of the cameras he seemed genial enough, a bit like he'd been with me once the hostage taking was over: rigid, ruthless, upright. Never one to gush. He's like the epitome of an early Calvinist, or one of those puritans who set sail for the New World. Paul Cousin is to capitalism what Torquemada was to Catholicism. The Grim Reaper's got nothing on him. As I said, the perfect man for the job.

"We could not stand by and watch the workplace turn into a crime scene," he said to the camera. Just picture it: if every unemployed person were to take their potential employer hostage . . . Imagine. Tremble at the thought. His message was clear: senior executives like him are acutely aware of their duty, and any wrongdoer seeking to harm their employer can expect to find a Paul Cousin blocking the way. All a bit terrifying when you think about it.

Throughout, Alexandre Dorfmann has been taking an Oscar-winning turn as "The Victim." Sober, solemn, and greatly saddened by these horrific circumstances. Let it be known that Alexandre Dorfmann is a CEO full of humanity, a CEO who has stood shoulder to shoulder with his executives in the face of terror. He has shown himself to be stoic, which is no surprise, considering the burden of his responsibility. And had it behooved him to lay down his life for his employees, let there be no doubt: he would have done so gladly and without hesitation. As for me, he had some stern words. I threatened his senior executives, which is not something he could ever forgive. The underlying message was clear: business chiefs are not going to be jerked around by some unemployed middle manager, gun or no gun. They will never be defeated. All bodes well for the trial . . .

When he stared into the camera, I had the impression that Dorfmann was looking directly at me. There was another, deeper message he was communicating: "Delambre, taking me for a prick was a very bad idea, and I'm not about to wait thirty years to string you up by the balls." So all bodes well for the next few months behind bars, too . . .

Seeing him speak to me like that made me realize I'll be hearing from him very soon. Let's not dwell on that for now. Suffice to say that when it does happen, I have no idea how I'm going to escape unscathed.

Next up, the report focused on me, on my life, showing shots of the windows to our apartment and the entrance to our building. Our mailbox. It sounds silly, but the sight of our name written like that on the little yellowed label, which dates back almost to the time we moved, was painful. I imagined Nicole shut away inside the house, talking to our daughters on the telephone in tears.

The thought still tears my heart to pieces.

It's incredible how far apart we are.

Lucie has explained to Nicole what to do when she's bombarded by journalists on the telephone, in the *métro* station, at the supermarket, on the pavement, or the stairwell, the foyer at the resource center, the elevator. The bathrooms of her fucking cafeteria. Her view is that if we ignore them, the newspapers will leave us alone until the start of the trial, which shouldn't be for at least another eighteen months. When the date was announced, I reacted as bravely as possible. I've done my math. Take the most clement verdict, subtract any special remissions I might hope for, then subtract the time spent on remand. Even then, the resulting sentence is unthinkably long. My age has never seemed like such a threat.

Besides all that, the TV coverage has let me enjoy my fifteen minutes of fame in jail: people discuss my case, everyone expresses their opinion, I'm asked questions. There are a lot of know-it-alls in here. Some figure I'll have extenuating circumstances working in my favor, which amuses those of the opposite persuasion: that I'll be held up as an example to other unemployed people who might be tempted by an idea as absurd as mine. Everyone measures my situation against their own, factoring in all their hopes and fears, their pessimism or optimism. They each have their own definition of the word "lucidity."

Some people call this "preventive detention," and that seems about right: if you forget the endless forms of wheeling and dealing that go on in here, you're prevented from doing pretty much anything. The only thing they take a liberal attitude to are the numbers. Instead of the four hundred detainees there should be, there are seven hundred. If you take the exact figure, it works out at almost 3.8 prisoners per cell. In other words, you'd need a miracle to avoid sharing a two-man cell with three others. At the start, it was really tough: in eight weeks, I changed cells or cellmates eleven times. Who would have thought that such a sedentary population could be so unstable? I've had a bit of everything: psychos, loonies, depressives, fatalists, armed robbers, junkies, suicide risks, druggy-suicide risks . . . It's like a trailer for what prison has in store for me.

The spirit of enterprise is alive and well. Everything here is bought, sold, swapped, exchanged, and valued. Jail is a nonstop marketplace for basic valuables. My flattened snout taught me a lesson: since then, I haven't kept anything, cutting my wardrobe down to two unspeakably ugly outfits that I wear on alternate weeks. I'm keeping a low profile.

Charles is my adviser. Apart from the girls (by which I mean Nicole and Lucie), he was the first to make contact with me. My letters to Charles arrive in three days tops, but when he writes to me, it takes at least a couple of weeks—his letter has to be screened by the investigating magistrate's office, which lets it through in its own sweet time. I picture my pal Charles in his car, pad resting on the steering wheel. The image of him deep in concentration comes naturally. The effort must be monumental. In his first letter, he wrote: "If you answer don't feel you have to but just tell me if Morisset is still there Georges Morisset he's a good guy I knew him from my time inside."

Reading Charles's literary output is much like listening to him speak. Free of punctuation, extremely long-winded stream-of-consciousness stuff.

A little later on, he wrote: "I will come and see you soon it's not that I can't where there's a will there's a way and all that but it brings back awful memories so I'd rather not but I do want to see you so I'll come anyway." The advantage to his prose style is that you can follow his line of thought nice and easily.

The Georges Morisset he mentions has one of the best reputations of all the guards. He has gradually worked his way up the rungs of the penitentiary ladder. I told Charles he'd been made a prison officer, and in his last letter he wrote: "Morisset officer doesn't surprise me cause he's a workhorse he's hungry and he's got the talent you'll see he's not going to leave it at that I wouldn't be surprised if he makes senior officer at the next round of exams you'll see."

There were a few other admiring lines. Charles was ecstatic about the meteoric rise of Officer Morisset. Of course it took going to jail myself to find out that my best friend—my only friend, in fact—had been locked up twice himself. And this was the very place he'd been remanded the first time. I have so far resisted the urge to ask him what he did.

In one of his letters, he also wrote: "As I know the lay of the land sort of I can help you see how it works cause at the start it's definitely hard and you're at a bit of a loss and maybe when you arrive you get smacked in the face so when you know things sometimes you can manage to avoid the most shitty problems."

This offer was timely, since I'd just been given two extra stitches beneath my left eyebrow following a contretemps (of the sexual sort, this time) in the showers with a somewhat simpleminded body builder who hadn't been turned off by my age. Charles is now my mentor, and I follow his advice to the absolute letter.

The advice about the clothes was one of his, along with a stack of other little things that have, by turn, let me: hold on to the best part of my lunch; not stray inadvertently into any of the different factions' "restricted areas," whose size and location seem to vary according to a baffling set of rules and customs; not be robbed of items the second I buy them; and not be flipped out of my bunk by new inmates too quickly.

Prompted by the news that I'd already had my face smashed in twice, Charles also explained that the worst thing of all was to be seen as a punching bag, the sort of guy you can rough up: "You will need to put a stop to that and reverse the tide and to do that there are two solutions first crack the biggest guy on your wing in the face or if you can't do that no offense but maybe that'll be the case with you then find protection from someone who can get you some respect."

Charles is right. These might be chimpanzee tactics, but that's how prison works. I've been keeping this in mind and have started trying to butter up the big guns in the hope that one of them will offer me protection.

First up I set my heart on Bébétâ. He's a guy of about thirty who must have been lobotomized at a very young age, with the result that he functions exclusively in binary mode. When he's pumping iron, he can only process two instructions: up/down. If he's eating: chew/swallow. Walking: right foot/left foot. Et cetera. He's waiting to be sentenced for beating a Romanian pimp to death (fist forward/ fist back). He must be about six foot six, and if you removed all his bones, there'd still be almost three hundred pounds of muscle. Inter- acting with him requires a scientific approach that borrows from the field of animal cognition. I have made preliminary contact, so he can register my face, a process that might take several weeks. I'm not even holding out hope that he'll remember my name. These initial moves have gone well. I've managed to effect a preliminary reflex: he smiles when he sees me. But it's going to be a long, long road.

For some reason, Charles's words about Officer Morisset kept simmering away in the background. At various points in the day, I would catch myself thinking about him, or notice him walking past my cell or in the yard during exercise time. He's about fifty years old, strongly built despite a slight paunch, and you get the feeling he's been at the prison for a while, and that if push came to shove, he wouldn't be afraid of a confrontation. He surveys everything with a keen eye. I even saw him reprimand Bébétâ once, who must be three times his weight. There was something in his manner with the big guy, his way of explaining to him what he was unhappy about, that intrigued me. Even Bébétâ can grasp that this is a man who breathes authority. That was when I had the idea.

I hotfooted it to the library and tracked down the details of the competitive examinations for becoming a senior prison officer. I checked that my intuition wasn't leading me up the garden path and that my plan had a vague chance of success.

"So, Officer, these exams . . . ? Not easy, from what I hear."

It was the following day, in the yard. The weather was nice, the inmates calm, and Morisset didn't seem the sort to throw his baton about. He smokes light cigarettes with meticulous concentration, as if each one is worth four times his annual salary. He holds his fag between thumb and index finger, cupping it with an almost maternal devotion. Quite odd, really.

"No, not easy," he answered, drawing delicately on the filter, where a little fleck of ash had settled.

"And what have you chosen for the written part: general dissertation or executive summary?"

That made him look up from his cigarette.

"How do you know about all that?"

"Oh, I know these civil service exams well. I've coached people preparing for them for years. All the government departments: health, labor, local authorities . . . The courses are all pretty similar—the core issues don't vary much."

I was worried I'd overplayed my hand with the "core issues" bit. Too impatient. I almost bit my lip, but I managed to restrain myself. The officer returned to his cigarette and kept silent for a long while. Then, smoothing over the fold in the paper with a fingernail, he said:

"You know what, I do struggle with the executive summary . . ."

Bingo! Delambre, you're a genius. You may well be looking at thirty big ones, but you've still got it when it comes to manipulation. All those years of management have really paid off. I let a few seconds pass before saying:

"I hear you. The problem is, almost every candidate chooses the dissertation. Because almost every candidate is the same as you—they're afraid of the executive summary element. So basically, if you play the percentage game, you can stand out in the eyes of the examiners. The numbers would work in your favor. And what's even better is that the executive summary, once you get the hang of it, is far more straightforward than the dissertation. It's more clear-cut."

This gave Officer Morisset plenty to think about. I had to be careful not to take him for a fool: I wouldn't gain anything by pushing him and risk losing the little ground I'd made. So I said:

"Well, best of luck, Officer."

And off I went into the courtyard. I'd hoped he would call me back, but nothing. The bell sounded, and after falling in line with the others, I turned to see that Morisset had disappeared.

29

In summer it gets very hot in prison. The air doesn't circulate, bodies sweat, the atmosphere grows heavy, electric, and the men become even more aggressive. Prison life has started to gnaw away at me like a cancer. I don't know how I'm going to endure the misery of finishing my days here.

Twice a week I go and correct Officer Morisset's executive summaries. He works like a Trojan. Every Tuesday and Thursday, he uses three hours of his time off to do his homework under exam conditions. Luckily for me, he's still way off the money, and his technique is appalling. He's fallen for the whole thing about making him stand out from his rival candidates.

The last topic I gave him was about the state of prisons in France. No less an authority than the European Committee for the Prevention of Torture had published a report on our prisons. When I handed it to him, he asked if I was mocking him, even though he knows full well that this is the sort of thing that might come up in the exam. I take care to drip-feed my pointers nice and slowly so that he requires my services for as long as possible. He's more than happy with the setup. Twice a week, he summons me to his office and we work on technique. I give him plans, advising him on how to structure his summaries. He doesn't get any support from the administration, so he's bought a flip chart and some felt-tips out of his own pocket. We work in two-hour sessions. When I leave his office, the other inmates joke around and ask me whether I've taken it up the ass from him or just sucked him off, but it doesn't bother me: Officer Morisset is respected, everyone knows where they stand with him. Most importantly, though, I've found my protection. For the moment.

Lucie was a good call, too. She's very proactive. There have obviously been a few issues with the investigating magistrate, who's a little skeptical about seeing such an inexperienced lawyer taking a case to the high court. She must be putting the hours in, because at every meeting with the magistrate she has the answer to any question put to her, expressing her views clearly, taking endless notes, and citing case law. Plus her face looks almost as tired as mine, even though we've still got months and months to go. The slow pace of the investigation suits her because it means she can keep up to speed. She's enlisted the support of a certain lawyer, Maître Sainte-Rose, and speaks about him regularly. If I express any doubt or start quibbling, she invokes him like some incontrovertible authority—must be a bigwig. He may well know his stuff, but he's not my lawyer. To him, my case is nothing but theory. Anyway, apparently he's got lots of experience and knows what he's doing. I'd be grateful if he could throw some of his legal jargon at the co-prisoner in the canteen who insists on devouring half my tray while his two cronies look on indifferently.

Lucie is going to an extraordinary amount of trouble. She's working even harder than when she was training, and she's never been under so much pressure.

She alone can save her father. It reads like a tragedy. And I trust no one but her, which is a drama in itself.

What's worrying her is the Pharmaceutical Logistics kerfuffle.

"The prosecution will be quick to point out that you floored your supervisor—head-butted him, no less—just a few days before taking these people hostage. He was off work for ten days. You'll come across as a violent man."

Hardly a shocking revelation to a guy who held twelve people at gunpoint with a loaded Beretta . . .

"Depends on your approach," I suggest.

"There is a chance," she says, flicking through her yellow folder, "that we'll go down the Logistics route. It would all be much easier if your former employer withdrew their claim. Sainte-Rose says . . ."

"They'll never agree. They even extracted a formal apology from me, the vampires. They're the sort who'll bleed a corpse dry before ditching it . . ."

Lucie has found the document she was looking for:

"Maître Gilson," she says.

"Yeeees . . ."

"Maître Christelle Gilson?"

"Maybe, I don't know, we were never that close . . ."

"Well, I was . . ."

I look at her.

"She was a friend of mine in college."

My heart skips a beat.

"A good friend?"

"Yes, best friends, in fact. Close enough to 'borrow' each other's boyfriends," Lucie says, grimacing.

"Who borrowed whose boyfriend?"

"I borrowed hers."

"You can't be serious . . . You didn't!"

"Oh, I'm sorry, Papa, but at the time I didn't know my father was planning on becoming a gun-toting maniac and that I'd need to defend him at the high court!"

"Okay, okay!" I say, holding up my hands in surrender. Lucie calms down.

"Anyway, I did her a favor. That guy was a complete jerk."

"Yes, but he was her jerk . . ."

This is a perfect example of the sorts of conversations Lucie and I have.

"Well then," she says. "I guess I'll have to pay her a visit."

Lucie explains that if she manages to convince her ex–best friend to mediate on her client's behalf to drop the charges and the damages claim, then I'll need to try the same tactic with Romain, our key witness. I hold my tongue. I make out that I understand, but for the moment, I'd prefer it if Romain was still officially an adversary. Keep it under wraps that he gave me a massive helping hand. It mustn't get out that he was complicit.

Over the course of our conversations, Lucie gives me news about her mother, who is terribly lonely. Early on I managed to call her on the phone. Lucie tells me she's worried because I don't anymore. I pretend that it's harder now, but the fact is that when I call Nicole, just hearing her voice makes me want to cry. It's unbearable.

Lucie informs me that her sister will be visiting soon. I don't believe it for a second. But it unsettles me, because I'm dreading the moment I have to confront her.

It's not easy to feel so ashamed in front of your children.

I have decided to start writing my story. It hasn't been easy, because it takes concentration, and wherever you are in this place, the TV is blaring all day long. At 8:00 p.m. it's a fucking racket, with everyone switching on their favorite news show at full volume. The headlines overlap and become virtually incomprehensible. France 2 (*With annual salaries of 1.85 million euros, French CEOs are the best paid in Europe*) vies with TF1 (*Unemployment is expected to reach 10 percent by the end of the year*). It's a complete shambles, but at least it gives you the overall picture.

It's almost impossible to escape the endless torrent of series, clips, and game shows. They drill into your head and follow you everywhere you go. Television ends up as part of your being. I don't get along well with earplugs, so I've bought a pair of real noise-deadening ear protectors. I forgot to specify a color, so I've ended up with a bright-orange set, which makes me look like one of those people who directs planes at the airport. The guys call me the "air traffic controller," but it doesn't bother me . . . I work better with them.

I'm not a great writer—always been better at speaking rather than writing. (My hope is that this skill will come in handy at the trial, even though Lucie tells me I have to let her do all the talking and that I can only say what I've learned by heart in the run-up to the hearings.) I'm not writing my memoirs, I'm merely trying tell my story. Mainly for Mathilde's sake, though I'm doing it for Nicole, too, since she doesn't understand the full extent of it. And for Lucie, because not even she knows everything. Seeing it in on paper, it's unbelievable how mundane I find my story. It is original, though, I'll give it that. Not everyone turns up to a job interview with a fully loaded Beretta.

Maybe that's a shame in itself. Surely one or two people have thought about it.

30

Ever since my arrival, and since Alexandre Dorfmann's first appearance on TV the day after the hostage taking, I've found the lack of word from Exxyal dispiriting.

It doesn't feel right. There's no way they can stay quiet for months on end.

Those were my exact thoughts when the word finally did arrive, as I was heading into the laundry room at about 10:00 this morning.

The inmate in charge took my bundle and disappeared into the bowels of the room.

A few seconds later, he was replaced by the hulking Bébétâ. I smiled at him and raised my right hand, as if I were taking an oath, which had become my way of greeting him. But my mind started racing when the figure of Boulon emerged from behind him. The guy they call Boulon is much smaller than Bébétâ, but infinitely more disturbing. A real sicko. He gets his nickname from the bolts he fires from his weapon of choice, a slingshot: a highly sophisticated piece of equipment with a tubular elastic armrest, which he likes to load with stones. But bolts are his favorite. When he was a free man, he carried bolts of every size around in his various pockets, and could hit targets dead-on from incredible distances. His final exploit was to bury a 13mm bolt right in the middle of a man's forehead from fifty yards. The bolt lodged itself in the center of his brain—a nice clean shot. He is known to have committed countless unspeakable acts but boasts that he's never spilled a drop of blood. Deep down, despite appearances, maybe he does have some heart.

As soon as I saw him emerge alongside Bébétâ in the laundry room, I realized I was about to receive some news from my ex–future employer. I turned to flee but Bébétâ's outstretched arm grabbed me by the shoulder. I tried to scream but in a fraction of a second he had spun me around and pinned me against him, his hand across my mouth like a gag. He lifted me off the ground without any effort whatsoever and squeezed me tight. I flailed my arms and legs in every direction as I tried to cry out. These men were going to kill me, I knew it. My efforts were in vain. Bébétâ carried me as though I were a living-room cushion. We were behind the counter, between the rows of sheets and blankets. He tried to put me down but I was so terrified that my legs couldn't bear my weight, and he had to support me. I carried on screaming with his hand over my mouth, emitting an inhuman wail in which I couldn't even recognize my own voice. I was like a car at the junkyard waiting to get crushed. Bébétâ held my head in place with one arm, still gagging me, and with the other he grabbed my left wrist and thrust it toward Boulon, who stared at me calmly, not saying a word. I thrashed my elbows, arms, legs, but all resistance was futile. I kept trying to scream. It was an utterly desperate situation. I felt appallingly alone. I was willing to give anything, to surrender. Anything. Nicole's face suddenly flashed before me. I held on to her image, but the Nicole before me was crying, about to watch me suffer and die as her tears fell. I tried to beg but no sound came from my mouth. Everything was happening in my head. Boulon said:

"I have a message for you."

That was it.

A message.

Bébétâ forced my hand flat on a shelf. Boulon took my thumb and snapped it back on itself. The pain was searing. I screamed. I felt like I was going mad. I tried to fight back, kicking my feet everywhere, especially behind me to make Bébétâ loosen his grip a bit, but Boulon had already taken my index finger and snapped it back, too. He grasped the finger and bent it until it reached the back of my hand. It made a sinister sound. The pain was blinding, nausea overwhelmed me, and I vomited, but Bébétâ kept hold of me, as if the capacity to be disgusted didn't enter his excuse for a brain. When Boulon took my third finger, I fainted. I think I fainted. But no, I was still conscious when the next finger was snapped back, sending an electric shock right through me. I couldn't even scream—I was well beyond that. My body was like a wet rag in Bébétâ's vise-like grip. I was sweating like a forsaken soul. I think that was when I shit myself. But Boulon wasn't finished. There were still two fingers. I thought the pain would kill me. It was so complete I thought I was going mad. Waves of it ran from my head to my feet; even the agony was wild and panic stricken. When Boulon did the little finger, the last one, my mind fled, my stomach churned, and it hurt so badly I wanted to die. Bébétâ let me go, and I collapsed to the ground screaming. I tried to clasp my hand. I couldn't even hold it against me, couldn't even touch it. I wailed. I was nothing but a giant surge of pain. I could no longer control myself—I'd been undone.

Boulon leaned down to me and, his voice still calm, said:

"That's the message."

I don't know what happened next because I fainted.

When I woke up, my hand was swollen like a pumped-up football. I was still crying, stretched out on a bed in the infirmary. I don't think I'd stopped crying since they'd taken me.

The pain was terrible, terrible, terrible.

I turned onto my side and curled up like a baby, my bandaged hand pressed into the hollow of my stomach. I cried. I was afraid. Horribly afraid. I didn't want that. I must get out of here. I don't want to die here.

Not like that.

Not here.

31

The good thing about prison is that the hospital stints are short. Four days. Reduced service. My disarticulated metacarpophalangeals, fractures, and dislocations were operated on and reset by a perfectly pleasant surgeon (as pleasant as the surgeon species permits, at least).

Several months of splints and casts lie ahead before I can expect a return to normality, something the specialist thinks unlikely anyway. I will live with the aftereffects.

As I come into my cell, a young man stands up and holds out his hand. He can't resist a smile as he notices the mass of bandages and offers me the other one. We shake the wrong way around—great start.

The only thing I want is to lie down.

Until yesterday, my hand was giving me unbearable shooting pains, and the nurse didn't have any painkillers that were sufficiently powerful. Either that or he didn't want to give them to me. Officer Morisset didn't just secure me a transfer, he brought me some tramadol, too. It makes me drowsy, but at least it eases the pain and lets me sleep every now and then. Morisset assured me they'll open an inquiry and told me I must hand over the names of my attackers, but he didn't even wait for an answer before leaving my cell.

Jérôme, my new roomie, is a professional conman of about thirty. He's got a handsome face, wavy hair, a reassuringly natural bearing, and if you picture him in a suit, he'd be the consummate executive. Face on, he's your bank manager; from behind, your real estate agent; right-hand side, your new GP; and from the left, your childhood friend who's nailing it as a stockbroker. He's got fewer qualifications than a shepherd from Sierra Leone, but he is very well spoken and has bags of personality and charisma. There's a bit of the young Bertrand Lacoste about him, perhaps by virtue of the fact they're both crooks. Since I have more than twenty years of management experience, we get along pretty well despite the age difference. He's a talented guy. Not talented enough to avoid prison, but a wily one nonetheless. He already has plenty on his CV: dozens of forged checks, tons of imaginary commodities sold for cash, genuine fake documents traded for an absolute fortune, fictitious jobs complete with bribes and state subsidies, and even shares transferred to foreign markets. What landed him in here was the presale of some nonexistent apartments just north of the Riviera—property of a hitherto-unseen luxury, quite literally in this case. He explained the whole ruse, but it was all far too clever for me. The guy is loaded. He could buy anything he wanted (well, with the exception of his freedom). His line of work must have been lucrative. I feel like a hobo by comparison.

I don't say anything.

Jérôme observes my head and my right hand, which is still very swollen indeed. He wants to know how I managed to get myself into such a fucking mess. It intrigues him. He's sniffing out a good business opportunity. I have to be careful of what I say and how I say it; what I don't say and how I don't say it.

My encounter with Boulon and Bébétâ has left me with post-traumatic stress, and I am terrified the moment I leave my cell. I scan my surroundings with apprehension, watching my back and all around me, permanently on the lookout. From a distance, I see Boulon going about his business, his dealings. He turns but doesn't seem to notice me. As far as he's concerned, I'm nothing but another transaction. I won't exist in his eyes until he receives a new order, at which point the only question he'll ask himself is how far he'll have to go, and whether he'll be paid enough for it. As for Bébétâ, when we cross paths he smiles, raises his hand with the palm facing me, the way I showed him, delighted to say hello to me, as if pulverizing each finger on one of my hands had somehow created a new emotional bond between us. What happened in the laundry room has already been driven out of the hole at the top of his spinal cord that serves as a brain.

Jérôme doesn't find me at all talkative. He, on the other hand, is extremely chatty. He needs to talk all the time. My thoughts are dark (possibly a side effect of my medication), and I obsess about the "message." The thing that worries me, of course, is the follow-up. That was the essence of the message: this is just the beginning.

Good Lord, I have absolutely no idea what to do.

Right from the start, I've been acting without any real notion of how this will finish. I'm improvising. I react when I'm staring a situation in the face.

I got a fist right between the eyes the second I arrived, but afterward I found Officer Morisset and earned his protection. They broke my fingers, but I managed to get a transfer into a two-man cell in a safer section.

At worst, I'll have to endure my fate.

At best, I'll manage to shorten my sentence.

But fundamentally, from the moment I realized that Exxyal was screwing me over, when I discovered that everything I'd done to get a job had been in vain, that I'd stolen my daughter's money for nothing . . . ever since I felt myself overwhelmed by that dark fury, I have been reacting, trying hard to come up with solutions, but without ever having an overarching strategy. No plan that could factor in the consequences. I'm no crook. I've got no idea what to do.

I'm in a real bind.

The fact is that if I had had a broad strategy, and it had brought me here, then at least I could say I'd had a strategy, albeit a piss-poor one.

The first message has very much arrived. What now?

One thing is for sure: I must find a way to prevent the second message from reaching me.

Curiously enough, it's the psychiatrist charged with my assessment who sets me on the right track.

He's fifty, and a proper, open kind of guy, despite all the buzz-words. Every sentence he utters is infused with meaning, betraying a lofty opinion of his function. While none of it rings false, the problem with my case is that it's pretty self-explanatory. You just need to put my file next to my CV and there's your diagnosis. I don't go to too many pains to convince him of what he already knows.

What does strike me is the question he uses to kick off the session: "If you were to tell me your life story, what would you say first?"

After the interview, I launch myself wholeheartedly into my work.

As I can't write, I ask Jérôme to help: I dictate, he writes, I reread, he corrects. It's going fairly quickly, though never quick enough for me. I'm trying to disguise the fact that I've entered a race against the clock.

If everything goes according to plan, the manuscript will be done in four or five days. I embellish my adventure, making no shortage of additions and inserting plenty of symbolic violence. I write in the first person, and I mix up the tenses to give it impact and pace.

And then I look into which newspapers might be interested.

Relations with Nicole have become strained. She is very depressed, living in a precarious state of limbo, and can see me getting the full sentence. She is lonely and in a terrible state, and there's nothing I can do for her.

She came to visit last week.

"I'm selling the apartment," she said. "I'll send you the paper-work. You have to sign it and send it straight back."

"Sell the apartment? Why?" I said, stunned.

"Your trial against your former employer is about to start, and I want to be able to pay damages if it comes to it."

"We're not there yet!"

"No, but we will be. And anyway, I don't need it—it's too big for me on my own."

It was the first time I'd heard Nicole so clearly state the incon-trovertible fact that I would never be coming back to live with her. I didn't know what to say. I could tell she was sad to have resigned herself to that truth.

"And then there are the legal fees," she continued, clouding the issue.

"But there are hardly any fees—we're not paying for a lawyer!"

Nicole seemed utterly dismayed, I wasn't sure why.

"Alain, I know things can't be easy for you here, but seriously, you've lost all sense of reality!"

I must have looked confused by these words.

"*I don't want Lucie working for nothing,*" Nicole said, hammering the point home. "I want her to be paid. She's quit her job to defend you, using her savings to replace the salary she's lost. And . . ."

"And what?"

After everything I've been through . . .

"And Maître Sainte-Rose is expensive," Nicole persisted. "Very expensive. And I don't want her to keep on paying."

This shocked me. First Mathilde, now Lucie plunged into debt by their father.

I couldn't look her in the eye any longer, and she couldn't look into mine.

Lucie's approach with Maître Gilson, her ex-pal from the univer-sity, has clearly been unsuccessful. Lucie didn't offer anything in exchange. All she did was ask for a bit of goodwill and clemency. No matter how much I told her that these were not qualities that

Pharmaceutical Logistics possessed in spades, she couldn't resist trying her luck. Lucie is a very good lawyer, but she's also naive. Must be a family trait. As it happened, the conversation soon turned to humiliation. Lucie's old friend seemed to revel in this opportunity for revenge, as if a simple refusal from her client weren't enough, and without showing the faintest compassion for what I'm going through and what I have at stake. As if stealing someone's boyfriend was really on a par with consigning a sexagenarian to thirty years in prison. It defied belief. In short, Lucie now wants me to approach Romain. If he agrees not to testify, Logistics will lose their only witness, which she figures will bring their whole case crashing down. She would then step into the breach and get all the charges dropped. I find it a bit silly to focus on this issue when I'm headed for the high court, but it seems that Sainte-Rose, her henchman, is adamant about this.

"He wants to clean up the case," Lucie explains to me. "We have to present you as a peaceable person. Show that you're not a violent man at all."

A nonviolent, Beretta-wielding man.

Terrific.

Anyway, I promise to send Romain a letter, or ask Charles to pay him a visit to talk about it, but I know I won't do anything of the kind. To the contrary: all my fortunes, not to mention Romain's safety, hinge on everyone regarding him as my foe.

32

Yesterday I found out that the second message was arriving.

I didn't sleep a wink.

"Visits" are announced the day before, but you're never told who's coming. Sometimes it's a surprise, and not always a pleasant one.

As is the case with me this morning. It's the messenger, I'm sure of it. Nicole isn't meant to be coming this week, and I gave up expecting Mathilde weeks ago. Lucie is welcome anytime (the procedure is different for lawyers). And anyway, she's working far too hard on my case right now to have any time to visit.

It's exactly 10:00 a.m.

We're standing in line in the corridor waiting for our names to be called. Some are excited, others despondent. As for me, I'm shit scared. Feverish. That was the word chosen by Jérôme, my main con man, when he saw me leave the cell. An inmate I know is staring at me. He's worried for me. So he should be.

David Fontana is wearing a suit and tie. Almost smart. If I didn't know what he was capable of, I'd think he was just a normal middle manager. He's a lot more than that. Even sitting in a chair, he's threatening. The sort of guy who picks Boulon as his messenger, though he'd much rather do the job himself given half a chance.

His eyes are gleaming. He hardly ever blinks.

His presence fills the atmosphere of the tiny booth, behind which a guard passes every forty seconds. Fontana radiates terrifying levels of power and violence. He could kill me with his bare hands in the interval between the guard's rounds, no doubt about it.

Just seeing him brings back the sound of my snapping fingers, and a shiver runs down my spine.

I sit down opposite him, and he smiles at me calmly. I'm not wearing a bandage anymore, but my fingers are still very swollen, and the ones that were fractured are still being supported in grubby splints. I look like someone who's had a terrible accident.

"So you received my message, Monsieur Delambre?"

His voice is cold, abrupt. I wait. Don't make him angry. Let him come to you. Play for time. But most of all—most of all—don't do anything to annoy him; don't make him give Boulon and Bébétâ the order to drag me into the workshop and crush my head in a vise.

"I say 'my message.' I really mean my client's message," Fontana corrects himself.

Sounds like there's been a change of client. Exit Bertrand Lacoste. The great consultant has been tried, tested, and found wanting. His little Polish intern has cast him into the abyss, and he's not getting out anytime soon. It doesn't look pretty for the Lord High Head-hunter. He needs to think long and hard about his fall from grace, and remember that you can never be too wary of the small fish, the mediocre ones. His ingenious hostage taking idea was an HR catastrophe of historic proportions. Exxyal will make sure everyone knows it. His career path has taken a major detour, and his firm's future looks about as rosy as mine.

So exit Lacoste, enter The Mikado. Alexandre Dorfmann himself is in the seat. Ex officio.

We're in a new category, now. Until now it's been the semiprofessionals—now we're into the big time.

The difference in approach between Lacoste and Dorfmann is immediately noticeable. The former makes promises about jobs, so no real consequences there. The latter engages Fontana, who deploys Bébêtâ and Boulon like a commando. Dorfmann will have said: "I don't want to know details." The gloves are off, but his hands are going to stay clean. Not that Fontana will mind: the need for total discretion in this operation means he can triple his fee, plus it gives him *carte blanche* to run things his own way (and I've already had a taste of what that entails).

Fontana waits as I piece the puzzle together. With the fake hostage taking for Exxyal, his role was largely organizational. Now he's in his element. He seems at ease taking me to task, like an athlete returning to the track after a niggling injury.

Did I receive his message? You don't say . . .

I swallow hard and nod in silence.

Not that the words would come anyway. Seeing him reminds me of my anger, of Exxyal, Bertrand Lacoste—everything that's landed me here in this mess. The vision of Fontana pouncing at me, teeth bared, comes flooding back. If he'd had the chance to kill me then, he would have done it. But he just hobbled to the window, his leg bleeding. Here in the visiting room, I can smell the cordite again, and in my hand I can feel the cold, heavy weapon I used to shoot the windows. I wish I still had that gun in my hand; wish I could hold it in my outstretched arm and slam two bullets into Fontana's head. But he's not here to get himself killed by my fury. He's here to take back what little I've won.

"Little . . . ?" he asks. "I hope you're joking!"

So here we are.

I don't move.

"We'll get on to that, but first, congratulations, Monsieur Delambre. Very nice move. Really, very fine work. I certainly fell for it . . ."

The admiring tone was at odds with his expression. His lips are pursed, his eyes boring into mine. Subliminal messages are oozing from every pore, and I'm picking up on each and every one of them.

They all revolve around the same theme: I'm going to crush you like a piece of shit.

"A rookie would say that you'd planned everything well, but I think the exact opposite. Otherwise you wouldn't be here . . . You're not a strategist. You're improvising, making it up as you go along. You should never do that, Monsieur Delambre," he says, wagging his finger. "Never."

I'm itching to remind him that his magnificent planning didn't prevent his hostage taking from going belly-up. But I'm spending all my energy on giving nothing away: poker face. My heart is beating at a hundred miles an hour. I hate him with an intensity that scares me. The man is capable of sending murderers to my cell, even at night.

"Although, that said," he continues, "for an improvisation, it was a decent performance, I must admit. It took me a while to figure it out. And of course, by the time I did figure it out, it was too late. Well, I say 'too late' . . . We'll make up for the lost time, Monsieur Delambre. You can be sure of that."

I don't even flinch, breathing from my stomach. Not a movement—mustn't let any emotion show. Stony eyed.

"Monsieur Guéneau was the first man you interrogated. That was your stroke of luck, I think. Because, despite appearances," he says, with a sweeping gesture that takes in the surrounding décor, "you have had some luck, Monsieur Delambre. Until today, that is."

I swallow hard.

"If Monsieur Guéneau had been interrogated later," Fontana continues, "your plan would have worked, but I'm not sure you would have gone through with it. You would have weighed up the situation more carefully. And ultimately, you wouldn't have risked it . . . But it was served up to you on a plate, so you couldn't help yourself. You couldn't resist the temptation. Do you remember how scared he was, Monsieur Guéneau?"

Jean-Marc Guéneau, eyes darting all over the place. I picture him sitting bolt upright as the young Arab fired him questions. And next to me, Lacoste's turkey, who . . .

But Fontana was front row for all that.

"Monsieur Guéneau's interrogation went badly wrong. You saw Mademoiselle Rivet wasn't up to the mark with her clumsy questions. She lost her footing, never managed to assert herself, and sure enough, Monsieur Guéneau started having his doubts, thrashing his head from side to side, not quite figuring out the game. The whole thing was seconds away from collapsing on itself. Then you decided to intervene . . ."

I remember approaching the microphone. And a few minutes later, Monsieur Guéneau had stripped down to his red-lace lingerie and was sobbing. Then he fell on the gun and swallowed the barrel.

"The man was desperate. You might not be much of a forward-planner, but you're not short of intuition."

There's that admiring tone again. Fontana's main aim is to shatter the icy wall I've put up against him. He's trying every trick in the book.

"You ruined him. He was willing to sell out his company, hand it to you on a plate. He was willing to give you anything: financial secrets, hidden deals, slush funds . . . And that's what you were hoping for."

True, that was what I was waiting for, even if I wasn't expecting it to come so quickly. And the fact that the first man to be interrogated was the one I'd been banking on was indeed a stroke of luck.

He had sat down at the desk indicated by the commando leader and plugged his Blackberry into the laptop computer before logging into the Exxyal Europe system.

He clicked once, twice, and opened the finance folder.

I waited a few seconds, watching him very closely.

He entered his personal passwords: the first, then the second.

I was looking out for that classic bit of body language that we all exhibit when our password is accepted. When the path is open at last and you can finally get to work, a minute reflex in the hands and shoulders that represents release.

"Then you stood up, and you said: 'Bastard.' Although I haven't stopped wondering whether I misheard and it was actually plural: 'bastards'?"

I don't move.

He carries on:

"The rest was all for show. You were terrified by what you were doing, and that played into your hands. Your fear was your trump card. Because your emotions were genuine, your terror was genuine—what you were doing took serious balls. Everyone read your fear at face value: an exec goes ballistic and ends up staging a spontaneous hostage taking. Of course he's scared! But the whole point was that this was a diversion."

I lined up the hostages, following Kaminski's instructions to the letter. I frisked them, spinning them around clockwise, fingers fully splayed. With my back to the door, I shot at the windows . . .

"And finally, the opportunity came to you through Monsieur Cousin. Ah, how he wanted to be the hero of the day, that guy! But if he hadn't provided you with your chance, it would have been someone else. It didn't matter to you. My cameo could have given you your opportunity—the only reason you repelled me was to give weight to your 'plan.' By that point, all you wanted was to fail. That's what no one could understand."

Paul Cousin, the specter. The color of chalk. He got to his feet and squared up to me. He was perfect. Precisely what I needed, it's true. When he intervened, he was the epitome of the company's values. Like a genre painting: *Outraged executive making a stand against Adversity.*

"You needed to appear defeated. That way you could keep us contained. You could pretend you were giving up and surrendering. Ultimately, you could do what you were planning from the start: go and tuck yourself away in the other room, where the laptop was still logged on thanks to Monsieur Guéneau. Open goal. The hostage taking gave you free rein over Exxyal's accounts. All you had to do was sit down, tap the keyboard, and help yourself."

David Fontana stops. He seems genuinely impressed. There's something fishy about his admiration—it's going to cost me dearly. It's intended to cost me . . .

"Ten million euros, Monsieur Delambre! You weren't messing around!"

I'm stunned.

Not even his client is telling him the truth.

I took 13.2 million.

I can't help but let the mask slip a little, and a glimmer of a smile crosses my lips. By now Fontana is over the moon:

"Bravo, Monsieur Delambre. No, really, bravo! I couldn't care less about the technical details. According to the IT specialist who examined the leak, you arranged a transfer to an offshore account without leaving a trace."

It was actually a lot cleverer than that.

When I left the hostages and sat down at the laptop, I only had fifteen minutes to spare, and my computer skills are minimal, to say the least. I know how to do spreadsheets and word processing. But anything beyond that? Well, I do know how to insert a USB stick and send an e-mail. Romain told me that would be enough. He'd worked almost thirty hours straight to sort everything out. The software he'd installed on the USB stick did all the hard work as soon as it was plugged in. Once I'd given him the access, it took Romain (working from his desktop at home) less than four minutes to release a Trojan horse into the Exxyal system. The malware he installed would allow him to reenter the system during business hours: enough time to access their accounts, secure the transfer to a tax haven, then delete every trace.

Fontana was right on this one point—the details don't affect the result.

"Especially well played, given you're acting with total impunity. Cleaning out an oil company's slush fund, one that's used for paying out bribes and kickbacks here, there, and everywhere . . . You can be sure they won't press charges against you."

No reaction.

He doesn't have the whole story, but he's got most of it.

The details don't matter at all.

Fontana doesn't budge. The seconds tick on.

"But ultimately, despite appearances, you haven't thought about a thing. What you did was motivated by pure anger. You took off with the cash, ran for forty yards, then stopped. And now here we are sitting opposite each other, Monsieur Delambre. What a miscalculation . . . In all honesty, I find it a complete mystery. Well, I have my theories. I don't think you were out to benefit yourself by taking this money. You're keeping it warm for your little family, not for yourself. After a hostage taking like that, you can't be under any illusions: best-case scenario, you'll be out in fifteen years. That's if you don't get cancer first."

Fontana leaves a heavy silence hanging.

"Or if I don't have you killed first. Because my client is very, very, very angry, Monsieur Delambre."

I can picture the fallout. The board of directors at Exxyal Europe won't have been given the details, but major shareholders can't be left in the dark. However much you love your CEO, a thirteen-million-euro hole in the finances is going to ruffle some feathers. Of course, a thirteen-million-euro hole in the finances isn't enough to get the boss of a big multinational fired—that would be absurd—but it's in everyone's interests for order to be restored. Capital on one side, unemployment on the other. Dorfmann must have given his shareholders some guarantees. He will have promised to recover the slush fund, to bring it home.

Fontana looks at my hand, and it starts hurting terribly.

"How much do you want?"

My throat is so dry that my voice doesn't carry. I'm forced to repeat the question.

"How much do you want?"

Fontana looks surprised.

"All of it, Monsieur Delambre. Absolutely all of it."

Okay. Now I see why Exxyal didn't give him the real number.

If I pay back the ten million they're asking for, that leaves me with three.

That's their offer.

Forget the bit after the decimal point. Let's not split hairs. Give back the slush fund, keep three million euros, save your life, and everything can go back to normal. Wipe the slate clean. That's what profits and losses are all about. If I deduct Romain's share, that leaves me with two million. Two million: easily enough to pay back Mathilde and Lucie, and to make Nicole change her mind about selling the apartment.

But I figure I'm entitled to a bit more than that. I've crunched the numbers in my head several times. The sum I took from Exxyal Europe is less than three years' salary for one of the top dogs. Okay, it's a millennium's worth if you're on the minimum wage, but fuck, I'm not the one who sets the rates.

I play my final card.

"And what about the payee list?"

My tone is the same. Fontana raises his eyebrows, but his question is a silent one. He hunches his shoulders a bit, like someone expecting a brick to land on his head.

I don't move. I wait.

"Explain that one to me, Monsieur Delambre."

"I understand your proposal regarding the cash. I just want to know what to do with your client's contact list. You know, the payees from this fund. Along with the details of the accounts their fees are transferred into for services to your client. There are all sorts in there: French deputy ministers, foreign politicians, sheikhs, businessmen . . . I'm just wondering what to do with it, since you brought it up."

Fontana looks extremely animated. Not only because of me, but because his client hasn't told him everything, which he finds very irritating. He clenches his jaw.

"I'll need some tangible proof for my client. A copy of your document."

"I'll forward you the first page. Give me an e-mail address to send it to."

I've sown some more doubt. Fontana's a prudent man. He'll look into this, and if I'm telling the truth, his client will have to tread very carefully with me. I've bought myself some time.

"Fine," he says at last. "I'll need to discuss this with my client."

"That seems very sensible. Discuss away."

I make my final play. I smile, full of self-confidence:

"Keep me posted, will you?"

Fontana hasn't moved an inch, but I'm already on my feet.

I walk down the corridor, legs like jelly.

In two days, three at most, Fontana will find out I'm bluffing and that there's no list whatsoever.

He's going to be livid.

If my new strategy doesn't yield any results in the next two days, Bébétâ and Boulon are going to quite literally make a killing themselves: my insides will be emptied onto the concrete of the exercise yard.

33

Day one: nothing.

As I move around, I keep an anxious eye on Boulon. As far as he's concerned, I don't exist. He hasn't received an order concerning me. I'm still alive today.

Keep faith.

It should work. It has to work.

Day two: nothing.

Bébétâ is pumping iron in the gym. He sets down his dumbbells to hold up his hand at me, because nodding hello while he's doing something else is beyond his capabilities.

You can tell right away with him: he hasn't received an order concerning me either.

The day goes slowly. Jérôme wants to chat, but he can see that now's not the time.

I only venture out of my cell once. I try to bargain for a blade from a guy I know. I want to be able to defend myself, even if I won't know what to do should the situation arise. He's not interested in anything I have to exchange, and I return to my cell empty handed.

I stop eating. Not hungry.

I can't stop running through everything in my head. It might work. Tomorrow's another day.

I hang on to that.

Day three: the last.

I can't see Boulon or Bébétâ.

Not a good sign.

Generally speaking, I know where I might find them. I don't want to bump into them, but not seeing them makes me even more anxious. I do a broad sweep of their usual hangouts as discreetly as possible. I look for Officer Morisset and remember that he's away for a few days. One of his friends is dying, and he's gone to his bedside.

I return to my cell and stay put. If they are looking for me, they'll have to come here.

I've been sweating since early this morning.

Midday arrives and still there's no news. Tomorrow, I'm a dead man. Why didn't it work?

And then it's 1:00 p.m.

TF1.

My face is on the front page. It's a work mug shot that dates back to the Jurassic. God knows how they got their hands on that one.

Right away, two, three, four inmates come rushing in to watch the rest of the story in our cell. They slap their thighs in excitement. Others say "*Shhhh!!*" so they can hear the anchorman better. There's a real crackle of excitement.

The journalist reports that this morning, *Le Parisien* published a double spread on me and my story, printing an extract from the first few pages of the manuscript I'd sent them. They went for the juiciest bits. I'm announcing the imminent release of my book, which tells the full story.

And, my word, if it isn't just the most heartrending testimony of a real-life victim of the crisis! Pitch perfect.

First, some background. Delambre. That's me. One of the inmates gives me a comradely slap on the back.

Delambre—an out-of-work senior in search of a job—and his professional background, his story, the good years followed by the scourge of unemployment later in life. The sense of injustice; the years in the doldrums. This man has been to hell and back. The humiliation before his children. His hopes of working again constantly frustrated, then the slide into hardship, and finally depression.

The hostage taking? An act of desperation.

The moral of the story? He's facing thirty years in prison.

The country's heart bleeds. My testimony is deemed "shattering." Archive images follow from a few months before: Exxyal Europe headquarters, the parking lot full of police, flashing lights, the hostages safe and sound in their foil blankets, then there's me, the guy they've trussed up and captured, being marched off at pace. The inmates in our cell howl with joy, and from elsewhere there's another "*Shhhh!*"

The guest analyst is a sociologist who has come in to comment on depression in executives and on social violence. The current system discourages and demotivates people, pushing them to extremes. The weakest feel like only the strongest can succeed. Older employees increasingly face the threat of exclusion. He has a question for the viewers: "In 2012, we'll have ten million seniors. Does that mean ten million thrown onto the scrap heap?"

My story becomes symbolic; the drama of my unemployment a fact of society.

Well played.

Fuck you, Fontana.

An inmate hugs me around the neck, delighted to be pals with a TV star.

Vox pops . . .

Ahmed, twenty-four, warehouse assistant: "I read the article in *Le Parisien* . . . I get it, I'm behind him all the way. Yeah, I'll read the book. It's all we can talk about at work. An unemployed guy in jail just for being unemployed . . . it's not right. Isn't the suicide rate high enough as it is?"

Françoise, forty-five, secretary: "I'm scared of being laid off one day. It terrifies me, in fact. I don't know where I'd go. And when you've got kids . . . I read the article in *Le Parisien* and I understood. In the office, we can barely talk about anything else. I'm going to buy a copy for my husband."

Jean-Christian, 71, retired: "It's all a bunch of nonsense. People who really want work can find it. They do whatever, but a job's a job, even if it's just packing boxes at a warehouse."

All the guys around me jeer. If I ever see Jean-Christian in the flesh, I'll shove my Pharmaceutical Logistics pay stub up his butt. Jerk. Not that it matters.

I catch Jérôme's eye. He's laughing. He gets it.

The TV and the papers all close with the announcement of the book's release: "A devastating account that is sure to turn political heads." I haven't found a publisher yet, but the last five minutes have left me confident that there won't be any trouble on that front.

From now on, I'm the most famous unemployed person in France.

A paragon. Untouchable.

I stretch. I breathe.

Boulon and Bébétâ are going to have to look for work elsewhere.

I stand up. I'm going to demand to see the warden.

Anything happens to me now, the prison administration are going to come under fire. They'll have to protect me. I'm a celebrity.

It's as if I've committed insider trading: I've bought myself a ticket to the VIP wing.

34

Usually, Lucie takes out the huge files and the reams (I mean *reams*) of notes filled out with her pretty, precise handwriting. Today, nothing. She doesn't move, her eyes fixed on the table. Her fury is bubbling with a delirious intensity. If I wasn't her father, she'd have smacked me outright.

"If you were a client, Papa, I'd be calling you a bloody bastard."

"I'm your father. And you did just call me that."

Lucie is white as a sheet. I wait, but she's waiting, too. I launch in. "Listen, let me explain . . ."

That was all she was waiting for. A trigger, a word. Her rage floods out like a river that's broken its banks.

Here are the highlights:

"This is a betrayal . . . You couldn't have done anything in the world more shitty . . . I don't want to defend you anymore . . . I caved in to your shameless emotional blackmail . . . Ever since, I've worked day and night to give us the best chance when it comes to the trial and you, behind my back, you write your fucking *memoirs* and go and send them to the press . . . Shows how little you appreciate

my work . . . How little you appreciate me . . . Because you can't
have written that shit overnight! . . . Days, weeks even . . . Days and
weeks when you were seeing me, speaking to me regularly . . . You've
made a complete *mockery* of me . . . But it's not even that . . . You did
it without telling me, because in your eyes, I'm of no importance
whatsoever . . . I'm just a little cog in the machine . . . Sainte-Rose
doesn't want anything to do with this case now . . . He's ditched me . . .
He said: 'Your client's more of a threat than the jury. He's a loose can-
non. You don't stand a chance, leave it.' . . . The investigating magistrate
asked me if I'm trying to put pressure on him or the jury by exposing
the case in the media . . . 'Maître, you gave me your word that the
investigation would proceed without any disturbance, and you've
just broken that promise. From now on, I know where things stand
with you.' . . . You've ruined my reputation . . . And Maman clearly
wasn't in on this either. Well, guess what—she is now! . . . Since seven
this morning there's been a mob of journalists downstairs screaming at her if she so much as opens the curtains . . . And there's no
hope they'll leave her alone anytime soon . . . The telephone's ringing
off the hook . . . She'll have to put up with this for months . . . Well
done! You've made everyone's life easier . . . I suppose you're happy . . .
You've got what you wanted: a bestseller! . . . Did you dream of
becoming a star? . . . Well, bravo—job done! . . . With all those royalties you won't struggle to find a lawyer you can piss all over as much
as you like . . . Because I've had enough of your bullshit."

End of highlights. And end of conversation.

Lucie picks up her bag and knocks angrily at the door, which
opens immediately, and she disappears without looking back.

Probably better that way.

After a tirade like that, any explanation would have fallen on
deaf ears.

And how do I explain myself to her, anyway? Maybe: "I'm staring
at a trial that may well result in me spending the rest of my life in
prison, as well as a vast sum of money in a secret account that I am
increasingly unlikely to be able to transfer to my daughters because

the people who want to recover it are a lot nastier and a lot more powerful than I could ever have imagined." Maybe not.

What about telling her that I'd never really thought about any of that?

Shit, I'm not some gangster . . . I'm just trying to survive!

How is Lucie going to defend me if she discovers that I freaked out and tried to make off with an oil company's slush fund? Plus I'm not about to tell her the tax haven I chose (it's St. Lucia, in the Caribbean); she'd fucking string me up.

If I manage to keep a small portion of this money, I'll give it to the girls the day I get sentenced. That's my only goal. I'm not going to escape a heavy punishment. I will die in here. But at least they'll have some money, provided I'm able to leave it to them. They can do whatever they please with it—I'll be dead by then anyway.

Living dead, but still dead.

Nicole hasn't visited for almost a month. With all the reports in the papers and on the TV, she already has enough on her plate. But mainly I think it's because she's furious with me.

My own cell: protection and television only when I want it—the dream.

I switch on Euronews: . . . *Twenty-five hedge fund managers who have each pocketed 464 million dollars a year . . .*

I flick to cable news: ". . . *State welfare will allow companies to lay off more than 65,000 employees this year . . .*"

I turn it off and relax for the first time in a long while. I feel as though I've been here for years, but it's only been a few months.

Not even six, a mere sixtieth of what I might end up with.

Journalists are wily jerks. Yesterday an inmate came up to me in the library and discreetly handed me a note, offering cash for an exclusive interview. This morning I saw him again and asked him about it. He didn't know anything: he received a hundred euros to give me the piece of paper from another guy who doesn't have a clue about it either. This note must have cost someone a thousand euros to reach me, which means I'm hot property in the eyes of the media. Other extracts from my story have appeared in the press, but the jackpot will be an exclusive interview. My response was to wait and hear their best price. In truth, I'll agree to it whatever the price, but I don't want to do anything until I've seen Lucie again.

I call her, leave messages, plead for her forgiveness. I say that I'll explain everything to her. I ask her not to leave me, telling her it's not how it looks, and that I love her. It's all true.

As I wait for her arrival, I try to hone my reasoning. I would so love to tell her that I'm fighting for her, for both of them, that I'm no longer fighting for myself. But love is no different from blackmail.

My story is being scrutinized in the business section of *Le Monde*. The labor minister giving his two cents. *Marianne* news magazine goes for the headline *The desperate victims of the crisis*. I've negotiated an exclusive interview for fifteen thousand euros, paid in advance to Nicole. They've forwarded me some questions and I'm agonizing over getting the answers just right. We agreed it would be published within a week. A second coat of paint for my budding notoriety. Now that I'm set on this path, I need to push on, to stay in the news and keep hitting the headlines. As far as the public is concerned, I'm just another human-interest story. I need to become a real person, real flesh and blood, with a face, a name, a wife, children—an everyday tragedy that could have happened to any old reader. I must become universal.

I'm told I have a visitor.

Fontana.

I stay calm as I make my way along the corridors. I've been sheltered from the other inmates, which means my strategy has worked. And if it worked on the administration, then it worked on Exxyal, too.

But it's not Fontana, it's Mathilde.

Seeing her stops me in my tracks. I don't even dare sit opposite her. She smiles at me. I turn my head to avoid meeting her eye. My physical appearance must have changed a good deal, because she bursts into tears almost immediately. She takes me in her arms and holds me tight. Behind us, the guard bangs on the metal with his key. Mathilde lets go of me and we sit down. She's still so pretty, my daughter. I feel enormous fondness for her, because I've taken so much from her, done irreparable damage, and yet she's here. For me. It moves me very much. She says she couldn't have come any sooner and is about to get tangled up in a futile explanation when I hold up a hand to show there's no need, that I understand. She seems grateful for that.

The world in reverse.

"I hear more of your news from the papers than the phone," she says, taking a stab at a joke.

Then:

"Maman sends her love."

And finally:

"Gregory, too."

Mathilde is one of those people who always says what ought to be said. Sometimes it's a pain in the ass. Right now it helps.

Their apartment fell through. She says it doesn't matter at all. On top of everything she lent me, they also lost a large part of their deposit since they failed to complete on the specified date.

"We'll need to start saving again. It's no big deal . . ."

She attempts another smile but fails miserably.

The truth is that part of her life has clouded over since her father's downfall, but Mathilde (something to do with teaching English, no doubt) has acquired something of the British stiff upper lip: she keeps her cool while the storm rages around her. She stops crying almost immediately. She's standing firm. Mathilde's motto must be "Dignity in all circumstances." The day after her wedding, she got rid of my name. She's one of those women who goes crazy over the idea of taking her husband's name. That means she's safe—her colleagues won't know that the poor loser in the papers is her father. But I'm certain that if they found out and asked her about it, Mathilde would boldly hold her ground, admit the truth and, despite her whole-hearted disapproval of my actions, say something like "family is family." I love her the way she is. She's been amazing to me, as if she's forgotten that I vanished away her savings and punched her husband in the face. What more could you ask for?

"Lucie thinks you can get extenuating circumstances," she says.

"When did she say that?"

"Yesterday evening."

I breathe. Lucie's coming back. I have to get in touch with her somehow.

"Have I aged that much?"

"No, not a bit!"

That says it all.

Mathilde talks to me about her mother, who's sad and shaken up. She'll come back as well. Soon, apparently.

Our thirty minutes are up. We stand and hug each other.

"I think the apartment's been sold. Maman will tell you about it next time she visits," she says just before leaving.

An image comes to me: our apartment, stickers everywhere, dozens of nonchalant buyers walking about in silence, picking up an object here and there with a look of mild disdain . . .

The thought kills me.

35

I didn't have to wait much longer for Fontana's return.

The man never wears the same suit. He looks a bit like me in the glory days, back when I had a job, although the blue of his suit is hideous and supremely vulgar. It must have cost him a fortune, but more than anything it reeks of bad taste. He's the sort of guy who wears a pocket square in an attempt to come across as a smart modern gentleman. His clothes are quite loose fitting. In his line of work, he needs to feel at ease—function over fashion. When he tries them on, I bet he pretends to punch the shop assistant in the face to see whether the sleeves inhibit his movements, or maybe he checks that the trouser leg has enough slack for a big kick in the poor man's balls. Fontana is nothing if not a pragmatist. That's what scares me about him. My scrutiny of his suit is a way of occupying myself because the thought of looking him in the face, of meeting his cold glare, completely terrifies me.

I need some composure. I won the first round by the skin of my teeth, but now we're squaring up for the second and I need to know what cards he's holding. I would be surprised if he'd turned up empty handed. Not his style. I'll need to be alert, stay focused. In the silence, Fontana's expression is blank.

"Well played again, Monsieur Delambre."

Subtext: Delambre, you piece of shit, just you wait. I'm going to destroy that other hand of yours.

I take a gamble:

"I'm glad you liked it."

My voice betrays my anxiety. I sit farther back in my chair, out of range.

"My client enjoyed it very much. So did I. Everybody enjoyed it, in fact."

I say nothing. I try to force out a smile.

"I see that you're resourceful," he continues. "There obviously wasn't any list. It took me two days to question my client. And then the IT specialist we enlisted to check it out lost us another good twelve hours. In the meantime, you managed to garner some interest in your case from the press, denying me any means of intervention. For now."

I make as if to stand up.

"Don't go, Monsieur Delambre. I've got this for you."

His voice remained level. He didn't think for a second that I was really going to leave. He's a skillful player. I turn around and let out a cry.

Motherfucker!

Fontana has just laid a large black-and-white photo on the table. It's Nicole.

I feel like my legs have been chopped off.

The photograph shows Nicole in the lobby of our building. She is standing with her back to the elevator. Behind her, a man wearing a black balaclava is pinning her against his body, face-on to the camera. His forearm is locked across her throat. She's trying to pull his elbow but she doesn't have the strength. Her struggle is futile. It reminds me of how Bébétâ held me. Nicole's face is petrified, her eyes bulging. That's why the photograph was taken. So I can see directly that Nicole's life is in extreme danger, so I can see her frenzied look.

Her lips are open: she's gasping for air, suffocating. She's on the tips of her toes, because the man holding her is much taller and pulling her off the ground. Strangely she hasn't let go off her bag, which she's holding in her outstretched hand. Nicole stares at me, full frame.

The man is Fontana. I can tell it's him despite the balaclava. He's wearing a pocket square.

"Where is she?" I yell.

"Shhhh . . ."

Fontana screws up his eyes, as if the volume of my cry had come as a tremendous inconvenience.

"She's gorgeous, Nicole. You've got good taste, Delambre."

No more Monsieur Delambre—straight Delambre, now.

Everything goes into overdrive as I grip the table without registering the pain in my fingers.

I'll kill this guy, I swear it.

"Where is she?"

"At her house. I was going to say: 'Don't worry about her.' But actually you should worry about her. That time, she got away with a fright. As did you. But next time, I'll break all ten of her fingers. With a hammer. And I'll do it personally."

He accentuates the "personally." With him, you get the impression that it won't be any ordinary hammer, and that there'll be a very deliberate technique for shattering the fingers. There's a grim determination in his voice. Then, seamlessly, before I can venture a response, he pulls out a second photo and slams it down violently on the table. Same style. Black and white. Blown up.

"As for her, I'm going to break both her arms and both her legs."

My heart lurches cruelly and my stomach turns. Mathilde. I think I recognize the place, not far from the *lycée*. The kids are walking behind the public bench where she's sitting. She's pulled the cling wrap to one side and is eating a salad from a see-through tub with a plastic fork. I never knew she did that. She's not smiling. Her hand is suspended in midair as she listens attentively, even curiously, to what the man sitting nearby is saying.

Fontana again. They're chatting—a typical conversation in the park. The scene is calm, ordinary in fact, but it is shattered as I imagine the aftermath: they stand up, take a few steps back toward the *lycée*, a car pulls up, and Mathilde is bundled into it.

Fontana, unsmiling, adopts an air of concern, as if a question is nagging at him. He's really hamming it up.

"And your lawyer, yes . . . Your other daughter . . . Does she need her arms and legs for work, or can she do it from a wheelchair?"

I want to be sick. Don't touch a hair on their heads. Shit, let me die if that's what it takes. Let Boulon come and break every bone in my body, every one, no holds barred, but don't lay a finger on my girls.

What saves me at this moment is my physical inability to articulate a single syllable. The words stay trapped at the bottom of my throat, frozen. I try to crank my brain back into action, but all the cogs have seized up and I fail to formulate any thoughts. My entire being has been consumed by the images of my girls.

I glance to my side, seeking something new to cling to. I clear my throat, still saying nothing. No doubt my eyes are like saucers, like a junkie after an all-nighter. All the blood has drained from me, but still I've said nothing.

"I will break all three of them. Together."

I make a conscious effort to shut down my sense of hearing. I'm aware of the words, but their meaning doesn't register. There is an urgent and overwhelming need to distance myself from these unbearable pictures, before I vomit or die. Any resistance is vanishing.

He's bluffing. I must convince myself that he's bluffing. I check. I look at him.

He's not bluffing.

"I will break every one of their moving parts, Delambre. They will be alive. Conscious. Let me assure you, what happened to you in here will be child's play compared to what I have in store for them."

He'll be enunciating their names. He'll be saying: "With Mathilde, I'm going to . . . ," "With Lucie, I'm going to . . ." His threats will be drawn from deep within him. "As for your wife, I'm going to tie her . . ." His threats are an extension of himself. He's saying bad things about them. When he refers to "all three of them," the anonymity sounds absurd, as if they were just things.

I need to keep talking to myself to maintain some form of defense, because I mustn't react. The photos are laid out in front of me so that I am left to fill in the blanks. He'll still be detailing everything he's going to do to them, in minute detail. I resist him with thoughts like this. My assessment of his persuasion technique? *Could do better.* It helps me hold my tongue. I forcibly dispel any notion of Nicole, even her name. I make her disappear from my memory. *My wife.* I repeat the words in my mind, repeat them ten, twenty, thirty times, until they are nothing but a string of syllables devoid of meaning. Endless seconds pass as I exercise my willpower. It enables me to continue my silence, buying me time despite my desire to cry, to vomit. *My girls . . .* I resist. *My girls my girls my girls my girls . . .* These words are emptied of meaning, too. I stare straight at Fontana without blinking. Maybe there are tears streaming down my cheeks that I don't notice, like when Nicole first visited. *Nicole Nicole Nicole Nicole Nicole Nicole.* Another word without meaning. Drain the words to drive away the images. Hold Fontana's stare. What do his eyes remind me of? Craters? I focus on his pupils, and soon it's Fontana's turn to be emptied of substance. I mustn't think about what he is. All this to stay silent for as long as possible. No, that's it, they're not craters. His pupils are like those random shapes you get on audio software, those ones . . .

Fontana buckles first.

"What do you say, Delambre?"

"I'd rather it was me."

That's the truth. I manage to avoid returning to reality completely. In my head I keep on repeating *Nicole my wife my girls Nicole my wife my girls Nicole my wife my girls Nicole my wife my girls Nicole my wife my girls.* It's kind of working.

"That may be the case," Fontana replies, "but this isn't about you. It's about them."

Clear my head. Nullify the words. Don't think about anything real. Stay in the realm of ideas—conceptualize. What words of wisdom from management theory?

Find a solution. I can't.

What else?

Bypass the obstacle. I can't.

"They are going to be in a lot of pain."

What else?

Propose an alternative. I can't.

Nicole's face comes back to the surface. I see her pretty smile, but I must chase it away. *Nicole Nicole Nicole Nicole Nicole Nicole Nicole Nicole.* It works.

There's another management technique—what was it again? That's the one: *Overcome the obstacle.* I can't.

Only one thing left for it: *Reframe the issue.* I can do that. At what cost? No time to think—I launch straight in:

"Is that all?"

Fontana frowns slightly. Good. That wins me a bit more time. *Reframe the issue*: maybe this will do the trick.

He cocks his head quizzically.

"I said, 'Is that all?' Have you finished your performance?"

Fontana's eyes widen. Lips pursed, jaw clenched. Cold, hard fury.

"Are you fucking jerking me around, Fontana?"

This might work. Fontana sits bolt upright. I go in for another dose:

"You're taking me for a prize prick, aren't you?"

Fontana smiles. He's figured out my game, but I can still sense an element of doubt, so I gather my words, my energy and all my strength, and give him both barrels.

"Even if you did . . . Can you imagine 'France's most famous unemployed person' standing in front of the press holding up photos of his crippled wife and daughters? Followed by accusations against a major oil company of kidnapping, unlawful confinement, abuse, torture . . ."

I have no idea where this came from. Reframing and a bit of quick thinking. Glory be to management! It's one messed-up discipline, but wonderfully effective all the same.

"And you're prepared to take that gamble!" Fontana says with false admiration.

I see him hesitate about showing me the photos again. Maybe he figures I've got the upper hand. I have a couple of extra rounds, so I reload.

"Is your client prepared to take that gamble?"

"Don't make me disappear your wife's body just so there won't be a photo," he says after a moment's consideration.

Reframe again: so far the technique's worked.

"Don't try any of that bullshit, Fontana. What do you think this is, for fuck's sake, *The Sopranos*?"

That pisses him off.

Reframe again: just the ticket.

"I'm who you need to speak to. Me and me alone. And you know it. So either deal with me, or slink off to your client empty handed. Your threats are starting to piss me off. Your client can't afford this sort of bullshit. So, what will it be? Me, or nothing?"

That's how success works. Like a necklace—remove the knot, and everything comes undone. Same with failure. I should know. To avert disaster, you need fiendish reserves of energy. Either that or a death wish. I seem to have a bit of both.

I have an idea. Who knows if it's good or bad, but it's the best I can do. That's what they call intuition. Fontana said I had it, and maybe he was right.

I've seized the initiative, and now it's action time.

"I'm willing to give back the money. All the money."

I said it without even realizing I was thinking it. But now it's said, I realize where it came from. I want peace. I don't want money.

"I want to get out of here. To be free."

There, that's what I think. I want to go home.

Fontana looks flabbergasted. I keep the momentum going:

"I'm willing to wait a bit. A few months, but no more. If I get out within a reasonable amount of time, I'll give back all the money. Absolutely all of it."

This knocks the wind out of old Fontana.

"A reasonable amount of time . . ."

He is sincere when he asks:

"And how do you intend to get out?"

Maybe my idea wasn't so bad.

I give myself four seconds to think it through.

One, Nicole.

Two, Lucie.

Three, Mathilde.

Four, me.

In any case, it's the only idea I have.

I go again:

"Your client will need to try very, very hard to get me out. But it's possible. Tell him that's all I'm asking of him, and that I'll give back the whole of the slush fund. In cash."

36

I have lied so much and so often that I'm walled in. Telling Nicole the truth now is beyond my strength. We have been robbed of any confidence in our life together, our safety, our future—everything I was so desperate to recover. How can I explain it to her?

The day after Fontana's visit, I send her a long letter through Lucie, for the sake of speed. Not entirely legal, but Lucie agrees it's vital.

I ask her to forgive me for everything she's been through. I understand her fear. I write that I'm sorry, that I love her, that everything I've done has been to protect her, that I am bound to end my days here, to die here, but that all I want is for her and the girls to be alive. I write that I've been forced to do things, but I swear that nothing will ever happen to her again, that she must keep faith. I write that if she has suffered because of me, then I'm sorry and I love her, I love her so much, and I write thousands of other words like this. Most of all, I want to reassure her. As I write the letter I am haunted by the image Fontana showed me, by Nicole's eyes drowning in fear. Each time I am overwhelmed by murderous thoughts. If I get my hands

on Fontana, he'll wish it was only Bébétâ or Boulon. But first I have
to reassure Nicole, tell her that it won't happen again, I swear, and
that soon we'll be together again. I write the word "soon" without
putting a date on it—for Nicole, "soon" might be ten or twelve years,
and I don't want to add another lie to the list.

After lights-out in my cell, I cry, sometimes all night. The idea of
anything happening to Nicole is unimaginable. Or to Mathilde . . .

I don't know what Fontana said through his ski mask. No doubt
he told her to keep her mouth shut if she wanted her husband to stay
alive behind bars. Nicole must have realized that the main point of
this episode was to take the photograph and for me to see it.

I know she hasn't pressed charges. Lucie would have told me.
Nicole hasn't said anything; she's kept it all to herself. She hasn't
written to me because all the letters have to go via the investigating
magistrate. Mathilde said she was getting ready to visit me, but now
I don't think she'll come.

Since then, time has gone by and nothing's happened. Days and
weeks have passed and I've heard nothing from her.

She must be asking herself how I managed to get into this mess,
and about what's going to happen to us.

To her. To me.

To us.

Maybe Nicole sometimes thinks it would all be easier if I were
dead.

To find peace, does she dream that I'm gone? Is that her way
of dealing with this thing that's killing us both?

Last night I woke up, delirious, and walked to my cell door. At
first I hit it once, as hard as I could, with my injured hand. The pain
was blinding and my wounds reopened immediately. But I carried
on because I wanted to punish myself, I wanted to end everything.
I was so alone. The pain was so intense, the worst I've ever experienced, but I carried on: right, left, right, left, harder, harder, harder.
I felt like the ends of my arms were stumps. I was sweating, yet still I
was punching the steel door. I collapsed on my feet, like a boxer on
the ropes. In my unconscious state, I carried on pounding away until

my legs gave way and I fell. There was so much blood that it flowed in rivulets through my bandages. Fists on steel—a lot of damage and not much noise.

In the morning, the pain was extreme. My fingers were broken and reset, and both hands are now bandaged up again. More X-rays and no doubt another operation.

Five more weeks pass, and still no news from her.

They could have put me in solitary, in a hole, in a dungeon. Anything would have been better than this.

My point of reference is not time or meals or noise or days turning to night.

Only Nicole.

My world is defined by her love. Without her, I no longer know where I am.

37

"And it has nothing to do with you?"

The news is so momentous that Nicole has decided to come and see me again.

I see the change close up, and it's terrible. She's been washed out by this affair, aging ten years in the space of a few months. I miss my Nicole, the one I relied on so much. I miss her horribly. I want to dispense with this new, shattered version sitting before me, and bring back *my* Nicole, my wife, my love.

"Did you get my letter?"

Nicole nods.

"Nothing else is going to happen to you, you know that?"

She doesn't answer. Instead she does something ghastly: she attempts to smile. Her way of saying, "I'm behind you"; of saying, "I have no words, but I'm behind you, I'm here, and that's all I can do." No questions. No reproaches. Nicole has given up trying to understand. A man assaulted her. She doesn't want to know who. He strangled her. She doesn't want to know why. Will he come back? She doesn't want to know. I promise her it was an accident, and she appears to believe me. What's hard for her is not that I'm lying, but that she can never believe me again. But what the hell can I do?

One thing has shifted between us, and it's what she's come to discuss. This is a game changer. I'm bursting to say:

"Did you see? I did it! How can you not believe in me anymore?"

But Nicole is drained. The bags beneath her eyes tell of hundreds of sleepless nights, but there is a small glimmer of hope, and I can feel it, too. Fucking hope.

"A colleague told me about the program. I went home early to record it and Lucie came over to watch it with me in the evening."

She's cross, but one of her great qualities is her total inability to lie (if I were like her, I'd already be dead).

"Lucie's wondering whether you've got anything to do with it," she says.

I make a show of looking outraged, but Nicole stops me dead by lifting her hand. With Lucie, lying is an option. With Nicole, it's not even worth considering. She closes her eyes for a second before saying her piece:

"I don't know what you're planning, Alain, and I can assure you that I don't want to. But don't drag our girls into this mess! It's different with me, it doesn't count—I'm with you. Fine if you had to do what you did. But not the girls, Alain!"

As she defends her daughters, she turns into a different Nicole. Not even her love for me would get in the way of this. If I only I could have placed her in front of Fontana when he threatened to dismember them. However, we might be past "not dragging our girls into this mess"—the two of them are already up to their necks in it. One of them has lost a vast amount of what little she had; the other has been instructed to get her father out of this quagmire.

"Please let me explain . . ."

All it takes is a shake of the head for me to stop.

"If it helps us, then great, but I don't want to know."

She looks down, trying to hold back her tears.

"Not our girls, Alain," she says as she pulls out a tissue.

The fact is that this might be a wonderful opportunity, and Nicole knows it.

"Do you think it's going to change anything?" she says, changing the subject.

"Did you get the money? For the interview?"

"Yes, you already asked me."

Various publishers have offered me advances of forty, fifty, sixty-five thousand euros, and good royalties, which will be paid straight into Nicole's account. Since I'm going to have to give Exxyal back all their money, this is undoubtedly all the girls will have left.

"I split your advance between Lucie and Mathilde," Nicole confirms. "It helped a lot."

I chose the most sensationalist, rabble-rousing publisher I could, the one who could make the biggest splash. The book's called: *I Just Wanted a Job . . .* with the subtitle: *Out of Work, Over the Hill, and in Prison*. It's coming out just a month before the trial. Lucie objected to the title, but I insisted. On the cover is a silver-gilt *médaille du travail* for thirty years of work with my mug shot superimposed over the face of the Goddess of Liberty. It's going to cause a massive stir. The publicist can barely cope on her own, so she's taken on an intern (unpaid, of course—no point wasting money). Lucie will be appearing on the TV and radio shows on my behalf, not to mention speaking to the papers. The first print run will be a hundred and fifty thousand copies, and the publisher thinks the trial will boost sales.

"I'm trying to take you out of harm's way . . ."

"So you keep saying, Alain. You want to protect us, but all you do is make things worse. I'd rather you did nothing at all—that way we'd still be living together. But you didn't want that life anymore, and now it's too late. Now I'm completely alone, can't you see?"

She pauses. We're like uncommunicating vessels—as soon as one of us goes up, the other goes down.

"I don't need money," Nicole says. "I couldn't care less. All I want is for you to be there, with me. I don't need anything else."

Her words are a bit disjointed, but I get the overall message: she's willing to resume our impoverished life from where we left off, even if it means being poorer.

"You don't need anything, but that didn't stop you from selling from our apartment!" I protest.

Nicole shakes her head, as if confirming my inability to understand a thing. It really gets to me.

"So do you think it'll make a difference?" she asks, changing the subject.

"What?"

"The interview."

I shrug, but inside I'm in overdrive.

"If everything goes according to plan, it should."

A long table. The media everywhere. The place was sizzling.

Behind the table, the entire wall was taken up with a banner bearing the EXXYAL EUROPE logo in enormous red lettering.

"It must be said, he's got stage presence, your CEO," Nicole says with a hint of a smile.

Alexandre Dorfmann was in his element. Last time I'd seen him he was sitting on the ground with my loaded Beretta resting on his forehead, and me saying, "So, your Higher-Than-Highness, how many exactly are you firing from Sarqueville?" or something like that. Not even a bead of sweat that day—a frozen-blooded animal. At the press conference, he was cool and calm, too. When he entered the room, it was as if I still had the Beretta held to his head. It might not have looked that way, but I've got him by the balls, old Alexander the Great. He entered the fray like a circus performer: solid yet supple movements, rigid smile, bright face. His lapdogs were lined up behind, stretching back into the wings.

"Were they all there?" asks Nicole.

"No, they were one down."

Right from the start, I noticed that Jean-Marc Guéneau, our red-lingerie-wearing friend, was late. Maybe he'd been held up in a sex shop—who knew. Something told me he wouldn't be joining the party. I hoped I wasn't in for a nasty surprise.

The stars' entrance had been edited, but I was able to catch a glimpse of the main characters: behind Dorfmann, Paul Cousin was first in line. He was standing so straight you'd swear he was a head taller than the others. Seconds later, there they all were sitting next to one another. Like the Last Supper. Dorfmann playing Jesus Christ, revving up to beatify the world with His word. Four brown-nosers instead of twelve: not bad going in these days of austerity. At the Lord's right hand: Paul Cousin and Évelyne Camberlin. At His left: Maxime Lussay and Virginie Tràn.

Dorfmann put on his glasses. There was a swarm of journalists and reporters, but silence fell as the crackle of flashes died out.

"The whole of France has been moved, and rightly so, by the unfortunate fate of a man, stricken by unemployment, resorting to . . . violent extremes during his search for work."

His announcement was prepared in advance, but this bombastic start to proceedings was not Dorfmann's usual style. He took off his glasses, more confident in his natural brilliance than his memory. He looked out to the assembly, staring straight at the camera.

"The name of our company has become embroiled in this regrettable matter because a man, Monsieur Alain Delambre, in a moment of madness, took several of our company's executives, including myself, hostage for several hours."

His expression hardened for a split second at the memory of the ordeal. Bravo—a marvelous turn. The faint shadow that crossed Dorfmann's face for a split second conveyed a clear message: we've been to hell and back, but we're not going to make a song and dance out of it; we have the dignity and the nobility to keep our pain to ourselves. The apostles flanking him joined in this almost indiscernible display of keen emotion. One looked down, desolate at the memory of the unbearable nightmare they'd been through; another swallowed hard, visibly racked by those hours of horror and the indelible mark they'd etched on her heart. Bravo to them, too! The vultures didn't miss out on any of it: flashes burst into action, seizing on this prize-winning pang of televisual suffering. Even I felt an urge to turn to my cellmates and applaud the show. But I was on my own (VIP).

"They're a real bunch of obsequious bastards, aren't they?" Nicole says.

"You could put it like that."

Dorfmann again:

"Whatever this job seeker's motivations, no circumstances—I repeat, *no circumstances*—can justify physical violence."

"How are your hands?" Nicole asks.

"Up to six functioning fingers. These four, and these two. So not bad—that's over half. The others aren't healing too well. The doctor hinted that bending them might not be easy in the future."

Nicole smiles at me. My love's smile, the entire reason for my fighting and my suffering. I could die for this woman. Shit, that's what I *am* doing!

Or maybe not:

"However," Dorfmann continued, "we cannot be deaf to the cries of the suffering. As business leaders, we must fight every day to win the economic struggle that would guarantee their return to work. We understand their frustration. And the truth is, we share it."

I would have loved to be watching the show in a café in Sarqueville. It must have been like a World Cup match. They'll have that little soundbite playing on loop.

"Monsieur Delambre's terrible misadventure perhaps epitomizes the tragedy faced by many unemployed people. That is why, on my initiative, Exxyal Europe has decided to drop all charges against him."

A huge commotion followed, with photographers greedily snapping the table of execs.

"My colleagues," he continued, with a proprietorial sweep of the hand that set off a stadium wave of earnest eye-closing from his subordinates, "have stood by me in this decision, and for that I thank them. Each of them, individually, had pressed charges. All of them have been withdrawn. Monsieur Delambre will face court action for what he did, but the state prosecution alone will be responsible for ensuring that justice is served."

The executives on either side of God the Father remained dead-pan, fully aware of their momentous role. Dorfmann had just unveiled a new stained-glass panel in the history of capitalism: *The Lord shows Pity to the Unemployed and the Needy*.

That was when I truly fathomed the value Dorfmann placed on his ten million. There must have been plenty of chatter backstage at Exxyal, because he'd just painted on another layer, and not just any color: a fine, virginal, almost Christ-like white. The white of innocence.

"Of course, far be it from either Exxyal or its staff to sway the scales of justice, which must be served with total impartiality. Our show of compassion is, nonetheless, a plea for lenience. A plea for clemency."

There was a general hubbub around the room. Everyone knows that CEOs are capable of superiority—just look at their bonuses—but this magnanimity . . . honestly, it brings a tear to the eye.

"Lucie thinks their dropping the charges might have a big impact on the verdict," Nicole says.

She said the same to me. I think it's far from enough, but I hold my tongue. We'll see. The trial will take place in three or four months, record time apparently. It's not every day that France's most famous unemployed person goes up to the high court.

Back on-screen, Dorfmann cranked it up:

"Having said that . . ."

Silence almost fell. Dorfmann hammered each syllable home, asserting His word.

"Having said that . . . this move will have no bearing on jurisprudence."

That's a tricky word for the mere mortals of a TV audience.

Simplify: return to the universal principles of communication.

"Our gesture is an exception. Anyone tempted to follow the example of Monsieur Delambre . . ."—cue rapturous applause in the cafés of Sarqueville—". . . should know that Exxyal Group will stand firm in its absolute condemnation of brutality and unreservedly support the prosecution of anyone who commits violent acts against any assets or personnel belonging to our company."

"No one seems to have picked up on that," Nicole says, "but it was weird, no?"

She sees that I'm not following her, so explains:

"Dorfmann spoke about the 'assets or personnel belonging to the company,'" says Nicole. "That's pretty serious."

No, still not with her.

"The 'assets,' fine, but the 'personnel,' Alain! They don't 'belong' to their company!"

Without thinking, I say:

"That didn't shock me. At the end of the day, didn't I do what I did to 'belong' to a company again?"

Nicole is appalled, but she lets it rest.

She supports me, no matter what. She'll support me to the very end. But our worlds are expanding in opposite directions.

"Here," she says.

She rummages in her bag and brings out some photographs.

"I'm moving in a couple of weeks. Gregory's being very good to me—he's coming with a couple of friends to do the heavy lifting."

I am only half-listening because my attention is on the photographs. Shots from various angles, ambient lighting . . . Nicole's gone to a lot of effort to make the place look nice, but it's no use. It's dingy. She's talking about the move, about the lovely neighbors, about taking a few days off, but I'm looking at the shots and I'm devastated. She tells me which floor it's on, but the number doesn't stick. Maybe the twelfth? I'm treated to several zoomed-out photos of Paris. When you're dealing with real estate agents, panoramic shots are rarely a promising sign. I don't even bother with the bird's-eye views.

"We can eat in the kitchen . . ." Nicole says.

We can puke in there, too. The patterned parquet is a real '70s throwback: a dull, right-angled affair. Just by looking at the photographs you can hear the voices echoing around the empty rooms and, come nightfall, the sound of the neighbors yelling at one another through the hollow partition walls. Living room. Corridor. Bedroom.

Another bedroom. Everything I hate. How much is a shithole like this worth? Did she really trade in our apartment for this, when we were so close to paying off the mortgage?

"Close to paying it off? With what payments? I'm not sure if you noticed, Alain, but we've got a few cash-flow issues!"

I sense that it's better not to test her. Nicole has reached a level of exasperation that is close to breaking point. She opens her mouth and I close my eyes in readiness for the tirade, but she goes for the underhand option instead.

"It's not like I'm the only one who's decided to move house," she says, motioning toward the décor around us.

That was below the belt. I toss the photographs onto the table and she gathers them into her bag. Then she looks at me:

"I don't give a damn about the apartment. I would have been happy anywhere so long as I was with you. All I wanted was to be with you. So without you, it's there or somewhere else . . . At least we'll be in less debt."

This new place perfectly matches my notion of where a prisoner's wife should live.

There's too much to say, so I say nothing. Save it. Keep my strength for the trial, my best shot at being allowed to come home to her soon, even if it's in that dump.

38

Everyone knows that there are good days and bad days. And you definitely want the day you go before the high court to be a good day. In fact, I'm going to need two of those days, as that's how long the trial is expected to last.

Lucie is buzzing. No more talk of Sainte-Rose, who withdrew his help after my previous antics. Curiously, as irritating as I found the presence of this phantom by Lucie's side (especially when I found out how exorbitantly high his fees were), seeing her reduced to making all these decisions by herself does panic me a little. What she said sixteen months ago about the need to be defended by a proper professional starts making perfect sense. I feel for her—her anxiety is overwhelming. The press have highlighted the fact that she's my daughter, and numerous photos of her have been printed alongside weepy headlines. I know she hates this, but she shouldn't.

My worry has increased in the run-up to the trial, but when she told me her line of defense, I once again found myself thinking I'd made the right choice. Broadly speaking, there are two potential strategies: political or psychological. Lucie is convinced the assistant public prosecutor will opt for the former, so she's gone for the latter.

Everyone is on standby.

Alexandre Dorfmann's press conference had been unanimously hailed a success. His magnificent gesture was all the more appreciated since neither he nor a single one of his executives had agreed to any follow-up interviews. This extreme modesty seemed to confirm—not that any confirmation was needed—that his move contained no ulterior motives whatsoever and that it was rooted in nothing but the purest sense of humanity. A few of the rags seemed skeptical, suggesting that there might have been some underlying, suspicious reason lurking behind his actions. But thankfully the majority of them fell in line with the broadcast media: in this tense period tarnished by labor disputes, with an almost permanent atmosphere of confrontation between business heads and employees, Exxyal's benevolent decision represents a new chapter in social relations. After two centuries of relentless class war, the torch of peace now shines bright on a new *entente cordiale*, marking a historic instance of reconciliation between leaders, workers, and employees.

In the meantime, Exxyal has made me confirm that I will indeed be paying back all its money.

The second promising sign before the trial was the U-turn from Pharmaceutical Logistics. Lucie's initial belief was that my former employer's position had been morally compromised by my heroic man-of-the-people status and that they were afraid of defeat at the tribunal, but we recently found out the real reason: their key witness, Romain, quit overnight and is not even replying to urgent e-mails from the head office. Lucie looked into it. Romain has gone back to his home province, back to farming the land. Gleaming new tractors, vast irrigation projects, the works. It seems the young man is pushing ahead with some ambitious investments.

Despite these good omens, Lucie still has her concerns. Trial by jury can, apparently, be somewhat unpredictable.

The day before the start of the trial, the radio and TV stations summarize the charges against me and rebroadcast the archive footage. I beg Lucie to be kind with her predictions: best-case scenario, she's hoping for eight years, four of which will be mandatory.

I do the math in my head and start panicking. Four years of mandatory prison means another thirty months inside! If I weren't already sitting down, I would collapse. Even if I manage to stay in the VIP section, I'm so exhausted that . . .

". . . I'll die!"

Lucie rests her hand on mine.

"You're not going to die, Papa. You're going to be patient. But I'm warning you, even that would be an absolute miracle."

I hold back my tears.

Last night, I didn't sleep a wink. Thirty months in here! Almost three more years . . . When I get out, I'll be an old man. And I will have given all the money back to Exxyal. I'll be old and poor. The thought is completely shattering and makes me feel so alone.

All this in mind, I enter the courtroom with my shoulders sagging and a washed-out complexion. I am a shadow of a man. It's not exactly what I had in mind, but it seems to make a decent impression.

The clutch of jurors has been picked at random from the kind of people I used to rub shoulders with on the *métro* back when I was employed. Men and women of all ages. But in the context of the high court, I find these familiar faces infinitely more sinister. Even though they've taken their juror's oath (". . . I do solemnly, sincerely, and truly declare and affirm that I will well and truly try the issues joined between the parties and a true verdict give according to the evidence . . ."), I'm on edge. These people are like me—I'm sure they're perfectly sensible.

I spot my little crew nearby.

Close family first: Nicole, more beautiful than ever, sending me discreet, confidence-boosting looks; Mathilde, on her own because her husband hadn't managed to get away.

A bit farther along there's Charles. He must have borrowed a suit from a better-heeled but much larger neighbor. He's floating in the clothes, which look as though they're being inflated by an air duct. Knowing from experience that he's not allowed to booze in the courtroom, he must have tanked up ahead of time. I saw him walking in earlier, determined but slightly wobbly. When he raised a hand at me to make his salute, he veered off-balance, forcing him to grip the back of a chair. Expressive as ever, Charles. He views the proceedings from some inner place, utterly engrossed. At every phase of the hearings, his face seems loaded with comments. Charles is almost a barometer for the entire event. He makes frequent sideways glances at me, like a mechanic looking up from under the hood to assure his client that, for the moment, everything's all right.

After the close family, the more distant relatives. Fontana, grave and earnest, calmly polishing his nails without looking at me once. His two colleagues are here, too: the young woman with the cold eyes, whose first name, Yasmine, was cited in the court documents; and the Arab who conducted the interrogations, Kader. They are on the list of witnesses cited by the public prosecutor. But first and foremost, they're here just for me. I ought to feel flattered.

Then there's the press and the radio and TV crowd. And my representative from the publisher, who'll be somewhere in the room licking his lips at the thought of how many sales this trial is going to rack up.

And Lucie, who I haven't seen wearing her official robe for ages. She has a good number of young colleagues in the room who, like me, must be shocked by how much weight she's lost this past year.

As the first day draws to a close, I simply don't understand why Lucie is predicting eight years. If the reporter summing up the courtroom action is anything to go by, the verdict will be nothing but lenient and the entire world is on my side. Except, of course, the assistant public prosecutor. A real shitbag, that guy. Bitter. He takes every opportunity to display his contempt for me.

It's perfectly clear from the statement made by the psychiatric expert: my physical state at the time of the events was marked by a temporary disorder that "completely eliminated [my] judgment and control over [my] actions." The assistant public prosecutor grills him, brandishing Article 122-1 of the *Code pénal* and seeking to emphasize that I cannot possibly be considered to have diminished responsibility on psychological grounds. All this wrangling goes over my head. Lucie contests his opinion. She has worked hard on this aspect of the case, which she sees as vital to the trial. The exchange between her and the assistant public prosecutor gets heated, and the judge has to call the court to order. In the evening, the reporter concludes soberly: "Will the jury deem Monsieur Delambre to be responsible for his actions, as the assistant public prosecutor strongly maintains? Or, as his lawyer insists, will they see him as a man whose judgment was severely impaired by depression? We'll know tomorrow evening at the end of the deliberations."

The assistant public prosecutor, for his part, glorifies in the detail. He describes the prisoners' anxiety as though he had been there himself. To hear his version, this hostage taking rivals Fort Alamo. He calls to the stand the RAID commandant who arrested me. Lucie makes few interventions. She's relying on the witness testimonies.

Enter Alexandre Dorfmann, lord of all he surveys. Tribute to whom tribute is due. His testimony has been hotly anticipated ever since that overblown press conference he gave.

I look over at Fontana, who is watching and listening to his boss with an almost religious devotion.

A few days before, I said to him:

"I'm warning you, I want my ten mill's worth! No way your client's getting away with the legal minimum, you hear me? For three mill, I'm a lost soul. For five, I'm a brave man. For ten, I'm a fucking saint! That's the way I see it, so go and tell that to your Lord on high. No way he's playing the CEO up there—this time, he's going to have to do some fucking work. For ten big ones and an honorable gesture from me to calm down his board of directors, he'd better bust his goddamn ass."

Dorfmann turns out to be a total natural.

Not even in her wildest dreams did Lucie expect such a testimony.

Yes, of course, the hostage taking was "an ordeal," but fundamentally the person before him was "no murderer, just a man who'd lost his way." Dorfmann looks pensive as he runs through his memory. "No, I never felt threatened. The fact is, he wasn't at all sure what he wanted." In answer to a question about physical violence, Dorfmann says, "No, none whatsoever." The public prosecutor presses him. I urge him on in my head: *Go on, your Excellency, one more kind word.* Dorfmann scrapes the barrel: "When he was firing, we could all see that he was aiming at the windows and not at anyone in particular. It was more like an act of . . . deterrence. The man seemed broken, exhausted."

The assistant public prosecutor goes on the offensive. He brings to mind Dorfmann's initial statements from a few minutes after the RAID operation, statements that appear "very damning for Delambre," and then from the press conference, which were "astonishing almost to the point of suspicion," in which Delambre was absolved of all wrongdoing.

"It's hard to keep up, Monsieur Dorfmann."

He's going to have to do better than that to throw Alexander the Great.

Dorfmann brushes aside this criticism with three clear arguments, emphasizing each salient point by turn with a wag of the finger at the assistant public prosecutor, a look over at the jury, and a prodigal hand gesture in my direction. A flawless performance. The fruit of thirty years of sitting on supervisory boards. By the end, no one has understood a word of what he's said, but everyone agrees that he is right. Everything seems clearer, logic perfectly restored. The assembly congregates reverently around the evidence Dorfmann puts before us. A business leader in full swing is as beautiful as an archbishop in his cathedral.

Lucie looks at me with pure elation.

My words to Fontana had been:

"I want everyone to be on their game! It's a team game, and for ten million I want real unity, real team spirit, got it? Dorfmann picks the gap and then the pack follows behind in a nice, tight formation. No weak links! Tell them to remember the management tips they give their underlings—that ought to help."

It does help.

Évelyne Camberlin steps up. A doyenne, dignity personified.

"Yes, I won't deny that I was scared, but I soon realized that nothing was going to happen to us. What really frightened me was that he might do something clumsy, a blunder of some sort."

As soon as the assistant public prosecutor intervenes, the audience starts jeering at him like a pantomime villain. He asks Évelyne Camberlin to describe her "terror."

"I was afraid, but I wasn't terrified."

"Oh, but of course! A man waves a gun in your face and you don't find that terrifying? You must be exceptionally cool under pressure," he adds with a derisory tone.

Évelyne Camberlin glares at him before smiling and saying:

"Weapons have little effect on me. I spent my entire childhood in a barracks—my father was a lieutenant colonel."

The audience is in raptures. I look at the jurors. A few smiles, but hardly all-out hysterics.

The assistant public prosecutor takes a sly turn.

"You dropped your charges entirely of your own volition, is that correct?"

"What you're really asking," she says, "is whether I did so under pressure from my employer. What would be the point?"

Deep down, this is the question on everyone's lips. It's at moments like this that we can tell whether the big man has got his case sewn up. With ten million on the table, I hope he has.

Before the assistant public prosecutor can respond, Madame Camberlin cracks on:

"Perhaps you're suggesting that my employers might stand to gain from projecting a generous image."

You're fired, Camberlin! If it were up to me, I would kick her out immediately for making that kind of insinuation. Where did she learn her public speaking? I'm livid. If she doesn't pull this one back, I'm making Dorfmann promise that her head will be the first to roll when the layoff plan gets underway at Sarqueville. She must have realized her error, because she backtracks:

"Do you really think Exxyal needs to boost its image in the eyes of the media by appearing charitable?"

Okay, that's a bit better. But I need you to hammer this into the jurors' heads.

"If so, why not ask whether I've been given a special bonus to testify before you? Or whether I'm being blackmailed with the threat of dismissal? Are these questions too tedious for you?"

There's a general hubbub, and the judge calls the court to order. The jury seems perplexed, and I panic that my plan's about to come apart at the seams.

"In that case," the assistant public prosecutor says after a pause, "if you and Monsieur Delambre are in such close communion, why did you press charges the day after the event?"

"Because the police asked me to. They recommended it, and at the time it seemed logical," Madame Camberlin replies.

Much more like it. Dorfmann's instructions were clear after all. There's a sense that all these people's futures are in the dock, too. That makes me happy—it makes me feel less alone.

Maxime Lussay falls in line with his colleague. His approach is less polished, a bit more rustic. He speaks in straightforward but effective terms, answering with a simple "yes" or "no." Low profile. Perfect.

Virginie Tràn, on the other hand, causes quite a stir. She's wearing a pale-yellow dress and a silk scarf. She is made up as if it's her wedding day, and she strides to the witness stand like a catwalk model. I can tell how badly she wants to please her boss. I figure she's still in bed with the competition. If I were her, I'd be treading very carefully.

She goes for the categorical approach.

"Monsieur Delambre made no demands. I struggle to believe that his actions were premeditated. If so, surely he would have asked for something."

Objection from the public prosecutor, and she gets a reprimand from both the assistant public prosecutor and the judge.

"We are not asking for your personal views on Monsieur Delambre's motivations. Stick to the facts."

She takes this onslaught as a chance to go all coquettish, lowering her eyes and blushing with embarrassment, like a little girl caught with her hand in the candy jar. This paragon of innocence would have made the most hardened soul burst into tears.

Up last is His Majesty Paul Cousin. He's the only one who takes a good look at me, square in the eye, as he walks to the stand. He's even taller than I remember. The audience is going to love him.

Me to Fontana:

"That tall bastard of yours is the key to everything. It's thanks to him that I'm behind bars, so you tell him that I want some serious tact. Otherwise I'll make sure he's back on fucking unemployment benefits until he retires."

Solemn and austere, Cousin seems aware of his big-man status. Calm and collected, he's an example to all.

With every question from the judge, with each cross-examination from the assistant public prosecutor, Paul Cousin makes a slight turn toward me. Before relaying his position, The Upstanding One observes The Lost One, then responds with a few sparse sentences. We barely know each other, he and I, but I feel like we're old friends.

He answers the judge by confirming that he is currently posted in Normandy. With a heavy heart, he announces that there'd been a vast restructuring program: a difficult operation, "from a human perspective." I hope he doesn't overdo that phrase, because it has a bizarre ring when he says it. He explains that Sarqueville is at the heart of the group's economic difficulties. In other words, he knows full well that times are tough. When they start quizzing him about his attitude during the hostage taking, we get a recap of the events: his opposition, his confrontation, his courageous dash for the exit . . .

"In order to stop you, Monsieur Delambre attempted to shoot you!"

A murmur of admiration goes around the room. Cousin swats it aside irritably.

"Monsieur Delambre didn't shoot me, that's all that matters. Perhaps he attempted to, but I cannot testify to that, since I never turned to see what he was doing."

The audience interprets this as modesty.

"Everyone else seemed to see it!"

"So ask everyone else—don't ask me."

Another murmur, and the judge calls Cousin to order.

"The overriding impression we get from your different, yet remarkably unanimous, testimonies is that this hostage taking was something of a picnic in the park. But if Monsieur Delambre really didn't represent any danger, why did it take so long for you to intervene?"

Paul Cousin shifts his whole body and stares right at him:

"In any situation, sir, there is a time for watching, a time for understanding, and a time for action."

Magnificent, Cousin.

The audience is mesmerized. Hats off.

I'd said to Fontana:

"What about old Jean-Marc Guéneau—he's not going to pull a fast one on us? If he tries anything, I'll have him back in his panties and sobbing before the jury!"

The man's a shadow of his former self.

I remember how he used to be all smartly dressed and swaggering. Now he's like a ghost. He confirms his identity and status: an out-of-work professional.

That's the nice, official way of saying "unemployed prick." Exxyal fired him two months after the event. He's clearly had a rough time, his employers would have said, but we simply cannot maintain our confidence in a finance manager who goes around with women's lingerie on under his suit. Despite being fired, Guéneau has agreed to testify, and he says exactly what's necessary. Because everyone knows it's a small world, and even if Exxyal is no longer his employer, the company still has a major say if he ever wants a job in the sector again.

I inspect him more closely.

Fourteen months out of work, and he looks like he's still firmly in the rut. Guéneau reminds me of myself after a year and a half of unemployment. He carries himself like he still believes. He's clinging on. I picture him in six months' time revising (downward) his expected salary by 40 percent, and then in nine months negotiating some temp work, and in two years accepting a low-level position to cover half the cost of his bills. In five years he'll get kicked in the ass by the first Turkish supervisor willing to stoop low enough to bother. At one point in his statement, I thought the sleeve of his suit might rip. The audience would have found that hilarious.

I also said to Fontana:

"As for that wanker Lacoste, make sure you keep him on a short leash. If he struggles to get the hang of it, you have my full permission to snap every single one of his fingers. I know from firsthand experience how much that helps clarify matters."

Fontana's face did something that no one except his mother could call a smile.

Lacoste's testimony is delivered with great humanity. His firm has gone into receivership—nothing to do with the present scandal, of course, but just another casualty of the economic crash. The very same crisis to which Monsieur Delambre fell victim, along with so many others. He does well, Lacoste. I hope that Rivet girl has given him his just deserts.

Lucie is looking at me more and more often.

Soon the assistant public prosecutor will be summing up on behalf of the enemy forces. Lucie has prepared for war, and all the combatants appear eager to sign the truce. She questions the witnesses with a light touch. She realizes that the odds are in our favor, but that we mustn't get ahead of ourselves.

The day before, Nicole had expressed her amazement:

"It's quite remarkable. Your father's going to the high court for a hostage taking, but no one seems fazed by the fact that a big company can arrange precisely the same thing to assess its staff. With complete impunity. If they hadn't organized the role play, there wouldn't have been a hostage taking, right?"

"I know, Maman," Lucie replied, "but what can we do? Not even the employees seemed to bat an eyelid . . ."

This argument has obviously played on her mind. She was even considering cross-examining the witnesses to put the matter in the spotlight, to push the point about the company's cruelty—to make Exxyal responsible for my actions. But aside from the fact that I'm on trial, not them, it's not even necessary anymore. At one point, Lucie looks toward me, concerned about the proceedings. I make a little two-handed gesture at her to show my surprise. I try to implore her as much as I can, but Lucie, seeming more and more dazed, has already turned back to attend to the litany of witnesses.

"As for you, Fontana," I said in the lead-up, "you're going to do what you do best: play the good little soldier. No doubt you're getting paid for results?"

Fontana didn't flinch, which meant I was spot-on: he's on commission. The more money Exxyal recovers, the more he pockets.

"I know you'd love nothing better than to crush me like a piece of shit, but you're going to be disciplined. You're going to go the extra distance for me. And I'll make it easier for you. For every syllable that's not perfectly on song, I'll take away one of those big ones that Dorfmann's hoping to get back. I'll let you explain that to him when he notices the shortfall and comes looking for an explanation."

You don't have to be a mind reader to guess that at that moment, if I didn't have such a strong advantage over him, he would have had no qualms about sticking my feet in a concrete block and dropping me into the canal Saint-Martin with an oxygen bottle and six hours of free time. What's going to happen when all this is over and I'm poor again? I hope he's not the sort to hold a grudge and get all personal about it.

In any case, for now, he's obedient.

He plays along with the general "not dangerous" analysis. Lucie makes him run through his credentials to lend weight to his opinion. David Fontana—a man who has rubbed shoulders with warriors, soldiers, and worse—can assure the court that Delambre, Alain, is a little lamb. His wound? Just a scratch. Any grievances on his part? Nothing of the sort.

Perhaps I laid it on too thick. We need to get the testimonies over and done with—all this unanimity is becoming a nuisance.

At the start of the afternoon, it's time for the defense's closing statement.

Lucie is glorious. Her voice is steady and compelling as she summarizes the arguments, carefully negotiating the witnesses' statements to avoid patronizing the jury. She addresses each juror in turn, both the men and the women, and does what she does best: explaining that my story could have happened to any one of them. And she does it well. She highlights her client's challenging living conditions, the decline of his self-esteem, the humiliation; then the brutal, incomprehensible action, then the turmoil and the inability to escape after cornering himself. Her client was alone and desperate.

She now needs to defuse the bombshell that is my book.

Yes, Monsieur Delambre wrote a book, Lucie explains. Not, as has been too often said, to achieve any sort of fame, but because he needed support. He needed to share his ordeal with others. And that's precisely what happened. Thousands, tens of thousands of others just like him saw their own plight reflected in his, identifying with his misfortune and humiliation. And they forgave his actions. Actions that, let us not forget, were of no consequence whatsoever.

Her client's extenuating circumstances are no different from the circumstances endured by anyone in a time of crisis.

It's really not bad at all.

If I weren't so afraid of the nasty public prosecutor, who's shaking his head throughout—at times scandalized, at others deeply dubious—I'd be saying that Lucie's prediction looked likely: no jury could ever acquit me. I came to the assessment with a loaded weapon: premeditation, pure and simple. You can't expect a thirty-year sentence to be lowered to under eight or ten years. Yet Lucie leaves no stone uncovered. And if anyone can reduce my sentence, it's her, my daughter. Nicole looks at her with admiration. Mathilde wills her on, giving her confidence.

Lucie was right: the assistant public prosecutor's case is exemplary. It rests on three pitilessly simple arguments.

One: Alain Delambre, three days before coming to the Exxyal assessment, had sourced, found, and purchased a pistol, which he had then loaded with live bullets. He evidently had aggressive, possibly murderous, intentions.

Two: Alain Delambre exposed his story to the media in order to sway his trial; to influence the jury by manipulating and intimidating them. The hostage taker has turned master blackmailer.

Three: Alain Delambre is setting a dangerous precedent. If his sentence does not serve as an example, tomorrow every unemployed person will feel entitled to take up arms. At a time when dismissed workers are resorting more and more often to brutality, arson, threats, looting, extortion, and kidnapping, can the jury really rank a hostage taking as an acceptable, legitimate form of negotiation?

In his view, this question answers itself.

We need an example. He continues addressing the jury:

"Today you are the last bastion against a new form of violence. Be aware of your duty. Realize that to afford mitigating circumstances when real bullets are involved is to prefer civil war to social dialogue."

We need a firm indictment. Fifteen years?

He calls for thirty. The maximum sentence.

When he sits back down, the crowd is left stunned.

Not least me.

Lucie is shell shocked. Nicole holds her breath.

Charles, for the first time in his life, looks sober.

Even Fontana lowers his head. Given how long I'm going to spend in jail, he won't be seeing his loot anytime soon.

As per protocol, the judge passes the floor back to Lucie for the final word. Inevitably it's the result of so many months of intense work and sleepless nights, but she chokes. She tries to speak, but the words don't come. She clears her throat and utters a few inaudible phrases.

The judge seems perturbed:

"We didn't hear you, maître . . ."

A heavy, stormy atmosphere has fallen on the room.

Lucie turns to me, tears in her eyes. I look at her and say:

"It's over."

She gathers her strength and turns to the jury. But it's beyond her—nothing comes out. The entire room holds its breath.

I'm right. It is over.

Lucie, deathly pale, raises her hand to the judge to signify that she has nothing to add; nothing she is able to add.

The jury is invited to deliberate.

Late that evening, to everyone's surprise, they still haven't reached a unanimous verdict. Deliberations are to continue tomorrow.

In the transport back to prison, I can't stop running through the possible scenarios. If they haven't reached a decision, it's because there are some sticking points. The trial went as well as it possibly could, but the verdict is set to go against me. If they were convinced by the prosecution, some will no doubt see themselves as upholders of justice and appeal for an exemplary sentence.

That night in prison is like being on death row, long enough to die twenty times over. My life flashes before me. All that for this.

I don't sleep a wink. Thirty years is unthinkable. Twenty years is impossible. Even ten years . . . there's no way.

An unbearable night. At one point I thought I was going to cave completely, but no, my anger returned, perfectly intact. A terrible fury, like in the good old days: death wishes about the injustice of it all.

The following day, I return to the courtroom white as a sheet. I've made a decision.

I closely examine the police officer in charge of transferring me. The doppelganger of the one guarding me in the dock. I scrutinize the lock system on the holster of his weapon. As far as I can make out, there's a large push-button that releases the tongue, leaving the gun to be lifted out unhindered. I rack my brains to recall Kaminski's information from before . . . Sig Sauer SP2022: no manual safety, but a slide catch lever.

I think I'll know how to use it.

I'll have to be very quick.

Once I'm in the dock, I see my opportunity: barge him power-fully, send him off-balance, and pin him with my shoulder. Then use my hand with the good fingers.

Lucie hasn't slept either. Nicole's not much better. Mathilde, too.

Charles is distraught. His anxiety has contorted his face into a dramatic mask. He tilts his head as he looks at me, as though deeply affected by my fate. I feel a terrible urge to say good-bye to Charles.

Fontana is prowling around the back of the room, as watchful and supple as a sphinx.

Suddenly Lucie leans toward me and says:

"Sorry. For yesterday . . . I just couldn't speak anymore . . . I'm sorry."

Her shattered voice rings in my ear. I squeeze her hand and kiss her fingers. She feels all my tension, says kind words that I don't listen to.

The policeman guarding me is considerably taller and chunkier than the one yesterday. Square jawed. It's not going to be easy, but it's doable.

I stand a little farther back in the dock. I need good, efficient leverage from my legs.

I can secure his weapon in under five seconds.

39

The jury returns. It's 11:00 a.m.

Solemn silence. The judge begins. Words pour out. Questions echo. One juror stands and answers.

No. Yes. No.

Premeditation. Yes.

Extenuating circumstances. Yes.

Verdict: Alain Delambre is sentenced to five years, of which he will serve eighteen months.

Shock.

I've already been remanded in custody for sixteen months.

With special remissions, I'm free.

My emotions overwhelm me.

The room erupts in applause. The judge demands silence but brings the session to a close.

Lucie hurls herself into my arms, screaming as the photographers flock around us.

I start crying. Nicole and Mathilde join us immediately. We become four sets of hugging arms, squeezing each other and choking on our tears.

I wipe my eyes. I could hug the entire world.

There's a commotion of some sort at the back of the room. Some shouting, but I can't make out the words.

Standing a few yards away, Charles lifts his left hand and makes his humble, complicit salute.

A little farther away, Fontana, flanked by his two minions, gives me his first proper smile, albeit with those predator's lips. He even stretches to a thumbs up.

Genuine admiration.

The only person hanging his head a little is my publisher: a good, chunky sentence would have really boosted sales.

The policemen pull me backward. I can't figure out why—everything is so unexpected.

"Just formalities, Papa, it's nothing," Lucie assures me.

I have to go back to prison to be formally released from custody and collect my things.

Lucie hugs me tightly again. Mathilde holds both my hands. Nicole has coiled up against my back, her arms around my waist and her cheek on my shoulder.

The policemen are still yanking at me. Not violently—just respecting the rules and evacuating the room.

The girls and I say silly things to each other, like "I love you." I hold Lucie's face in my hands, trying to find the words. Lucie plants an enormous smacker on my lips. She says: "Papa."

This is the last word.

It's time for our hands to unlock, our fingers to part. Except Nicole, who continues to cling to me.

"That's enough, madame," says one of the officers.

"It's over," Nicole says to me, kissing me passionately on the lips.

She extricates herself from me, crying and laughing all at the same time.

I would do anything to leave with her now, right now. A quick getaway with Nicole, the girls, my life—everything.

Mathilde says: "See you tonight." Lucie nods as if to say, of course, she'll be there, too. Tonight, all of us together.

Time to leave. More hand gestures, promising each other a thousand things.

From the other side of the room, Fontana smiles at me with a barely perceptible nod of the head.

His message is clear: "See you very soon."

40

I come to my senses in the bus on the way back to prison. The news has spread like wildfire among the inmates. I hear tin trays banging on iron bars. Congratulations. A few whoops and cheers. Returning here knowing I'm a free man is almost a pleasant experience.

Officer Morisset is on duty, and he pays me a visit to offer his congratulations. We wish each other good luck.

"And don't forget, officer: outline your argument *in* your introduction, not after."

He smiles at me and we shake hands.

I walk into my cell for the last time, piss in the latrine for the last time. Everything's for the last time.

Sixteen months in jail.

What will I have to show for it all?

I try to fast-forward to tomorrow. My girls. I start crying again, but they're good tears. My fingers feel better, even though a couple of them, the left index and the middle right, don't bend like before.

I get back my civilian clothes. They're fairly worn out—last used during the hostage taking. For my official discharge through the custody office, lots of things need signing, and I'm handed endless papers that I shove in my pocket. A painfully slow process, lots of waiting. I'm sitting on a bench.

A creeping bitterness overwhelms me as I add up the damage on my crooked fingers. I have:

> aged ten years in here.
> ruined Mathilde.
> extorted Lucie.
> drained Nicole.
> estranged my son-in-law.
> sold the apartment.
> spent the proceeds from my book on the trial.
> postponed my retirement indefinitely.
> wound up in a depressing one-bed.
> still haven't found a job.

I'm back to square one.

It's been a story of abject failure, and it's unbearable.

All I wanted for tonight was my freedom, but now that I have it, I see that it's not enough.

I have to give back the money now; what little I've won will end up in the hands of those institutional crooks.

But have I lost everything? I can't let this happen to me.

There's just one last question.

Is there still a way for me to keep my hard-earned cash: yes or fucking no?

I think hard, turning all the options over in my head. Only one solution presents itself.

Sarqueville.

Let's pay Paul Cousin a visit.

41

The doors open and close. There's a positive feel to the dreary thud, yet I'm scared. I've come out alive and in one piece, with the exception of a few fingers. I don't want to make one more mistake.

And when I step through the prison door, I'm still not sure whether I'm going to attempt one last play.

As ever, I'm going to let circumstances decide for me.

The street is divided into a perfect triangle.

There's me with my back to the prison gate, empty handed and wearing my last remaining suit.

To my left, on the other side of the road, there's Charles. Good old Charles. Confronted with the dual challenge of staying both upright and stationary, he is leaning against a wall. As soon as I get out, he lifts his left hand as a sign of victory. He must have come by bus which, if true, is nothing short of miraculous.

There to my right, on the far pavement, is David Fontana, who gets out of an enormous 4×4 to intercept me. Full of exuberance, Fontana, with that same dynamic stride.

And no one else.

Just the three of us.

I look left and right to find Nicole. The girls are meant to be join-ing us later for dinner, but Nicole . . . where is she?

On seeing Fontana heading my way so purposefully, my gut instinct is to look for help. I take a backward step.

Charles has kicked into gear, too. Fontana turns and points a finger at him. Clearly intimidated, Charles stops dead in the middle of the street.

Fontana's in front of me, a few feet away. He is radiating a nega-tive aura. I know that if he pretends to smile, it gets even worse: he exudes ferociousness.

He pretends to smile.

"My client has kept his side of the deal. Now it's your turn."

He rummages in his pocket.

"Here are your keys. The keys to your apartment."

My internal alarm is triggered.

"Where's my wife?"

"As you've never been to the place before," he adds, ignoring my question, "I've made a note of the address. And here's the number for the keypad."

He holds out a piece of paper, which I grab. His steely eyes don't blink.

"You have one hour, Delambre. One hour to make the transfer into my client's account."

He nods toward the piece of paper.

"The bank details are at the top."

"But . . ."

"I can assure you that your wife is eager to have you home."

I try to support myself, but behind me is just empty space.

"Where is she?"

"She's safe, don't panic. At least she'll be safe for the next hour. After that, I'm no longer answerable for anything."

He gives me no time to respond. His cell phone is already in his hand. The blood drains from my face. Fontana listens, then holds it out to me.

"Nicole?"

I pronounce her name as if I'd just come home and couldn't figure out where she was.

"Alain . . ."

She pronounces my name as if she were on the brink of drowning but trying to remain calm.

Her voice pierces me and runs right down my spine.

Fontana snatches the phone out of my hand.

"One hour," he says.

"It's not possible."

He already looked set to leave, so I blurted this out with as much conviction as I could manage. Fontana glares at me. I take a deep breath. Crucial to speak slowly, to make my sentences flow.

Another golden rule of management: *trust in your skillset.*

"The money's stored in various accounts, all of them offshore. What with the different time zones and stock exchange trading hours . . ."

I egg myself on: *Believe in yourself! You're an international finance expert; he's just an asshole! You know what you're talking about! He's got no fucking idea! Keep hammering it home!*

". . . the time needed to verify sales, redeem shares, process payments, approve passwords . . . It's just not possible. I'll need at least two hours. More like three, in fact."

Fontana didn't see this one coming. He thinks about it, looking for a shred of doubt in my eyes, a bead of sweat on my forehead, or an unusual dilation of the pupil. Then he looks at his watch.

"You've got until 6:30 p.m."

"What guarantee do I have . . . ?"

Fontana wheels around furiously.

"None."

He doesn't pick up on my distress. I, on the other hand, have just noticed a crucial development: for Fontana, this is no longer simply about sealing a deal; I have become an object of personal hatred. Despite all his experience, I've caught him off-guard several times. For him, this is now a matter of honor.

In a few seconds, the street is deserted. Charles, who'd managed to make it as far as the street lamp, resumes his journey along the pavement unaided.

I rest my hand on his shoulder.

Charles is all I have left.

We hug each other. It's weird, but he reeks of kirsch. It's been ten years since I smelled that.

"I get the feeling you're in deep shit," Charles says.

"It's my wife, Nicole . . ."

I have no way of explaining why I hesitate. I should already be sprinting to the nearest computer, getting online, fetching the lucre, filling up the bucket, and dumping it in Exxyal's coffers. I'm holding the keys to our new apartment. There's a little label on a green plastic thing, like a real estate agent's set. I read the address. My god, it's on avenue de Flandre. There's nothing but dreary low-rise buildings and anonymous apartment towers out there. I could have guessed as much from the photos. This settles it for me.

"Your wife not there?"

Whenever I've thought about this money, I've pictured maybe twenty, a hundred, a thousand times the sort of immaculate apartment Nicole and I would be able to afford. The girls, too.

"Don't worry sure as anything she'll be there waiting."

In this place, I imagine Nicole laying out the same worn-out kitchenware. In the sitting room, the carpet will be as frayed as her cardigan. Fuck. After all we've been through, we can't just let it all go. Rouen's two hours away. It's doable. They can't do anything to her. They won't touch her. But first I have to call her.

"Have you got your cell phone?"

It takes Charles a bit of time to grasp what I'm talking about.

"Your cell phone . . ."

Charles twigs. He goes in search of his phone—this could take all day.

"Here, let me."

I sink my hand into the pocket he was heading for, grab the phone, and punch in Nicole's number. I picture her with her cell phone. The girls have teased her about it for years. It's an ancient thing she's never wanted to part with. A horrendous orange job, virtually first generation, that weighs a ton and barely fits in her hand. There can't be another one like it anywhere in the world. She's always telling us to leave her old gizmo alone—it's hers and it works just fine. When it dies, how will she be able to pay for a new one?

A woman's voice. It must be Yasmine, the young Arab woman from the hostage taking.

"You calling your wife?" Charles asks.

"Put my wife on!" I scream.

The girl weighs it up, then says: "Wait there."

Then it's Nicole.

"Have they hurt you?"

That's my first question. Because in my head, they've already done awful things. I feel a tingle in each of my knuckles, even the ones that don't work anymore.

"No," Nicole says.

I barely recognize her voice. It's completely hollow. Her fear is palpable.

"I don't want them to hurt you. You mustn't be afraid, Nicole. You have nothing to be afraid of."

"They say they want the money . . . What money, Alain?"

She's crying.

"Did you take their money?"

Too complicated to answer that.

"I'll give them everything they want, Nicole, I promise you. Promise me they haven't touched you!"

Nicole can't speak through her tears. She utters syllables that I can't make out. I try to keep her on the line.

"Do you know where you are? Nicole, tell me if you know where you are!"

"No . . ."

Her voice is like a little girl's.

"Are you in pain, Nicole?"

"No . . ."

I've only heard her cry like this once before. It was six years ago, when she lost her father. She collapsed on the kitchen floor in tears, screaming endless words, in a horrendous state. She had the same sobbing, high-pitched voice.

"That's enough," says the woman.

The line goes dead. I'm rooted to the pavement. The silence is brutally abrupt.

"That your wife?" Charles asks, slow on the uptake as ever. "You in the shit then?"

He's a sweet man, Charles. I've been paying him no attention, but he's still there, waiting patiently, bathed in his *eau de kirsch*. He's worried for me.

"I need a car, Charles. Now. Right now."

Charles whistles. Yup, that really is a thinker. I keep going:

"Listen, I don't have time to explain . . ."

He stops me with a direct, almost precise gesture, not the kind I would usually associate with him.

"Don't mess around with me!" I say.

A short silence, then:

"Right," he says.

He pulls a few crinkled notes out of his pocket, unfolds them, and starts counting.

"Cabs are over there," he says, jerking his head somewhere behind him.

I don't need to bother counting—I know how much the custody office lot gave me. I say:

"I've got twenty euros."

"And I . . ." says Charles, counting shakily.

It takes him a crazy amount of time.

". . . I have twenty, too!" he yells suddenly. "Snap!"

It takes a moment for him to come back to earth after this giddying revelation.

"It's not quite enough for a full tank, but it'll have to do."

42

The taxi hardly waited around. I'm buzzing, adrenaline coursing through my veins as fast as a galloping horse. It takes me less than ten minutes to jack up Charles's Renault 25, kick away the blocks, and get it back on its tires. Charles is swaying back and forth, always a few steps behind. Everything's going hellishly fast for him. So fast, in fact, that while he's still filling up at the Center Leclerc on the corner at 3:45 p.m., we're actually zooming past Porte Maillot. Five minutes later and we're joining the *autoroute*, where the traffic is fine. The car's steering is pulling hard to the side, and the fact that half my fingers are in a mush doesn't help the matter. I compare my watch with the clock on the dashboard.

"Aha, look no further," Charles says, waving his gargantuan watch, "this puppy doesn't lose a minute in three months!"

A quick bit of arithmetic tells me I have just over two hours left. I call directory assistance and request the Exxyal refinery in Sarqueville. "I'm putting you through," the voice says. I ask for Paul Cousin. I get pinged from one secretary to another. I ask for Paul Cousin again.

Not there.

I slam on the brakes.

Charles, his bottle of kirsch clenched between his thighs, looks around as quickly as he can, peering through the back window to check whether we're about to be crunched by a truck.

"How can he not be there?"

"He's not here yet," says the girl.

"But he'll be in today?"

The girl checks her calendar.

"He'll be in, but it's a bit of a difficult day . . ."

I hang up. For me, he'll be in. Meetings, appointments, whatever—he'll be there. I chase away the thought of Nicole, the sound of her voice. I don't know where she is, but nothing will happen to her before 6:30 p.m. By which time I'll have solved the problem.

Fuck you, Fontana.

I clench my jaw. If I could, I'd clench the steering wheel, too, destroying my joints that are already in pieces.

Charles watches the traffic race past. He puts his bottle of kirsch back in its spot under the seat. The enormous chrome bars that serve as bumpers come a third of the way up his windshield and stick out into the other lane a bit. I have no idea what the police will say if they stop us. I don't even have my license on me.

In theory, Charles's home is a six-cylinder, 2.5-liter turbo V6. In theory. In reality, it maxes out at 70 miles an hour and shudders like a Boeing 747 preparing for takeoff, with noise levels to match. We can barely hear each other. I stick firmly to the fast lane.

"You can give her some more, you know!" Charles says. "She's not shy!"

I don't want to upset him by telling him that my foot's down as far as it'll go. He'd be so disappointed. We surrender to the sound of the engine. The car stinks of kirsch.

About an hour in, I tap the dial with my finger. The gauge is going down so fast I can scarcely believe my eyes.

"Yup," says Charles, "she's a thirsty girl!"

You're telling me. She's sucking it down at twenty-five miles per gallon, no problem. It should get us there, but only just. I do everything I can to keep Nicole from my thoughts. The farther I get from Paris, the closer I feel to her, to saving her.

Fucking hell, I will do this.

I hold the wheel tight because the steering's wildly, dangerously off-kilter.

"Sore is it?" Charles asks, pointing at my bandages.

"No, that's not . . ."

Charles nods in agreement. He thinks he knows what I mean. It suddenly strikes me that since his first greeting outside the prison gate, I have taken his cell phone, his twenty euros, and his car, subjecting him to this hazardous journey without saying or explaining anything to him. Charles hasn't asked me a single question. I turn to him. As he watches the landscape flash past, his face enthralls me.

Charles is a beautiful man. There's no other word.

He has a beautiful soul.

"Let me explain . . ."

Charles doesn't look away from the landscape, but just lifts his hand as though to say tell me what you want, when you want, if you want. Don't fret.

A beautiful, big soul.

So I start explaining.

In doing so, I replay everything. Nicole. The last few years and months. I relive the pathetic hope of landing a job at my age and I see Nicole's face again as she leans against the door of my office, holding the letter and saying: "My love, this is unbelievable!" The tests, the interview with Lacoste, all my idiotic preparation.

"Ah well, holy shit!" Charles says admiringly. He is deep in thought, his eyes fixed on the passing *autoroute*.

I talk about my stubbornness and Nicole's anger. Mathilde's money and my fist in her husband's face. The hostage taking. It all comes out.

"Ah well, holy shit!"

By the time he's digested all the information, we've made another eighteen miles.

"This Fontana," he says, "is he that squat guy with metally eyes?"

Charles had been struck by him at the trial, too.

"Always on the lookout, that guy! And he had some backup as well. Tough bastard that one. What did you say his name was again?"

"Fontana."

Charles mulls over the name for a long while. He murmurs "Fontana," chewing on each syllable.

The dial continues its breakneck descent. You'd think there was a leak in the fuel tank.

"She's going at less than twenty-five miles per gallon!"

Charles looks skeptical.

"I'd say more like twenty . . ." he says at last.

Perhaps Renault 25 actually means liters . . . At this rate, we won't have enough. He offers me the bottle but thinks better of it.

"No, that's true—you're driving."

However hard I try to concentrate on other things, I am assailed by the thought of Nicole and her tears over the phone. I'm confident that they haven't hurt her. They must have grabbed her at the bottom of the building. Adrenaline pumps through my veins faster and faster, surging from head to toe. I picture Nicole sitting tied to a chair. No, that's crazy—if there are still hours to go, she'll be free to move. What use would it be to tie her up? No. They're just keeping an eye on her. What sort of place? Nicole. I think I might be sick. I concentrate on the road ahead. Paul Cousin. Sarqueville. All my thoughts must stay focused on that. If I win this round, I win the whole thing. Nicole will be back, back with me.

I lied to them: transferring their money would have taken half an hour. By now, it could be back in Exxyal's account.

Nicole could be free.

Instead, I'm getting as far away from her as this old banger will allow.

Have I completely lost my mind?

"Mustn't cry, my man . . . ," Charles says.

I hadn't even noticed. I wipe away my tears with the back of my sleeve. This suit . . . Nicole.

Criquebeuf: almost seventy miles to go. The fuel gauge is sputtering like a candle.

"There's no way she's even doing twenty, Charles. Come on, it's got to be less!"

"Could be . . ."

He leans toward the dial.

"Oh yeah, look at that! Well then, we'll need to have a think about that . . ."

A sign indicates it's about four miles to the next service station. It's 5:00 p.m.

We've only got four euros and some change left.

A few minutes later, the Renault 25 starts juddering. Charles grimaces. I feel ready to cry again and start smacking the steering wheel like a maniac.

"We'll find something," Charles assures me.

Will we now. The car bunny-hops more and more severely, so I pull into the slow lane and ease off the accelerator to save the last few seconds. The engine stalls, but I manage to use our momentum to carry us onto the exit for the service station. We can put in four euros of petrol. The car doesn't so much stop as collapse. It dies. Silence inside. Despondence. I look at the time. I have no idea what to do. Even if I were to change my mind and make the transfer right away, how would I do it? Where would I go?

I'm not even entirely sure where we are. Charles frowns.

"Hold on!" he yells, pointing at the *autoroute* behind. "Back there! I saw it: Rouen, fourteen miles!"

Another twenty-five miles to Sarqueville, and the car has drunk its last drop.

Nicole.

Think.

I can't thread two thoughts together. My brain stopped functioning with the image of Nicole and the sound of her voice on the telephone. I didn't even notice Charles open the passenger door. He's embarked on a roundabout route toward the service station.

Think.

Thumb a lift. Find another vehicle. There's no other choice. I drag myself out of the car and run to catch up with Charles. He's already in discussion with an enormous blond-haired man with a red face and a grubby cap. Charles motions toward me as I approach them.

"This is him, my pal . . ."

The guy looks at me. He looks at Charles. We must seem a funny pair.

"I'm going the other side of Rouen," he says.

"Sarqueville?" I ask.

"Not far from there."

"You can take my pal, then?" Charles says, rubbing his hands.

These words reveal where dear Charles's strength lies. No one can resist him. His sincerity is so disarming, his generosity overwhelming.

"No problem," the guy says.

"Well, no time to lose," Charles says, still rubbing his hands.

The man is shuffling impatiently. Charles and I shake hands, and he senses my embarrassment.

"Don't worry!" he says.

I rummage in my pockets and give him the four euros.

"Bah, what about you?"

Without waiting for an answer, he gives me back three.

"Share like brothers," he chuckles.

The driver says:

"Look, gents, sorry but . . ."

I hug Charles. He barely touches me. He takes off his massive green fluorescent watch and hands it to me. I strap it to my wrist and squeeze his shoulder. He looks to one side and nods to indicate that the driver's waiting.

As I watch him disappear in the side mirror, he gives his salute.

It's a huge semi. He's transporting stationery, a heavy load. We're hardly going to be blasting down the *autoroute*. Is this turning into a suicide mission?

Nicole.

Throughout the journey, the guy respects my silence. I play back the image of Nicole over and over. At times, it's like she's already dead and I'm remembering her. I dispel this idea as forcefully as I can and try to focus on something else. A few headlines. *This year's unemployment forecasts of 639,000 are set to be exceeded, according to the Ministry of Labor.* Good of them to be so honest.

When the truck drops me at the Sarqueville exit, it's 5:30 p.m. One hour to go.

I have to call. I go into a telephone booth on the roadside that stinks of cigarettes and put in two coins.

Fontana picks up.

"I want to speak to my wife."

"Have you done what you were supposed to?"

It's like he's here, standing in front of me. My heart's pounding at a hundred thousand beats per minute.

"Everything's underway. I want to speak to my wife!"

My eyes fall on the plastic-covered sheet with all the international dialing codes and user instructions, and immediately I realize my error.

"Where are you calling from?"

It doubles: two hundred thousand beats per minute.

"From an online connection, why?"

Silence. Then:

"I'm handing you over."

"Alain, where are you?"

The anxiety in her voice sums up her distress. She starts crying.

"Don't cry, Nicole, I'm coming to get you."

"When?"

What am I supposed to reply to that . . .

"It'll be over soon, I promise."

But my tone is too harsh for her. I shouldn't have called. She starts screaming:

"Where are you, Alain, where the fuck are you! Where are you? WHERE ARE YOU?"

The last bit gets lost in her sobbing. She breaks down, overcome by her tears. I feel desolate.

"I'm coming, my love, I'll be there soon."

I say that, but I'm light years away from her.

Fontana comes back:

"My client still hasn't received anything. What stage are you at exactly?"

I feel feverish. The screen in front of me is flashing. I put in another coin. My credit's being guzzled as quickly as the fuel in the Renault 25. The cost of living is crazy now. I've had enough.

"I've already explained: nothing can be done in under three hours."

I hang up. He's going to run a search on the number that came up. In five minutes he'll know I'm near Rouen. Will he make the link? Definitely. Will he realize the significance? I don't think so.

5:35 p.m.

I sprint toward the tollbooth. I make for the right-hand side of the first car. It's a woman. I crouch down and knock on the window. Alarmed, she gathers her change and drives off like a shot.

"What are you doing?" asks the girl in the booth.

Twenty-five, at a guess. Big girl.

"I ran out of gas," I say, pointing back down the *autoroute*.

She makes an ambiguous sound.

Two more cars turn me down. *Where are you?* The words are still ringing in my ears. I sense the girl's irritation increasing as I hassle the drivers. Can hardly blame her . . .

A van. A big, dog-like face. A setter, perhaps. The man's about forty. He leans across and opens the door. I glance at my watch.

Where are you?

"In a hurry?"

"Yes, yes I am."

"Typical. Always happens when you're in a hurry . . ."

I don't listen to the rest. I say: "Sarqueville . . . The refinery . . . Five miles."

We arrive in the town.

"I'll drop you off," offers the setter.

The town's deserted. No one in the streets. Shops closed and banners everywhere: NO TO THE CLOSURE! . . . *VIVE* SARQUEVILLE! . . . YES TO SARQUEVILLE! NO TO SARKOVILLE!

No wonder Paul Cousin's not in the office—his work is already done.

"The town's dead. Everyone's getting ready for the march tomorrow."

It's really not my day. Where will Cousin be? I remember the secretary's hesitation on the phone.

"When is it?"

"The march? On the radio they said four o'clock," the guy answers as he drops me at the barrier. "They're aiming to be outside the refinery in time for the seven o'clock news on France 3."

"Thank you," I say.

The refinery is a monstrosity, all cylinders, overhead tubes, giant ducts, and pipes of every size. Never-ending smokestacks tower into the sky. Red and green lights flash away on the sides of vats. The whole thing takes your breath away. It's like the site is dormant. Operations on hold. Banners beat in the breeze. Same slogans as in town, but here, engulfed the vastness of the factory, they seem pitiful. Everything is dominated by the pipe work. The defiant words spray-painted on the flags are a rallying cry for a struggle that seems over before it's even begun.

Paul Cousin's done a fine job: all the baying, the blustering, the howls of indignation are happening down the road, out of sight. At the refinery, there's not a single burning tire, no barricades or vehicles blocking the way, no picket lines of protesters stoking empty oil drums to grill their sausages. Not even a leaflet littering the ground.

I hesitate for a split second before walking past the barrier as confidently as possible. I don't get away with it.

"Excuse me!"

I turn to the guard.

Alain? Where are you?

It's true: What the fuck am I doing here? I walk up to the booth, go around the side, and climb two steps. The guard scrutinizes my suit, which by now has certainly seen better days.

"Sorry. I have a meeting with Monsieur Cousin."

"And you are . . . ?" he says, picking up his telephone.

"Alain Delambre."

If Cousin hears my name he might think twice, but he'll definitely see me. I look at Charles's watch. So does the guard. Between my tattered suit and my fluorescent timepiece, I seem an unlikely candidate for a meeting with the boss. Time passes at an alarming rate. I pace about next to the booth, trying to look relaxed.

"His secretary says that you don't have an appointment. I'm sorry."

"That must be a mistake."

The way the guard spreads his arms and looks at me leaves no room for doubt—I'm dealing with a stubborn bastard. The sort who really believes in his job. The worst sort. If I keep pestering him, it's only going one way.

Normally speaking, a man in my position would look surprised, take out his cell phone and call his contact at the refinery to clarify matters. The guard eyes me closely. I figure he thinks I'm a tramp. He's begging me to try and jump the barrier. I turn, take a couple of steps, pretend to dig around in my pocket and take out an imaginary phone. I look up at the sky as though I'm deep in thought, all the while getting farther and farther away. The refinery is served by a single S-shaped strip of blacktop. Over on the *autoroute* the traffic is getting thicker and thicker, but here there's no one. Still engrossed in my pretend conversation, I end up in a spot where the guard can't see me anymore. If there were any vehicles passing by I'd be able to hop aboard, but there's zero movement on this side of the refinery. It's 5:45 p.m. Barely forty-five minutes left. Whatever happens, it's too late. Even if I wanted to reverse everything, I can't.

Alain?

Nicole's somewhere over there with the killers. She's crying. They're going to hurt her. Will they snap her fingers, too?

Can't find Paul Cousin.

No cell phone and not a cent on me.

No car.

I'm alone. The wind picks up. It's about to rain.

I have absolutely no idea what to do.

Alain?

Where are you?

43

What's the point in coming all the way to Sarqueville only to wander aimlessly around the streets? It's not like I'm going to bump into Paul Cousin in town, visiting the cemetery before the battle commences. I stay put, shifting from one foot to the other.

The *autoroute* runs all the way down one side of the refinery. The traffic's mounting up. Ahead of tomorrow's march, police vehicles are starting to pile into the area, followed by coachloads of riot police. They're all converging on the town in preparation for the protests. On my side, the refinery side, everything's dead calm. It starts drizzling a little after 6:00 p.m.

A few minutes later, it's pouring.

I'm in no-man's-land. I have to speak to Nicole. No, to Fontana. I have to come up with a reason to push back the deadline.

I can't. Nothing.

The rain gets even harder. I flip up my jacket collar and walk toward the refinery once more, racking my brains as I go. I draw on every last weapon from my arsenal of management-speak. Hypothesis after hypothesis, what-if after what-if, but nothing works.

I attempt to run through the list of possibilities, but still nothing comes.

My brain is refusing to function. I'm back in front of the booth, pummeled by the rain. I look like an unemployed man fresh out of prison. I'm Jean Valjean.

The guard looks at me through the water running down his window. He doesn't even flinch. I go up on my tiptoes and knock on the glass. Still no movement. He's just standing there. This can't be happening . . . I tap again. He makes up his mind and opens the door. Not a word. I hadn't noticed before, but he's about my age. More or less my height. He's got a tummy on him, a belt propping it up from underneath. Apart from that and his mustache, we look more or less alike. Give or take. The rain is dripping down the collar of my drenched jacket and pouring down my face. I have to screw up my eyes to make out the guard, who's still standing in the open door, looking at me without moving.

"Listen . . ."

The rain, my saturated suit, my stance, my bandaged hand tugging at my tieless collar, my humiliation . . . everything about me screams rock bottom. He cocks his head, a motion I am unable to decipher.

He's a guard. About sixty. Same age as me.

Alain?

I've got less than half an hour left. I don't know what else I can do to rescue the situation. All I know is it involves getting past him. He's the only living being between me and my life.

The last one.

Where are you?

"Listen . . ." I repeat. "I really must make a call. It's very urgent."

I've just thought of something. Dead battery. My cell phone's bust. He can't hear me over the sound of the rain hammering on his booth. He moves closer to the door, leans his head out slightly and stoops down to me. A drop of water on his neck startles him. He recoils and angrily brings a hand to his collar. He looks at me again, before saying:

"Get the fuck out of here! Now!"

Those are his words as he slams the door violently. What really riled him up were those drops of water on his neck. That's what tipped him over the edge.

So no help, no telephone, no nothing. Nicole might suffer, I might die, the refinery might fire everyone, the town might become a wasteland, the civilized world might disappear. But he—he has shut his door. Must be one of the few who kept his job.

It's over. In a few minutes, Fontana will walk up to Nicole and fix his steely eyes on hers. I'm at a loss. I'm a hundred and fifty miles from her, and she's going to suffer horribly.

The guard pretends to peer into the distance through his rain-spattered window, like the captain of a cargo ship. I reach a conclusion with absolute certainty: this man represents everything I abhor; he is my hatred in human form.

The only sensible course of action is to kill him.

I stretch my neck muscles, climb the two steps, and open the door. The guy takes a backward step as I pile into him.

This man is the Enemy: killing him will save us all.

My fist makes contact at the precise moment that the image of Nicole arrives. She's sitting in a chair, tied up, a large piece of duct tape over her mouth. Someone's holding her hand, preparing to break her fingers, and the guard falls back and cracks his head on the desk, his chair rolling toward the door. Fontana looks Nicole in the eye and says: "You do know that you can't count on your husband," and suddenly snaps back all her fingers. Nicole screams, a bestial, primordial cry, the same sound I make when the guard knees me in the balls. Nicole and I scream together. We're being tortured together. We're twisting in pain together. We're going to die together, I've known it from the start. From the start. Death. I stagger back two paces toward the door and the guard's back on his feet. Nicole has fainted. *Alain? Where are you?* Fontana slaps her cheek and says: "Wake up, time for the other hand," and the guard hits me, I'm not sure what with, but it knocks me into the swivel chair, which tips over and sends me flying out of the booth, completely off-balance as I bounce down the steps, rolling backward, skidding down the slick concrete. Nicole can't bear to look at her hands, the pain's too much, and I'm floundering, battered by the rain. My head cracks into the ground first, and Nicole is in so much pain she can't even scream, nothing comes from her throat and her eyes are bulging out, mesmerized by the agony—*Alain? Where are you?*—and my head bounces once, twice as I close my eyes and everything stops and I clutch my skull, feeling nothing.

I'm a body without a soul, from the start I've had no soul.

My hand covers my eyes and I try to figure out what position I'm in, try to turn over but I can't—I might die here—car fumes hit my sinuses, and through squinting eyes I make out the edge of a chrome exhaust pipe, big tires, silver rims, then shoes, perfectly polished shoes, and a man is standing over me, and I rub my eyes as the figure towers above me, his legs firmly set, and I notice how very tall he is.

How thin he is.

It takes me two more seconds to recognize him.

Paul Cousin.

44

It's really a deluge now, the rain coursing down the windshield and drowning the scenery in a milky blur. The daylight is fading. I think of the demonstrators on the far side of the *autoroute* who are preparing for tomorrow. They must be keeping a close eye on the gray sky. It looks leaden for another generation at least. Paul Cousin can rest easy: even the elements are working in his favor. It's like a sign from heaven.

St. Cousin is at the wheel. He doesn't bother with the wipers. Instead his severe, puritanical eyes are trained on my suit as it drips on the floor of his car. My whole body is shaking. I should be with Nicole. Nicole is with Fontana, and I'm here, lost. The back of my head's bleeding. I'm struggling to breathe—must have cracked some ribs. Nicole's right . . . I do screw up everything. I've taken off my jacket and I'm clutching the rolled-up sleeve against the top of my skull. Cousin's not hiding his disgust.

He managed to calm the guard.

We're in his parking space at the refinery. Swanky car. Cousin has both hands on the wheel. He is projecting a patient demeanor, but the underlying message is clear: don't abuse the situation.

"Any chance of turning that off?" I ask.

The air conditioning is freezing. I'm chilled to the bone. It's arctic, very much Cousin's style. I picture him rubbing his torso with snow. His Reverend Dimmesdale side.

Luxury dashboard for a luxury car.

"Company wheels?"

Cousin doesn't move. Of course it's a company car. It's only the second time I've seen him close up: the size of his head is simply astonishing. It gives me the creeps. All this is giving me time to focus. I compose myself, determined not to rush headlong into the fray. Only twenty minutes to go. The Patron Saint of Lost Causes has let me get away by the skin of my teeth. I can't make the same mistake I did with the guard and blow my last chance. I take a deep breath. Nicole's fear is at the forefront of my mind.

I can't miss this last chance.

Cousin's patience is wearing thin.

"It's not like I don't have better things to be doing!" he snaps at last.

If that were really true, we wouldn't be here in this stationary car, the rain hammering down, on the day the whole region is rallying against the layoff plan he's enforcing, in the shadow of a substantial police presence. It doesn't add up.

I keep quiet because I can tell Paul Cousin is on edge. Despite all my instincts to get moving, and fast, I know that would be the best way to ruin everything.

The last time Cousin saw me was yesterday, in the dock. He testified in my favor on the orders of his boss. And now, twenty-four hours later, he finds me—coming apart at the seams in more ways than one—smacking the guard in the face at his factory, which happens to be on strike. It doesn't bode well at all. If anything, I'm here to make demands. Yet St. Paul seems intrigued. Ever since I saw him enter the courtroom, I could tell he was furious with me, because he knew full well that he'd been screwed over. Only he doesn't know to what extent, and that's what intrigues him—he's itching to know. The fact is, he's the one who should be making demands. He did me a favor. He contributed to my freedom. Somehow I've become his boss's protégé, the man he's gone to extreme lengths to help. But Cousin doesn't know what demands to make. Seeing me here, destitute, has flipped his world on its head. My patience pays off. Cousin can't resist:

"During the hostage taking," he says, "you let me go on purpose, didn't you?"

"Let's say I wasn't opposed to the idea."

"You could have shot me."

"That wasn't in my interests."

"Because you needed someone to escape and warn the police. Didn't matter who. Me or any of the others."

"Yes, but I hoped it would be you."

I inspect my jacket sleeve: I'm still bleeding, so I press it hard against the top of my head again. This dithering annoys Cousin, since it forces him to wait. I will myself to take my time, which is no mean feat because I can't help glaring at the clock on the dashboard every other second. *Nicole.* The minutes drag. I continue distractedly:

"I was so pleased when you became the hero of the day in your boss's eyes. It was just what you needed to be welcomed back into the company fold after slogging it out free of charge for all those years. I was glad you were the first to stand up and be counted. You were the one I wanted. You were my favorite. Call it solidarity for the unemployed."

Cousin turns all that over in his enormous head.

"What did you take from Exxyal?"

"How do you know about that?"

"Come on!"

He's in a huff, old Cousin. He continues:

"Alexandre Dorfmann organizes a press conference to announce loud and clear that Exxyal is dropping all charges, and demands his execs testify in your favor at the trial . . . It's not hard to tell that you've got him cornered. So I'll ask you again: what did you take?"

The moment of truth. I've got fifteen minutes left. I close my eyes. I look at Nicole. All my courage lies with her. I ask the question calmly:

"How pissed off will Dorfmann be when he finds out the two of us are in agreement?"

"Agreement over what? Agreement over nothing!"

Cousin's outraged, shouting.

"Yes, agreement over nothing . . . But only me and you need to know that. If I tell him that we've agreed to screw him over, who's he going to believe? You or me?"

Cousin concentrates hard. I set out my argument:

"The way I see it, he's going to let you handle things at Sarqueville because it's a shitty business. Both hands deep in the shit. CEOs don't tend to be too excited about that. Then afterward, when you've fired everyone, your head will be the next to roll. And this time, you won't be bailed out by a courageous unemployed person who's no longer eligible for unemployment benefits."

His fury seems to fill his entire head, which is saying something.

"And what exactly are we agreeing on?"

I wheel out the big guns.

"I ran off with Dorfmann's slush fund. My plan is to tell him that we've gone halves on it."

You might expect him to be scandalized, but not a bit of it. Paul Cousin thinks about it. He's a manager. He assesses the situation, runs through the various strategies, analyzes his objectives. In my mind, he could buy himself some time by considering how fucked he is. I try to jog him:

"You're pretty fucked, my friend."

I jog him because I'm in a chronic state of urgency. I hope Fontana hasn't stuck a clock in front of Nicole. He's capable of it. He's capable of counting down the minutes, the seconds. I go for a second volley.

"I'm giving you three minutes."

"I doubt that."

He needs to reframe the issue. Eight minutes to go. Nicole.

"How much did you take?" he asks.

"Tut tut tut."

Nice try, but I'm not going to fall for that.

"What do you want?"

Fine application of the reality principle.

"Some dirt on Exxyal. Something really dirty. I want to blow Dorfmann out of the sky. Give me what I want and I'll make it worth your while. A seven-figure bribe, a disgraceful kickback, a deal with a terrorist state, a nasty payoff . . . I don't care."

"And how would I know about any of that?"

"Because you've been here for twenty years. You've spent more than fifteen at the top. And you're the kind of person who laps up the shady stuff. Why else would you be here in Sarqueville? I'm not asking for the whole file—just a few highlights will do. Nothing more. You have two minutes."

Make or break.

"How can you guarantee me confidentiality?"

"It has to be something from the company system, that's all. I hacked into Exxyal's servers. I could feasibly have snatched anything from in there. I'm not asking for a top-secret document . . . it doesn't even need to be confidential. All I want is some key information— I'll take care of the rest."

"I see."

Sly dog, Cousin.

"Three million."

Even slyer than I thought.

Nothing if not pragmatic. It took him just a few seconds to analyze the situation in front of him and weigh up the pros and cons before deciding to up the ante. Three million euros. I have no idea how he came up with that number. He knows I ran off with the slush fund. He's made an educated guess. In his mind, what percentage does that represent? I'll try another round. Got to wrap this up.

"Two," I say.

"Three."

"Two and a half."

"Three."

"Okay, three million and thirty thousand."

Cousin looks surprised, but my face is deadpan.

"Deal," he says.

"Give me a name!"

"Pascal Lombard."

Holy shit. A former interior minister. I'm blown away. The guy's face comes to me clearly. Prime example of a slippery politician: no shortage of talent; murky past; relentlessly cynical; a few past misdemeanors that investigators were never quite able to untangle; hounded for fifteen years but still holding forth noisily at the Assemblée, crapping all over public morality. Reelected time and time again. Two or three sons in business or politics. Classic.

"What about him?"

"Insider trading. 1998. The time of the merger with Union Path Corp. Textbook stuff: when he heard the news from Dorfmann, he bought up a whole stack of shares from one of his sons, and three months later, when the merger was announced, he sold them all."

"Profit?"

"Ninety-six million francs."

I dial Nicole's number on the car phone. Fontana picks up after the second ring.

"Let me speak to my wife."

"I hope you've got some good news for me."

"Oh, I do. Some excellent news!"

"I'm listening."

"Pascal Lombard. Union Path. 1998. Ninety-six million."

Silence. I give it time to sink in. You don't need to be a senior-ranking intelligence agent to realize that this involves something fishy. Pascal Lombard's name is infamous. He's a political Pandora's box. Fontana's silence confirms I'm right. All the same, he gives it a shot:

"Don't play with me, Delambre."

I think I can hear a sound from behind him. I can't help blurting out:

"I want my wife! Let me speak to her!"

My voice fills the car. Paul Cousin looks at me, finding me increasingly dazed.

"Sorry, Delambre," Fontana says, "but my client hasn't received anything, and you've missed your deadline."

"What's that sound behind you? What is it?"

He doesn't like failure, Fontana. And right now, things might be bad for me, but they're bad for him, too. That's what I'm banking on. His client has enlisted his services, and right now everything's going down the tubes.

"Call your client," I say. "Speak to Alexandre Dorfmann in person and simply tell him this from me: 'Pascal Lombard. Union Path. 1998.'"

I gather my strength and wait a few seconds.

Ready:

"Just say that, and all your problems are over, Fontana. Because that'll put his mind to rest immediately."

Aim:

"But if you choose not to call him, he's going to be very, very, very angry with you."

Fire:

"And if that happens, think hard about how powerful Dorfmann is: my problems will pale compared with yours."

Silence.

Good sign. I breathe. Well handled.

"How do I call you back?"

"I'll call you, but first let me speak to my wife."

Fontana hesitates. He really doesn't like having his hand forced like this.

"I said let me speak to my wife!"

"Hello."

It's Nicole. No more fear. We're beyond fear. Her voice is so weary it sounds lifeless.

"Alain? Where are you?"

"I'm here, my love, I'm with you. It's all over."

My voice catches a little as I try to reassure her, to give her some grounds for hope.

"Why are they keeping me?" Nicole asks.

"They're going to let you go, I promise. Have they hurt you?"

"When will they let me go?"

Her voice is thin and shaky, tense and bruised.

"Have they hurt you?"

Nicole doesn't answer. She asks me question after question with a mix of anguish and despondency. Her mind is stuck on one point:

"What do they want? Where are you?"

No time to reply because the phone changes hands.

"Call me back in ten minutes," Fontana says.

He hangs up. My stomach lurches so violently that I retch from the nausea. All the while, Cousin's been drumming his fingers on the wheel.

"I've got a lot of work to do, Monsieur Delambre. Perhaps it's time to formalize our deal, wouldn't you say?"

Indeed, time for formalities. He suggests we agree on the practical aspects of our transaction without delay. Cousin is shafting his boss in the same methodical manner he serves him. A true professional.

As for me, I'm badly shaken up by Nicole's words.

"Just one thing to finish with . . ." Cousin says.

"Yes, what?" I say, still in a daze.

"Why the thirty thousand?"

"Three million into your account."

I pat the dashboard.

"Plus your car. It's coming with me."

45

"I'm sorry, but I haven't received any instructions along those lines."

"Fuck you, Fontana!"

I'm screaming. Back on the *autoroute* to Paris and I'm doing well over a hundred, my palm flat against the horn. The car in front is dawdling and refusing to budge, so I honk even harder.

"Things have changed, you piece of shit!"

Even if I wanted to, I'd struggle to remember the terror Fontana inspired in me not long ago. I know I'll win, I can feel it all the way to the tips of my fingers, but more than anything in the world I want Nicole.

I keep going:

"I'm the one giving the orders now, you hear me, dickhead?"

The dickhead stays quiet. The mere mention of the names Pascal Lombard and Union Path made Alexandre Dorfmann instruct him to suspend the operation until he has met me in person. He's expecting me at his office in less than two hours. Even if I allow myself the luxury of being forty minutes late, I figure he'll change his appointments to see me. I've turned the speakerphone up to full volume, and I carry on shouting as I weave in and out of the traffic, a hundred and twenty on the dial:

"And I can even tell you how this is going to end up, you bulldog. In one hour, you're going to release my wife and go running back to your kennel. And let me assure you, if there's so much as a hair missing from her head, your antics in Sudan will feel like the fucking *Rescuers*!"

Words fail me for a moment.

"So listen to these instructions, you prick, and follow them. I want three photos of my wife immediately. The first of her face, the second of her hands, and lastly I want one full-length. All of her. Do it on your cell phone. And on each one I want today's date and time. Send them to . . ."

I scrabble around for the number in the car telephone. I take one hand off the wheel and lean toward the screen, pressing one button, then another. *How does this bastard thing work?* A deafening horn blares out and I look up immediately. The car has swerved dangerously left into the oncoming traffic lane and is heading at full speed toward a Dutch semi that is honking its foghorn as loud as it'll go. I barely have time to register the situation, flinging the wheel to the right to avoid the truck I'm bearing down on at the speed of light. It doesn't even occur to me to brake. The dial says I'm going 114 mph.

I yell out the car phone number to Fontana.

"I'm giving you five minutes! Don't make me call back, or I swear, every last cent I extort from your boss will go toward ripping off your balls!"

I continue slaloming across the four lanes. I have to calm down. No big deal if I'm flashed by a radar gun, but getting myself stopped by the police is not a good move. I stick to the fast lane and ease off the accelerator. Ninety-three—that's reasonable. Every ten seconds, I glare at the screen. I'm desperate to see the photos of Nicole. I picture Fontana rushing to get me what I want. There are a few minutes to go.

To try and relax, I look around the inside of Cousin's car. It's a luxurious one. A real gem of French engineering, which seems pretty damn cynical when you consider his job is to close down industrial sites. I fiddle with the controls and find a radio station. I end up on France Info. . . . *last year John Arnold, a thirty-three-year-old trader, earned between 2 and 2.5 billion dollars. Then came . . .* I switch it off. The planet never stops spinning in the same direction and at the same speed.

I make sure the call waiting option is activated and dial Charles's number. One ring, two, three, four.

"Hello!"

Good old Charles. Sure, his voice doesn't exude freshness, but the tone is there, buoyant and bighearted.

"Hi, Charles!"

"Whoa it's you damn yeah I was expecting you where are you calling from?"

All that in the same stride. Charles is delighted. He's relieved, thrilled that the effort he put in to answering the phone has paid off.

"I'm on the *autoroute* to Paris."

The information swirls around the remaining brain cells bobbing up and down in his kirsch-soaked head. I don't wait for the next question before explaining everything: Cousin, Fontana, Dorfmann.

"Ah but damn!" Charles says over and over once I've finished my account.

He is flabbergasted by my performance. I keep on the lookout for Fontana's call—the time seems to be dragging horrendously. I ask Charles where he is.

"Like you, on the *autoroute*."

Good god, Charles is behind the wheel!

"Massive stroke of luck," he continues. "I call my pal and guess what his brother-in-law has a little place two shakes from the service station where we broke down and he filled me up didn't I tell you it was lucky?"

"Charles . . . are you driving?"

"Weeell doing my best."

It knocks the breath out of me.

"I'm being sensible you know," Charles assures me. "I'm staying in the slow lane and not going above forty."

The best way to get hit from behind and stopped by the police.

"Hold on . . . how far along the *autoroute* are you?"

"That I cannot really tell you because the signs are all written so small you see."

I can imagine. But just as I start answering, I make out his scarlet car with its immense chrome bars in the distance, hogging the right-hand lane, with a thick cloud of white smoke stretching behind him like the train of a wedding dress. I slow down slightly, and once I'm alongside him, I honk my horn. He seems so small, as though he's been compacted, his eyes barely higher than the steering wheel.

It takes him a couple of seconds to take stock of the situation.

"It's you! Ah well damn!" he screams when he recognizes me.

He's giddy with joy. He gives me his little salute, beaming from ear to ear.

"I can't hang around, Charles, they're expecting me."

"Don't worry about me," he answers.

There are so many things I'd like to say to him. I owe him so much. I owe him an enormous amount. If everything works out okay, I'm going to change Charles's life. I'm going to give him a house with a cellar full of kirsch. There are so many things I want to say to him.

I put my foot down and start racing again. In a few seconds, the white cloud and the red body of his car are just blurs in my rearview mirror.

"Everything should be all right from now on, Charles."

"Ah well good," he says, "easy as pie."

"Easy as pie" . . . he must be the only person left in the world who uses phrases like that. I round things off:

"I'm meeting Dorfmann . . . just dropping in to nail his balls to his desk, then I'll pick up Nicole. After that it's finished."

Charles is over the moon, thrilled.

"I couldn't be happier for you my friend. You deserve it!"

Hearing that from Charles sends me over the edge. To be so genuinely happy for someone else . . . I'd never be capable of that level
of selflessness.

"You already shafted that other prick whatshisname again
Montana?"

"Fontana."

"That's the one!" Charles shouts.

And he's off again on another round of jubilant celebrations.

My victory is certain. The meeting called by Dorfmann is in itself
an order to fall back, a thinly veiled request for an armistice. I will
get Nicole released and meet her at the apartment. We'll take home
the compensation we've earned, the fair price for all our misfor-
tunes. Our miserable existence will come to an end. I want Charles to
be with us. Nicole will love him.

"Ah well no," says Charles, "after all this you have to just be with
your sweetheart you don't need me there standing around!"

I insist.

"I want you to be there, Charles. It's important to me."

"You sure?"

I fumble in my pocket, unfold the piece of paper Fontana gave
me and read him the address.

"Wait," says Charles.

Then:

"Say it again?"

I read it again and Charles lets out a shriek.

"Ah you have to say that's strange I lived in that neighborhood
when I was a boy no even younger than that when I was a nipper."

That'll help.

"Listen wait," Charles continues, "I've got to make a note of the
number of the street because I'm not sure I'll remember it."

I picture him lurching spectacularly from left to right then
pouncing toward the glove compartment.

"No!" I shout.

In his state, if he doesn't remain completely focused on his
driving, it's going to end in disaster.

"Don't sweat, Charles, I'll send you a text message."

"As you wish."

"Okay, let's do it that way. Shall we say eight-thirty? I've got to go now. Promise? I'm counting on you, all right."

The first photograph is of her hands, and I'm completely fixated by it. No doubt this is because mine still hurt so much, and because driving for the first time in months has made me aware that they will never work like before, that some of my fingers won't bend until I die, or even after I die. I recognize her wedding ring. The sight of her two hands, open and exposed as though waiting for the hammer, leaves a horrible impression. The second photo is marked with the right day and the right time, but it's of the wrong Nicole. My Nicole from before, from always, has been replaced by a woman in her fifties with graying hair and drawn features, and she's standing facing the camera with a combination of fear and defeat. Nicole looks ravaged by this ordeal. In the space of a few hours, she's become an old woman. It tears at my heart. She looks like one of those pictures of hostages you see on television in Lebanon, Colombia, or Chad, her eyes inexpressive, blank with anxiety. In the third image, her left cheekbone is marked by a cut, around which a violet bruise has spread. From a fist, or maybe a baton.

Did Nicole fight back?

Did she try to escape?

I bite down on my lip until it bleeds. Tears prick my eyes.

I smack the wheel, screaming. Because that Nicole, the one in the picture, is my doing.

I mustn't let the guilt overwhelm me. I have to pull myself together. No giving up now. Must stay focused for the home stretch. I sniff and wipe my eyes. Quite the opposite—seeing her like that on the screen must renew my strength. I will fight to the very end. I feel happy in the knowledge that what I'm bringing her will reconcile everything: it will heal all the wounds, erase all the scars. I'm coming home to her, with all the riches to secure our life and our future. I'm coming home with the solution to each and every one of our problems.

All I want now is for the time to pass quickly, for her to be freed, to come home; to hold her in my arms.

I must call her. The tone barely rings before Fontana answers with a clear, firm, definitive "No." I'm about to unleash more insults but he's faster than me.

"You're not getting anything else until I've received instructions from my client."

He hangs up right away. The fine thread between Nicole and me has been broken. Everything is in my hands. I must free her, save her, right now.

I step down on the accelerator again.

46

La Défense.

I look up. At the summit of the gleaming glass skyscraper, a fiery gold sign bearing Exxyal Europe's name and logo spins on its axis. You can imagine it turning into a deity when night falls, transfiguring into a tremendous, shining beacon that lights up the world.

Paul Cousin's car is equipped with a device that can open the garage gate remotely. It's past 7:30 p.m., but on the second level, which is reserved for company executives, most of the spaces are still full. Space no. 198 lights up automatically as my car enters and the aluminum barrier sinks into the ground. I park and walk quickly toward the elevator. Cameras follow my every move. They are everywhere, making it hard to concentrate. I'm unsure about my destination, so I push the button that shoots me to the top floor of the building. This is where the gods have resided since the dawn of time.

Stylish, luxurious elevator, postmodern design, with uplighting and a plush carpet. I look like a rag doll in my rumpled, horribly out-of-date suit. As the floors file by, a creeping anxiety comes over me.

This is how battles are lost.

Management theory says: avoid irrational behaviors and choose to deal in what is real and measurable.

I take a deep breath, but it doesn't help. Alexandre Dorfmann—big French business leader, pillar of European industry—is about to greet me. Confronting one so powerful is getting the better of me. I run through the facts, and one doubt still lingers: why does he want to meet me?

He doesn't stand to gain anything from it.

All he needed was to relay his instructions anonymously. Proposing to meet me seems an imprudent move on his part. I feel certain he doesn't know the details of Nicole's kidnapping—he pays Fontana handsomely enough to be exempt from knowing details, making sure he is safe from any allegation of wrongdoing.

So why does he feel the need to step into the ring himself?

There must be something I haven't considered. The cards have been stacked without me noticing. I'm convinced he's going to squash me beneath his thumb. He's going to skin me alive. Such an easy victory against a man like this is simply not possible. It never happens. I'm climbing the scaffold. When the elevator door opens, I'm already half defeated. There's a veil before my eyes, and printed on it is Nicole's beleaguered face. I, too, am drained as I step out of the elevator.

Up here, the secretaries are all men. Young and highly qualified. They're called advisers or associates. One of them flashes me a corporate smile. Very professional. The sort of guy who's never happier than when he's at some smug media event with all his pals. He's been briefed: "Monsieur le Président" will see me.

A quilted, carpeted, padded antechamber. I stay on my feet. I know the rules of the waiting game—long simmer over a low heat. My breathing is steady, but my heart must be racing at 120 beats a minute. Clearly I don't know the rules, because there's no wait at all: thirty seconds later, the door opens, and the young associate makes himself scarce.

I am summoned.

The first thing that strikes me is the unbelievable beauty of the city glittering through the enormous floor-to-ceiling windows. God has a wonderful view over the world. One of the many perks of the job. Alexandre Dorfmann is engrossed in some paperwork, but he pulls himself away from his desk. Despite the interruption, he removes his glasses in a dignified manner. His face transforms as he directs a smile at me that's as thin as a blade.

"Ah, Monsieur Delambre!"

The voice alone is an instrument of domination. Immaculately honed, down to the smallest intonation. Dorfmann takes a few paces toward me, shakes me warmly by the hand, all the while holding my elbow with his left one, before drawing me to a corner of the room covered with bookcases, a small library that screams: "I am a business leader, yes, but above all I am humanist."

I sit down. Dorfmann takes his place next to me. Casual.

My feelings at this point are indescribable. This man has an astonishing aura. Some people are like that: electrifying. They emit waves.

Dorfmann radiates power in the same way Fontana radiates danger. He personifies the instinct for mastery.

If I were an animal, I'd start growling.

I try to remember him on the day of the hostage taking, sitting mute on the ground. But neither he nor I are the same men as then. Here we are back in the real world. The social order has corrected itself. I might be wrong, but I think the real reason we're here face-to-face today is to explore just that: what I put him through.

"Do you play golf, Monsieur Delambre?"

"Er . . . no."

They say prison ages you, but surely not so much that I look like a fucking golfer now?

"That's a shame. I had a metaphor in mind that summarizes our situation nicely."

Dorfmann waves his arm as though swatting a fly away.

"No matter," he says, before adopting an air of regret and spreading his arms in apology:

"Monsieur Delambre, I don't have much time . . ."

He smiles at me. An outside observer would swear that he felt a deep fondness for me; that I was a dear old friend with whom he'd love to talk at length if the circumstances permitted.

"I'm rather pressed myself," I say.

He nods, then pauses, looking me up and down for a long time in perfect silence: observing me, detailing me, studying me without the slightest embarrassment. Finally he fastens his dispassionate eyes on mine. He keeps them there for a long while, and it unsettles me right down to my belly. This moment feels like a distillation of every fear I have endured throughout my professional life. Dorfmann is an expert in the intimidation department: he must have terrorized, tortured, and frightened an incalculable number of colleagues, secretaries, and advisers, filling them with enough panic to want to throw themselves out of a window. His entire bearing is an assertion of one simple, clear truth: he's where he is because he's killed the competition.

"Good . . . ," he says at last.

The reason for my presence before him finally dawns on me.

From a technical perspective, it's impossible to justify. In practical terms, everything advises against it. But he wanted to make absolutely sure. From the start, this conflict has involved two men who have virtually never seen each other, with the exception of a few minutes when I had a Beretta pressed against his temple. It's not Dorfmann's style to conclude business in this manner.

In any professional contest, there has to come a moment of truth.

Dorfmann couldn't let me go without satisfying the burning need to see me in the flesh, to assess whether his power really has been put in check.

And, by extension, to see whether I represent any threat to him. He's measuring any potential risk.

"We could have settled this over the telephone," he says.

Evaluating the harmfulness of my intentions toward him.

"But I wanted to congratulate you personally."

Deciding whether I'm waging all-out war, a challenge he'd have no qualms in accepting.

"You have handled this affair masterfully."

Or maybe he's figuring out whether he can take my word. Simply put: Can a pair of bastards like us trust each other?

I don't move a muscle. I hold his stare. The only thing Dorfmann trusts is his intuition. This may well be the key to his success: the certainty that he will never be outmaneuvered by another man.

"We should have given you the job," he says at last, almost to himself.

He laughs at this notion, all on his own, as if I weren't there.

Then he returns to earth, like someone reluctantly coming to from a waking dream. He shakes himself, then smiles to indicate a change of tack:

"So, Monsieur Delambre, what are you going to do now with all this money? Invest it? Start your own business? Launch yourself into a new career?"

This is the final test in the conclusive assessment he's just made of me. It's like he's handing me an invisible check for thirteen million euros but holding it tight between his fingers, forcing me to pull harder and harder. For now, he's refusing to relent.

"I want rest and relaxation. I just want a well-deserved retirement."

I'm clearly offering him a truce.

"Goodness, don't we all!" he assures me, as though he, too, only ever dreamed of the good life.

On the balance of this, after a final second's reflection, he releases the invisible check.

This is what baffles me more than anything: the sum is of no importance whatsoever. It'll simply be written off.

In Alexandre Dorfmann's world, the sum is not what makes him tick. The sum is not what he's fought for.

The idea that I've extorted him of a slush fund evaporates. I'm just a minnow leaving with a handful of change.

47

The car is as comfortable as it gets, but it's still taking unbearably long. 8:05 p.m. It's the tail end of people leaving the office. Most employees are heading back to their cars, apart from the execs, who are staring at another two or three hours' work, best-case scenario. Even though I've been given the definitive green light, I don't let myself think it's over, that I've won, that I've nabbed the pot once and for all. My eyes are glued to the car phone. Nothing's happening. Nothing. I reason with myself: for now, there's nothing to worry about. I run through the numbers again, extending the margins of safety and rounding everything up: it all depends how fast Dorfmann relays his instructions. I look at the clock on the dashboard again: 8:10 p.m.

I keep myself occupied, sending Charles a text with the address for the apartment. Quick glance at the dashboard: still nothing. I'm tempted to look at the photos of Nicole again, but I resist. They'll scare me, and I have to believe that it's futile to fear that everything is over. It's counterproductive. I'm a few minutes away from the most important moment of my life. If everything goes well, this will be a great day for making amends.

8:12 p.m.

I can't bear it any longer. I dial Nicole's cell phone number. One ring, two, then a "hello" at the third: it's her, straight through to her.

"Nicole? Where are you?"

I shout this. It takes her several seconds to answer. I'm not sure why. It's as if she doesn't recognize my voice. Maybe my screaming has sent her into a panic.

"In a taxi," she says eventually. "What about you, where are you?"

"Are you by yourself in the taxi?"

Why is she taking so long to answer my questions?

"Yes, they . . . they let me go."

"Are you sure?"

What a stupid question.

"They told me I could go home."

There it is. I breathe. It's over.

Victory. I've won.

An irrepressible wave of joy washes over me.

My chest opens, and I feel an urge to shout out, to howl.

Victory.

Move over job-center Delambre, here comes wealth-tax Delambre. Without the tax. I could cry. In fact I'm already crying, gripping the wheel with all my strength.

Then I smack it furiously.

Victory, victory, victory.

"Alain . . . ," Nicole says.

I shriek with joy.

Fucking hell, I managed to sink the lot of them. I can't help gloating.

I can spend 50,000 euros a month for the rest of my life. I'm going to buy three apartments. One for each of my girls. The whole thing's unbelievable.

"Alain . . . ," Nicole repeats.

"We won, my love! Where are you, tell me, where are you?"

I realize that Nicole is crying. Very softly. I hadn't noticed right away but now that I'm listening more closely, I can hear her little sobs, which are causing me so much pain. It's normal, a normal aftereffect of fear. She needs reassurance.

"It's finished, my love, I promise you it's finished. You've got nothing to fear anymore. Nothing else can happen to you. I need to explain . . ."

"Alain . . ." she says again, unable to go any further.

She repeats my name on a continuous loop. There are so many things to explain to her, but that will take time. First, I must reassure her.

"What about you, Alain . . . ," Nicole asks. "Where were you?"

She's not asking me where I am right now, but where I was when she needed me. I understand, but she doesn't know the full extent of the problem. I'll need to explain to her that I never left her, that all the time she was so afraid I was scoring a definitive victory over our miserable existence. For both of us. In the time we've been speaking, I've started the engine, left the Exxyal garage, and am heading for the fast lane back into Paris.

"Right now, I'm in La Défense."

Nicole is taken aback.

"But . . . what are you doing in La Défense?"

"Nothing, I'm coming home. I'll explain everything. You've got nothing to fear. That's the most important thing, right?"

"I'm scared, Alain . . ."

We're having a lot of trouble understanding each other. She's going to need to get over all this, forget everything she's been through. We'll have to work on it together. I join the ring road.

"There's no reason to be scared, my love."

I'm repeating myself, but what else can I do?

"We'll be together again in no time."

I'm going as fast as possible so I can hold her in my arms.

"Do you know what we're going to do?"

I must encourage her.

"We're going to start from scratch, a brand-new life, that's what we're going to do. I've got some big news for you, my darling. Some really big news! You can't begin to imagine . . ."

But for now, telling her all this isn't making any difference. She's still crying. I can't do anything while she's in this state.

"I'm going to be . . ."

I want to say "at the house," but I can't bring myself to use that word for the place I'm meeting her. Physically impossible. I try to find the words. Nicole's still going in circles ("Alain, Alain . . .") and it's unsettling me. It's making me nervous.

"I'll be there in half an hour, okay?"

Nicole takes this in.

"Yes," she says eventually, sniffing noisily. "Okay."

Silence on the line. She hung up before me.

Five minutes later, I've reached Porte de Clignancourt. I call back. It's ringing. Once, twice, three times. Voicemail. I redial. Porte de la Villette. Voicemail again. I feel waves of dread. I don't even dare think the name *Fontana,* but he's there in front of me, all around me, everywhere. I tap the steering wheel nervously. I've won and I refuse to be scared now. I try Nicole's number again. She finally picks up.

"Why didn't you answer? Where were you?"

"What?"

Her voice is vacant, mechanical.

"I was in the elevator," Nicole says at last.

"Are you . . . Have you arrived? Are you back, have you shut the door?"

"Yes."

She lets out an immense sigh.

"Yes, I've shut the door."

I picture her taking off her shoes like she always does, the tips of her toes pushing against the heel. Her sigh is one of pure relief. For me, too.

"I'll be there in fifteen minutes, my love, okay?"

"Okay," Nicole says.

This time it's me who hangs up. I punch the address into the GPS and come off the Périphérique. By some miracle, I'm at avenue de Flandre just a few minutes later. But my heartache isn't over yet—the roads are jam-packed with parked cars. I turn off in search for a space. Is there a public car park around here? I look up at the high-rises. Hideous. I smile. This apartment that Nicole bought, I'm going give it to that charity, Emmaüs. I take a right, then a left, then go back on myself, scanning the vehicles parked along the street. I go farther, then come back, mapping out concentric circles that start to make me prodigiously angry. Crawling along, I look closely at the cars lining the right- and left-hand pavements.

Suddenly my heart skips a beat and my stomach churns.

No, it can't be possible. I saw it wrong.

I swallow hard.

But something tells me that yes, it is possible.

My reflexes were good—instead of stopping, I carried on driving. I must be absolutely sure. My hands are shaking because this time, if I'm right, it's a catastrophe. I'll be dangling in midair without a safety net. I take a right, then another, then a third and find myself back on the same street, going faster now, keeping my head firmly upright like a man absorbed in his commute or lost in thought. As I drive past I can clearly see a woman sitting behind the wheel of a black 4×4: Yasmine. She's wearing an earpiece.

It's her, no doubt about it.

She's waiting.

No—she's on the lookout.

If she's there, parked on a street a hundred feet from where Nicole lives, then it means Fontana's there, too.

They're on the lookout for me. They're on the lookout for us. Nicole and me.

I keep driving, turning at random. I need some time to figure out what's going on.

Dorfmann gave his instructions. Fontana obeyed. His assignment is over.

It's not a hard one to deduce: his contract with his former employer is over, so Fontana has decided to go it alone. Nothing like thirteen big ones for an incentive. It's enough to see out your days, no trouble whatsoever.

And that doesn't even factor in his personal hatred for me. I've tripped him up time and again, and now the bell's rung for last orders. He's only got one boss now: himself. No strings attached. The man is capable of anything.

Fontana is using Nicole as bait, but it's me he wants. He wants to make me spit out my bank details one hammer blow at a time. To make me pay in every sense of the word.

I think he'll attempt to take both of us. He'll make Nicole scream until I give him everything, everything, everything.

And afterward he'll kill her.

He'll kill me, too, no doubt reserving some special fate for me. Fontana wants to settle a personal difference with me.

I have absolutely no idea what to do, turning and swerving from one street to the next, making sure at every cost that I don't get too close to the surveillance vehicle again. Fontana must have positioned himself somewhere he can apprehend me as soon as I arrive. I've managed to avoid his eye so far because he didn't imagine I would arrive by car. They're probably expecting me to come in a taxi or by foot, who knows.

If Fontana lays a finger on us . . . I can already picture Nicole tied up in a chair. This isn't possible. I'm at a total loss, and I also don't know the area. I unfold the piece of paper with the address. Nicole is on the eighth floor.

My thoughts are confused, all over the place. Is there a garage? I must not be seen. But what can I do?

I can only see one way out. The worst option, but it's the only one: go in guns blazing (albeit unarmed), then flee. It's not ideal, but I don't see any other option. This trap has made my brain shut down.

I reach out for the car phone but my hand's trembling so much I drop it. I recover it with difficulty and clamp it against my chest. A space is free in front of the entrance to a building; I pull in for a moment and leave the engine running. I have to call Nicole. I dial her number.

"Nicole, you have to leave," I say as soon as she picks up.

"What? Why?"

She's lost.

"Listen, I can't explain. You have to leave right now. This is what you're going to do . . ."

"But why? What's happening? Alain! You're not telling me anything, I can't take this anymore . . ."

She realizes my panic and understands that the situation is serious; sensing the danger ahead, her voice fails her and gives way to violent sobbing. The terror of the last few hours returns intact.

"No, no," she says again and again. I have to get her moving. I come out with it:

"They are here."

No point saying who. Nicole sees Fontana's face again, Yasmine's, too, and a fresh wave of fear grips her.

"You promised me this was over, Alain," she sobs. *"I'm fed up with your crap, I can't take any more of it."*

She's leaving me with no choice. I need to scare her even more to get her moving.

"If you stay there, Nicole, they'll come and find you. You have to leave. Now. I'm downstairs."

"Where are you?" she screams. "Why aren't you coming?"

"Because that's what they want! It's me they want!"

"Fucking hell, who are 'they'?"

She's howling in sheer terror.

"I'm going to lead you through this, Nicole. Listen carefully. Go downstairs, turn right, and that's rue Kloeckner. Take the right-hand sidewalk. That's all you have to do, Nicole, nothing else, I swear, I'll take care of the rest."

"No, Alain, I'm sorry. I can't anymore. I'm calling the police. I can't take this, I can't."

"DON'T DO ANYTHING! YOU HEAR ME? DON'T DO ANYTHING EXCEPT WHAT I TOLD YOU!"

Silence. I keep going. I have to make her.

"I don't want to die either, Nicole! So do what I say, nothing else! Come downstairs, turn right, and do it now, for fuck's sake!"

I hang up. I'm so scared for us both. Deep down, I know my plan is rubbish, but I've thought hard and it's the best I can do. Nothing else for it. I wait for three minutes, four . . . how long can it take to make up your mind and come downstairs? Then I start the engine. No one's expecting to find me in this car. Not even Nicole.

Act fast.

All guns blazing.

I speed down rue Kloeckner and from a distance I see Nicole's outline on the right-hand sidewalk; I drive up behind her and see how labored her walk is, so stiff, and as I come level with her she makes out the sound of an engine, quietly and to her left, but she doesn't turn to look; she's expecting the worst at any split second, and her stride is still rigid, like she's walking to the gallows. I stay alert for the right moment, see there's nothing in front, nothing behind, then accelerate, overshoot her by ten feet, brake hard, pile out of the car, leap onto the sidewalk, and grab her by the arm; she lets out a yelp as she recognizes me but before she can do anything else, I open the passenger door, bundle her into the car, run around to the other side, and get back behind the wheel. The whole thing takes no more than seven or eight seconds. Still nothing in front or behind. I rev the engine softly as Nicole stares at me, then at the car, then back at me, everything seeming intensely strange to her, and it's hard to know whether she's less scared now that she's in this silent car, sliding along like a wave, with me at the wheel; but she closes her eyes as I gingerly take the first right, still nothing in front or behind, and I shut my eyes, too, for a moment and when I open them, I recognize the catlike figure of Fontana a hundred feet ahead, sprinting along the sidewalk and then disappearing. I speed up without thinking, overtaking the point in the street he dove into, the point from where the tip of a black 4×4 as high as a bus is emerging. I trigger the central door locks, startling Nicole, and I put my foot down. The car surges forward and Nicole lets out a shriek as she's pinned against her seat by the acceleration. Fontana's car turns behind us and I veer left, already speeding, clipping the back of a stationary car as I pass, my car lurching, forcing another cry from Nicole, who grabs her safety belt and fastens it with a sharp click. In this neighborhood the traffic's not so bad: everything converges on two large boulevards that thrust into the center of Paris or retreat to the suburbs. I cross the next intersection without even slowing down and a red Renault 25 with enormous chrome bumpers stops abruptly to let me pass. Charles is back in the picture.

I'd forgotten all about Charles.

He sees us tear past at top speed and barely has time to raise his hand before we are well beyond him, a black 4×4 seconds behind us in pursuit. I know it'll take Charles a bit of time to figure it out, but he'll get there eventually, and anyway I don't have time to think about it because I'm on the boulevard, in the right-hand lane, where stationary cars are stuck bumper to bumper in a traffic jam. If I stop now, Fontana will rush us, shoot out the windows, tear open the doors, and I'll be helpless. All he needs is for us to stop for just long enough to pounce and he'll take care of the rest, lodging a bullet straight into Nicole's head to paralyze me, before knocking me around and stuffing me into Yasmine's 4×4 . . .

We come up behind the final car in the line and I've got no idea what to do. Nicole clamps both hands on the dashboard as she sees the line of stopped cars closer and closer before us, and I ram the steering wheel roughly to the left, accelerate, and head back up the left lane in the wrong direction, horn full blast and lights full beam. Fontana does something I never saw coming: he sets off a flashing police light, stretches an arm out the window, and sticks it on the roof—a ballsy move that says a lot about his determination—and now anyone who sees us will think it's a chase and won't move an inch to let me through. We're being hunted down and the whole city will turn against us. I've no idea how (we must have taken symmetrical routes) but again Charles's car is speeding toward us. I swing right to avoid it and then left to straighten up, flinging Nicole against the door. Her feet are buried beneath her seat and her head's tucked down, hands crossed behind her neck, as if she's trying to protect herself from the roof caving in. As soon as she hears the police siren she turns to the rearview mirror, her eyes bright with hope, but the second she realizes it's a trap, she resumes her fetal position and starts moaning.

As he whips past us, Charles is wide eyed and looking right at me, then at the car pursuing us.

I'm not thinking anymore, I'm just a bundle of reflexes, pinballing between horror and joy, invincibility and mortality, and I turn violently to the left up a street, then left and right again, without any idea where I'm going. The moment an obstacle appears I turn again, one street, two, three, skimming cars here and there, avoiding pedestrians and bicycles, and scraping a bus down the left-hand side as it pulls away from its stop. Fontana is still behind us, however close or far, and I don't know which way to go before suddenly, strangely, we're on a one-way street running alongside the Périphérique.

It's walled in on both sides by parked cars.

Long and straight as an arrow.

One-way, single lane.

We can barely see to the end.

I put my foot down, and in the mirror I see Fontana. My driving's not quick enough, the hands he destroyed not strong enough. Fontana retrieves the flashing light and pulls it inside and shuts off the siren, the 4×4 sticking to a constant speed fifty yards behind us because there's no escape.

I don't manage to keep in a straight line, drifting constantly and hitting the cars on my side as well as Nicole's.

At the end, a few hundred yards away, there's a red light where the street hits a wide boulevard that's thick with moving vehicles. Another wall. I accelerate even faster toward this desperate impasse.

I know it's over. Nicole knows it, too.

The boulevard we're heading toward is a fast lane: stopping there with Fontana behind us would be like getting out of a car on a Formula 1 track, blasting our way through the traffic like taking on a bullet train.

Nicole pushes back in her chair, bracing herself for the merciless obstacle ahead.

The rear window explodes. Fontana's shooting at us. Saving himself some time for when it comes to the collision. It feels as if the inside of the car is being ripped apart and the wind is rushing through the shattered glass. Nicole shrinks into her seat.

And now for the final scene.

Here's how the story ends.

Right here, in the space of a few seconds.

In the space of a few hundred yards.

In this immensely long, straight street that we're driving down at almost 75 miles an hour, chased by a black, metallic beast with its headlights glaring.

The image haunts me still, all these months later.

It will never go away.

For many years to come I'll see it over and over, dream about it, inquire about its mysterious, tragic meaning.

Nicole has looked up again and is hypnotized by our rapid advance toward the wall of cars barring our way.

And the two of us, both mesmerized, witness before us the sudden eruption of a red car equipped with a vast, gleaming bumper and spewing out a great plume of white smoke. It has just turned in to the far end of the road and is driving directly toward us, the wrong way. Two hundred yards apart, our cars are bearing down on each other at full speed.

I start braking lightly, at a loss about what to do next.

Death is hovering over us.

Charles, on the other hand, is accelerating. When his car is barely more than a hundred yards away, I can make out his face between the chrome bars of his front bumper.

The final message.

Charles puts on his turn signal.

The left one.

There's nowhere for him to turn, and I realize that's not the message. It's not about which direction Charles wants to take. He's showing me the direction to take. It's a message: *turn right.*

I speed up and desperately scan the uninterrupted line of cars parked to my right. Charles is now less than sixty yards away now. His face is growing, starting to fill up the screen. We're tearing toward each other faster and faster, drawn together into the eye of the hurricane.

Suddenly I see the exit.

It's a dead end. It opens out on our right a few dozen yards ahead. I yell over at Nicole. She grabs her seat belt and thrusts her legs far out in front, pushing back against the footwell. I slam on the brakes and thrash the wheel around. The car skids, striking an obstacle at the back that I don't see before bouncing roughly into the little alley and smashing straight into a van. The airbags burst open, flattening us against our seats. The car comes to a halt.

Now that we've made way, Charles and Fontana's cars are left face-to-face in the dead-straight road.

They smash into each other like meteorites.

When he sees Charles's bright-red banger in his headlights, Fontana tries his best to stop, but of course it's too late.

The two cars pile into each other at a combined speed of more than 110 miles an hour.

I can still see Charles's final gesture in slow motion.

In the moment his car comes in line with us, I see it, clear as anything. He's sitting very low behind the wheel, his head turned toward me, smiling.

Charles's wonderful smile, brotherly and generous. The same as ever. *Don't you worry about me.*

He looks me in the eye as he goes past and lifts his arm toward me: his regular signal.

The next second, the crash is hideous.

The two vehicles smash into each other at full speed, then fall on top of each other tangled, crushed, fused.

The body parts that don't disintegrate in the collision are shredded by the metal carnage, and flames overwhelm them.

Now it's over.

EPILOGUE

Dinner at Mathilde's. I buzz and wait on the landing. I've brought flowers and I'm wearing a smart suit, a raw-silk pinstripe number. And my enormous diving watch with its fluorescent green strap, which never leaves my wrist, much to everyone's astonishment. As always, it's Gregory who opens the door, while Mathilde, tucked away in the kitchen, calls out excitedly: "Oh, Papa, you're here already?" My son-in-law's handshake is so firm that I can feel the challenge, the macho gauntlet being thrown down. But I never fight back. Those days are over.

Mathilde emerges when I enter the sitting room, always saying the same thing as she fixes her hair: "Oh my god, I must look dreadful. Papa, help yourself to whiskey, I'll be back in a second."

She then disappears into the bathroom for a good half hour, leaving Gregory and me to exchange various pleasantries, sticking to the safe, uncomplicated ground that experience has shown us.

Gregory has gained in self-confidence since taking office in the brand-new apartment I bought them, a large five-room place in the heart of Paris. The way he handles the decanter, the haughty postures he adopts . . . you'd be forgiven for thinking that his fortunate circumstances are due to his own considerable merits, his undeniably superior qualities. The two of us are like boxers: we owe our success to being smacked in the face. I never say anything. I hold my tongue. I smile. I tell myself it's fine, that I'm just waiting for my daughter. Eventually she'll arrive, each time wearing a brand-new dress that she twirls on entry.

"What do you think?" she asks, as though I'm her husband.

I try to mix up my compliments. I really ought to start a list of adjectives for future evenings, because these monthly visits (always the second Thursday) will make my dwindling linguistic resources dry up before long.

I always feel unprepared. Sometimes I say "Marvelous!" but that seems too old-fashioned, or maybe "Amazing!"—that sort of thing.

Charles's words, I suppose.

From the window you can make out the spires of Notre-Dame. I sip the whiskey that Mathilde buys specially for me. My own bottle at my daughter's house. In spite of this, please don't assume I'm becoming an alcoholic. Quite the opposite—I'm doing everything I can to stay in shape. Nicole is very appreciative of my attempts at self-maintenance. My discipline. I've joined a gym near her place. It's pretty far, I'm not sure why I chose that one, but that's how it is.

We sit down for dinner. Mathilde has the presence of mind to give me a quick update on Lucie, because she knows I'm eager to hear her news. It's my only link with her since the end of all that.

With Lucie, it finished in the apartment on avenue de Flandre. I hadn't been expecting anyone, but the doorbell rang, and when I opened, Lucie was there.

"Oh, it's you," I said.

"I was in the area and decided to drop by," she replied.

And she came in. It wasn't hard to see she was lying. She hadn't been in the area—she'd come specially. Her face said it all. Anyway, she got to the point immediately. She's not as polite as the others, so no attempt to keep up appearances.

"I've got some questions for you, now," she said.

No talk of sitting down, going for dinner, or any of that. Her "now" resounded heavily, so heavily, and I looked down expecting the first barrage, knowing how difficult it was going to be.

"But," she continued, "I'm going to start with the main one: Do you really take me for a complete fucking idiot?"

Terrible start.

The whole thing had finished barely two weeks earlier.

The day before her visit, I'd written checks for everyone. Big checks. Mathilde looked at hers and took it for what it was: an unimaginable Christmas present, smack in the middle of the year. It was like she'd won the lottery.

In reality, these were fake checks. Just to mark the occasion. I explained to them that their millions of euros were stashed in off-shore accounts and that using such sums would require various precautions regarding the tax authorities. We'd need to get creative with our accounting. Nothing major, but just be patient, I had it all under control.

Nicole laid hers on the table carefully. She'd already known about this for several days. I'd explained it to her right away. With Nicole it was different, it wasn't like with the girls. She put her check in front of her as you might place a napkin on the table at the end of a meal. She said nothing. There was no point in her repeating herself. Quite simply, she didn't want to ruin it for the girls.

Lucie looked at her present, and it was obvious that it had plunged her into a state of deep reflection. She stammered "thank you" a few times, listening to my enthusiastic explanations in a manner that was both attentive and absentminded, like she was hearing a different speech in parallel.

That evening, I told my two girls that whatever happened, their futures were assured. They could use what I'd given them to buy themselves an apartment (or two or three) and do whatever they wanted to feel safe. This was a gift from their father. I was paying everyone back.

I'd split it three ways. I was paying everyone back a hundred times over. I even thought my gesture might earn me a bit of respect.

It did, but only in part. Mathilde was in raptures; Gregory asked endless questions about the practicalities. I said as much as I could without giving away the essentials, all the while feeling like it wasn't going at all as I'd planned, nothing like I had dreamed.

And the following day Lucie was back, asking: "Do you really take me for a complete fucking idiot?" It was nonstop because, as it always is with Lucie, she provided the question along with the answer to the question. Because she hadn't stopped thinking from the first second she saw her enormous check, from the moment it had dawned on her.

"You manipulated me in the most contemptible way possible," she said.

She spoke without anger, her voice level. That was what scared me the most.

"You hid the truth from me throughout because you thought that, in my naivety, I would defend you better if I thought you were innocent."

That hit the nail on the head. I'd had a thousand opportunities to explain what I'd really done, but I thought it would have undermined her defense. And I had my reasons. If I had given her the full picture, I would be in prison right now for a very, very long time.

Until the very last second, I never thought I'd be certain to hold on to the money.

Could I have reasonably told them about it, raising their hopes about a life finally free of need, only to pull the carpet out from under their feet if I didn't manage to see my plan through?

I tried to make her appreciate all this, but she cut me dead:

"You wanted me to come across as genuine. You made a spectacle of our relationship. You did everything in your power to make the press think that this was about a poor victim of unemployment being defended by his well-meaning, generous daughter. You got exactly what you wanted when I choked up in front of the jury. Maybe that final moment was what exonerated you the next day. That single second was the culmination of months and months of lies, of making me believe the same as everyone else. You wanted me to defend you because you wanted someone hardworking and credulous, someone clumsily honest. And to achieve that, you needed me to be a silly little girl. I was the only person in the world who could play the dummy so perfectly. I was a shoo-in. Your best shot at being let off was to have a muppet at your side. What you did was disgraceful."

Exaggerating as ever.

But that's in her nature, it's how she is—she can't resist taking it a bit further.

Lucie is always mixing up cause and effect. I need her to realize that there was never any strategy. At no stage did I think she needed to be a dummy to be effective. She was an incredible lawyer. I couldn't have asked for a better one. All that happened was I realized—too late in the day to tell her the truth—that even her *faux pas* would work in my favor. That's it.

Things are not at all the same when seen from her angle and from mine.

I needed to say all this, but Lucie didn't give me a chance. Not another word. An argument would have reassured me. I would have taken insults, but this . . .

Lucie looked at me.

And she left.

It kills me when I think back to it. I stayed there for a while, frozen in the middle of the room. She left the door ajar. I went as far as the landing and heard the little click the elevator makes when it reaches the ground floor. I returned to the apartment, battered with exhaustion and feeling totally demoralized.

On the doormat there was a scrunched-up piece of paper that I picked up and unfolded. It was Lucie's check.

I can't stop thinking about that, and it breaks my heart.

Gregory is still talking as we sit at the table, regaling me with the latest drama at work, from which, of course, he emerges the hero. Mathilde stares at him, transfixed. He's her big man. It makes me want to kill myself, but I weigh in with a "No?" or a "Nice one!"—not listening to a fucking word.

Lucie hasn't called me once for almost a year.

All I have left are these monthly conversations with Gregory.

I'm finding life pretty tough.

So I drift off and think of Charles.

Of Nicole.

I picture us a year ago. God, it was miserable.

After Charles died, when everything was over, we stayed together for two days in that gloomy flat on avenue de Flandre. We stayed by each other's sides, lying on our backs for hours at a time, simply holding hands like a pair of petrified snow angels.

And on the third day, Nicole said she was leaving. She told me that she loved me, but that she just couldn't go on. She couldn't—something was broken.

Finally, my epic ego trip had come to an end. We had to go through all that for this simple realization to dawn on me.

"I need to live, Alain, and that's not good enough for you," she said.

She and Lucie stood in exactly the same place when they left me. Lucie threw away her rolled-up check as she left; Nicole gave me one of those smiles that I never come away from unscathed. I'd just said to her:

"But Nicole, it's all over and we're rich! Nothing can happen to us anymore. Nothing can stop us from being everything we've ever dreamed of!"

Apparently I had some nerve saying that.

Nicole simply touched my cheek and shook her head, as though she were thinking: "Poor thing."

After a bit, she said:

"My poor love . . ."

And she left, perfectly calmly.

In this respect, Lucie reminded me of her mother a great deal.

I'm not sure, but maybe this is why I decided to stay living at avenue de Flandre, despite being capable of buying myself a stunningly expensive place.

I filled the ordinary flat with ordinary furnishings, with ready-made ideas straight out of an IKEA catalog.

And to be honest, I don't actually mind it that much.

Nicole moved into a place in Ivry, I'll never understand why. It was impossible to persuade her to let me buy her a beautiful apartment like Mathilde's. Absolutely impossible to discuss it with her. It was a no, and that was that. She didn't even let me buy her the place in Ivry. She pays the rent herself out of her salary.

We have dinner from time to time. At first, I'd take her out to one of the grand Parisian restaurants. I was aiming to sweep her off her feet again, trying to look all handsome in my first-ever tailored suit. But it didn't take long to realize she wasn't impressed. She'd eat in virtual silence, then head home on the *métro*, not even agreeing to a taxi.

Now, we don't see each other so often. Before, I suggested endless outings to the opera, the theater; I tried to give her books on art, weekends away, things like that. I told myself that I had to win her back, that it would take time and no little sleight of hand, but that bit by bit we would find our way back to each other, that she'd realize how wonderful our new life could be. That's not how it went. She said yes to one or two things, but after a while she stopped. For a while, I called her all the time; then one day she told me I was doing it too often.

"I love you, Alain. I'm always glad to hear you're doing well. But that's all I need to know. I don't need anything more."

At the start, without her, time went slowly.

I felt like a moron in my sparse apartment with my made-to-measure suits.

I've become a sad man.

Nothing disastrous, but I don't get the enjoyment from life that I'd hoped for. Without Nicole, nothing has any real meaning.

Without her, nothing has any meaning at all.

The other day, something came back to me that Charles had said in those bizarre sentences of his: "If you want to kill a man start by giving him what he seeks the most. More often than not that's enough."

I miss Charles an awful lot.

I've put the rest of the money in accounts opened under the girls' names. I don't pay much attention to it. I know it's there. It's what I won. That's all I need to know.

The first few months were terribly long, being alone like that.

But then I started a new job a few weeks ago, a volunteer position: a "senior consultant" at a small charity that helps young entrepreneurs.

The fact is I can't help it: I can't not work.

Vézénobres, August 2009

ACKNOWLEDGMENTS

My first thought is for Pascaline, of course. For her patience and her tireless rereadings. For her presence.

Afterward, thank you as ever to all the following:

Samuel, for his constant advice and repairs (at times up on the high wire), which have proved unfailing and valuable companions. My thanks to him for understanding so well that meaning must prevail over precision . . . He is not answerable for any of the lingering errors.

Gerald, for his helpful remarks at a time when the text needed them.

Joëlle de Cubber, for being so responsive to my requests for medical advice.

Eric Prungnaud, whose reading and observations were of great comfort at just the right moment.

Cathy, my affectionate sponsor.

Gérard Guez, for being so welcoming and kind.

Charles Nemes, who came up with the title for this book over a meal (a relatively dry one, by the way).

A huge thank you, of course, to the whole team at Calmann-Lévy, my French publishers.

Finally, readers may well have picked up on references to Alain, Bergson, Céline, Derrida, Guilloux, Hawthorne, Kant, Mailer, Marías, Onfray, Proust, Sartre, Scott Fitzgerald, and others.

Each one of these references can be considered an homage.

PIERRE LEMAITRE was born in Paris in 1951. He worked for many years as a teacher of literature before becoming a novelist. For *Alex*, he was awarded the Crime Writers' Association International Dagger, alongside Fred Vargas, and was sole winner for *Camille* and *The Great Swindle*. In 2013, *The Great Swindle* also won the Prix Goncourt, France's leading literary award.

SAM GORDON is a translator from French and Spanish. His previous translations include works by Karim Miské, Sophie Hénaff, Timothée de Fombelle, and Annelise Heurtier.

ABOUT THE TYPE

Typeset in Minion Pro Regular, 11.5/15 pt.

Minion Pro was designed for Adobe Systems by Robert Slimbach in 1990. Inspired by typefaces of the Renaissance, it is both easily readable and extremely functional without compromising its inherent beauty.

Typeset by Scribe Inc., Philadelphia, Pennsylvania.